A PROMISE
OF FIRE

AMANDA
BOUCHET

D0317852

PIATKUS

First published in the US in 2016 by Sourcebooks, Inc.
First published in Great Britain in 2016 by Piatkus

1 3 5 7 9 10 8 6 4 2

Copyright © 2016 by Amanda Bouchet

The moral right of the author has been asserted.

*All characters and events in this publication, other than those
clearly in the public domain, are fictitious and any resemblance
to real persons, living or dead, is purely coincidental.*

All rights reserved.
No part of this publication may be reproduced, stored in a
retrieval system, or transmitted in any form or by any means, without
the prior permission in writing of the publisher, nor be otherwise circulated
in any form of binding or cover other than that in which it is published
and without a similar condition including this condition being
imposed on the subsequent purchaser.

A CIP catalogue record for this book
is available from the British Library.

ISBN 978-0-349-41254-2

Printed and bound in Great Britain by
Clays Ltd, St Ives plc

Papers used by Piatkus are from well-managed forests
and other responsible sources.

MIX
Paper from
responsible sources
FSC® C104740

Piatkus
An imprint of
Little, Brown Book Group
Carmelite House
50 Victoria Embankment
London EC4Y 0DZ

An Hachette UK Company
www.hachette.co.uk

www.piatkus.co.uk

For my family, near, far, and beyond the stars.
You have supported me in every way, always.
Thank you.

CHAPTER 1

I PLUCK AT MY CRIMSON TUNIC, TENTING THE lightweight linen away from my sticky skin. The southern Sintan climate isn't my worst nightmare, but it sometimes ranks pretty high, right along with the stifling layers of cosmetics masking my face, my leather pants, and my knee-high boots.

Heat and leather and heels don't mix, but at least looking like a brigand means blending into the circus. Here, discreet only gets you noticed.

Craning my neck for a breath of fresh air, I navigate my way through the beehive of tables already set up for the circus fair. The performers on the center stage are the main attraction. The rest of us surround them, carving out places for ourselves amid the crowd. Tonight, hemmed in on all sides in an amphitheater lit by hundreds of torches and filled to capacity, I feel like a Cyclops is sitting on my chest—suffocated.

Damp curls cling to my neck. I peel them off and tuck them back into my braid, scanning the crowd as I walk. I recognize some of the regulars. Others I don't know. My eyes trip over a man and get stuck. He's looking at me, and it's hard not to look back. He's striking in a dark, magnetic way, his size, weapons, and bearing all telling me he's a tribal warlord. His build is strong and masculine, his gait perfectly balanced and fluid. He walks with predatory confidence, unhurried, and yet there's no mistaking his potential for swift, explosive violence. It's not latent or hidden, just leashed.

Watchful, alert, he's aware of everything in his vicinity. Especially me.

Our gazes collide, and something in me freezes. His eyes remind me of Poseidon's wrath—stormy, gray, *intense*—the kind of eyes that draw you in, hold you there, and might not let you go.

Adrenaline surges through me, ratcheting up my pulse. My heart thumping, I blink and take in the rest of him. Intelligent brow. Strong jaw. Wide mouth. Hawkish nose. Black hair brushes a corded neck atop broad shoulders that have no doubt been swinging a sword since before he could walk. Body toned to perfection, skin darkened by a lifetime in the sun, he's battle-chiseled and hard, the type of man who can cleave an enemy in two with little effort and even less consequence to his conscience.

He keeps staring at me, and a shiver prickles my spine. *Is this man* my *enemy?*

There's no reason to think so, but I didn't stay alive this long without the help of a healthy dose of paranoia.

Wary, I sit at my table, keeping an eye on him as he weaves a bold path through an array of potions, trinkets, and charms. He's flanked by four similar men. Their coloring varies, but they all have the same sure look about them, although they pale in comparison to the warlord in both authority and allure. The man with the gray eyes is a born leader, and only an idiot would mistake him for anything else.

He stares for so long that I start to wonder if he can somehow bore through my layers of face paint and unmask me, but I've never seen him before, and he can't possibly know the person underneath. I'm from the north of Fisa, where magic is might. He's from the south of Sinta, where muscle and cunning decide who lives or dies. Our paths would never have crossed in the past, and warlords don't usually frequent the circus.

I look away, hoping he'll do the same. There are plenty of reasons a man stares at a woman. An exotic face and generous figure attract as much attention as a good mystery, if not more, and the warlord's intense scrutiny feels more appreciative than alarming.

Ignoring the flush now creeping into my cheeks, I smooth the wrinkles from the coarse wool blanket covering my table and arrange my paraphernalia like usual. My glittering, gold-lettered sign advertises *Cat the Magnificent—Soothsayer Extraordinaire*, even though flashes of the future only come here and there, usually in dreams. Luckily, it only takes a few questions for truths to reveal themselves like flowers opening for the sun. I read people's body language and glean who they are, what they want, and maybe even what they're capable of. It's about knowledge and illusion. I get a copper for it, which is more than a fair deal for me. I won't peddle futures. I have an idea of my own, and that's more than enough.

My leg starts a nervous bounce. Prophecies can be interpreted loosely, right?

The audience gasps, and I turn to see what's happening on the stage. Vasili is throwing knives at his wife. She's strapped to the flat side of a vertical, rotating wheel, and he's blindfolded. He's never hit her, but my heart still comes to a complete standstill every time they perform. Tonight is no exception, and I hold my breath, both riveted and terrified, until he runs out of knives.

The crowd is too caught up in the circus to take advantage of the fair, so I get up again and head to the performers' gate to watch the end of the show and put some distance between the warlord and me. He's still looking when he shouldn't be.

The air coming through the gate is fresher, bringing with it the sound of Cerberus's chuffing breaths and the scent of sweaty dog. He's Hades's pet, so I doubt the heat bothers him. I toss him a wave, and two of his three upper lips curl in a snarl of acknowledgment. One of these days, I'll get all three, although in eight years I never have. I think his middle head just doesn't like me.

Finished with his performance, Vasili unstraps his wife while Aetos launches himself onto the stage with a triple flip and lands in a fighter's crouch that shakes the platform. The solid wood creaks under his colossal weight, and the rapt crowd murmurs in awe. Aetos straightens, pounds his chest, tears the horse pelt off his giant back, and catches fire. His roar shakes the amphitheater. No one can roar like Aetos. I've seen him perform hundreds of times, and I still get chills.

Seven-and-a-half-feet tall, muscle-bound, and tattooed blue from head to toe with Tarvan tribal swirls, he moves his hands in an impossibly fast dance, weaving fire until he's encased in a sphere of living flame. He bursts through the crackling barrier with another roar. The explosion blasts the hair away from my face and dries out the inside of my nose. I'm forty feet away but feel like I'm in the furnaces of the Underworld. Fanning myself is useless. I'll never get used to the southern heat, and with Aetos performing, it's even worse.

The Sintan Hoi Polloi can barely contain themselves. It's like doing tricks for children—everything enchants. For them, the circus is a whirlwind of power and impossible magical delights. Everywhere from the hard-packed dirt floor surrounding the fair tables and stage to the high, far reaches of the circular stone seating, people jump up and down, hooting and stomping their feet.

My feet tap along with the crowd's, my eyes following
Aetos around the stage. What a relief to be back in Sinta,
even with all the dust and heat. I do whatever I can to stay
on the west side of Thalyria. Our recent sojourn in the
middle realm of Tarva made my lungs tight and my fingers
itch for a knife. I'd probably start jumping at shadows if the
circus ever went all the way east to Fisa. Just the thought of
my home realm makes my sweat turn cold.

Sinta. Tarva. Fisa. West to east. Here to… Nothing I'm
going to think about.

The audience whoops in approval of Aetos's fiery
moves. Hoi Polloi in the amphitheater are ecstatic—and
not only with the show. They've been celebrating ever
since a warlord from the tribal south hacked his way north
to Castle Sinta to put his own sister on the throne. You'd
think Dionysus had dumped a three-month supply of wine
over the entire realm. Temples have been overflowing with
Sintans offering prayers of gratitude, their holy men overcome with gifts to help clothe and feed the poor. Statues
of Athena, who is apparently well loved by the conquering warlord, are being spontaneously erected in towns
and villages from here to the Ice Plains in Sinta's north.
Happiness and generosity abound, and I don't even want
to think about how many sheep have been slaughtered for
celebratory feasts.

For the first time *ever*, the magicless majority is in
charge, and Hoi Polloi are literally dancing in the streets—
but only when they're not throwing themselves in abject
loyalty at the feet of the new royal family. Or so I've heard.
I haven't actually seen the new royals, but news spreads
fast when there's something to say. After the warlord
and his southern army secured the Sintan throne during
the spring, his family took weeks just to move north. Not

because they're slow, but because of the sheer number of adoring people in their way.

It's no secret the northern-born Magoi royals here in Sinta were despots, just like everywhere else in Thalyria. Hoi Polloi know they're better off with one of their own in charge.

But royals without magic? My cynical snort is lost in the boisterousness of the crowd. *It'll never last.*

Sweeping the horsehide back over his shoulders, Aetos takes a mighty leap into the air and doesn't come back down. He hovers well above the open-air seating and shoots flames into the darkening sky. They drizzle down in a shower of sparks that char the raised wooden stage and add to the oppressive heat. He lands with the last of them, tramples a budding fire under his huge boot, roars, of course, and then takes a solemn bow.

I cover my ears, grinning. I might go deaf from the applause.

Aetos stomps to the exit in a swirl of black cape and red flame, nodding to me as Desma takes the stage for her Dance of a Thousand Colors.

She moves to the melody of a kithara, starting out slowly and building speed until she's whirling around the stage in a kaleidoscope of color. Her feet barely touch the ground. A rainbow shines from every pore, from every strand of hair and eyelash, illuminating summer's twilight with an impossibly complex brightness. Her eyes glow with more shades of color than even the Gods have names for. Inconceivably beautiful, Desma is the grand finale, and the crowd worships her.

I'm as spellbound by Desma's dance as everyone else, and Vasili startles a squeak out of me when he nudges me in the ribs with the blunt end of a knife.

"You should be out there with her, Cat. Make a new act and call it the Fantastical Fisan Twins."

I whip the knife out of his hand, flip it, and nudge him back. "Twins look alike."

He looks back and forth between Desma and me. "Short. Long, dark hair. Bright-green eyes. Fisan."

Okay. He has a point. We're even the same age—twenty-three.

I sweep a hand down, indicating my curvaceous figure, and then point to Desma's much straighter frame.

Vasili grins, and his wide mustache spreads out, nearly meeting his bushy eyebrows on either side. "There is that. Desma should eat more."

I snort. "Or I should eat less."

"You're a woman, Cat. That's how you're supposed to look."

I make a face at him. Vasili has treated me like family since the day I showed up—fifteen years old, emaciated and dirty, with blisters all over my feet. "There's nothing like starving to make a person appreciate food," I say, my eyes roaming the place where I first saw Selena's traveling circus in action. Eight years have passed, but this southern Sintan dust heap is still my favorite venue.

Vasili grabs his knife back and twirls the base of the hilt on his palm, spinning it on an imaginary axis.

I watch the whirling blade. "You know I wish I could do that."

Smiling, he increases the speed until the knife is nothing but a blur.

"Show-off," I grumble.

He chuckles, backing up so that Desma can make her way through the gate. She keeps moving, swaying rhythmically, and I turn to follow. We all know from experience that she can't just stop, or the colors will build up inside her, the pressure unbearable. She takes my hands and spins me into her dance, our feet stirring dust into the shimmering air. We pass Cerberus on our way out, and one head pops up, ears twitching.

Desma's colors skitter over me with tiny teeth, nipping at my skin. Her rainbows jump to me, eager, and I absorb them so fast the magic leaves me breathless and floating.

"You soothe me, Cat." She guides us along the rough stone wall as we travel down the back side of the amphitheater. "You're a balm to my soul."

"I'm a bucket of water to your torch."

She laughs at my tart response, colors pouring from her throat and sinking into me.

It doesn't take long for Desma to stop glowing, and her power leaves me energized enough to forget the stifling heat. Rainbows fly from my fingertips, painting the evening shadows with splashes of color. I draw a picture of the Minotaur on the wall and then aim harmless ribbons of magic at friends who pass. Tadd and Alyssa launch into tumbling runs over the burned-out grass to avoid the beams. Zosimo and Yannis take my colorful volley head-on before staggering to the ground with imaginary wounds.

"Cat! You're a menace!" Aetos booms from behind me.

Laughing, I whirl and hit him with everything I've got left. The magic can't do more than tickle, but he acts like he's on the glaciers again, pitting himself against the man-eating Mare of Thrace.

His face contorts, turning more menacing with every step. I eye his hulking form and the giant horsehide flapping behind him like dark wings and wish I'd braved the Ice Plains, defeated a monster, and made an offering like that mare's head to the Gods.

What did I do to deserve my magic, apart from survive?

Aetos wades through the color-thick air and then grabs me, crushing me in a bear hug. "Who's laughing now?" he rumbles somewhere above my head.

"Too tight." I gasp, the magic fizzling as my bones shift.

"Sorry." He lets go, and I breathe again. His eyes, glacial blue like the Ice Plains, narrow when he gets a good look at me. "Zeus! You look like you're forty." He taps a finger against my cosmetic-layered nose. "Your face paints are so thick I can hardly see what's under there."

"That's the idea," I say with a cagey grin.

His expression sobers. "Who are you hiding from, Cat? Who are you?"

I clam up, humor draining from me like someone else's magic. Aetos hasn't looked at me like this in years. Not since he stopped asking where I ran from and why I scream at night.

I force a cocky smile. "I'm Cat the Magnificent. Soothsayer Extraordinaire."

He doesn't smile back, only letting me off the hook once he gives me a look that says he's not done fishing. "Time to dazzle some Sintans, Cat the Magnificent. Soothsayer Extraordinaire."

The tension I hate so much breaks when Desma pats my rump. "Either those pants shrank or you're eating too many spice cakes again."

I make a sound of disgust. "Why is everyone ganging up on me?"

She grins. "Because you're weird, and nobody knows who you are."

"My pants are fine." Actually, they're verging on truly uncomfortable, but I'm not about to admit it now.

Aetos crosses his arms, frowning. "They *are* too tight.

If I see anyone looking at you for more than five seconds, I'll tear his bloody head off his bloody body."

My right eyebrow creeps up. "Then everything will be very bloody."

"Laugh all you want," he growls. "Just don't get splashed."

I make a sign to the Gods on Olympus. "Grant me patience."

"Seriously, Cat." Desma grabs my arm, unexpected urgency in her grip. "Those face paints and that outfit make you look a lot older and more experienced than you are. Tread carefully in the crowd tonight."

I roll my eyes. "I have done this before."

"I know." She releases me as abruptly as she grabbed me. "But things are different in Sinta now, especially in the south. These people have realized that muscle *can* overcome magic. Hoi Polloi have been feeling feisty all spring and summer, and you wouldn't want to kill anyone by accident."

Everything in me stills. "What makes you think I can do that?"

Desma shrugs. Aetos looks way too interested, so I shift the focus to him.

"You can kill with fire."

"I can kill with one finger," he scoffs, snapping for good measure. "Fast, too."

Desma's small hands land on her narrow hips. "We're talking about magic, not obscenely overmuscled Giants."

"Who are you calling obscene, rainbow woman?" Aetos's barrel chest heaves with indignation, thunderclouds gathering in his eyes.

"Stop!" I cut off their bickering before they have a chance to warm up. The Fates got everything backward with these two—a huge, tattooed southerner with fire and flight and a tiny Demigoddess with nothing to show for her Olympian heritage except rare beauty and a colorful glow. What a pair. I wish they would finally sleep together and get all the repressed emotion out in the open. "I have to go. My table's up."

Aetos winks. "Careful out there."

I shove him. It's like ramming my hand into a marble statue. "Why does everyone suddenly think I need protection? Didn't you just decide *I'm* the menace who can kill by accident?"

"So you can?" Desma asks.

I shake my head. "Of course not." I hate lying to my friends.

A boy with a berry ice in his hand and red dripping down his chin passes me three times before he finally stops.

I point to the chair across from me. "Sit."

Looking skittish, he lands on the edge of the seat. "Can you see my future?" he asks.

"Maybe." Never commit to something you probably can't do. I can try to have tea with Zeus. That doesn't mean I'll succeed.

His expression turns belligerent. "Does that mean you can't?"

"Let's make a deal." I lean forward, lowering my voice. "If you don't think I do a good job, you don't have to pay me."

Hazel eyes sharpen, and he nods.

"Say it," I prompt.

"It's a deal."

I sit back, satisfied. "What do you want to know?"

He shifts uncomfortably. His face, boyish and awkward

now, but promising to break hearts in a few years, scrunches up. I wait, trying to look patient until his question finally pops out.

"Will I ever have magic?"

I stifle a sigh. You're either born with magic or you aren't. Magoi or Hoi Polloi. It seems cruel to dash his hopes too fast, though. "Give me your hand."

Trusting, he holds out his right hand.

I wipe my slippery palm on my leather pants, which does nothing, and then take his hand in mine. His is sticky with berry ice juice, and our hot skin fuses.

Palm reading is an ancient ritual, one that holds no bearing on anything whatsoever. You can't read a damn thing from the lines on someone's hand, but if the boy has even a tiny, glacial shard of the Ice Plains inside him, I'll feel it. His power will want to come to me the same way mortals reach for the Gods.

There's nothing. He's warm, sticky, and smells like kalaberries. His hand holds no power, although that doesn't mean magic is forever out of his reach. I hesitate before sending him on a dangerous path. "Why do you want magic?"

His cheeks color. "I'll never be as smart and strong as the tribal warlords. If I don't have magic, I won't have anything."

That's not true. He has a brain. He seems healthy. He can do anything he wants. The boy believes what he's saying, though, or else my magic would react to the lie.

"Are you brave?" I ask.

He looks surprised. "I-I try to be."

"Do you love your mother?"

He nods, his brow creasing at my question.

"Say it out loud," I insist.

"I love my mother."

"Is your family good to you?"

He starts to nod, and I raise a warning finger with my free hand. I have to hear it. There's magic in spoken language. It's binding. There's a reason people ask for someone else's word. Every sentence a person utters can be a promise—or a betrayal.

"They're good to me," he answers.

A loving family. How novel.

"If you saw a child being beaten, would you walk away or would you intervene?"

His eyes widen. "But what could I do?"

"That doesn't answer the question." A hard edge creeps into my voice, and he pales.

Note to self: Don't scare children.

His shoulders straighten. "I would intervene."

I brace for a ripping in my soul. Surprisingly, none comes. He's told me the truth, which makes him worthy of my advice. He's also courageous and has a family that will support him, which means he might actually survive it.

"The Gods favor kindness and selflessness." Some do at least, and despicable people like Cousin Aarken get chomped. *Ha!* "Under the right circumstances, goodness and honesty can be rewarded."

The boy looks confused. "I have to be good and ask the Gods for magic?"

I sit back, releasing his hand. "Yes, but you can't just go to the temples, pray, and say, 'please, please.' It doesn't work that way. You have to prove yourself. When you're older, wiser, and much stronger, choose either the Ice Plains or the Lake Oracles."

"You mean go north." His freckled nose wrinkles in distaste.

"That's where the magic is. Here, we're so far from Olympus that it's weak and diluted in the people who possess any at all. Even Magoi have trouble this far south. It's harder for most of us to wield our power."

"Most?"

I wink conspiratorially. "Most."

The boy chews on his berry-stained lip with teeth that are white and straight. "Which should I choose?"

He's so earnest that something in my chest tightens. I'm pointing him toward vicious magical creatures or Oracle fish the size of Dragons. What if I'm sending him to his death?

"You have to be very strong to survive the Ice Plains. The Oracles are capricious but usually the safer bet."

He nods, storing the information away. I should charge two coppers for this kind of thing, especially in southern Sinta. There's more ignorance of magic and history here than anywhere else in Thalyria.

"Which lake?" he asks.

Make that three coppers. Maybe even four...

"That's your choice, and it depends on which God you want protecting you." I pitch forward and then say in a low voice, "But if you're anywhere near Fisa and you see Poseidon's three-tentacled trout, tell it Catalia says hello." I draw back, alarmed. *What in the Underworld?* I don't blurt things out. I don't just hand over information about myself that I've never told my friends, including my full name.

The boy's eyes go as round as clay pots. "You've been to an Oracle?" he says far too loudly.

My stomach lurches while I wonder when I stopped being in control of my own mouth.

Damn meddling Gods. What do they want with this kid? Or worse—with me?

I reluctantly nod. "And came out the right end. Not the

back," I clarify. I don't even want to think about being digested by a giant fish. "Oracles will look you in the eye, poke around in your head, and then taste you. If you're lucky, they'll help you. If you're not worthy, they'll swallow you whole."

He pales. "Eat…people?"

"Even Oracles need to eat. I have a cousin who found that out the hard way."

The boy's jaw practically hits my table.

"Oh, he deserved it," I assure him. Mother knew Aarken and I were rivals and informed me with her usual cruelty and disappointment that I should have taken care of him before the Oracle did. Kill or be killed—the family motto.

"You're amazing." The boy sounds breathless.

I laugh. Sort of. "Everyone thinks so."

He grins at my obvious humility and starts digging around in his pocket for a copper.

"Keep it," I tell him. "Buy yourself another berry ice and bring one back for me." It's so hot I'm tempted to let one melt down the back of my neck, but I'm sticky enough as it is.

"Thanks!" He grins even wider.

I hope the information I've revealed about myself remains between us. His smile is charming, and I don't want another enemy. "How old are you?"

"Thirteen," he answers proudly.

It's only a small deception. Pain still rips my soul. Flames sear me from the inside, igniting in my core and lashing out to char my bones. I lock my body down, holding still until the burning passes.

"You're eleven," I say coolly. "Why would you lie?"

His face falls, and he stares at his feet. "I wanted to impress you."

"Lies never impress." I try not to grit my teeth and scare him. "Remember that when you see the Oracle, or you might come out the wrong end."

He nods without looking up.

Sweat breaks out on my upper lip. A bead of moisture slips down my spine. Between the southern climate and the boy's lie, someone's going to have to peel me out of my pants. I hope Desma's up for the job.

"What's your name?" I ask.

"Jason." He's still hanging his head.

"Go get me that berry ice, Jason of Sinta. I'm melting in this heat."

He flashes me a relieved smile and then dashes off.

I lean back in my chair, fanning myself and longing for the cool north, a view of the Ice Plains, and a way to take back certain parts of what I just said. At least the kid doesn't realize it's important. Poseidon and Fisa are worlds away to a southern Sintan boy. Catalia doesn't mean anything to him.

I'm just starting to convince myself that my unprecedented slipup wasn't so colossal when a deep voice rumbles behind me, making me start.

"The Gods don't favor kindness and selflessness. They favor strength and courage."

CHAPTER 2

THE LOW VOICE WASHES OVER ME LIKE THE INCOMING tide on a dark night, chilling despite the heat. I turn, my heart leaping into my throat. The warlord who was staring at me earlier steps closer, his long fingers nearly brushing my shoulder as he points to the banner proclaiming me a soothsayer. "You planted an idea. You didn't tell him his future."

"These conversations are supposed to be confidential!" I snap, springing to my feet. *Oh Gods! How much did he hear?*

"The boy asked if he'd have magic, and you never told him if he would."

My jaw unhinges. How dare the brute listen in! "I gave him a way to get magic. That's better than answering a yes-or-no question."

"So will he get it?"

I have no idea. That depends on the Oracle. It depends on Jason. "That's none of your business."

"You went to an Oracle. Which one?"

I feel the blood drain from my face. "That's none of your business, either."

His eyes narrow, and he stares down that hawkish nose at me. "What did you whisper to the boy?"

My heart stutters. "That's none—"

"—of your business," the warlord finishes dryly.

If looks could kill, I'd be dead. I don't respond well to threats, even ocular ones, and my spine shoots straighter than Poseidon's trident. "If you're trying to intimidate me, then don't bother. It won't work."

His full lips curve into a cool smile. "In my experience, I can intimidate anyone."

I huff, incredulous. "Do you want my services? If you do, sit down. Otherwise, go away. You're scaring people off with that look."

His expression darkens. "What look?"

"That one." I wag my finger in his face. "The one that says *I'm big, I'm bad, and I can chew you up, spit out your guts, and use your bones for toothpicks.*"

The warlord's face blanks with surprise. You'd think I just morphed into the Hydra and grew some extra heads.

One of his four men, an auburn-haired ax-wielder to his left, can't repress a snort and gets the back of the warlord's fist in the gut for it. Not too hard, but hard enough that the end of the laugh comes out as a wheeze.

I glare at the semicircle of large, muscular men now cutting me off from the noise and bustle of the rest of the circus fair. My table is at my back, they're at my front, and I can't walk away, even if I want to. "Take your violence elsewhere. This is a peaceful table."

Peaceful? Me? Ha!

"A fragile flower," the warlord mocks, magnetic gray eyes looking me up and down in a way that makes my temperature rise. He studies me intently and a little too long. "And wilting in the heat."

I scowl, repressing the urge to wipe my sweaty palms on his white tunic. He's too clean for a tribal warlord. He doesn't even smell bad, and his slightly wild, jet-black hair is shiny, curling softly around his neck. There's not a drop of perspiration on him, which infuriates me. I contemplate the sword with its two-handed hilt poking up over his shoulder from the leather harness on his back, pretty sure I can't even lift the monstrosity. Good thing I have other strengths.

The sharp pinch of magic stings my skin, and I turn. Aetos is watching.

"Either sit down and get a question answered, or that man over there"—I point to my painted friend—"is going to pop your skull like a cherry in a crow's beak."

The warlord's teeth flash in the way of wolves before they pounce. "You think he can?"

"I know he can."

The idiot actually chuckles. "He wouldn't know what hit him."

I snort. "He'd incinerate you."

"He could try."

His tone is utterly unconcerned. I grit my teeth. Typical warlord: huge ego, huge sword, huge ass. Figuratively— the rest looks just right.

"Go." I point away from my table. No one insults my friends.

His eyebrows lift. "*Go?*"

"Do you need me to say it in sign language?" I make a rude hand gesture that universally conveys my meaning.

Setting his jaw, the warlord circles my table. I turn, too. His men follow, and the semicircle of muscle moves to the other side, guarding the warlord's back and leaving mine once again open to the circus fair and a dozen very powerful people who will come running if I need them.

The warlord sits in the chair the boy used, dwarfing it. "You're awfully small to be making threats," he remarks casually.

"It was more of a message," I reply, still standing.

His gray eyes turning steely, he rises halfway, plants his

hands on the table, and leans forward until we're practically nose to nose. "Send that message again, and I'll teach you how to make a real threat, and carry through on it."

My scalp tingles. I have to give him credit; the warlord does menace with a capital *M*. But I grew up on a steady diet of terror, and I know true malice when I see it. This isn't it. This is banter to people like us.

Baring my teeth in what could hardly be called a smile, I throw his words back at him. "You could try."

"Don't tempt me," he growls softly.

"Trying to scare me?"

"Glad it's working."

I laugh—although maybe I shouldn't. He *does* look miffed all of a sudden.

In magical fights, I can absorb other Magois' powers and then turn their own abilities back on them. If I have to fight a Hoi Polloi, I need to be faster, stronger, or smarter, or else I'd better have some useful magic stored up. Right now, I don't have anything. I doubt I'm faster, and I know I'm not stronger than the warlord. As for brains, the jury's still out. At least I have my sense of humor.

Deciding to test his, I glance up at the night sky and then cringe like something terrifying is coming straight for us. As if on cue, the warlord surges to his feet, drawing his sword and looking spectacularly ferocious. His free arm sweeps out over the table, pushing me roughly back. I stumble, see red, and then gear up to fight back when I realize he's trying *to protect* me.

Under the heat of his hand, something in my chest contracts with a sharp twist. His piercing eyes look up, around, everywhere, vigilantly scanning the amphitheater for threats. There's nothing, of course, and his arm drops.

"Don't scrunch up your eyebrows like that," I scold, a little out of breath for no good reason. "You'll give that pretty face wrinkles."

He's not pretty. He's far too masculine for that, with his intense gray eyes and powerful body. A fresh scar cuts diagonally through his right eyebrow. Along with his wide mouth and hooked nose, it gives him a piratical look that does strange things to my insides.

When he swings his gaze back to me, I have no idea what to make of his expression. The auburn-haired man is turning red from trying to hold in a belly laugh, so I cringe again and cover my head with my hands.

"*What* are you doing?" The warlord sits again, resting his sword across his lap.

"The Gods might punish your gargantuan ego, O Scary One. I'm trying to avoid the lightning bolts."

The ax-wielder guffaws and then takes a hasty step back.

"Is this how you treat all your customers?" the warlord asks.

My surprise must be obvious. "So far, no question has been asked, and no money has been exchanged. I wouldn't call you a customer. You're more of an eavesdropper and a bully."

"Good Gods!" the ax-wielder booms. "She has bigger balls than I do."

Humor flashes in the warlord's silver-hued eyes. "Balls don't necessarily come with brains."

"Mine do." If my smile were any more syrupy, my teeth would rot.

He arches a dark eyebrow, as if daring me to show him the goods. I'm not sure whether to laugh or run. In the face of indecision, I turn to the auburn-haired warrior. "Want your fortune read? Half price."

F/23444570

"Sure." He adjusts the ax on his shoulder, catching the torchlight and sending a sudden glare into my eyes.

I move to the side. Being blind is too much like being in the dark—never good.

"I have a question," the warlord interrupts.

Curiosity sparks. "Finally." I let out a beleaguered sigh and flop back into my chair. It's probably safe to sit down again. While the warlord is far from harmless, I'm not getting the impression he's out to harm *me*. "I was beginning to think we'd be here all night."

He levels a flat stare at me that would wither a person who hadn't been tortured, beaten within an inch of her life, and nearly murdered six times in her own bed before the age of fifteen.

"Around me, big mouths are attached to dead bodies," he says.

I sigh, shaking my head. "What kind of person goes around threatening death?" *And by that, I mean* besides *most of the people I grew up with.*

He leans forward again, one eye closing in a quick and unexpected wink that takes the dangerous edge off his words. "The kind who can."

Butterflies tickle my insides. "You either have an Olympian-sized sense of self-importance, or you're overcompensating for a lack of confidence."

The warlord's gray eyes crinkle at the corners, and his lips jump up for the briefest of smiles, taking his face from striking to far too appealing in less than a heartbeat.

"Peace?" he offers, his deep voice sincere.

I bite my lip, taming the reciprocal smile I can't quite help, and pretend to think about it. "Fine. But don't go releasing any white doves yet."

He chuckles, the warm, appreciative sound sending a

wave of heat through me that has nothing to do with the southern climate. My words come out surprisingly husky when I ask for his question.

Sitting back, he indicates the four men around him. "Are my companions loyal to me?"

And just like that, I'm uncomfortable again. His question smacks of another life, one where people tortured me for truths.

"Soothsayers predict the future." I force an even tone despite my suddenly thumping heart.

He rephrases the question, never taking his eyes off me. "Will my men *remain* loyal to me?"

I try not to squirm, not liking his revision much better.

The warlord frowns at my hesitation. "What's more important than loyalty?" he asks.

There's a hardness to his tone, and his question strikes a nerve. *Have I been disloyal? Does running away make me a traitor, or smart?*

Who cares? I'd rather be disloyal than dead.

My eyes dart to the men behind him. "All four?"

"All four." He nods to his crew.

I swallow my misgivings. The warlord doesn't know me. He doesn't know what I'm capable of. "Four coppers then. One for each."

He puts the coins on the table, and I pocket the money, turning to the ax-wielder first. "What's more important? Your warlord's life or your own?"

"My warlord's."

There's no hesitation. No soul ripping.

"You have to choose between this *savage*"—I sink a lot of sneer into my voice just for the fun of it—"or your wife. Who do you choose?"

"I have no wife."

"But if you did?"

"If I choose to marry, my wife and children will come first."

No searing flames. No melting bones. No pelting truths to outweigh the lie.

I let my eyes glaze over and place my hands on my crystal ball, pretending to do soothsayer-like things for an appropriate amount of time. I should probably make up a chant, but I can't bring myself to do it.

"Your man is loyal," I finally announce. "But I don't advise using his future family against him."

"I'll have a family?" The ax-wielder's face splits into a wide grin.

Eh... "Yes. Lovely wife. Several strong children," I lie. Or maybe I don't. How in the Underworld should I know?

The warlord's unwavering stare has me shifting uncomfortably in my chair. "Step back, Flynn," he commands. "Carver, you're next."

A dark-haired man approaches, moving forward with a confident stride. He's about my age, lean and tall, and looks like he'd be mean in a fight. He's the type of sinewy swordsman that can move like a shadow and strike before you blink. I know his kind. He's the kind you want watching your back, not sneaking up on it. There's a resemblance to the warlord in his facial features, black hair, and gray eyes, but the similarities end there. The warlord outweighs him by about sixty pounds and is probably ten years older.

The man—Carver—smiles at me. There's a disarming, rather friendly gleam in his eyes, but I have no doubt his easy smile could turn sharp with menace.

"Is loyalty important to you?" I ask.

"Yes."

I point to the warlord. "Would you follow this man into a fight?"

Carver nods.

"Say it," I prompt.

"I would. I have, and I would again."

I glance at the warlord. His expression is unreadable, but his eyes feel like a Cyclops's foot on my face. I ask for Carver's hand, feeling awkward. Even if palm reading is a hoax, his rough skin still tells a story of battles and blood. "Would you die for this man and his cause?"

"Yes." A simple, one-word, truthful answer.

I stare at Carver's long, powerful, callused fingers. What is the warlord's cause? From what I heard, the new royal family outlawed warring among the Sintan tribes. They're all supposed to get along now that one of theirs has taken over.

I repress a smirk. *Good luck with that.*

"I would bleed for him. I would die for him."

Carver's truth is so strong that it carries a word— brother. Shocked, I drop his hand like a poisonous snake. I almost never hear an echo from truths.

The word still bouncing around inside me, I say, "Your brother is loyal, but I think you already knew that."

"Hmm."

I scowl at the warlord. "What's that supposed to mean?"

"I never said he was my brother."

Damn it! Who stole my filters tonight? "You look the same."

"Not that much."

I wave my hands above my table. "Soothsayer, remember? I *know* stuff."

He tilts his head, looking hard at my eyes. He keeps up his scrutiny until unease ripples through me, making me squirm.

The warlord breaks eye contact. "Basil," he calls out flatly, motioning another man forward.

A blond man takes Carver's place. He's handsome without being remarkable, strong without being overwhelming. He blends in. I guess that's what he's good for. Warlord, Flynn, and the fifth man don't blend. They're too big, too powerful. They demand attention. Carver doesn't blend, either. He's lean and angular, with wily eyes. Basil is just... *blah*, as far as I can tell.

Basil moves to the right, away from the warlord and closer to the fifth warrior who has watchful blue eyes and a colossal mace that could probably crush three skulls at once. Basil's movement is minute, and I only notice because I've trained myself to look for body language that will help me fool people into thinking I'm not a fraud.

Great. The warlord's question suddenly makes sense. This is a party to out Basil. Too bad I'm invited.

"Basil, is it?" I ask even though I already know. I'm just stalling the inevitable.

The man nods.

I take a deep breath and lock my muscles, bracing for a false answer. "Where do your loyalties lie?"

Basil looks smug. Like most southerners, he has no idea of the power of magic and words. If he did, he'd be running away.

Fire explodes in me at his deceitful answer, agonizing. Bones fry. Organs roast. I try not to blanch as truths ignite along with his lie, scorching my insides like red-hot coals.

In a sudden burst of movement, the warlord disarms Basil and grabs him by the throat. "Who do you work for?"

"I'm loyal!" Basil squeaks, looking as stunned as I feel.

His lie blasts me again.

"I saw the look on her face." The warlord squeezes

Basil's neck until the other man gasps for air. "You're a liar."

He saw my pain? I'm more worried about *that* than I am about anything else. I controlled my reaction. I always do. How does some Hoi Polloi warlord know what a little flinch means anyway?

Basil plunges his hand into his pocket and pulls out a thin, glass vial filled with gray powder that glitters silvery in the torchlight and impresses the magic out of me. He draws back a gloved hand, ready to smash the poison into the warlord's face.

I leap over the table, taking its black wool covering and my fake crystal ball with me, and latch on to Basil's arm. It takes all my weight to keep his hand from moving.

"Back off," I warn the warlord. "It's Medusa's Dust. It'll turn you to stone."

He uncurls his hand from around Basil's neck and steps back, leaving me dangling like an idiot from the traitor's wrist.

"How do you know that?" His question sharp, the warlord shifts his focus to me, and I think maybe I should have let him die.

"Poison expert." Sort of. I blow a damp curl out of my eye. The only thing keeping Basil from shaking me off is Carver's very long and very lethal sword at his back. We're surrounded by big men with scary weapons, and no one's *doing* anything. "Someone cut off his arm. Or kill him. If I let go, he'll throw dust all over the place."

Flynn hefts his ax. "That would be suicide."

"Thank you, Flynn." I roll my eyes in the auburn-haired man's direction. "Do you really think he cares?"

Flynn shrugs. "He's dead anyway."

Exactly. So get on with it.

Before I can say as much, Basil twists his arm with me still holding on and somehow smashes the vial against my neck. My eyes shoot wide as Medusa's Dust burrows deep into my skin, the powder as hungry as a swamp leech. The onslaught of magic shatters my equilibrium, and I stumble back against my table, gasping for air, giddy and slightly outside of myself.

His face turning terrible, the warlord roars and lunges for me.

"Don't touch me!" I cry, evading. As soon as the magic works its way into my system, the poison will infect anyone who touches me. I don't know how long that takes. It's fast for a normal person. Longer for me.

My limbs get heavy quickly. More slowly, my skin hardens, turning gray. I'm not worried. Medusa's Dust is magic-based. My body will chomp the poison like lamb steak for dinner. Force enough toxic berries down my throat or stick a few adders in my bed and I'll die like anyone else, but magic won't kill me.

The warlord watches my skin lose all color, his eyes somber, his jaw tight, and his hands clenched at his sides. Something in his gaze shocks me. I don't ask why he cares, although I almost tell him that in a few minutes, I'll be pink and soft and poison-free again, but that's not something he needs to know.

I turn to Basil. He's smirking, obviously glad he took that pesky soothsayer down with him.

"Thanks for the present." I offer him a smile fit for the bloodthirsty maniac I was meant to be. "Here's one for you."

I grab his wrists with both hands, just above the gloves that protected him from the poison. Medusa's Dust races up his arms. He hardens, freezing solid on a gasp, his mouth half-open and his eyes wide with terror.

I let go, disappointed. "That was fast."

The warlord stares at me, his expression almost comically thunderstruck. "Why aren't you dead?"

I throw him a saucy look. "You think I'm that easy to kill?"

Relief floods his face. He grins, and a tiny lightning bolt zings down my spine. "She's the one," he announces to his men. "I want her."

Whoa. What?

Who? Me?

What for?

His warriors close in. I throw out my arms, creating a poisonous perimeter. "Back off or you'll end up like Basil."

"Is there a problem, Cat?" Aetos's blue face towers above their heads. The warlord looks small in comparison, despite standing over six feet.

I shake my head. "Tell Selena we have a new gargoyle. She likes that kind of thing." I slide a look toward Basil, trying to ignore his petrified expression and crooked teeth. His nostrils are flared, like he's still trying to suck in air.

After sparing the human statue a quick glance, Aetos arches his eyebrows at me, picks it up, and then carries it away. Desma and he were right. I might accidentally kill someone tonight. Or not so accidentally.

Annoyance flits across the warlord's face. "I've been trying to flush him out for days. Now I have no one to interrogate."

"Some Tarvan woman wants your head in exchange for Basil's brother's life." Shock vibrates through me. The words slipped out without my consent. I swear to the Gods I hadn't even formed the thought before they were out there, hovering damningly between us. Who in the Underworld is in control of my mouth tonight, because it is *not* me!

The warlord's lips part, not in surprise, but in some kind of satisfied expression I don't understand and don't like.

My gut clenching, I turn my hands palms up and shrug. "Soothsayer, remember?"

"You're exactly what I think you are, aren't you?"

The woman who divines the truth through falsehood? The most coveted diplomatic weapon in the realms? The Kingmaker?

I back my still-toxic self away, careful not to bump into anyone. I feel like the Gods are peeing on me from Mount Olympus. I was happy here. The circus was my family.

"There's one of you every two hundred years." The warlord stalks me through the crowd, his long strides devouring the space between us. "Kingdoms rise and fall for you. *Because* of you."

His intense gray eyes are readable enough now. He's thinking of ways to contain me, to catch and use me. He'll expose me. He'll put me in a cage and make me sing like a siren.

Strike that. He'll *try* to make me sing like a siren. "Touch me and I'll kill you."

His mouth flattens. "You could try."

If it means getting away, I'll expose another talent in front of all these people. It doesn't come to that, thank the Gods. I slip backward through the performers' gate, and Cerberus steps between us, blocking the warlord's path and making him draw up short. The hound's enormous fangs glint in the torchlight, drops of venomous saliva hissing when they hit the ground. Three low, ominous growls shiver through the dark passageway as I quickly exit the amphitheater. Hades has a thing for Selena, and his watchdog guards her circus instead of the gates to the Underworld. Cerberus will hold the warlord back. Too bad he'll keep Jason and my berry ice away, too.

CHAPTER 3

I wish I didn't have to move on. Thank you for taking me in. "Oikogeneia."

I say the word for family out loud as I write it in the ancient language of the Gods, hoping someone in the circus can read it and knows the power and promise it holds. Aetos doesn't have that kind of schooling. Desma and Selena might, and I trust them to use the magic only if they have to. Aetos would die for me. Desma would die for me. Vasili and Selena might, too, and probably a dozen others. If they call me, there isn't a threat in the three realms that will keep me from coming back to them.

Before I came to the circus, there was only one person I wouldn't have been willing to kill, if it came to that, or let die for me. Now there are more than I have fingers and toes, and it makes me weak.

Family.

It irks that a word so contaminated in my mind contains such power. I gave it power and gifted it to my friends. I would kill myself before letting it cross my lips for any of my remaining blood relations.

My few belongings are packed in the old brown satchel I stole off a sleeping merchant on the Fisan coastal road eight years ago. Some clothes and a pair of old boots, a cloak, three throwing daggers, a few hair ties, a comb, and my stage cosmetics—everything I possess. I strap the circus's bedroll and blanket to the ties at the bottom of my bag. I don't think Selena will mind. It's hardly theft at this point.

Straightening, I think about my next step. When Poseidon gave me my gifts, he also gave me his obsession. The frigid northern lakes and the Fisan Ocean are both about three weeks out of my reach. As usual, that means settling for a Sintan stream. It's still water, even if it's warm. I'll stop at the creek, somehow get out of my pants, clean up, cool down, and then... I don't know. Nothing will ever change, no matter where I go. I'll still live in fear, the black crow of dread circling my head.

The circus was different. With Selena and Cerberus here, I almost felt safe—safe until that dratted warlord decided to stick his big, hooked nose into my life.

Growling in frustration, I look around my tent for the last time. No one will see me leave. Where I'm concerned, stealth reaches an entirely new level.

The warlord's taken this from me. Home and family mean something to most people. I never understood what it was until Selena took me in, and Aetos and Desma decided I was theirs. They're mine, too. Leaving them is like cutting off a limb.

Deep breath in. Long breath out. *Cats don't cry.*

My tent flap snaps open, and the warlord fills the doorway, a mass of shadow and steel.

I freeze, stunned. Disbelief leaves a sour taste in my mouth. "H-How did you get back here?"

He steps inside, crosses his arms, and leans casually against the tent post. The torch pops, sending a flicker of firelight over him that illuminates his inky hair and sunbronzed skin. The wavering glow highlights the hard muscles rippling under his rolled-up sleeves, tapering down to corded forearms, thick wrists, and powerful hands. Hands that could break me in two.

His teeth flash. Wolfish. Confident. "I have my ways."

My mouth falls open, and a shiver scrambles down my spine. I'm rarely at a loss for words.

"You took my copper and didn't evaluate my last man." He nods to his final companion. "Kato. You're up."

The last man ambles forward, casual, followed by Carver and Flynn. They're all so relaxed. What's wrong with these people? Don't they know the world is falling down around my ears?

The man called Kato stops a few feet from me. I take him in with a glance. He's big, blond, and almost impossibly handsome, with startling cobalt eyes. The mace he carries tells me he'd rather bludgeon than slice. I get that. There's something satisfying about whacking people over the head.

Backing up, I dig around in my pocket, which is *not* easy, and pull out one of the warlord's coppers. "Here's your coin. Now get out." I throw the copper at him.

He catches it on reflex and then tosses it back, hitting me in the chest.

I glare at him, fuming.

"I'm loyal," Kato volunteers cheerfully. He looks like he's always happy. There are smile lines etched into the tanned skin around his mouth and eyes, and perfect teeth like his are just made to be shown off with a grin.

I scowl at the blond warrior now, reluctantly noting that he's a rather perfect specimen of a man while giving him a heaping dose of the evil eye. There's no soul ripping this time, and everyone knows it.

Apparently satisfied, the warlord steps closer. "Now that that's settled, you're coming with me."

I snort, stepping back. "Never in a billion suns. Not even if Zeus showed up as a swan and tried to peck me in your direction. I wouldn't go with you even if my other option was Hades dragging me to the Underworld for an eternal threesome with Persephone."

The warlord pierces me with a hard stare. "We can do this the easy way, or the hard way."

"Or no way," I retort.

He lunges for me. The tent is small, and he's shockingly fast. His hands close around my upper arms, and satisfaction flares in his eyes. "Not poisonous anymore?"

"A shame." I stomp on his foot, crushing with the heel of my boot.

He laughs. *Bastard.*

I disappear. I'm still there, just invisible, and he lets go. They always do. The warlord lets out a sound somewhere between a snarl and a grunt and stares at his empty hands. It never occurs to people to just hold on.

I inch away, silent. Four men block the door. They shed their casualness like it's a second skin, becoming battle ready in an instant, alert, the air around them charged with tension.

"Guard the door," the warlord rumbles. "She's still here."

Gods damn it! I glance around. There's no escaping under the tent. The material is tight and flush to the ground. Aetos drove the spikes in for me, and it'll take Aetos's muscles to get them out again. There's a knife in my belt. I could slice the canvas, but by the time there's an opening I could fit through, the warlord would be on top of me. My only option is to draw them away from the door. If Flynn and his giant ax would move about a foot to the right, I could probably slip through.

The silence in the tent is absolute. I don't even hear them breathing. Then the warlord turns and looks straight at me. *Impossible.*

Still one moment, he pounces the next, grabbing me.

I'm so shocked I lose my concentration and pop back into sight. One big hand is clutching the better part of both breasts, and the other is clamped over my ear, his fingers digging into my braid.

I suck in a sharp breath and pound on his wrist, trying to dislodge his hand from my chest, shaken by how large the warlord is, and how ungodly hot his hands are on me—a firestorm of muscle, sinew, and bone.

His eyes flaring, he adjusts his grip, banding hard fingers around my left arm. I fly at him with my right fist and punch him in the neck. He jerks, taking the blow on the muscular column instead of the sensitive front. I draw back for another hit, but he plucks my fist out of the air and then forces it down, easily shackling both wrists in one hand. He uses his other hand to disarm me, slipping the knife from my belt and into his own.

I nearly cringe at my own stupidity. Eight years with the circus has made me soft. I had a knife, and I didn't even think of stabbing him when he couldn't see it coming.

Snarling, I bang my forehead into his jaw.

A muscle feathers along the warlord's cheek. Grasping my upper arms, he lifts me clear off my feet. "That is *not* a good idea."

He's conveniently put his nose within reach. I drive my head toward it, but he dodges, growling a curse as my nose slams into his cheekbone. Pain makes my eyes water. Gasping my next breath, I go still, dreading the gush of blood. When there isn't any, I screech like a Harpy and kick him in the shins.

With eyes like thunder, he sets me down, spins me in his arms, and then crushes my back against his chest. "Settle down, Soothsayer."

Settle down? Settle down!

"Could you see me?" I wheeze, his heavy arm compressing my rib cage.

"No, but I knew where you were." The warlord sniffs loudly and then exhales, his hot breath tickling my ear. "You stink."

Lovely. "Who *are* you?"

He turns me back around, keeping hold of my arms. "Beta Sinta."

I go numb with shock for the split second before fear surges through me in a paralyzing rush. *This* is the warlord who put his sister on the throne? *This* is the Hoi Polloi who somehow overcame the previous royal family's magic? *This* is the man now second in command of all of Sinta?

No wonder he got past Cerberus. All he had to do was order someone to bring him back here. He owns us all. He could have Desma arrested, Aetos executed, Tadd, Alyssa, Vasili, and all my other friends tortured until they begged for mercy. Selena deprived of her life's work. No explanation necessary. He's Beta Sinta.

"The better question is who are *you*?" He studies my face. "Fisan. I can see that even through all the paint."

I almost say I'm Beta Fisa just to see his eyes bug out, but that joke wouldn't really be funny for anyone. "Cat," I answer tightly. I don't deny being Fisan. My olive skin, light green, elongated eyes, dark hair, and long, straight nose give me away. It doesn't matter. A lot of people are Fisan.

"Just Cat?" He cocks his head. "I don't believe you."

I stare at him, an inferno of hatred in my eyes.

Beta Sinta's mouth flattens into a hard line as he nods to Kato. The Adonis-like blond takes a rope from Beta Sinta's belt and then ties one end loosely around my waist and the other around Beta Sinta's. The second we're attached, the warlord lets go. I start working on the knot, and no one tries to stop me. It's more of a bow. There's nothing to it, so why won't it budge?

"An enchanted rope." Beta Sinta's smug announcement has my eyes widening in astonishment. "Only I can untie it."

My mind rebels. "You don't have that kind of magic." He doesn't have any magic.

"You'd be surprised at the treasures one can find in the bowels of a despot's castle."

Actually, I wouldn't. "But the Medusa's Dust…" I sputter a curse. "I saved your life!" Obviously one of my stupider ideas. I used to be good at this stuff. If people could have gotten the better of me this easily when I was a kid, I'd be dead.

"You *think* you saved my life, but I appreciate the gesture, which is why you're still conscious."

I gasp and swing at him again.

He catches my fist before it can connect, crushing it slightly. "Control your temper," he advises, releasing my hand with a soft shove.

There are some things about my blood even I can't deny. Temper is one of them. "I'll show you temper, you oversized, egomaniacal, murdering son of a Cyclops!" I ram my foot into his groin.

Beta Sinta doubles over with an explosion of breath. I'd do it again, but I'd rather run. I swipe my knife from his belt, bring the blade down hard on the rope, and plow my way toward the door.

A second later, I'm on my ass. The rope is perfectly intact, and three men are looking down at me, identical smirks needing to be wiped off their faces. Permanently.

Flynn's foot lands on my wrist, stomping just hard enough to make me let go of the knife. Beta Sinta uncurls himself, glaring at me while he picks up my blade and slips it into his boot.

I change tactics and start sucking the magic out of the rope. Power nips at my skin and seeps into me, but the rope retains its enchantment. I keep sucking, and it keeps giving—a perpetual supply of magic!

Gods damn it! I pound both hands on the ground and howl.

"Up," Beta Sinta orders.

I twist and lash out at him with my feet. He jumps to avoid my sweeping kick, and fury erupts in me. I'm fast and well trained, but he's always a step ahead. Part of me is awed by his speed and agility. Most of me wants to grab Kato's mace and thump Beta Sinta over the head with it. Repeatedly.

He fooled me at the fair, this man with the quick smile and midnight hair. I thought the warlord was just another warlord. I flushed at his interest and jumped into his dance of teasing threats. I had fun. Now, looking at him reminds me of something much stronger than fleeting attraction. There's nothing in this world or the Underworld I hate more than royals.

"I'd rather let Cerberus slobber me to death with poisonous drool than go anywhere with you."

His jaw muscles flexing, Beta Sinta pulls on the rope until I'm forced to either scramble to my feet or get dragged to his. "Come and I won't have your friends arrested one by one while you watch."

I feel myself pale. There's no lie in his words. He's not bluffing.

So this is it, exactly what Mother was trying to teach me, to pound and torture into me. Love is weakness, an exploitable flaw.

My surroundings fade, and I feel her sharp-nailed fingers digging into my chin as she turns my face and forces me to watch my older brother gut my nursemaid, the only woman who ever held me. Mother beat me when I cried, gave me a puppy the next day, and then ten months later, just when I loved that dog more than anything except for my sister, started the lesson all over again.

I blink, and Beta Sinta's handsome, treacherous face comes back into focus.

Poseidon, protect me. I pick up my satchel, swing it over my shoulder, and don't look back.

CHAPTER 4

HOME. GONE.

Friends. Gone.

Captured by a ruthless Hoi Polloi warrior who's going to use me to keep the kingdom he stole.

Can life get any worse?

Let me think... I'm tied to the warlord atop his huge horse, I stink, and my skintight pants are driving me insane.

We ride through the night, the enchanted rope keeping me from jumping off the horse. By dawn, I'm sore and exhausted, my whole body limp with fatigue. My nose still hurts, and my bottom half, which hasn't been in contact with a horse in years, is aching fiercely, but I keep yawning, and my eyelids feel like someone's hung marble statues from them. Rage and anxiety usually keep me nice and alert. Right now, they can't even keep me awake. I slump against the warlord's back as the sun rises on our right, my last conscious thought that I hope my caked-on cosmetics leave a grimy face print on his clean, white shirt.

I only wake up because someone is fiddling with the rope. Cracking open an eye, I see lean, tall Carver retying it so that Beta Sinta and I are not only strapped together at the waist but under the armpits as well. I didn't even feel Beta Sinta untie the rope to begin with and scowl at the lost opportunity. I could have turned invisible and bolted from the horse.

Carver pulls the knot tight, tugging me hard against his

brother's back. "You sleep like the dead. Kato and Flynn are already betting on when you'll fall off."

I give him the evil eye, and Carver chuckles, flashing that easy smile. *Does he think this is funny?*

By noon, the sun is high and hot, beating down on my dark hair and crimson-clad back. My leather pants are officially one of the worst things in my life right now, and that's saying *a lot.* I still manage to go back to sleep. I haven't slept like this in years, maybe in my entire life. I may be strapped to a man I hate, but he would probably do a lot to keep me alive. He might even be good at it. Ironically, I feel almost safe.

I'm going to escape. *After* I sleep.

The afternoon heat is unbearable enough to wake me up for good and make me want to claw off my skin. Beta Sinta is throwing off more than his fair share of heat as well, and all I can think about is dumping buckets of icy water over us both. I keep sane by thinking about the north, the cold, the fiery glow of sunshine through a curtain of ice, and the soft chill of snowflakes frosting my skin, but all that does is fill the hollowness inside me with an even deeper ache. Longing for things I can't have is useless, just like wishing for freedom and a life no one wants to steal out from under me.

Stifling a sigh, I blink against the dry summer brightness and look around. Dust, dust, and more dust. *Fabulous.*

My stomach wakes up with a low rumble. "Don't you people eat?"

"We ate. You slept through it."

Beta Sinta's deep voice vibrates through my rib cage, and I wiggle back as far as the rope will allow.

"I have to get down."

He glances over his shoulder at me. "Now?"

"I have to… You know…"

There's a slight pause. Of course he knows.

"There are woods and a stream up ahead. We'll stop there."

I squint and can barely make out the greenery on the horizon. It's miles away. What does he think I'm made of? "I have to pee *now*."

Wordlessly, he reins in his mount, loosening the rope to give me about four feet to work with.

I slide to the ground and land on wobbly legs, bracing myself against the horse's steaming flank. I glare up at him. "You have to get down. Or untie the rope."

Moving with easy, masculine grace, Beta Sinta swings down, still irritatingly fresh except for the sweaty face print on his back. *Ha!*

"Some privacy?" I grind out.

He arches one eyebrow. You'd think I'd just asked him to catch Pegasus and fly him to the moon. There's no privacy anyway, not even a bush to squat behind, just sunburned plains, heat haze, dust, and tumble bumbles.

Shrugging, I turn invisible, taking the rope and the warlord along with me. His men shout in alarm.

"It's all right," Beta Sinta calls. "I'm still here."

He can't see me, though. Right now, he can't even see himself. Anything attached to me turns invisible right along with me. Clothes, ropes, warlords… It's a great way to scare the life out of someone. They think they've died and become a realm-walking spirit. Nobody wants to end up like that.

The second we pop back into sight, Beta Sinta mounts his big, brown beast and reaches down for me. I'm so stiff I can't get back on the horse. None of my muscles comply with my brain, and he has to haul me up like a sack of grain.

"Go easy, Griffin," Flynn rumbles on our left. "She's not used to riding."

I almost throw him a grateful glance but then turn it into a scowl, which is easy since I'm squinting into the sun, and Flynn's shock of auburn hair is so shiny it's practically a weapon in its own right.

Beta Sinta ignores Flynn's advice in favor of getting to the woods—and shade—faster, setting a pace that makes me wish my seat bones were even better padded than they already are. I sink my nails into his sides, half to hold on, half to maim him, but he doesn't even react.

Griffin. I turn the name over in my head, reluctantly curious. A griffin is an exceptionally rare creature, a mix of lion and eagle, king of beasts and king of birds. His parents must have been the pretentious sort. Then again, he did take over Sinta.

He finally slows to a walk, I think for my sake even though we're not yet to the forest. My stomach growls, louder this time, and he fishes around in his saddlebag, handing me something wrapped in grape leaves. It's smelly and not quite firm. Goat cheese. *Gag!*

"Got any bread to dilute this?"

"Dilute?" Beta Sinta sounds like he's laughing. There's definitely a smirk in his voice.

Kato's blue eyes dance with humor as he hits me with a dazzling smile that's almost as bright and sunny as his hair. "Griffin ate it all."

I huff. "There's no need to be so merry about it. Did you abduct me just to starve me?"

"I was hungry, you were sleeping, and you're hardly being starved," Beta Sinta says.

It's hard to argue with that around a mouthful of cheese. I swallow and ask, "Why Beta? Why crown your sister Alpha when you're the one who did all the work?"

It doesn't seem like he's going to answer, so I take

another bite of cheese and keep eating until I devour the entire chunk. It turns out goat cheese is edible if you're really hungry.

We're almost to the edge of the woods when he finally speaks. "When I was a boy, royal soldiers used to tear through our tribe, searching our homes for twice the taxes we owed, at times abusing our women, and often taking our men for their endless wars. We collected nothing of value because it would be stolen, and thatched our roofs with simple hellipses grass because half the village would be burned to the ground. We'd cut down fields of the stuff for weaving and thatching. It's supple yet strong. And abundant. We'd rebuild, over and over again, making everything we could from that bloody grass."

He turns, and I see him in profile, his sharp gaze scanning the meadow rolling right up to the forest. He's probably noting the abundance of hellipses grass. The tough, long stalks are the only thing that really grows here unless there's shade, a natural water source, or irrigation. It's all over the north, too, but greener and softer there, like the springtime grass here before it dries and yellows from the heat.

"One day, my father decided he was done with blind subjugation. He challenged for leadership, won the tribe, and then did the same from village to village until he'd unified a swath of people and land across southern Sinta. Before the royals even noticed, he created an army right under their noses. The next time soldiers came, they only took the taxes we owed, they left our men and women alone, and they didn't light up a single home." He pauses to hand me his water gourd, drinking after me before continuing.

"I know what one decision—one *person*—can change.

But I form and execute plans. I don't second-guess, and I rarely call myself into question. That's not all Sinta needs. Our goal isn't just to dominate, like previous royal families. It's to rule."

Reality douses the spark of interest flickering inside of me. It's only been a few months. What will his attitude be once the power and wealth sink in? Will the Beta position still satisfy him? And, if it lasts that long, what will his future children's attitudes be once they start vying for the throne? From what I've heard, Alpha Sinta is unwed and too old to bear children anyway. That means Beta Sinta will succeed his sister on the throne, likely sooner rather than later, and then his offspring will come after him. Probably in every sense of the words. "How terribly noble."

"Egeria's warm," he says, ignoring my sarcasm. "She smiles at people. She has ideas for healing centers and schools. She knows how to comfort widows and orphans. She compensates for what I lack."

"Humanity?" I ask snidely, not really meaning it despite my own unfortunate circumstances.

He shrugs. "In a way."

I snort, not having expected him to agree. "If you're trying to scare me, it's not working." I know what an utter lack of humanity looks—and feels—like. If he had no humanity, he would have taken the throne for himself. He wouldn't be interested in showing his sister's softer face to Sinta, or in *ruling* instead of *dominating*. And I'd be unconscious over his horse's rump.

That doesn't mean I like him any better.

"I'm not trying to scare you, Cat."

"So what *are* you doing?"

"Explaining. Like all the realms, Sinta was being beaten into the ground by bloodthirsty, selfish royals. Things had to change. I don't lack humanity. I just do what needs to be done."

I frown at the back of Beta Sinta's tanned neck, noticing a smattering of freckles across it. I could almost agree with that, if "what needs to be done" hadn't included abducting *me*.

The ancient forest rises like a sentinel wall, its trees gnarled and old, its canopy thick and high overhead, providing instant relief from the heat. I tilt my head back, breathing the shady air deep into my lungs. "Please say we're stopping," I mutter on the exhale.

"Up ahead," Beta Sinta answers. "By the stream."

For a second, the thought of water—rejuvenating, curative water—distracts me from everything else. "How long will we stop?"

"Until tomorrow. We need to hunt."

"Thank the Gods," I groan.

Carver, Flynn, and Kato smother laughs, and I narrow my eyes at them. "You won't be laughing with my knives in your hearts."

They chuckle outright, as if I were joking.

Flynn stretches his upper body, adjusting his ax. "She talks big, but she's made of custard."

"Fluffy and full of cream?" Kato wiggles blond eyebrows at me.

Carver grins. "Think she's sweet, too?"

My eyes spit fire. "Bite me. You'll find out."

They burst out laughing, the deep, booming sounds driving the birds from the nearby trees. A tremor even ripples up Beta Sinta's back, and I have the almost uncontrollable urge to sink my teeth into him.

It takes forever to reach a clearing suitable for making camp. There's enough shade that the grass is still fragrant and green, and the air smells fresh, like foliage and fertile soil. Beta Sinta's horse starts grazing before he even dismounts, swinging his leg over the big animal's neck and sliding easily to the ground. There's not enough slack in the rope, and it snaps taut, jerking me to the left and chafing my hips.

I stiffly regain my balance, grumbling a curse that would make Aetos proud.

Beta Sinta looks up, unexpected humor softening his eyes to a warm silver-gray. "What are you still doing up there? I thought you couldn't wait to get off the horse." A teasing smile lifts one corner of his mouth, and my heart thumps hard in my chest. *Stupid heart.*

I swivel my head and stare straight ahead. It's either that or kick him in the teeth.

I'm seriously considering the kicking option when he reaches up, plucks me off the horse, and sets me down, holding on to my waist while I get my feet under me. My hands land on his biceps for balance, and I gain a whole new appreciation for his battle-hardened physique. The steely strength coiled under my fingers makes me wonder what kind of magic I'll need to come across to overpower him, what I'll have to expose him to in order to get away.

Not that I care.

His grip on my waist tightens, and a tremor unfurls through me at the subtle pressure of each warm, blunt fingertip. Eyes hooded, darkening, he murmurs, "You'll recover."

Traitorous heat rises in my belly and fans out across my chest. "Dazzle me with your sympathy. Oh wait! You don't have any. Big, bad Beta Sinta has to hide behind his sister so he won't scare widows and orphans. How many widows and orphans did you make with your war? Was it worth it, *Beta Sinta*? How long do you think you'll rule?"

His previously warm gaze turns cool and flinty as his hands fall away, leaving my whole midsection suddenly cold. "Longer—now that I have you."

His words hit me like a punch, driving the air from my lungs. "I'd rather die than spend the rest of my life as an information slave, getting fried by diplomats' deceit and sycophants' lies." I back up a step, shaking my head. "You can't use me. I won't let you."

The tightness in his expression eases. "It's not a question of getting used, Cat. We'll work together. You'll see."

My mouth gapes. I have no idea what to say to that bit of insanity.

"Hoi Polloi have never ruled in Thalyria. Don't you think I know I need Magoi on my side? *At* my side?" he asks. "Magoi are a powerful minority in Sinta. They could be catastrophic for us if they ever decide to turn against us, especially with the northern nobles supporting them. My family and I managed to recruit a few Magoi advisors who actually seemed more interested in the realm than in the blood flowing through our veins, but that's not enough. I need more than that."

He looks at me intently, leaning slightly forward. His hands curl at his sides, almost as if he's resisting touching me again. "That's why I went searching across Sinta for Magoi, but no one felt right. Not until you. You felt exactly right." His voice deepens in pitch, smoothing over me like a velvety secret I shouldn't want to know.

My breathing shallows. Strange sensations dart through me, and I stupidly echo, "Exactly right?"

He nods. "I need someone in my inner circle, someone who will make other Magoi think twice about rebelling.

Someone who might even make them wonder what I have to offer. Someone powerful and trustworthy."

I blink, stunned by his apparent blind faith in me. "You don't know anything about me!"

"I know you're the Kingmaker, and I also know you didn't hesitate to put yourself in danger to protect a southern Sintan Hoi Polloi stranger and his men."

Bollocks! Bollocks! Bollocks! Why did I do that? Stupid Medusa's Dust. Stupid Basil. Stupid *me*!

Beta Sinta's eyebrows draw together in a sudden frown. "Don't do that again."

I snort. "Don't worry. I won't."

He nods, like I didn't just splash him with the acid in my voice.

"Come." The conversation about upending my entire life for his political gain evidently over, he tugs on the rope. I have two options—put one foot in front of the other, or get dragged around. I put one foot in front of the other.

Once the horses are seen to, Beta Sinta sends Kato and Carver hunting and tells Flynn to guard the camp. Flynn has been carrying my satchel, and I grit my teeth while Beta Sinta goes through it, tossing my stuff around like he owns it. He sniffs my citrus soap, takes out the throwing knives and hands them to Flynn, goes through the pockets of my different pairs of pants, and then lobs the bag at me. "Time to get rid of your stink."

I glare at him. "Charming."

"Warlords don't need charm."

Maybe not, but royals do.

He leads me to the stream and looks at me expectantly. It turns into an epic staring match, and I finally throw my hands up in frustration, despising myself for cracking first.

"You can't possibly think I'm going to strip naked and bathe in front of you."

"Turn invisible."

"I won't even make it to the water with four feet of rope!"

"True." He pulls his tunic over his head, revealing a sculpted torso, powerful and scattered with scars. Most of them are small, but there's a big one under his left arm, snaking around his rib cage from the back. The skin is jagged and raised, a shade lighter than the rest of his sun-browned hide. No healer mended that. "I'll bathe, too."

My eyes lock on the hard ridges of his abdomen. *He's not serious.* His belt drops to the grass. *He is!*

He starts sliding his pants down his hips, and I vanish in a panic, taking Beta Sinta into invisibility with me. His clothes reappear in a neat pile to my left just before his voice rumbles out of thin air. "Tug on the rope when you're ready. And don't forget the soap."

With my heart racing like a herd of Centaurs, I need a moment to recover the power of speech. "Use your own soap!"

"Yours smells better."

My jaw drops, not that he can see. Of all the weird and uncomfortable situations I've ever been in, this one tops the list. I'm about to get naked with a Hoi Polloi Beta Sinta. Mother would have a fit, which almost makes being here worth it.

That in mind, I unbuckle my belt and pull off my tunic. My boots follow, but I can't for the life of me get out of my pants. Not sure what else to do, I throw my tunic back over my head, and we reappear. Beta Sinta is a lot closer than I expected, and he whirls, his elbow colliding with my chin.

"Cat!" He reaches out to steady me as pain rockets

through my jaw. One warm hand curls around my shoulder. The other tilts my face up, inspecting the hit. "Are you hurt?"

I bat his hand away. Of course I'm hurt, but one bash in the face isn't the worst I've had.

He frowns. "What's wrong?"

What isn't? I flush hot and red and focus on his chest. It's a pretty spectacular chest. I refuse to look lower. I close my eyes and mumble, "I can't get my pants off."

There's a beat of silence. Then he laughs—*really* laughs—and my eyes fly to his face. I ball up my fist, wondering what he'd do if I hit *him* in the chin.

Still chuckling, Beta Sinta says, "Don't look so furious. I'll help."

"Stop laughing," I demand through clenched teeth.

Surprisingly, he makes an effort. His lips press together, but his eyes stay bright, leaving an intriguing mix of humor and hardness on his face.

I take a deep breath and reluctantly uncurl my fist. Right now, Beta Sinta is the lesser of two evils.

His eyes drop to my chin again. "You handled that hit well. Like a man."

"Is that supposed to be a compliment? The last thing I want is to be hairy and stupid."

He grins, surprising me. "Not everyone knows how to take a hit. Personal experience?"

I don't respond. I'm not about to spill my life's story.

Beta Sinta shakes his head. "Cat, this doesn't have to be—"

"Don't bother." I hold up my hand, cutting him off. I close my eyes again since I don't want an eyeful and then sit, leaning back on my elbows. The second I sense him reaching for me, I turn us invisible.

"How am I supposed to help you if I can't see you?" he asks.

"I'm right in front of you," I mutter. "Do it by feel."

He grumbles something that sounds like "stubborn soothsayer" before one hand lands heavily on my stomach, just below my breasts. His fingers slide toward my hips, bumping over the rope. Shivers skate across my skin. I feel warmth through my tunic and then calluses as he pushes the material aside. Tension locks me in place. Having Beta Sinta's hand on me is strange and disturbing. I'm repulsed. *Definitely* repulsed.

His other hand joins the first, sending a jolt of heat through me. I press my lips together, wholly unsettled.

It takes a few hard tugs before I'm finally free. "I'm going to burn those," I groan in relief.

"Don't." His disembodied voice carries a rough edge. "I like them."

His tone nearly scares the magic out of me. The last thing I need is to get distracted, lose my invisibility, and end up sprawled naked on the ground with Beta Sinta.

I blink, banishing the image. "All the more reason to burn them."

"I'm not your enemy, Cat."

I scramble back as far as the rope will let me. "Everyone is my enemy."

Silence. I guess he has nothing to say to that. I throw off my tunic, pick up my soap, and tug on the rope.

The stream is revitalizing despite not being as cold as I'd like, and the water helps wash away the memory of a hard, hot hand sliding down my belly, of rough fingers on my hips, dipping under my—

Stop!

Flushing, I scrub every inch of myself, feeling like I can

finally breathe again without my layers of cosmetics and yet dreading being seen without them. When I grudgingly give the soap to Beta Sinta, it's an awkward exchange in which we grope for each other's hands and touch way too much skin. While he's washing, I float, the rope keeping me close.

"That's not helpful," he gripes, giving the rope a hard tug.

I zip through the current, stream water washing over my face. "Too bad," I sputter, letting myself drift back downstream.

"Aren't you cold?"

"Cold?" I almost laugh. "I grew up swimming in the snowmelt from the Ice Plains. This is a thermal bath to me."

His pause makes me realize what I just gave away. *Filters, Cat. Filters.* They don't seem to exist around him. Even southerners know the most powerful Magoi come from that far north. And from Fisa, to boot.

"Let's go," Beta Sinta eventually says, climbing the bank and dragging me with him.

"I don't have a drying cloth."

"Use your tunic." He must sweep his hand toward my clothes because his fingers accidentally brush my lower back. He inhales sharply, and I jump forward, shocked and confused by the strange sensation of lightning webbing out under my skin from the point of contact. I'm suddenly way too hot, with a pounding heart, and wondering what the not-altogether-unpleasant but very real zapping is all about.

Tingling from head to toe, I release a slow breath, hating that it shudders on the way out. "My tunic's too dirty."

"Then use mine," he offers gruffly.

Biting my lip, I scoop up his tunic and gingerly pat myself dry. The masculine scent of salt and sunshine teases my nose and imprints on my skin, lingering when I wish it wouldn't. When I'm done, I toss the shirt down, aiming for a spot where the grass is thin. As luck would have it, the tunic reappears sweaty face-print up. Beta Sinta sees it for the first time and curses. *Ha!*

His tunic disappears again along with the rest of his clothing.

Ridiculously warm, I take my time combing and braiding my hair, trying to soak up the relative coolness of the evening air.

Beta Sinta curses softly under his breath. "What in the Underworld is taking you so long?"

I don't answer and get dressed slowly, knowing it'll irk him. I also can't believe he's about to see me without my face paints on.

Finally, I can't stall anymore. "Here I come. And you too," I add, doing my best to sound like I'm sucking on a lemon.

We pop back into sight, and he looks me over with disconcerting thoroughness, something hot and alarming in his gaze.

I blush, and the warmth in my cheeks makes me want to hit him. Or kick dirt in his face. "What?"

He flashes me a lopsided grin, brief and tinged with surprise. "You're a lot younger than I thought."

My face is clean, unmasked, and my sable hair is drawn back in a simple braid tied with a leather cord and swinging halfway down my back. I'm wearing loose, brown traveling pants, soft leather boots, and a light-green, sleeveless tunic that does nothing to hide the scars on my arms. I wonder if Beta Sinta knows what they are. I haven't been this exposed outside the circus's protection in eight years, and it terrifies me almost as much as the heated look in Beta Sinta's eyes.

Awareness thunders through me, unwelcome. The

longer he stares at me with that smoldering intensity, the wilder the tiny, sizzling flames licking through my lower abdomen become. After a moment of utter stillness, when I'm shockingly conscious of my own rampaging heartbeat, he turns and walks away.

With Beta Sinta's back to me, I remember to breathe again. Brutally forcing my inner turmoil into the *do not open ever* compartment of my brain, I follow, dragging my feet to make him shorten his stride every time the rope cuts into his hips.

Carver, Flynn, and Kato stare at me when we arrive back at the camp. "Who are you, and what have you done with Cat?" Flynn jokes.

I throw him a sour look. "She's out chasing mice."

Carver looks at me and then at his brother. The silent communication that passes between the two men sets my nerves on edge. When I escape, I need a new disguise. Forty and curvy just got busted. Well, forty anyway.

Last night, surrounded by friends and the glow of the circus torches, I thought the warlord couldn't intimidate me. I thought I was safe. Hidden.

It turns out I'm an idiot.

CHAPTER 5

I'VE NEVER HAD THE BEST SENSE OF DIRECTION, BUT even I know we've passed the same egg-shaped boulder twice on the third day after my abduction.

"Why are we going in circles?" I ask. The rope is as short as ever. There are about three inches between Beta Sinta's back and my front. And he's so bloody hot! Sitting this close to him makes me want to dump snow over his head.

"We're being followed."

My heart jolts in my chest. Are Aetos and Selena coming for me?

I doubt it. They read my note. They would think about it, fight about it, but in the end, they would leave me be.

"How do you know?" I ask.

"I saw smoke from a campfire twice in the last two days."

"Maybe it's a coincidence."

"That's why we're going in circles. To find out if they're really following."

"I hope they are," I announce.

"Why's that?" He doesn't sound even mildly concerned.

"Because then there'll be a fight. If I'm lucky, someone will kill you, and I can finally untie this stupid rope." I have to eat next to him, sleep next to him, bathe next to him, pee and...other stuff next to him. It's horrible and humiliating. It's a worse punishment than Prometheus getting his liver eaten every day by a giant eagle.

Poseidon, why are you doing this to me?

If I have to wake up with my nose in Beta Sinta's chest one more time, I think I'll scream.

"I've fed you, I haven't harmed you, and I haven't asked you to do anything in particular. Your situation could be far worse," he argues. "With whoever might be following us, it could be."

"First of all, abduction is a major strike against you. Second, they won't necessarily catch me. Third, you hit me in the face."

His back tenses. "That was unintentional."

"It still happened."

"You hit me often enough," he mutters.

"Good idea." I grind my fist into his kidney, feeling no remorse. He snatched me from the circus and threatened the people I love. He deserves that, and worse.

Gray eyes glint at me over his shoulder. Beta Sinta's voice turns a little too calm for comfort. "Cat…"

"Your Highness?" My tone is a sweet-and-sour masterpiece.

"Have a care." His eyes narrow, and he takes his time turning back around.

After we set up camp, earlier than usual, Beta Sinta unties himself for the first time and links me to Carver. Unease grips my stomach in the strangest way.

"What are you doing?" I demand.

"They're following us. See the smoke?" He points at something that looks like a cloud. "I'm going to investigate."

"Alone?"

He smiles faintly, angling his body toward mine. His warmth burns a flush into my cheeks. "Worried about me?" he asks.

"What? No! I hope you die."

His smile fades. Straightening abruptly, he tells Carver, "You know what to do."

Carver nods and claps his brother on the back. After acknowledging Kato and Flynn, Beta Sinta prowls away without a backward glance. The send-off is pretty minimal, if you ask me.

"What are you supposed to do?" I ask when Beta Sinta is out of earshot.

Carver tugs me toward the campfire, and I drag my feet. Southerners always want to be where it's hot. "If he doesn't come back, I'll take you to Sinta City myself. To Egeria."

If he doesn't come back, he's dead, and his rope won't work unless someone else claims it. That someone will be me, and I'll be long gone before we reach Sinta City.

I watch Beta Sinta disappear on foot up a rocky hillside scattered with scrub. "Good riddance."

"You don't mean that," Flynn says.

I cross my arms, frowning. "Yes, I do."

"Why?" Kato asks. His golden hair glows almost celestial white in the strong beams of the setting sun, and I have to squint to look at him. "He's been decent to you."

"If decent means abducting me and keeping me tied up, then I guess he's been decent, by your standards."

Carver moves, forgetting I'm attached, and I lurch, falling to my hands and knees. A stone digs into my palm, and I hiss a breath between my teeth. Grating a curse, I grab the rope and give it a hard enough yank to make Carver stumble.

"I hate this bloody rope!" None of these people have magic. There isn't a dribble of power to steal, nothing to get me out of here.

Flynn is instantly by my side, reaching down to help me up.

I shove his mammoth hands away. "Don't touch me. I hate you all."

He looks sympathetic, which makes me want to throw him under a Cyclops's boot. "That's not true."

I glare at him. "I have no freedom, no privacy, and now I don't even get to have my own mind? Don't tell me how I feel!"

Flynn sets his ax down with a sigh. "You hate Griffin, even though you shouldn't, and the rest of us are just lumped in because that's easiest for you."

I roll my eyes as I contemplate making a lunge for the ax. I would if I thought I could lift it. "Spare me your psychological ramblings."

"Do you want a bath?" Carver asks, his question cutting straight through our argument and ending it.

We're fifty feet from a stream with a tempting clear pool. I'm hot and dusty, and I desperately want to jump in. Swimming is in my blood. I'm a fish in Poseidon's sea.

I plant my hands on my hips. "No."

He shrugs. "It's just that you and Griffin keep going off for long baths."

My mouth drops open. *What in the Underworld is he implying?* "He doesn't give me any choice! Apparently, I stink."

Kato leans over and sniffs me, his cobalt eyes dancing with humor. "You don't smell that bad."

That bad? "That's because I bathe."

Carver glances at the water, then back at me. The rope hangs loosely on his narrow waist. "Except for tonight?" He has the nerve to look like he might laugh, so I level the same cold look at him that I used to give my siblings. It's my *The Ice Plains will melt away and the Underworld will freeze over before I give one* inch *to you* look.

Carver arches dark eyebrows, looking annoyingly like a certain warlord whose ass I'd like to kick from here to a Harpy's nest. "Suit yourself."

A bitter smile curves my lips. "Always." It's a good thing my own lies don't burn me.

I *hate* stinking. I hate it with the passion of the Gods. I regret my stubbornness before dinner, and even more after when I'm forced to lie down next to Carver, who smells even worse than I do. Kato is on watch, Flynn is already snoring, Beta Sinta is off in the brush, and Carver doesn't feel right. His body isn't solid enough. He doesn't smell of citrus soap and sunshine. He's just...not the same. As much as I hate to admit it, I was getting used to his brother.

Sleep takes a long time coming and then is fitful, troubled by memories that resurface in dreams. Anxiety bubbles in my stomach, acidic and sharp. The churning has me fumbling in the dark, tumbling in the undertow, getting dragged out to places I don't want to be.

The first scorching blast sinks into my belly, and I snap awake with a startled cry. He only attacks at night, when I'm asleep and can't see. I don't know how he gets past the locks on my door, but it's him, always the same one. He wouldn't dare come after me when I'm ready and alert. I'm too good with a knife.

His magic rips through me. Fiery needles pierce my skin, burning deep into the heart of me. I arch off the bed, throbbing, and scream until my throat turns raw, blind with pain. Red with fury.

He lets up, and I just barely suppress a whimper. He's not strong enough to keep going. If his magic were mine, I could go for hours, slowly cooking him until the last breath left his body. He's not me. For every five minutes of torture, he needs one to recover. That's when fists fly.

I block, curling into a ball until either I can strike back without leaving myself too open, or Thanos comes to pull him off me. He hovers over me, fingers digging into my shoulders and pushing me down. His hands on my blistered skin are excruciating, but I thrash to loosen his hold, shrieking for all I'm worth, and then hammer a fist into his throat.

My knuckles connect with flesh, and everything suddenly feels too real. My eyes fly open, and Carver is doubled over me, grabbing his neck. His eyes are bulging, and the breath he finally manages to drag into his airway rattles in his throat.

Seeing him, I go limp with relief. A shudder tangles in my chest. *I'm not there.*

"What in the Underworld was that?" he rasps, rubbing the Cat-sized fist mark already shadowing his skin.

I glance at my shaking hands, expecting to see red bubbles and slashes, blood turned to lava in my veins. They look normal, but I know the truth; they're stained.

"Nightmare," I croak.

Carver sits back on his heels. He shoves a hand through his hair, frowning. "You were twisting and howling like a damned lunatic. Scariest thing I've ever seen."

I clamp my mouth shut. If I open it, I might scream.

Drawn by the commotion, Kato and Flynn exchange a look. Flynn drags his bedroll closer until I'm pinned between Carver and him, and Kato sits down near my head, using one of my knives to carve a likeness of Athena into a chunk of fragrant cedarwood.

I should tell them all to go away. I really should. I unlock my jaw, and something else comes out. "Why Athena?"

"Wisdom and war," Kato answers. "What every man needs."

"Not home and family?" I ask.

He grins. "Not a young man. A hearth and a wife are for later, when the battles are won."

"Haven't you won? Sinta is yours."

"Sinta is Egeria's," Kato says. "There are battles yet to come."

His cryptic words send a chill down my spine. Is Tarva next? Fisa? "What makes you think she'll rule any better than the royals before? Capricious, violent, cruel, bestowing favors only to take them away…"

"You'll understand when you meet her."

That'll never happen. I'll escape soon. I have to.

"That was more than just a nightmare. Who hurt you?" Flynn asks. He sounds angry, and his genuine concern leaves me feeling raw and exposed.

I press my lips together and stare up at the night sky. I have a better question. Why haven't I had my daily dose of nightmares since Beta Sinta abducted me? That is, until tonight?

The next morning, Beta Sinta still hasn't returned. No one seems particularly worried, and they don't break camp. I grit my teeth and hint that I might want a bath. Even Poseidon is telling me I stink.

Carver grins. "So how does this work?"

"How do you think? We both turn invisible. The rest is pretty much self-explanatory."

Chuckling at my crankiness, he wiggles his eyebrows at Kato and Flynn, who joke about wanting their turn at an invisible swim. I roll my eyes and make a rude hand gesture. Then we disappear before they can retaliate.

On the bank, I strip and grab my soap. "You ready?"

"Naked as the day I was born," Carver answers, sounding far too proud.

I tug on the rope and lead him into the stream. The pool on the east bank is perfect, four feet deep with a sandy bottom and a light current.

"Too bad I can't see you," Carver says.

"What?" I feel my cheeks heat. "Why?"

"That would be more fun," he answers matter-of-factly.

I can't help laughing. "Splash."

"What for?"

"So I know where you are."

The water sloshes about three feet from me, and I hurl the soap at him. Carver lets out a satisfying grunt.

"Don't flirt with me."

"Why not?" He sounds completely innocent. The rascal.

"Because I'll kill you."

"You could try," he says, imitating his brother's deeper voice.

I snort, smothering another laugh. "Is that the new royal family's motto? Very plebeian. Perfect for your lot."

"What's wrong with plebeian?" Carver asks. "I'd rather be us than them."

He means Magoi nobles and royals. "So would I," I answer truthfully.

I dive under and blow bubbles. Carver must see them because he hits me with a huge splash when I come up. Sputtering, I splash him back, or at least I think I do. Sometime in the middle of a full-on water fight, I realize I'm having fun. I shouldn't be enjoying this, but I can't help it, and being strapped to Carver is so much better than being attached to Beta Sinta. That's all weirdness and tension.

"You win!" Carver cries, a shiver in his voice. "I'm turning blue."

"How do you know? You're invisible."

"I can feel it. Trust me."

Trust you? Not likely. "You southerners are so fainthearted."

Water droplets appear out of nowhere, splattering all around me.

"Shake your hair over there!" I yell, flicking water back.

He must jump away because the rope snaps taut, yanks me, and I face-plant into the stream. I right myself, cursing colorfully between coughs.

Carver laughs. "I'm surprised Griffin hasn't drowned you yet. I keep forgetting you're attached."

I think back over the last few days as we climb the bank. Beta Sinta is surprisingly conscious of the rope, almost never jerking me around.

Frowning, I gather my hair and start wringing the water from it. "I need a drying cloth. And more soap."

"Ask Griffin," Carver says.

I huff. "Forget it." I finger-comb my tangled curls, air-drying the rest of me before dressing. I leave my feet bare. "You ready?"

"I'm always ready."

I let go of our invisibility, and Carver is still completely naked, his clothes clutched in one hand.

"That's not ready!" I cry, slapping my hand over my eyes. "You're an idiot!"

"But an impressive idiot."

"No!" I screech. "Oh Gods! Now I have to replace my eyeballs!"

He laughs, his clothes rustling. "You asked if I was *ready*, not if I was *dressed*, but it's safe now."

"I don't believe you." I keep my hand where it is even though I'm tempted to split my fingers and take a peek.

"Then walk blind." Carver moves forward, the rope pulling me along.

A moment later, I take my hand down and walk straight into Beta Sinta, bouncing off his formidable frame. He grabs my arms to steady me, lifting a little at the same time. I end up on my toes, tipping into him, my hands flat against his chest.

Startled, I tilt my head back and find him looking down at me, his thundercloud eyes shaded by thick, dark lashes. His eyes flare a heated silver, something shockingly possessive roaring to life in his hooded gaze.

Heat sizzles through me, coiling deep in my belly. My lips part on a silent gasp, and his eyes drop to my mouth. Stark hunger hardens his striking features, and an unexpected thrill skims down my spine. The low sound that rumbles out of him is raw, primal, and utterly male. He looks ready to slam his mouth down on mine.

Instinctively, my eyes lock on his mouth. He has the kind of generous lips that look like they would be hard and soft at the same time, that would demand and coax, and set nerves on fire and melt resolve.

He drags me closer, and my heart leaps wildly in response. *Stupid, stupid heart.*

"Breathe," he murmurs.

My eyes widen, and I suck in a huge breath because it's either that or pass out.

He chuckles. *Bastard.*

Scowling, I push off, getting nowhere because Beta Sinta doesn't let go.

"*You.*" I must manage to look as scornful as I sound because he stiffens, finally releasing me. I drop, landing hard on my bare heels, the strangest chill rattling through me at our sudden separation.

His eyes go from blazing quicksilver to frosty granite. "Having fun?"

"Not anymore."

"Cat..." Carver warns, dragging his tunic over his head.

"What?" I snap.

"You're neither a guest nor a friend," Beta Sinta grates out. "Speak respectfully."

"If you don't like my big mouth, then let me go!"

Beta Sinta's eyes narrow on his brother before swinging back to me. His gaze is dark and unnervingly intense. A muscle pops in his jaw. I have no idea what *he's* so mad about. *I'm* the one getting dragged around Sinta by a magic rope.

I bend down and jerk on my boots. "No? Then just kill me and get it over with."

"I have no intention of killing you."

My temper ignites. "You want to use me! You ripped me from my home because you think it's your right. Beta Sinta can do anything he wants. Ruin anybody's life he wants. Royals!" I spit. "You're no different from the rest of them—Sintan, Tarvan, or Fisan."

"It's not like that," Carver interjects. "You'll have a good life."

I turn a blistering look on him, only vaguely registering that I detect no lies in either of their words. "A good life? Living in fear? A captive? Waiting for someone to steal me? Torture me? *Murder* me?"

Beta Sinta's eyes drop to the scars on my arms, comprehension flitting across his otherwise stony visage. "So that's what happened to you."

My chest erupts, a thousand moments of terror and pain

suspending my heartbeat and stopping my breath. I reel back, the bitter tang of residual fear splashing in my throat.

"And at the circus?" he asks softly.

My eyes feel like they take up half my face. I swallow, but my mouth is so dry it hurts. "There, nobody *knew*."

Most of the irritation vanishes from his expression. "You can relax, Cat. I'm not planning on flying a 'Kingmaker' banner from the castle gate." His voice is level, reasonable, almost soothing. It makes me want to explode. Or vomit. Or both.

"It starts with four people," I say hotly, waving my hand toward our camp. "And turns into four hundred!"

"It won't." He reaches out, gently closing his fingers over mine.

I'm so shocked by the intimate touch and the sheer warmth of his skin that it takes a moment to rip my hand away. I give it a sharp tug, and he lets go. "You don't know that!"

Beta Sinta unties the rope from Carver and straps me back to him. I feel like a bloody dog. On a leash. With a Gods damn owner! Apparently, the argument is over. He even gets to decide that. *Son of a Cyclops!* It takes all my minimal self-control not to start kicking him in the shins.

"I've already heard from Kato and Flynn. Anything to add?" Beta Sinta is looking at the bruise on Carver's neck. The others obviously told him about my nightmare. Did they also tell him how they surrounded me like a flock of oversized mother hens?

Carver grins, rubbing his neck. "She packs a mean punch."

Beta Sinta doesn't smile back. "Maybe you slept too close."

CHAPTER 6

BETA SINTA POINTS SOUTHEAST—AT LEAST I *THINK* IT'S southeast. "Six males. Tarvan. They're definitely following us."

"Tarvan?" Flynn scratches the auburn stubble on his jaw. "What could they want?"

Everyone looks at me.

I shake my head. "No way. I haven't attracted attention in years." No wonder my guard was so low when Beta Sinta showed up at the circus.

"Four to six." Carver's long fingers glide over the hilt of his sword, flexing. "We can handle those odds."

"One's a Giant," Beta Sinta says darkly. "They must have brought him down from the north."

Silence. *Don't you people know anything?* "Giants are easy." Sort of.

Four sets of eyes turn to me again, and I wonder why I opened my big mouth. We joke about Aetos being a Giant, but he's really just a very large man. Real Giants are stupid and slow, but with such thick hides, they're hard to cut through. Accomplished warriors have been pummeled to death simply because they couldn't get their swords in deep enough.

"Aim for the eyes. If it can't see, it falls to its knees, panicked. It's a reflex. Then you have to get to its head. The vertebrae make good climbing holds, and Giants are... lumpy to begin with." I grimace, remembering gristle, fat-pocked muscle, and tough, weathered skin. "Chop through the spine at the base of the skull, where the skin is thinnest, and so is the bone."

Hope sparks in their eyes, and I sigh, disgusted with myself. "Flynn's ax will do."

"How do you know how to fight a Giant?" Kato looks impressed.

Satisfaction swells in my chest. I can't help it. I like impressing people twice my size. I shrug. "Maybe I'm lying so you'll all get killed."

There's no reaction, not even a raised eyebrow. How come they never get riled up? It's not normal.

Kato turns back to Beta Sinta. "How much time do we have?"

"A few hours," he answers. "At most."

"So do we ride and make them chase us, or do we wait for them to come?" Carver's hand is still twitching near his sword. He's like me with my knives, and I feel a surprising surge of kinship.

What's wrong with me? I must be coming down with something, like empathy. *Gah!*

"We wait. We'll be fresher that way, and there's a cave just to the north. We can hide the horses and gear in there." Beta Sinta jerks his head toward me. "And Cat."

"You are *not* tying me up in a cave!"

Flinty eyes swing my way. "I can't have you attached to me while I fight."

"Untie me, then!"

He snorts, and I roll my eyes.

"Two hours, then the cave," Beta Sinta says. "Enjoy the sunlight."

"I can fight. Help even the odds."

He shakes his head. "You'll turn on us."

"You don't even know if they're enemies!"

Sternness overcomes his features, startling me with how different it makes his face. "Everyone's an enemy."

"Learn that from me?" My frosty, snide tone shocks even me, turning my voice disturbingly like Mother's. I swallow the panic rising in my throat. What if the olive really *doesn't* fall far from the tree?

Beta Sinta levels his hard look at me. "I don't need a petulant soothsayer to teach me what every conqueror already knows."

Frustrated beyond belief, I'm tied to a big, fat rock in a stuffy cave that smells like horse dung. At least I have four feet of rope.

Shouts and clashing metal eventually disturb the murky silence. I hate not knowing what's going on. I could help, especially if the Tarvans have magic. Not that I *want* to help, but I can put a dagger into a Giant's eye from forty feet away, and I doubt any of the Sintans can do that.

Restless, I pluck at the frayed edge of my boot. They're fighting a Giant, a creature from the Ice Plains. A monster. I've seen one in its prime. It was colossal, and as ugly as ugly gets.

Mother glances down the hill, the chill wind tossing her hair and slapping pink across her cheeks. "It'll either rape you or eat you. Possibly both, so I suggest finding a way to kill it quickly."

Icy snow stings my face and hands. Looking down the frozen slope into the gaping hole of the Giant's lair, I shake even though I'm not terribly cold. "Any other advice?"

She arches one perfectly sculpted eyebrow, imperious.

"Do you have any other advice, Mother?" I correct.

A thin, hard smile curves her lips before she grabs my shoulders and shoves.

At least she left me my knives. I blinded the Giant on instinct, paralyzed it with a well-placed jab, and then sawed its head off with a throwing knife. I was eleven, and there was nothing quick about it. At least all the gore kept me warm. And Mother got what she wanted. She tested me, and she covered me in blood.

The knowledge of what to do came out of nowhere that day, guiding me. The Sintans won't have that. It's not written in their bones.

Anxious, I force my hands to my sides before I tear my boot apart.

Outside, something stomps hard enough to shake the ground. Dirt and pebbles cascade from the cave's dark ceiling, and I duck, covering my head with my arms.

Did they listen to me about the Giant? I was telling the truth.

My gut churns as I pull on the knot Beta Sinta tied, blind to the battle outside, listening to deep bellows, clashing metal, and growls, and snorts, and pounding. Anything could be happening out there. A victory. A massacre. This could mean my escape. And why that thought makes me feel like there's blood on my hands is anyone's guess.

Finally, I can't take it anymore, and I wrap the rope around both hands and pull on the rock with all my might. It slides a few inches across the dirt. I pull again, and again, slowly moving toward the mouth of the cave until I'm panting and sweating and quietly cursing up a storm.

At last, I can lean far enough out to see the battle. With practiced efficiency, I count heads. Auburn. Blond. Two dark as midnight. Three Tarvans are left.

Then there's the Giant. It's hard to miss.

Breathing heavily, I swing my gaze back to Beta Sinta. He's locked in combat with two of the remaining Tarvans. Carver is taking on the other while Kato and Flynn dodge the Giant's club, trying to get close enough to blind it. Flynn throws a knife at its head, but his aim is off. Kato shouts something and tosses another knife to Flynn, who's closer. Flynn tries again just as Kato moves in and distracts the creature with a hard strike to its lumpy calf. They're coordinated and working together as a team, but they won't get far if they can't blind the Giant and bring it to its knees. Its skin is just too tough.

As if drawn by an irresistible force, my eyes find Beta Sinta again, taking in every powerful sweep of his sword, agile step, and cunning feint. He's impressive, to say the least. So are the Tarvans. These are no ordinary bandits. They have the kind of skills that only come with years of training and real-life practice. Just looking at their weapons and the way they fight, I know a spectacular amount of gold went into buying their services and sending them after Beta Sinta and his men.

But Beta Sinta is still better with a sword. So is Carver. They won't stay outnumbered for long.

Seconds later, Beta Sinta brings down one of his opponents with a hard slice across the man's middle. He doesn't even slow down as he whirls to face the other, blood flying out from the tip of his blade. There's no emotion on his face, only focus and steely resolve. My breath catches. Chilling determination. Efficiency. This is the man who conquered Sinta, the warlord who could be king.

On Beta Sinta's left, Carver gains the upper hand in his fight, driving his adversary back and out of my line of sight. Beta Sinta and the remaining Tarvan follow the same path, their swords clashing in a blur. The Giant moves after them, probably magically bound to the mercenaries in some way, and Kato and Flynn disappear as well, still trying to blind the monster with knives.

My hands already raw from before, I haul on the rope again to move farther out of the cave. The heavy rock won't budge, and I turn to find it wedged fast between two other stones.

Damn it! I can't see anymore!

I wrestle with the big rock, curse at it, go back and try to lift it, and get nowhere.

Time seems to slow down, and the wait to know what's happening becomes interminable. The sound of fighting gradually fades. Pacing in front of the wedged rock, I watch the entrance to the cave. Then, strangely hesitant, I tug on Beta Sinta's knot again. When it doesn't give, an odd feeling stirs inside of me. I'm not relieved. *Definitely* not relieved.

A few minutes later, all four men walk in, blocking the light from the cave's narrow entrance. They look surprised to find me so close to the exit.

My chest deflates as I exhale the breath I was holding. "Really? *None* of you died?"

"Don't sound so disappointed," Flynn chides, grinning like a fool. "And thanks for the advice." He nods to me, but I don't nod back.

"A blind Cyclops throws better than Flynn," Kato teases. "He lost six daggers, including yours, going for the Giant's eyes before he finally got one."

One? Who got the other?

Who cares!

"Mine?" I turn to look outside. "I have to find them!"

"It's a mess out there. We'll buy more knives," Beta Sinta says, pointedly adding, "for Flynn."

"No. They're mine, and I want them back!" Vasili gave them to me. I threw my Fisan knives down a sinkhole in Tarva four years ago. I was trying to "let go." It didn't work, of course.

I give him my death glare until Beta Sinta finally agrees to look for my knives before we leave.

"How do you know so much about Giants?" he asks. His gray eyes tell me he's wondering what else I know, how much information he can get out of me. I should really stop giving it away for free.

I wave my arms around. "Soothsayer, remember? I *know* stuff."

His grin surprises me. Straight, white teeth flash in the shadows, and a bolt of lightning thunders down my spine, splashing warmth along my nerves. I blink and turn away, off balance and alarmingly hot.

"Give me my knives back, and I'll teach Flynn to throw something other than his ax," I offer peevishly, my insides in a knot and my fingers itching for a blade.

Beta Sinta unties the rope from the rock and reties it around his waist. "We'll see."

At least it's not a flat-out denial. Surprised, I glance up, my uncooperative eyes snagging on the shadowed planes, angular jaw, and aquiline nose of his arresting profile. He leaves the cave, and I follow, my stomach doing an annoying little flip when he catches my hand and helps me over the brambles at the entrance. I didn't need help, and he knows it.

My hand still tingling from his warmth even after he lets go, I ask, "What did the Tarvans want?"

He shrugs. "They didn't stop to talk, so neither did we."

"Mercenaries are notoriously tight-lipped."

He nods, and I can't help thinking they'd only come

after a small Hoi Polloi group with a hired Giant to assure the kill. I'm sure they weren't here for me, so I have to wonder who's after Beta Sinta's blood—and who has the coin to buy it.

We ride north for the next several days, our pace sedate because of the pounding summer heat, our path dictated mainly by sources of water and shade. Beta Sinta gives me my knives back for target practice with Kato and Flynn. It's a moderate show of trust, and I almost wish he hadn't done it because I can't seem to despise him as much since the day he handed over my blades.

I could have stabbed him right then. I thought about it. I really did, but some part of me just didn't want to. I don't know why, since Beta Sinta drives me insane. He's always there, infuriating and practically on top of me, and I hate the fact that I'm getting so used to him.

Weighing the knife in my hand, I judge the distance to Beta Sinta and think hard about what I'm willing to do to escape. I never miss.

He's alone right now, sitting with his elbow on one knee and his chin propped in his hand. A breeze lifts his hair, exposing the broad, masculine lines of his tanned and somewhat weathered face. There's a crease between his eyebrows, and his preoccupied expression gives me the strangest urge to ditch throwing practice and ask him what's wrong.

Ignoring that bit of lunacy, I turn back to the target, a silver birch with a knot in the trunk six feet up. I take aim and hit the knot. "Vasili has a knife-throwing act. There's no one faster with a blade. He throws ten knives at his wife in ten seconds. He's never hit her once."

Flynn grunts, eyeing the birch. "Sounds like a lethal son of a Cyclops. He taught you?"

For the last three evenings, we've been attached at the hip—literally—and Flynn hasn't gotten much better. It must have been sheer luck that he helped blind the Giant. Or an intervention from the Gods.

That thought raises too many questions, so I shut it down. "I was good with a knife before, but Vasili made me better. It's about balance and anticipation. Feel where your target is. Figure out how it's moving."

"Trees don't move," Flynn grumbles.

"They do if there's wind."

He gives me a cross look, throws, and misses, cursing when his knife scrapes a chunk of bark off the side of the tree and then crashes to the ground.

"Only let go when the tip points directly at the target. And don't rush," I say for the fifteenth time.

"It's hard not to rush when a Giant is swinging a ten-foot-long spiked club at you."

I roll my eyes. "You got too close."

"I couldn't hit it otherwise!" He rakes his hand through his hair, spiking it into an even wilder mess.

I bat Flynn's hand down. "You're going to turn yourself bald. 'Don't rush' doesn't mean you can't move, or fight. Just relax, and don't rush the release. Wait until it feels right."

His mouth flattening, he concentrates and throws again. The knife sticks a good two feet below the knot and a little to the right. Flynn shouts in triumph.

"Good!" I say. "You got him in the stomach. Belly wounds are the worst."

He glances at me. "Speaking from experience?"

I arch a brow. "As if I'd let some idiot impale me."

Flynn makes a strangled sound.

"What?" I ask.

"You're right, Cat." Coming up next to me, Kato seems terribly serious all of a sudden. "Don't let just anyone impale you. Only someone special."

My mouth falls open. It's possible to turn kalaberry red, and if the heat in my face is any indication, I do. They're ridiculously pleased with themselves, grinning like sirens with sailors on the horizon. I shake my head, but the corners of my mouth jump up in an involuntary response that has nothing to do with my having fun. Because I'm not. *At. All.*

"Concentrate!" I snap, turning back to the target. If I had a whip, I'd crack it. Or maybe not. They'd have too much to say about that.

Chuckling, Kato picks up a knife, draws back, and then throws. The hilt bounces off the base of the tree, and his lips purse in annoyance. "This is harder than it looks."

"That's one of the lighter knives, a floater. It's not as stable, and the target is too far for it. Try this one." I hand him a heavier blade and then guide his hand around the hilt as if he were holding a hammer. "Remember, stiff wrist or you can't control the rotations."

His blue eyes narrowing on the target, Kato takes a deep breath, getting a feel for the knife in his hand. When he throws, he hits the bottom of the knot and lets out an ear-shattering whoop. I can't help smiling—a huge, idiotic, smeared-across-my-entire-face smile. Three days ago, neither of them could hit a tree.

Beta Sinta wanders over, ruining my mood. "It's good that you're teaching them, Cat. You're good at that."

"At teaching or at throwing?" Instead of looking at him, I release one of my daggers, burying it to the hilt in the center of the knot. It's so close to my other knife that the two vibrate against each other in a metallic song.

"Both," he answers.

"And I'm supposed to care what you think?"

His jaw works like he's grinding his teeth—or chewing up an irritated response. "I'm glad you're working with them," he says evenly. "It was a compliment."

I put my hand over my heart, inhaling dramatically. "That makes abducting me and threatening my friends so much better."

A frustrated sound rasps in Beta Sinta's throat. "You never let up, do you?"

I glare at him, my voice cold enough to sprout icicles. "Why would I? I'm neither a guest nor a friend."

A muscle bounces in his cheek. He takes a knife from his belt, buries it in the birch next to my two, and then walks away.

I huff. At least *he* doesn't need throwing lessons. "Why didn't he blind the Giant?"

"He got the other eye." Flynn shrugs. "And I needed the practice. You shouldn't goad him, you know."

I snort. "It's the only fun I have."

Flynn sighs, a gusty sound full of censure. "You helped us with the Giant. You're teaching Kato and me to throw. You've told us things about magic and the north, things we never would have known. You're part of this team now, and half the time you even act like it, whether you mean to or not. It's not a bad place to be. We watch each other's backs."

"I watch my own back." I always have.

"It's better to have friends doing it," Flynn says.

"I have friends! They're at the circus."

His lips mash together. He can't argue with that. "You're

not a guest, that's true. Whether you're a friend, though, Cat...that's up to you."

My whole body goes still. My heart rate accelerates. Flynn is extending an olive branch. I can practically see it in his hand. I can also think of about a hundred nasty things to say, but they just won't shove past the lump in my throat. *Gods, I'm such an idiot.*

"We worked hard and fought bloody battles to be where we are," Kato says. "People will be jealous of how you just danced into the inner circle."

"I didn't dance here. I was dragged."

He hands me a knife, grinning. "I keep forgetting that."

Even if it's a joke, his lie still ignites an inferno in my bones. Pain roars through me, and I shudder. Hiding it seems pointless now.

"Sorry," Kato murmurs, frowning at the blast of internal fire he knows he inadvertently caused.

I shake off the burn and throw the knife, hitting the target again.

"You're an asset," Flynn continues, sweeping his big hand toward the knot with my blades dead center. "Good for more than just your magic."

He's pointing to the target, but I get the feeling he's talking about knowledge as well as knives.

"And you won't believe the riches and luxuries in the castle. You'll think you've died and gone to the Elysian Fields instead of the Underworld." Flynn's deep, animated voice reminds me of a rumble of thunder in the north. Something about him puts me in mind of home—the good parts—even though he's a southerner to the core. Maybe it's his size. Everything is big in the north: big lakes, big mountains, big Oracles, big magic. "You can have a room filled with gold furniture, the finest linens, gowns, and feather pillows." He chuckles. "You can lounge around drinking wine and eating sugared fruit all day long."

I look up at him, confused. What makes Flynn think I'll be in the castle when both he and Kato have talked about living in the barracks? Anyway, locked up is locked up, even if it's in a gilded cage. "The Elysian Fields are reserved for those favored by the Gods, and I refuse to be a drunk with rotten teeth."

Flynn laughs, smiling broadly before his expression turns unnervingly serious. "You'll be protected."

"Protected?" My eyebrows nearly shoot off my head. "Who will protect me from Beta Sinta?"

Flynn's eyebrows nearly shoot off *his* head.

"Oh, never mind," I mutter. "I'll protect myself."

He frowns, shaking his shaggy auburn-haired head. "You haven't realized it yet, but you're part of Griffin's team. He won't let anything happen to you."

A disconcerting wave of warmth rolls through me. "*He's* the problem. And for the rest, he can't control everything."

"Don't tell him that," Carver says, ambling over. Carver hasn't shown any interest in target practice. He's been polishing his sword until the long blade gleams like frost on a frigid dawn.

"Don't tell him what?" Beta Sinta asks, startling me. The man moves like a shadow, despite his size.

I turn and scowl at him. "That I'm not an actor in your Sintan tragedy."

He gives me his hard stare, widens his stance, and crosses his arms. Apparently, he's here to stay.

"If you're loyal to Griffin," Flynn says soberly, "he'll be loyal to you."

"And what's more important than loyalty?" My tone mocks Beta Sinta's at the circus fair.

"Well?" Beta Sinta asks. "What is?"

"Freedom. Choice." I face the target and throw, hitting the knot again. There are no more knives, so Carver sheaths his sword and goes to retrieve the daggers, returning three to Flynn, three to Kato, and Beta Sinta's to him. I don't get to play this time. Maybe Carver's afraid I'll stab his brother.

"What are freedom and choice without honor?" Beta Sinta demands.

"What honor is there in keeping me against my will?"

"What honor is there in letting go of an important weapon just because she complains all the time?" he practically snarls.

"I don't complain all the time!"

His eyes flash silver. "You do!"

My jaw drops, but before I can respond, Kato jumps in. His voice rises, mimicking mine. *"I hate this rope. I want bread. There's no more fruit. It's too bloody hot. Let me gooooo!"*

"That doesn't sound anything like me!" I punch Kato in the arm. Hard. "And I *do* hate this rope! And I want bread. And fruit. You people eat meat at every meal, even for breakfast. It's not normal. And don't get me started on all that goat cheese!" I make a face because I just can't help it.

"Cat, you know things, things about Magoi and royals. Things about Giants, and Oracles, and Dragons from the north. Things we know next to nothing about. Plus, there's your Kingmaker power. You're very valuable to us." Beta Sinta flicks his hand toward the birch. "And you're not bad with a knife."

Not bad? Not bad! I cross my arms, sullen. "It all comes down to how much use I can be."

"That's what it comes down to for everyone. How much

use we can be." Beta Sinta comes toward me until I have to tilt my chin up to look at him or step back, which I refuse to do. His gray eyes are stormy, and a tremor runs through me. It isn't fear, and it makes me want to squirm.

"I conquered a kingdom and found a treasure." His voice turns gravelly, low. "I won't let you go. Not now. Not ever."

A fluttering stirs deep in my chest. Something new. Something strange. I beat it down and turn, nodding to Flynn to get his daggers ready. "Yeah, I get it. You won't let me go." I guess I'll just have to escape.

So why is some small part of me considering helping these people? Sinta has been both a home and a refuge. I've watched Sintan faces split wide with wonder and delight. I've given advice and seen what's in a thousand hearts. Most of it's not bad. I've been protected—by Selena, by loyal friends, by Cerberus guarding our gates, by Poseidon when he feels like it. Most Sintans have no magic and no refuge, and the Magoi royals were like Gods. They maimed, struck, killed, and rewarded at their fancy. Sintans didn't necessarily live badly, but they lived in fear. The takeover has been a source of new hope. For the first time, a Hoi Polloi family is in charge, and the majority of Sintans think that will be better for them.

I can't help thinking they're right, and it's making me sloppy. I keep letting things slip, as if my mouth and my brain aren't connected anymore. Last night, I told the men all about Dragons. The Fisan royals have Sybaris, a terrifying She-Dragon whose favorite pastime is to chomp mortals. They don't use her to take over Tarva only because Tarva has Scylla, the She-Dragon's sister. They're both magic-bound to protect their realms, but the two won't fight each other. Generations ago, Dragon use turned into a giant stalemate with lots of huffing and fiery puffing, but no army eating. Most people don't even remember the Dragons are still there. Sinta had Echidna, the third sister, to ward off the other two. As soon as royal magic wasn't containing her anymore, anyone with an ounce of sense and some knowledge of Thalyrian history knows Echidna must have flown off to the Ice Plains. Before, everyone had a Dragon. Now Sinta is the only realm without.

"How do you fight a Dragon?" Beta Sinta's voice is deep and right in my ear. I have two feet of rope and not enough space.

"With another Dragon."

"How do you get a Dragon?"

"With magic."

He looks at me, but I don't look back. My eyes follow the sparks popping from the campfire.

His tone grows clipped. "And if you don't have magic?"

"Then you don't have a Dragon."

My wandering mind snaps back to birches, daggers, and Sintan warriors. "Find me fruit and bread, and I'll consider being less of a pain. And no more goat cheese!"

Beta Sinta looks at me for a long time and then walks away.

Okay then. I turn back to Flynn. His auburn hair catches the last few rays of dappled sunshine sneaking through the canopy of leaves, framing his strong, square face in a red-gold glow. He looks pleased and claps me on the back like I'm part of the team. He hits me so hard I nearly fall on my face.

I don't want to like him. I don't want to like any of them. I don't want to be part of their team.

"I might be able to drive a Dragon." *Gah! Where did that come from?*

Carver, Flynn, and Kato cheer loudly, drawing Beta

Sinta's attention. He looks curious, and I turn my back on him, feeling vaguely ill.

Twenty minutes later, Flynn lands two daggers near the edge of the knot, and I can't help it. I jump up and down and clap.

CHAPTER 7

I SQUINT INTO THE HEAT HAZE, WONDERING IF I'M hallucinating. "Is that a town?" I was starting to think we'd go all the way to Sinta City without ever staying at an inn.

Sleep in a bed? With Beta Sinta?

My stomach flips over at the thought, even though I've been sleeping next to him on the ground.

Maybe he'd just tie me to the bed?

What flashes through my mind makes wildfire splash across my cheeks when I should be seething. I *am* seething. Beta Sinta keeps me infuriatingly close—on horseback, at meals, in streams. At night. His scent is constantly in my nostrils, the heat of him always scorching my skin.

"Better. A market town." He turns, smiling at me, and the outside of his thigh brushes the inside of mine. My pulse picks up, and there's an excited leap in my chest. My unruly physical reaction to him makes me want to kick myself in the head. Or kick *him* in the head.

"Why now? Not that I'm complaining." I can put a muzzle on my animosity for a few hours in exchange for a market town.

"You said you'd be less of a pain in exchange for fruit and bread. And no more goat cheese."

I fight the smile tugging at my lips. "I said I'd *consider* it."

"For more soap and a drying cloth, maybe you'll get us a Dragon," he adds hopefully.

Of course the others told him about that. They're worse than a bunch of gossiping fishwives. I can't even yawn without it being reported back to Beta Sinta within the hour.

"I'll need more than that for a Dragon. And I don't even know if I can."

"You could try."

I snort. "That's not *my* motto."

I can't see his face, but I know he's grinning. His high spirits make me want to grin back, which worries me. Does Beta Sinta think he's won? How did I even end up here?

"What were you doing at the circus only a few months after taking over Sinta? Didn't you have other things to do?"

He chuckles, a deep, vibrating sound that rumbles through my body. That fluttery feeling irritates my chest again.

"I told you, I need Magoi on my side. The circus is full of them, but from what I could see, they're not the usual pretentious, prejudiced lot."

True. "And abduction seemed like a good idea?"

"I asked first."

"More like ordered. And threatened my friends."

He shrugs. "I told you. I do what needs to be done."

My hackles instantly rise. "Who are you to decide what needs to be done? That's subjective by nature. No two people think alike."

"Someone has to decide. Without rulers, there's chaos."

Damn it! That's true. "We had rulers. There was order."

"There was oppression."

Damn it! That's true, too.

"Hold on," he says. My hands automatically land on his waist while he urges his horse to jump a lightning line. The mark of Zeus stretches as far as the eye can see in both directions, a charred scar cutting across dust, stones, and yellowed grass, proof that the Gods are never far from Thalyria.

Beta Sinta reins in, waiting for the others to catch up. "Character, past, and environment all affect the choices we make. The trick is choosing a path and following it. Make a decision, and don't turn back."

"What if it's wrong?"

"I don't know." He winks at me over his shoulder. "It's never happened."

I roll my eyes, torn between laughing and pulling my hair out. "Since kidnapping clearly doesn't bother you, why me? I can't do anything. If I could, I'd be long gone."

He turns again, his dark eyebrows raised. "Does my rare and surly Kingmaker really need me to answer that?" he teases.

His? My pulse speeds up. "Okay. Fine. Besides *that.*"

He doesn't turn back around. His eyes travel an unhurried path over my face, and I can almost feel the heat in them on the curve of my cheek, and then on my mouth. His burning gaze snags on my braid, following it across my shoulder and over the swell of my breast. As his eyes dip, his lips part, and his fingers twitch on his thigh.

My breathing turns shallow. Muscles I'm not usually aware of clench deep inside me, growing achy with tension and warmth. The heat simmering in my core quickly spirals through the rest of me, flushing my face with color. I hate that I react this way to him. And I hate that it shows.

Scowling, I flick my braid over my shoulder.

Beta Sinta blinks and turns back around. "*That* was it, at the time. The Kingmaker. But you're a lot more than that, aren't you, Cat?"

The blood still climbing to my face plummets like Icarus falling to the sea. Gods, magic, and the prophecy I try so hard to ignore all collide in my stomach in an explosion of secrets and dread. Anxiety coats my tongue while an icy chill slides down my spine. The feeling is so familiar, and yet it freezes me solid every time.

I take a deep breath and let it out as silently as I can. "Not really." My voice comes out light and steady, even though I'm about two Hydra heads away from having a panic attack. "I'm from the north. Knowledge of creatures and magic is normal for us."

He grunts. Agreement? Skepticism? I can't tell.

I bite my lip, wondering what he really knows. "Why focus on me?"

Beta Sinta shrugs, rolling his muscular shoulders right in front of me. His lightweight tunic doesn't hide much. It's hard not to stare.

"I don't need more brute strength," he says. "I won this war. There are politics to deal with now—Magoi nobles, and Tarvan and Fisan royals. I need to know who's lying to me. I need to know the truth so Sinta can avoid more war."

"The warlord wants peace?" I scoff.

"Am I lying?"

I grit my teeth. "No." Of all people, I should know. "Power corrupts."

"Power corrupts the weak."

Gods! I hate it when I agree with him. "How did you even know what I can do?"

There's a slight pause. "At first, without drawing attention to myself, I was trying to get a feel for the different Magoi at the circus, but I found myself always watching you instead. First outside Sinta City when the circus crossed back over from Tarva. Then I went to a few performances in Kaplos. When the circus moved south, I decided to follow. I knew there was something different about you, something special, but I couldn't figure out what."

His words stun me into silence. Beta Sinta watched me

for *weeks* without my even realizing it? I'm not careless, or oblivious. None of this makes sense—not him focusing on me, and not my runaway mouth at the last circus fair. And since. Information is valuable, and I've been spewing it out like it's worth copper instead of gold.

"How did you figure it out?" I finally ask.

His pause is longer this time. "Strangely enough, it was a dream. I dreamt I was swimming in a vast and stormy ocean in the dead of night. When I couldn't swim any longer, I sank to the bottom, and you were there. You lit up the dark like a lightning bolt, took my hands, and pulled me to the surface. You told me we could change everything— that you knew the truth."

My heart seizes and then crashes violently against my ribs. An oracular dream! Beta Sinta was gifted with an oracular dream—*Poseidon's* oracular dream—and he doesn't even know it.

Queasiness turns my insides upside down. *Poseidon, why have you betrayed me?*

My mind races while my stomach ties itself in knots. What in the Underworld is going on? Why is Poseidon even interested in Sinta? There's no ocean in the west, his Oracles are on the other side of the realms, and magic has always been weakest here. The Ice Plains get diagonally bigger as you go east. Sinta has the narrowest strip. As the middle realm, Tarva has twice as much glacial territory, and Fisa, in the east, has even more. To core Olympians like Poseidon, these dusty hills, plains, and old forests are an afterthought. As much as I love Sinta, it's the runt of the realms.

"From there I started thinking about old legends," he continues. "I went to Mylos for the knowledge scrolls and found you, or the equivalent of you. The Kingmaker—the

woman who hears the lie and knows the truth. Basil was
the perfect test. I knew he wasn't who he said he was. I
was constantly drawn to you. The dream told me I needed
you. After I saw your reaction when Basil lied, I knew
what to do."

Constantly drawn to me? A weird spasm twists my
chest. *Focus!* "Snatch me with a magic rope?"

He laughs. "Exactly."

My hands, which for some reason keep ending up on
his waist lately, curl into fists. Beta Sinta grabs one and
holds on.

"Let go," I demand.

"No."

My eyebrows snap together. "Why not?"

"Because your gut reaction is always to punch, and I
don't like being tickled."

Tickled? Tickled! Indignation swamps me. I'll show
him *a tickle*.

Before I can move, he drops the reins and captures my
other hand, easily maneuvering both my hands into one
of his. He picks the reins back up with the other. As usual,
he gains the upper hand with disgustingly little effort, and
I end up with both arms around him, my face buried in
his back.

Beta Sinta's crisp, masculine scent of citrus and sunshine fills my nose. Hard muscle ripples under my cheek.
I'm frighteningly aware of all the places his broad, powerful body touches mine, and I shiver despite the heat.

"Let. Me. Go," I grind out.

"I. Said. No."

I open my mouth, teeth bared.

"If you bite me, I swear to the Gods I'll dump you off
this horse and make you walk."

I close my mouth. The town is still miles away. "I won't bite."

"Or punch."

I grit my teeth. "You're asking a lot."

"Am I?" he drawls, tightening his grip on my wrists until I hiss.

"Ow! Fine. Or punch."

His fingers loosen. "Is that your binding word?"

My eyes widen. Beta Sinta says he needs me for information, but he already knows more about the ways of magic than is good for *me*.

"Fine. It's my binding word." It's like pulling my own teeth, but I'm desperate to stop hugging him. He's too hot and…and…*something*.

"Ever," he stipulates.

Something between a laugh and a snort explodes from me. "Don't push your luck."

"A day, then. Starting now."

"Fine. A day," I agree, fuming.

He lets go of my wrists. I sit up so fast I almost tumble off the back of the horse. Beta Sinta's chuckle is almost as irritating as the jolt of magic that seals the deal. Hoi Polloi can say one thing and do another, even if they shouldn't. They may feel guilt, or regret, or possibly nothing at all, but there are no physical consequences. I can't get away with that.

An epic scowl on my face, I wiggle back, rubbing the finger marks on my wrists and thinking about Poseidon. Between Beta Sinta's oracular dream and my out-of-control mouth, there's no doubt the God is sticking his trident where it doesn't belong. When Gods dabble in the affairs of men, anything can happen. It's definitely not something to ignore. If my God Father wants Beta Sinta and me together, he must have a very good reason for it. Or at least I hope so.

We stable the horses at Pan's Pavilion, a completely innocuous inn on the west side of town. Why Beta Sinta is entering a conquered city with so little fanfare is beyond me. What's the point of taking over a realm just to wander around like a nobody?

He laughs when I ask. *Laughs*. What is *wrong* with these people?

"If anyone finds out who I am, we'll be thronged," he explains. "Better to just be a nobody if we want to make it to Sinta City before winter."

I guess that explains his avoidance of populated areas up until now. I roll my eyes. "Oh, the woe of being adored."

Beta Sinta grins. "It's a hard life."

I harrumph. Too bad I made that vow not to hit him. It would be pretty satisfying to smack the smug look off his face right now.

The five of us head straight to the market. The streets are narrow and shaded in the inn's vicinity, but the closer we get to the agora, the more they widen, letting the afternoon sun beat down. It's as merciless as Zeus on the top of my dark head. I can't help wondering where a glacial lake is when I need one. Or a hat.

The architecture changes near the heart of the city, becoming ornate. Temples dot the central neighborhood, a steady flow of people moving in and out of them for prayer.

I insist on going into a sanctuary dedicated to Poseidon. There are only a few coppers in my pocket, along with the obol I wouldn't even consider giving up. That coin is for Charon, and it'll stay in my pocket until the day I need to pay the ferryman to row me across the Styx and into the land of the dead.

Settling on my knees in front of a huge statue of the Sea God, I bow my head, say a silent prayer of safekeeping for my friends at the circus, and then put two of my three coppers into the polished bronze bowl at Poseidon's feet. It's not much, and Poseidon's followers are many, but I hope my coppers will eventually find their way to providing for people who need them more than I do.

Beta Sinta kneels beside me and takes a handful of silver coins from the pouch at his side, dropping them next to mine. My eyes practically pop out of my head at the sight of so much money.

"I usually give to Athena and her cult." He shrugs. "But since we're here…"

Carver, Flynn, and Kato all kneel and give up a silver coin as well.

After the holy man bestows a blessing on each of our bent heads, we head back out into the blinding sunlight. The heat sinks into my scalp, driving me crazy. Squinting and fanning myself, I look around at the stone buildings adorned with fluted marble columns and carvings of creatures and Gods. What I see makes the geography of our convoluted travels finally click into place.

"This is Velos," I say.

Beta Sinta glances at me, seeming surprised. "You've been here?"

"No, but Apollo and Artemis are everywhere, and Velans worship the twins." They're on nearly every facade, in all their naked glory. "Velos depends on game from the forest to the west. Along with the market, meat and leather are what make the city prosper. It's logical to worship the Gods of archery and the hunt."

"How do you know so much about Velos? The circus travels a route farther to the west."

Hours of schooling and a tutor with a whip? "I've met people, heard things," I say offhandedly.

Beta Sinta stops, his mouth flattening in obvious irritation. "Help me, Cat. Or at least tell me the truth. I know when you're lying."

"Oh?" My heart trips over its next beat.

"Your eyes get twitchy."

"My eyes do not get twitchy!"

"This one gets narrower." He touches the tip of his finger to the corner of my right eye, and a little jolt zips through me. "It's as if you're expecting the lie to hurt, but it doesn't because it's your own."

I jerk my head away and start walking again. "Thank you for telling me. I'll have to work on that."

"Cat..." he growls, stalking after me. "Everything would be so much easier if—"

"—you let me go."

Beta Sinta shakes his head. "I can't. You're too valuable."

"Aren't you the lucky despot? The one who caught the Kingmaker. Forgive me for not being overjoyed about becoming your slave."

"Not a slave." He grabs my arm, swinging me back to him. "One of us."

Incredibly, he believes what he's saying, even if I don't. I wrench my arm from his grip, feeling each long finger like a brand on my skin. I wish my eyes could shoot flames. Or my hands. Or really, any part of me would do. "I'll never be one of you."

Beta Sinta spears a hand through his black hair, tugging a little. "You're too stubborn for your own good."

I glare at him. He simply looks back, and his calm

makes me want to hit something. Or *someone.*

Our small group continues before stopping again in front of a row of colorful market stalls. A light breeze slips over my shoulder, and I turn into it, trying to cool down while Beta Sinta opens his leather pouch again and produces four silver coins.

Flynn rubs his hands together, his eyes brightening. "Payday!"

Flynn, Carver, and Kato each take a coin, leaving one in Beta Sinta's palm.

"Cat." He extends the coin to me. "Your pay."

Of all the things I imagined he might say, that wasn't one of them. I snap my jaw shut and turn away. I have my last copper.

He doesn't insist, dropping the coin back into his pouch. "I'll hold it for you. I know what you want. You complain about it often enough."

I look up sharply and find his eyes brimming with humor. *Is he teasing me?*

We approach the vendors, the enchanted rope tugging me along. I wonder what would happen if I sat down and refused to budge. Would I get dragged around on my ass? Tossed over one shoulder? The possibilities keep my feet moving.

Beta Sinta buys enough apricots and oranges to last a week; four loaves of bread; normal, hard cheese; and green grapes. I want the red ones, but since I refused the money, I keep my mouth shut. He finds a soap seller next and takes forever sniffing the different scents.

I roll my eyes. "You're worse than a woman. Just take the yellow one. It's always the best."

He picks it up and inhales. "Lemon. Smells like you."

I don't know if it's the way his voice turns rough, or how

his thick, dark lashes dip, fanning his cheeks and shading his eyes, but my insides turn revoltingly mushy.

"And *you*," I sputter. "My soap should have lasted another month."

"We'll take two," he tells the vendor, paying and then continuing down the row of stalls.

"There is no *we*. Don't act like I have a say in any of this."

Beta Sinta whirls, frustration darkening his eyes. "You *could* have a say. And you could bloody well choose your own soap!"

"I did! I told you to take the yellow one."

"And I did!"

Muttering a curse, he walks off so fast that the rope pulls, jerking me into someone. Or maybe the man stumbles into me. His eyes are unfocused, and he's listing to the left.

Magic bites my skin. My body responds instantly. I feel the vortex. I let it expand, readying the whirlpool that'll pull the stranger's magic into me and make it my own.

I reach out with a shudder. Aside from the steady, light nip of the rope, which I hardly feel anymore, I haven't been in contact with magic for nearly two weeks, and whatever is coursing through this man's veins is exciting and potent. I don't know what it is, but it might mean my escape.

I grab his shoulders, feeling like a child in a kitchen full of cakes. I'm going to stuff myself until I burst.

CHAPTER 8

"Cat?" Beta Sinta sounds far away. "Cat! What are you doing?"

Laughing, floating, I release the man only when there's no magic left to take. Turning, I stumble into Beta Sinta. He catches my bare arms, and I gasp. Eyes like a storm. Fingers *so* warm.

"You're pink!" I giggle, the sound strange and unfamiliar to my ears.

He frowns, and it makes me laugh. His face fades in and out of focus. Everything is hazy, rosy, and not quite upright. The world is buzzing. It's turned elastic, and it vibrates at the edges.

Dizzy, I lay my hand on Beta Sinta's chest for balance. His heart beats under my palm, and the steady rise and fall of his chest mesmerizes me. *Up. Down. Up. Down.* It seems perfectly normal to time my breathing to match his.

"*Poseidon's balls!* What in the Underworld did you do to me?"

I turn to the red-faced, raging man whose magic I took. A person's natural magic will come back in a matter of hours, but this feels like a spell. I blink him into focus, tilting my head so he's not sideways. He staggers, and tremors rack his wiry frame. He's pink, too, and madder than the Minotaur in his maze.

Beta Sinta tenses under my hand.

"That dose was supposed to last all day!" the man

snarls. "I paid good silver for it. Give it back!" he thunders, lunging at me.

Beta Sinta's arm snakes around my waist, and he spins me out of the way. The man howls, but all I can do is laugh, even when he draws a knife and waves it at me, a manic look in his eyes.

An enraged sound rises in Beta Sinta's chest. His free hand shoots out and knocks the knife from the man's trembling grip. The next thing I know, Beta Sinta has the other man by the throat. It's impressive. Fast.

One of Beta Sinta's arms is still wrapped around me, plastering me to his side. The other is extended in front of my nose. Powerful without unnecessary bulk, tanned, corded, chiseled—the whole arm is almost too appealing to resist. Muscles bunch and roll, and I have the hardest time not reaching up to squeeze his biceps.

He tosses the man to the ground. Kato, Flynn, and Carver take up positions around us, looking wonderfully lethal. I clap and grin—I *love* a good fight, not that this one seems very fair—and then blink. Flynn either just grew three feet, or I'm hallucinating.

"Dose of *what*?" The deadly undertone in Beta Sinta's voice makes the tiny hairs on the back of my neck rise. A shiver rattles me, and his grip around my waist tightens.

When the man just gapes at us, prostrate, Beta Sinta draws a knife from his belt and throws it without a second's hesitation. It sticks not even an inch from the man's ear, slicing off a hunk of matted brown hair.

"The next one lands somewhere that hurts," Beta Sinta says in a low, furious voice.

I wrinkle my nose. "Brutal."

Thundercloud eyes flash to mine. "No one touches you."

I chew on my lower lip, confused. "You're touching me."

His eyes dip to my mouth. "I'm the exception."

The breath stalls in my lungs. Everything inside me suddenly feels liquid and light. He reminds me of a pirate again. Dark. Sharp. Fierce. I smile up at him, wondering if it would be all right to jump into his arms and bury my face in his neck.

Our eyes meet. His are like molten silver, and my legs turn weak. I sway into him, and Beta Sinta's fingers convulse on my hip, tugging me closer. His eyes close for the space of a deep breath. When he opens them again, his jaw hardens, and he turns back to the man on the ground with a snarl. "I'm waiting."

I turn back, too, narrow my eyes, and point an accusing finger. "Answer or die!" The man's face drains of what little color it had left, and I burst out laughing.

"Euphoria," he wheezes, struggling to sit up. "Paid five silvers for it, and the little leech stole it with one touch." He spits in my direction. The gob lands about a foot from my boot. It's pink.

The rumble in Beta Sinta's throat reminds me of a volcano about to erupt. This could get messy. I'm not in the mood for messy.

"*You* bumped into *me*." At least I think he did. I peel Beta Sinta's arm off me and walk away, finding it takes an unusual amount of effort to put one foot in front of the other. The rope pulls, and I totter. Beta Sinta steadies me with a firm hand on my lower back, hesitating before following. I almost ask if he'd like to beat the man to a pulp before we move on but, really, this *is* Beta Sinta. There's no need to be polite.

"What about the addict?" Carver asks in a low voice, handing Beta Sinta back the knife he threw.

"Leave him," Beta Sinta answers, sheathing the blade.

He's at my elbow, his heat searing my arm. "Make sure he's not following."

The addict slips from my mind as soon as he's out of sight, growing hazy like everything else. Cheerful, carefree, I hum, floating up and down the market rows. There's something else I need. *What?*

Can't remember. Don't really care.

I stumble. Beta Sinta catches me, his hands circling my waist.

"You're high on euphoria." He's holding on to me. I think he's holding me up. His large hands skim up my ribs, steadying me. "A strong dose, calibrated to a man twice your size." He gazes down at me, and I see my face reflected in the darkest part of his gray eyes. "How did that happen?"

I motion for him to lower his head so I can whisper in his ear. His cheek brushes mine, and warmth rushes through me. I press into his jaw, curious about the feel of the two days' worth of beard on his skin. It prickles, but not unpleasantly.

"I can steal magic," I tell him. "If you had any, I'd steal yours."

He lifts his head, his eyes shadowed. I don't know what to make of his expression. I don't know what to make of anything. I've never felt this way before—disconnected from myself, confused, and happy. It's a relief not to be scared anymore. So freeing. I should do this more often. I'm having the time of my life!

"I can give it away, too." I direct some euphoria at Beta Sinta. It bounces back to me with a shudder, and I frown. "You don't want any?" *Is he supposed to have a choice?* I try again, and the same thing happens. "There's something very strange about you." For some reason, that makes me laugh so hard I sound like a donkey.

After I stop braying, it occurs to me that the problem might be me. I wiggle out of Beta Sinta's grasp and throw some magic at Kato.

Kato grins and leans to the left. "Everything's pink!" He turns, loses his balance, and upends an entire display of boots, belts, and other leather goods.

"For the Gods' sakes!" Beta Sinta mutters. He hands the furious vendor a silver coin for the inconvenience. "Flynn! Take care of him. Take him back to the inn. Make sure he doesn't do anything stupid, knock anything else over, or kill anyone by accident."

"Oh, no!" I cry. "We mustn't kill by accident. Only on purpose."

"My sentiment exactly," Beta Sinta grumbles, taking my hand and pulling me down the street. He looks a lot like I might be on his kill list.

I giggle. Carver follows.

"Where are we going?" I dance a Fisan jig around Beta Sinta, making him turn in circles. The dust I kick up shimmers like ice crystals under a winter sun. I long for the cold, the kind of cold that makes your brain freeze.

Where is my brain? I can't feel my head!

My hands fly up, and I dig through my braid, pulling it apart until I feel scalp. *Oh, good. Still there.*

"We have one more thing to buy," Beta Sinta says.

"I knew it!" I yell, clapping in triumph. "What?"

"A drying cloth."

That sounds boring. Something shiny catches my eye. I veer to the right, taking Beta Sinta with me. "A sword! I want a sword. Can I have a sword?"

"You can't even lift a sword," he says, but he follows me along the vendor's table anyway.

"I can. Watch me." I reach for the biggest, shiniest

blade in the merchant's wares. It won't budge. "That's odd. Someone must have glued it." I lean over the sword and keep going until my face lands on metal.

"Ow!" I rub my nose, and my finger comes away bloody. Seeing the red smear should worry me, but I can't remember why.

"Blood." Mother's voice haunts me from far away. *"Spill it. Shed it. Bathe in it. Make people fear you."*

Laughter bubbles up inside me. I've never found Mother funny before. This euphoria stuff is great!

Beta Sinta leans close to inspect my nose. He brushes hair out of my face with callused fingers that are light and warm.

On impulse, I lift my hands and trail my fingers over the dark stubble shadowing his cheeks. "Hmmm. Scratchy."

He stares down at me as he catches my hands and slowly lowers them, keeping my fingers trapped loosely in his. His thumbs skate over my knuckles, and a lovely flutter tickles my ribs.

"The cut's nothing," he says, his voice unusually soft. A few heartbeats pass before he lets me go and turns to the vendor, nodding to a half-sized sword at the far end of the table.

The merchant hands it to him, and Beta Sinta inspects the weapon, testing its weight and balance and making sure the blade is straight.

"We'll take it," he finally says. "And your smallest sword belt with dagger loops."

"You're buying me a sword? And a belt for my knives?" Thrilled, I leap on him like an octopus, clinging to him with arms and legs. So more like a quadropus. Does that even exist?

Gods! His skin is on fire!

Beta Sinta's arms lock around me. Thunder rolls in my ears, and I cock my head, listening for more. He goes utterly still. Does he hear it, too? Then he inhales so deeply that his chest expands, pressing into me. A dizzying sensation sweeps through me. Against my neck, his shuddering exhale stirs my hair and sends a rush of goose bumps down my spine.

I shiver, giggling breathlessly. "Ack! That tickles!"

With a strained chuckle, he untangles my limbs and sets me back on my feet, standing protectively over me. I can't help smiling up at him. He's such a contradiction. So arrogant and yet so reasonable.

"The sword's really for me?" I ask.

His hands linger on my waist, his splayed fingers pressing lightly into my sides. "You said you wanted one."

My smile widens. "In that case, I want *two*! One for each hip." I can already imagine my swagger.

He laughs, his expression a disconcerting mix of humor and indulgence. "Let's start with one," he says, pulling me a shade closer.

I gaze up at him. My brain is fuzzy, my limbs are light, and no one has ever looked at me the way he does. The undisguised heat in his quicksilver eyes makes it hard to breathe.

Beta Sinta pays for the sword. It's short, about two and a half feet long, with a rounded guard shaped like a loosely woven basket of laurel leaves.

"Can I have it?" I ask, bouncing next to him. "Can I? Can I, please?"

"No."

"Why not?"

"You can have it when I can trust you."

That sounds logical. "Okay."

"*Okay?*" He arches dark eyebrows. "That's it?"

"What's it?" There's a bee buzzing in my ear. I swat at it, laughing. It turns into a Centaur and gallops away. "Did you see that?" I cry.

"See what?"

"The bee. The Centaur bee. The pink one."

Beta Sinta rolls his eyes—something I never thought he'd do—grabs my hand, and drags me through the market. Colors, sounds, and spicy scents swirl through the fog in my brain. I float through them. I have to dance. I dance and skip like the child I was never allowed to be. I'm happy. I fear nothing. I don't have to watch my back. There's a giant butterfly doing that.

It lands on my shoulder, flaps powdery wings, and whispers, "I'll take care of you."

I look up, beaming. "Thank you."

"You're welcome," Beta Sinta says.

"Not *you*."

He frowns, and I laugh, dancing some more. When I fall, Carver helps me up. I smile and give him my best curtsy. It's really well done. There isn't a princess in the three realms that could do better.

Carver bows back, and it's awful. I laugh until I snort. Mother would *not* approve.

Beta Sinta lightly tugs my hand, and I stumble to the right, landing in a sea of drying cloths. They hang and flap, rainbow sails in the afternoon breeze. I jump, trying to touch the highest one while he plows through the stock on the table, looking for something in that efficient manner of his.

"This one," he tells the merchant. It's mid-sized and a disgusting shade of yellow.

"Is that for me?"

He nods, and I scrunch up my nose.

"Not that one. It looks like Cerberus threw up on it." I look around. "I want *that* one!" It's bright red and three times too big. *I love it!*

He throws the yellow cloth back on the table and buys the red.

Done with the market, he tows me back toward the inn again. Suddenly light-headed, I plop down in the middle of the cobbled street, hearing Beta Sinta's grunt when the rope cuts into his hips.

I squint up at him. "Serves you right. You could just untie me. Or let me go."

He smirks. "And miss all this fun?"

I burst out laughing. A second later, he grins back. His smile is broad and makes my heart thump an irregular beat. His nose is a bit hooked, but that makes his face different, interesting. So does the scar. I can't remember why I don't like him. In fact, I—

My head snaps around. I felt something. I *want* it. I jump up, my feet flying.

"Where are you going?" Beta Sinta falls into stride next to me. Carver is on my other side, easily keeping pace.

I don't answer because I don't know, not until we turn a corner and race up the steps of a bathhouse. I barrel through the front doors, startling a couple on their way out. Their white robes are cinched with matching hammered-gold belts. *Shiny!*

I reach for the woman's belt. She slides away from me, and I let her go. There's something more important here.

There's a side for women and a side for men. I don't care which is which, and I don't stop to find out. I turn right and run down the marble hallway. There are waves under my feet. Cool foam curls between my toes. I shriek with laughter as a Satyr chases me, trying to pinch my cheeks.

A tall, heavy door stops me in my tracks. I reach for the latch, but for some reason, I keep missing it.

"I get the feeling you've never been high before," Beta Sinta says, leaning around me to open the door.

"Have you?" I ask.

He shakes his head. His eyes dance with silver streaks. They glitter like far-off galaxies in the deep of night. I stare into the scatter of stars, falling, falling...

"Looks like fun," Carver says, pulling me out of space.

I turn to the wiry swordsman. "Want some? It's fabulous!"

"No thanks." Carver grins. "Offering anything else?"

I giggle and blush. Then my smile turns into a pout. "Don't flirt."

Carver does his best to look stricken, ignoring Beta Sinta's glare. "Why not?"

"Don't you know? Poseidon sent your incredibly annoying brother to me with an oracular dream. Once-in-a-lifetime thing. Except for most people. Most people never have one. Anyway"—I roll my eyes—"he probably thinks it *means* something." I snort. "I'd rather eat goat balls. Or goat shit." I frown, confused. "Or goat cheese!" I shout triumphantly.

They stare at me. I could catch flies in their open mouths. I don't want any flies, even pink ones.

"Oracular dream?" Beta Sinta says.

"She's a wealth of information," Carver murmurs.

"What? Never heard of one?" I shrug. "I'm hot." Remembering the water, I turn, trip over my own feet, and crash to the floor.

Beta Sinta sets me upright. I run again, driven by blind need. Booted footsteps follow. The rope draws taut and then gives as we burst into a bathing chamber with three naked men. I laugh at their startled expressions and then yank my tunic over my head.

Beta Sinta's eyes widen. "For the Gods' sakes, Cat!"

I keep stripping, tossing my clothes into a messy heap.

"Out!" he barks to the room.

There must be something scary about him because all three men jump out of the pool and run, leaving puddles on the floor.

They disappear, and I turn back to Beta Sinta. He doesn't look that scary to me. I tilt my chin, inspecting him. His hair is the color of a starless night, shiny, and curling softly around his neck. I reach up, playing with the silky strands. They look like ink splashed across my fingers.

Smiling, I smooth stray locks away from his face and then pat his head. "Good Beta."

There's a low rumble in his throat.

"Woof!" I bark back.

He grins. Then his eyes drop to my bare chest. His smile freezes, his nostrils flaring as his hands curl into fists.

Heat explodes inside me along with a thousand tiny wings. A flush sweeps up my neck. My nipples harden under his smoldering gaze, and I'm suddenly intensely aware of my own breasts—the sway and the weight, the roundness of them. A muscle ticks in his jaw before his eyes drift down, taking in the rest of me. His expression reminds me of a starving man who just stumbled upon his next meal. Focused. Hungry. Ready to pounce.

"Untie me or get in." My voice is husky. There's a butterfly colony inside me.

Beta Sinta steps closer to shield me from Carver's view, ordering his brother out of the room. Carrying most of our purchases, Carver backs away with his usual bravado. I blow him a saucy kiss over Beta Sinta's shoulder, startled when a violent sound rattles in Beta Sinta's chest.

Carver laughs his way out of the room. Quickly.

Warm air brushes my skin. *All* of it. It's Beta Sinta's heat. He's that close. I think I'm forgetting something important.

Silver eyes meet mine. "Give me your binding word you won't leave without me."

"All right."

"Say it."

I roll my eyes and bow, adding a pompous hand flourish. "I won't leave the bathing chamber without you, O Imperious One."

His mouth twitches, and I preen, oddly elated that I make him laugh.

Beta Sinta unties the rope, which I think I should care more about. His fingers barely brush my waist, but the contact makes my breath catch and my belly tighten. Tiny flames lick my skin where he touches. I shouldn't like it, but I do.

The moment the rope drops away, I take a deep breath, dive into the pool, and swim the entire length underwater. *Bliss.*

I pop up, laughing, and then swim for what feels like hours. My hands and feet wrinkle like month-old grapes, but I keep swimming, Poseidon's ocean in my ears. Beta Sinta paces the length of the pool, shadowing me. I splash him, and he frowns. I invite him in, and he shakes his head. I don't know why he won't join me. I haven't had this much fun in...well, *ever*. Too bad he's such a grump.

Sometime after dark, exhaustion hits me like a Cyclops's fist. I go limp, my muscles used and tired and so heavy I can barely move. Nothing is pink. Nothing is wonderful. I'm not dizzy or happy, and Beta Sinta watching me swim around naked isn't even remotely funny anymore. Gasping, I try to turn invisible—that important thing I was forgetting earlier—and can't. I'm too weak. I try again, but nothing happens. The blood drains from my face so fast I see spots.

Beta Sinta's eyes sharpen. He takes a step forward, hesitates, and then stops, hovering on the edge of action.

My face flames as humiliation sweeps me into dark places. I'd rather take a hundred beatings than this. *This* is torture.

My eyes sting, and I fight back tears. *Cats don't cry.* But this time, I think I might. Years of dread crash down on me, and I shudder, wondering if I can just let myself drown to save the realms from the calamity of Cat.

Standing in the water, I hang my head, my dark hair floating around my shoulders like a peacock's fan at midnight. I can see my toes through the water. I can see everything. So can he.

"That's why addicts stay high," Beta Sinta says from the side of the pool. "It's too awful when it ends."

I sniff. I can't look at him. I won't.

"Come." He holds out the gaudy red drying cloth I chose. It's hideous and oversized.

He averts his eyes while I crawl up the steps. My eyes hurt. There are shooting pains in my head. I'm shivering. I'm not cold, but I can't stop shaking. My teeth even chatter, which is an entirely new experience.

Barely holding myself upright, I let Beta Sinta wrap the cloth around me. He pats me dry, his hands surprisingly gentle. His touch is efficient, not overly invasive, and—*good Gods, I can't believe I'm even thinking this*—oddly comforting.

I squeeze my eyes shut, for once hating myself more than I hate him.

"Why did you take it?" He leans over me to wrap the

cloth more snugly around me. Sooty lashes shield his eyes. Black hair sweeps forward, brushing my bare shoulder.

A tremor runs through me, warmer this time.

"The magic wanted to be inside me." My voice is as weak as a wisp of smoke. It sounds like I feel. "I couldn't control it. I-I didn't even try."

"It wasn't his magic. It was a spell." Beta Sinta straightens. Shadowy in the torchlight, his eyes are like the ocean at night, dark and deep. He's close, too close, but I don't have the strength to step back or even look away.

"It doesn't matter," I say listlessly. "It's the same to me."

He fiddles with the cloth again before tugging lightly on my elbow. "Let's go," he says, his voice thicker than usual.

I'm not sure I can. I locate my clothes, take one step, two, and then sink to the floor and curl up on my side, my cheek pressed to the cool marble.

Beta Sinta gathers my things, then puts one arm under my knees and the other behind my back, picking me up like I weigh nothing. I can't find the energy to protest, and my head flops against his shoulder, soaking his tunic. I close my eyes, feeling the heat of my breath circle back to me from against his neck.

"You never smell bad," I mumble.

"Should I?"

"It would make you mortal, like the rest of us."

"I am mortal. That's why I need—"

"—your help," I finish wearily, forcing my leaden eyelids up.

"This isn't a game, Cat."

"Just leave me here," I moan. "You can't carry me all the way back."

He grunts, like I should know better. "And leave behind my most valued treasure?"

Despite my magical worth, I've never been anyone's most valued treasure. "I won't be used."

A smile curves his wide mouth. His lips are expressive, and so...*close.* "Egeria will win you over."

I doubt that. I yawn noisily, the tip of my nose accidentally brushing Beta Sinta's neck. Drawn to his warm, solid strength, I'm tempted to burrow closer. I'm about to give in when a stab of panic slices through me.

Oh Gods! It's all over. Eight years of hiding, and now this.

I didn't think it was possible to hate myself any more right now, but I was wrong. "It won't get that far."

"You're wrong. You're wrong about a lot of things."

I let that go. I have bigger problems. "I bled on that sword and didn't dilute it." I didn't care at the time. It's true what they say—drugs make you stupid. "They'll track my blood. It's been hours. They're already on their way."

He tenses, and his voice turns into a knife's edge—hard and sharp. "Who?"

I yawn again. Apparently, even the most terrifying people in the realms can't compete with bone-deep fatigue and drug withdrawal. "It's your fault. You exposed me."

His arms tighten, locking me against his chest. "I'll protect you."

My eyes drift closed, darkness enveloping me like a shroud. Not for the first time, I wonder how long I'll live.

Beta Sinta's heart thuds under my hand.

"You could try," I whisper, fading into oblivion.

CHAPTER 9

CONVERSATION WAKES ME UP. MY HEAD IS POUNDING, I'm on a mattress, still wrapped in my drying cloth under a lightweight blanket, and my wrist is tied to the bed. I obey my first instinct and tug on the knot. When it doesn't move, I feign sleep and listen. The first thing I hear is Flynn's gruff voice asking who's after me.

"That's what I'd like to know." Frustration colors Beta Sinta's answer. He's pacing, his long strides beating a steady rhythm on a wooden floor. "She told me everyone is her enemy. At the time, I thought she was exaggerating, but any royal or noble would kill to get their hands on the Kingmaker. She can steal magic. Turn invisible. She might even be able to drive a Dragon. The Gods only know what else she can do. She's even handy with a knife."

Handy? Handy! My eyes almost pop open out of indignation.

Beta Sinta's footsteps stop next to the bed. Warm fingers brush mine. "Who wouldn't want her?"

Something in his tone makes my stomach tumble. That horrible mushy feeling hits me again.

Carver joins the conversation, sounding broody. "There's more here than we know. More to her." He exhales loudly. "Can we protect her?"

I doubt it.

"Can we hide her?" Flynn asks.

Maybe.

"We have to get her to Egeria," Beta Sinta says.

Gah! Her again.

"Our first problem is who's coming now," Kato says. "We'll deal with the rest later."

Good old Kato. He knows how to get rid of the dung and clear out the stench. Behind closed eyelids I see broad shoulders, Adonis-like features, smiling blue eyes, and sunny blond hair. In my mind, he's winking at me, his three knives planted in the knot of a tree. I showed him that.

"I could ride hard and fast, bring back a third of the army," Flynn offers.

"No. They're protecting the castle." Beta Sinta's voice rings with finality, and I mentally roll my eyes. *They're protecting the castle—and his darling Egeria.*

"We could find more Magoi and pay them for protection," Carver suggests.

"That would only expose her more," Beta Sinta says, pacing again.

Other footsteps join Beta Sinta's. The tread is heavier, less precise. "So what do we do?" Flynn asks.

No one says anything for a while. Then Beta Sinta's voice rumbles above me, low and sure. "Stay together, like we always have. The four of us have never come across an enemy we couldn't best."

A hollow feeling spreads through me. I could be lying on my circus cot, listening to Aetos, Desma, Vasili, and Selena having this same conversation. But they've loved and protected me for years. Beta Sinta only wants me alive so he can use me.

I want to live. At least one of our interests converges.

I let out a sigh and start talking. "They'll start by sending armed men. At least twenty, and some with magic. If that doesn't work, they'll resort to creatures. Centaurs, Kobaloi…that kind of thing. Maybe even a Dragon." I open my eyes. My head throbs, and the glow from the oil lamp feels like a dagger through my skull. "By the way, I hope Lamia drains your blood and eats your hearts."

Carver grins. "Lamia only eats children."

I huff. "That's what you think."

"Welcome back." Flynn pats my foot through the blanket.

I sit up with a groan and grab my head.

"The headache is a whole Harpy's nest of fun," Kato says, his expression strained, his face paler than usual. "Thanks for that."

I scowl at him. "Sarcasm is not favored by the Gods."

"Do you see any Gods here?" he asks, spreading his hands wide.

"That's the whole point. You don't see them until they're firing lightning bolts at you."

His lips twitch with a weak smile before his eyes squeeze shut, and he drops his head, pinching the bridge of his nose.

Great. I brought down Adonis with a hit of euphoria. I feel like a delinquent.

Beta Sinta crouches by the bedside, eye level with me. "How do you know what's coming?"

I look away, flushing. I can't help remembering his heated gaze on me in the pool, or the way his arms tightened around me before sleep robbed me of conscious thought.

My eyes lowered, I pluck at the blanket. "Experience. And just a hunch. I could be wrong."

"Are you ever wrong?" he asks.

"Yes. Unfortunately."

His weight dips the mattress. "Work with us, Cat. We'll help you."

My eyes jerk back up. "I wouldn't even be in danger if it weren't for you!" At least not immediate danger. "I'm not part of your team. When will you get that through your head?"

"You'll have everything you need," Beta Sinta argues. "Coin, shelter, protection."

Does he really think that's all a person wants? I could sell myself to any number of Magoi nobles for that. "Do *you* need protection?"

"Sometimes."

"I don't. I don't need anyone." *Is that my eye twitching?*

Beta Sinta watches me, his expression sober. "That sounds like a lonely life."

A familiar hole gapes wide inside my chest, and I swallow, closing my eyes against the four of them. When I open my eyes again, they're still looking at me, and I can't seem to muster all that much hate. Well, Beta Sinta gets some, but it's not that dramatic, even in my own head. It feels like another defeat. He caught me. He kept me. And now I don't even truly despise him anymore. It's humiliating. I've already been humiliated enough for one day.

I disappear.

"Cat?" Beta Sinta calls. I don't know why. I'm still attached to his bloody rope, which is attached to the bloody bed, which is now bloody invisible right along with me.

"I'm getting dressed." I push the blanket back and reach for my clothes. I manage well enough except for my tunic. I pull it over my head, slip my free arm through one sleeve, and then tug the rest of it down enough to cover most of me before reappearing. "You have to untie the rope."

Beta Sinta's eyes lock on me when I reappear, their burning intensity turning my temperature volcanic. His gaze keeps coming back to my hair. It's almost never loose, but now it's a wild mess, falling to my waist in waves.

Almost hesitantly, he reaches out, lightly touching a dark curl. "You're too young to be so cynical."

I shiver, growing horribly self-conscious. Being mostly covered just reminds me of being completely naked, and I blush uncontrollably. Even my toes turn red.

As my color rises, Beta Sinta's mouth curves a little too smugly for my taste. He wraps hot fingers around my free wrist, slowly reaching across me to untie the rope with his other hand. As soon as I can, I punch my arm through my tunic, ignoring the traitorous tightening in my stomach and the Gods-awful fluttering in my chest.

He tugs me off the bed and then gets Carver to tie us back together around the waist. I feel unsteady, and not because of the euphoria.

"Is that really necessary?" I ask, glaring at the rope.

"You make it necessary," Beta Sinta responds.

He's right. I'd be gone like an arrow from Artemis's bow-string if I could get away. "Did you really think I'd hand over my loyalty just because you say you won't randomly massacre Sintans, and your sister, the Alpha, is 'so nice'?"

"I thought you'd see reason," he says stiffly.

"Reason and I don't mix."

"I can tell," he mutters.

My blood instantly boils. Everything about him sets me off, builds up pressure I don't know how to deal with. With no other conceivable outlet for my visceral reaction to him, I swing at Beta Sinta, my fist connecting with his gut.

Pain explodes in a flash of blistering heat, fracturing my body into brittle shards. I crumple to the floor, my cry muffled by a clap of thunder so violent it rattles the inn. I scream. On fire. Burning up. Ripping apart. Lies are nothing compared to this. This is Olympus raining fire, scorching my skin, my eyes, my soul!

I claw at my throat and chest where the burning is excruciating. The room echoes with a long wail. It's me. The wail is me!

Beta Sinta grabs my hands and hauls me back up. "You're hurting yourself!"

I fight him, kicking and screaming, thrashing like the Furies. *Oh Gods! The Furies!*

"What in the name of Zeus is wrong with her?" Flynn demands, joining in the struggle to keep me still.

I whip my head around. My skull splinters, leaving me half-blind with pain. "Get it out! Get it out!"

"What? What, Cat?" Flynn looks as panicked as I feel.

"It's the betrayal." Beta Sinta's hands are like manacles on my wrists.

"What betrayal?" Flynn asks.

"She gave me her binding word she wouldn't punch me for a day. She broke it."

I can't believe I swore a false oath. I've never broken a vow. Only Beta Sinta could make me mad enough to forget my binding word. I had no idea what the Furies would do to me, but I never imagined this—frantic to tear myself apart, consumed by fire, screaming my head off. What about a lesser Goddess slap on the wrist? An annoyed zap from the Underworld? No one ever told me about *this*!

I fight like a caged beast. I could rip the fire from my flesh if Beta Sinta would *just let go.*

Carver grabs me around the waist and stops me from kicking his brother. "I'd hardly call that a betrayal," he grates out, barely holding on to me.

I'm wild, frantic. Pain rages inside me. Blinding. Jagged. "Burning" doesn't even begin to describe it. It's *unbearable.*

"She's practically made of magic!" Beta Sinta snaps. "What do you expect?"

"But she punches you all the time," Flynn says, grunting when I elbow him in the ribs.

"And I'm supposed to let her?" Beta Sinta snarls.

"What do you expect when you keep her tied up? Tied to *you*?"

"I'd had enough!"

"*She's* had enough!" Flynn thunders.

"Whose side are you on?" Beta Sinta thunders back.

"Fix her!" Flynn roars.

"I don't know how!" Beta Sinta hauls me against his chest, pinning my arms down with his much heavier ones.

I go limp, in too much pain to fight anymore. I'm sobbing now. I haven't sobbed in years. Tears stream down my face, salty and wet.

"What do I do?" His voice urgent, Beta Sinta crushes me against him. The weight of his arms makes my bones ache. "Tell me, and I will. Tell me!"

I can only guess. It's not something anyone ever talks about. When you make a vow, you don't break it. Period. Now I know why.

It takes all my strength to scrape two words from my throat. "Release. Vow."

"I release you from your vow." His breath rushes over my temple. "I release you, Cat. Be well again. Be well."

Something inside me shifts. The vow dissolves instantly. The pain melts slowly, leaving me shaking.

Beta Sinta's arms stay locked around me. "Cat?"

My nose is buried in his chest. I leave it there, breathing raggedly. Breathing him.

"Are you all right?" he asks.

My skin stings where I scratched it, and I must have bled, but that doesn't matter right now. I peek at my hands, thinking they're charred black. They're not. They look normal except for the bloody fingernails, but they feel fried, like the rest of me.

"I'm alive." My throat hurts from screaming. My voice is a hoarse rasp. "That's all you need."

He blows out a long breath, stirring the hair at the top of my head. "You do realize you're both stubborn and infuriating?"

I don't answer. Does he really expect me to agree?

"If I didn't need you so much I'd have—"

"—killed me by now?" I supply.

He chuckles. The sound vibrates through me, disturbing and much too intimate. "Let you go. Just to be rid of you."

I lift my head enough to glare.

As if it were a normal thing to do, Beta Sinta sweeps his hand up and down my spine in slow, soothing strokes. "Come eat something. You haven't eaten in hours, and we finally have food you like."

Warmth follows the path of his hand, heating more than just my back. I feel it in the strangest places. Coiling deep inside of me. Spiraling through my belly. Tingling along my ribs.

Neither of us moves. I eventually gather the strength, or maybe the will, to push off and stumble away from him. I get this awful feeling the second I leave his arms—I want to be back in them.

My eyes wide, I back away, a tangle of fear and emotion knotting in my chest. I'm used to being scared, but this time is different. This time, I'm afraid of myself.

Beta Sinta changes his mind about going straight to Sinta City. We stay in Velos for nearly a week and then wander the nearby countryside like vagabonds, waiting for something to happen. I keep saying we should run. Hiding is what I do, but he wants to find out who's chasing me, and I won't tell him.

At this point, I'd be safer in Sinta City, in the castle. There's an army there. But he doesn't want to draw mysterious enemies into the heart of the realm, and he wants to protect his family and his perfect sister who smiles for widows and orphans and has Sintans falling on the ground to kiss her feet. *Gag!* She won't last another month as Alpha.

On the bright side, I get to have an opinion now. What do I want to eat? Do I need to get off the horse? Do I want three or four feet of rope? Which side do I sleep on?

Fruit, I'm used to the horse, four feet, and on the left.

Beta Sinta even offers to show me how to use the sword he bought me in Velos. In his arrogance, he actually thought I'd need lessons. As soon as he hands me my blade, I nick his chin and draw blood.

His eyes narrow as he wipes his chin on his sleeve. "I thought you knew knives."

"I'm better with knives." I thrust again. He blocks this time, throwing me back so hard I almost fall over. I might have, if not for the rope. It's awkward sparring like this, but I'm too happy to be doing something different to complain. "That doesn't mean I can't use a sword."

"You fight dirty," he mutters.

I grin. "Is there any other way?"

He plays with me for a while. I hold my own because he's holding back. One swing with his true strength and I'd buckle instantly.

"Can't beat a girl?" I taunt, knowing he won't hurt me. Not much, anyway. "Has the big, bad warlord gone all soft?"

"Do you have a death wish?" Beta Sinta stalks forward

and nearly knocks the sword from my hand. The vibration rattles my bones from fingers to shoulder.

I roll my eyes. "I wish. That would make my life—or lack thereof—so much easier."

Flynn, Kato, and Carver chuckle on our right. I flick my braid over my shoulder and give them the evil eye. "Laugh all you want, ladies. You're next."

"No thanks," Flynn says. "I wouldn't want to hurt you."

"Poor Flynn." I sigh. "So scared."

They laugh. Unfortunately, I do, too. I drop my guard, and Beta Sinta steps in, disarms me, and sweeps my legs out from under me. I crash to the ground, the wind knocked out of me. He follows me down, pinning me with a classic grappling move I saw coming from miles away but was too slow to do anything about.

He ends up on top of me, his face mere inches from mine. The air flees my lungs again but for entirely different reasons. I can't help wondering about the laugh lines around the corners of his eyes, or noticing how the outer rims of his irises are more silver than gray. He hasn't shaved in days, and the beard shadowing his cheeks looks almost long enough to be soft. The dark whiskers frame his wide mouth and highlight the sensual curve of his full lips—lips I keep looking at.

His hair falls forward, caging us. His eyes turn that stormy gray. They remind me of the ocean on a wild, windy dawn just before the sun kisses the horizon. I bet if he looked at me a certain way...

Dear Gods, is he looking at me that way right now?

I panic and slam my forehead into his nose.

"Zeus's bollocks!" Beta Sinta bellows. Blood spews from his nose, drenching me.

"That's disgusting," I sputter. "Get off!"

His hooked nose is crooked now, too. *Oops.*

"You're as heavy as a horse." I ram my palms into his shoulders, trying to dislodge him. I can feel every steely inch of him. That's way too much, and he's way too close.

Something dangerous sparks in his eyes. "Concede I've won."

"What? No! In your dreams. Of the non-oracular kind." I jerk my head up again, the effort only halfhearted. He dodges, and my forehead glances off his scruffy cheek.

His voice deepens to a growl. "Concede I've won."

"Not a chance."

He settles more heavily on top of me. I can hardly breathe. "Are you sure that's wise?"

"Do you need me to say it in sign language?" I lift my head and bite him where his shoulder meets his neck. He tastes like salt, sun, and citrus. He tastes like he smells. My tongue apparently has a mind of its own because it snakes over his skin, tasting more.

He stops breathing. He doesn't fight me. He doesn't even move.

What in the name of Zeus am I doing? I release the bite and spit on the ground. "Gross!" I cough out, trying my best to believe it.

Beta Sinta lifts his head, anger and something else, something intense and shiver-inducing, flashing in his thundercloud gaze. I feel frozen in place and all jumbled up—belligerent, remorseful, excited…kind of worried.

He rises, roughly hauling me to my feet. He attaches me to a tree and leaves me there while he washes the blood off his face and tries to straighten his nose. I'm covered in his blood, too, but he doesn't seem to care.

More or less alone for the first time in days, I find a spot without any rocks or roots and stretch out, making a big deal about how great it is to finally have my own space. Which it is. Sort of.

Lacing my hands behind my head, I stare up at the leaves, a heavy feeling settling in my chest. I didn't mean to break his nose.

An hour later, Beta Sinta brings me to the stream in silence. His nose is swollen, and both his eyes have dark bruises under them. Instead of turning invisible for a bath, I wash my face, neck, and hands and then start chanting. He looks wary but doesn't try to stop me. When I'm done, I plunge my hand into the water and snatch the salamander I conjured out of the mud before it can swim away.

I rinse it off and then shove it in Beta Sinta's face. "Here. Eat this."

"Why?"

"It'll fix your nose."

He eyes the wriggling creature with suspicion. "How?"

"How do you think? With magic."

"Are you a healer, too?"

"No, but I know some tricks." I've needed them. "Go on. Eat. And no swallowing it whole. You have to chew. Crunch. Crunch," I say, dangling it in front of his nose.

He looks disgusted, and a little cross-eyed because it's so close. I'm surprised when he opens his mouth. I toss the salamander into it, and Beta Sinta crunches down. He gags, his eyes watering at the vile taste, but he still chews and swallows.

I grimace. "I can't believe you ate that."

"Why? You said I should." He clears his throat, visibly nauseated.

"Because it's revolting. And how do you know I didn't just poison you?"

"Did you?"

"No, but I could have."

He shrugs, completely unconcerned.

"By the way, you could've swallowed it whole."

Now he looks annoyed. *Ha!*

"And just so you know, never eat a blue amphibian. Most colors are fine, but blue is bad news."

He touches his nose, wiggling it back and forth and then scrunching it a few times. There isn't a trace of damage left. "I'll remember that if anyone ever tries to serve me a toad."

I make a face and roll my eyes. "I've never seen anyone conjure a magic toad. Toads are mostly terrestrial, anyway. I don't think they count."

"I'm not surprised. I just wanted to see you make a face and roll your eyes. It's adorable."

Adorable? My jaw hits the riverbank. No one's ever accused me of *that* before.

Great. Now I can't make faces or roll my eyes. My life just got bleaker. So why do I feel like smiling? *Gah!*

After dinner, Beta Sinta ties me to the tree again, apparently to have a conversation with Carver that I'm not allowed to hear. I don't mean to, but I fall asleep watching the moon hang in the sky. I wake up screaming, my knuckles flying toward Beta Sinta's throat. He catches my hand and holds it. My fist uncurls as where I am and who I'm with push the nightmare aside.

Past shadows fade as he traces slow circles on the palm of my hand with the pad of his thumb. I'm not sure he even knows he's doing it, but it's suddenly all I can think about—that hot, rhythmic circle on my hand. The rough skin combined with the soothing touch heighten the shivery sensations building inside me. I don't pull back. I'd be disgusted with myself, except this sure beats reliving needles of fire and a fist the size of my face.

Wordlessly, Beta Sinta reattaches us at the waist and then leads me over to his bedroll, spreading mine out on the left. I lie down, staring into the darkness and rejecting the completely irrational feeling of relief being next to him brings.

"Who did that to you?" he asks in a low, furious voice.

I stiffen under my blanket. "It doesn't matter."

"It matters to me."

My whole body goes still. "Why?"

"Because I punish people who hurt women."

My chest tightens painfully. It's a feeling I keep getting lately. I don't like it. "I wasn't a woman then. I was just a girl."

A savage sound rumbles in his throat. He sounds like the lion hybrid he's named for. "Who?"

"Like I said, it doesn't matter anymore."

"How can you say that?" He turns to me, his eyebrows drawn into dark, angry slashes. "Don't tell me you're the forgiving type."

I snort. "The person who gave me nightmares was punished a long time ago. Kill or be killed. That's the way of my world." I roll onto my side to face him. "*I'm* still here."

His mouth opens, but I cut him off. "Drop it, Beta Sinta."

His eyes are black in the moonlight. I can't tell what he's thinking.

"I have a name," he finally says.

I stay silent. His name doesn't change anything, and Beta Sinta is what he is.

He lifts up on one elbow and props his head in his hand, clearly with no intention of dropping it. "There were others, though. People who hurt you."

It doesn't sound like a question. I wouldn't answer anyway. I roll over, turning my back on him and closing my eyes. A face fills my mind—beautiful, olive skin, dark hair, eyes as cold as ice. She laughs. *"You* are *me. Don't even pretend that you're not."*

I shiver so violently that Beta Sinta must see it. The scars on my arms burn. Chills run through the rest of me. I'm not her. Not yet, anyway. The problem is, I might be worse.

It takes a long time for sleep to come. Close to dawn, I wake up way too hot with a warlord plastered to my back. One heavy arm is draped across my waist, his big hand splayed possessively over my stomach, tucking me against him.

My heart slams in my chest, and a frightening, warm sensation infuses that empty part of me. Something in the warmth flutters, cautious, like a nascent bird's wings. Like a fledgling, though, I don't know whether I'll crash or fly.

CHAPTER 10

IT TAKES TWELVE DAYS FOR THE ATTACK TO COME, long enough for my enemies to cross Fisa, Tarva, and half of Sinta at a grueling pace. I was wrong about twenty men; she sends thirty. "I told you we should've run."

Kato and Flynn adjust their weapons, mace and ax ready. Carver draws his sword, his eyes as sharp as his blade.

"Thirty to four," Beta Sinta says. "I've seen better odds."

I gape at his casual tone. He gets all worked up over my being snarky or not controlling my temper very well (at all!), but *this* doesn't faze him? What is *wrong* with him?

"Thirty to five," I correct, itching for my knives.

"They're Fisan."

"I know." Their snow-white standard undulating with blue waves brings on a mess of emotions. "So?"

He turns in the saddle. "Not interested in returning to your home realm?"

No.

Really, no.

A thousand trolls worth of no.

"If I wanted to be in Fisa, I would be."

He faces forward again and kicks his horse. I grab his waist, and we gallop for higher ground.

"I thought you weren't one of us," Beta Sinta calls over his shoulder.

"I'm not. Maybe you'll kill each other off, and I'll get away."

"This could be your lucky day," he says somewhat grimly.

It's not. I know it the second I see who's leading the Fisans. In all the realms, he's one of the few people who actually wants me dead, not just captured. And here I thought she'd send someone to bring me back. I might have to reevaluate my worth.

Beta Sinta stops and squints at the riders, focusing on their leader. "Gods, what did you do? Eviscerate his mother?"

I laugh. It's high-pitched and completely inappropriate, but I can't help it. He's right about the way Otis is looking at me. *Hate, hate, hate.* It doesn't bother me. I'm pretty sure I hate him more. "People don't think when they're angry."

Beta Sinta grunts. "You should know."

My nostrils flare. I'm nothing like Otis. If I were, I'd still be in Fisa. "This isn't the time for snide remarks. They're going to massacre us."

"They can try."

I smile at that. It's more a baring of teeth.

Beta Sinta glances at me. "I thought there was no *us*."

Did I just use the u-word by accident? "Untie me," I say, ignoring what I can't explain and don't want to think about. "Give me my weapons."

"I don't trust you."

"You can't fight tied up like this, and neither can I!" I feel him hesitate. "Oh, for the Gods' sakes! I give you my binding word I won't escape during the fight." That doesn't mean I can't escape later, and I'd rather stay with Beta Sinta for now than battle Otis like a sitting duck. At least the Sintans don't want me dead.

Gray eyes lock on mine. "You won't try to escape?"

I shake my head, unable to look away. "No. I swear it."

"Ever. You won't try to escape me *ever*. Not as long as I live."

My eyes widen, and I gulp down a scathing retort. "That's a lot to ask," I say roughly.

"I have a lot to lose," he answers just as roughly.

My heartbeat pounds against my ribs. Otis or Beta Sinta? Fisa, possibly death, or this, whatever *this* is. "It's out of my power if I'm captured."

His expression hardens. "Then I'd better not let that happen."

I swallow the sick lump in my throat. As far as choices go, it's not the hardest I've faced. Poseidon set us on this course. Would my God Father steer me wrong? He sent Beta Sinta to me with an oracular dream. What am I supposed to do with him? Probably not let him die. Or get killed myself.

My lungs feel scratchy, and I have to rip the words from my throat, regretting them as soon as they're said. "I won't try to escape you as long as you live."

The vow takes hold with a jolt of magic, jarring me. Scaring me.

A look of pure triumph crosses Beta Sinta's face. "I'll protect you, Cat. I swear it."

My heart clenches violently in my chest. "Don't make promises you can't keep. It displeases the Gods."

His deft fingers work fast, untying the knots. He stuffs the rope into his saddlebag, drags me onto his lap, and then plants his mouth on mine.

The kiss sizzles through me, quick and rough and shocking me to my toes. My lips tingle from hardness and warmth. Heat explodes through the rest of me, racing under my skin like a storm on the wind.

He pulls away, glaring at me. "Whatever happens to the rest of us, *you* live."

My pulse going wild, stunned, I shove him and sputter, "Gross!"

Sort of.

Not really.

Damn.

Beta Sinta grins and dumps me off the horse. "Go. Turn invisible and hide."

My jaw goes slack. "I'm not running away!"

His eyebrows slam down. "You'll do as I say!"

"Yeah, when has that ever ha—"

My head whips around. Power stings my skin as an arrow whistles past, trailing Chimera's Fire in its wake. My blood pulses, grabs the magic, and stops the arrow inches from Flynn's chest. Flynn of the belly laugh. Flynn who defended me, who fought for me when I was in pain.

Fury paints the world red. I gather the scorching magic, flip the arrow around with a swipe of my hand, and then fling it back toward the bowman, ramming it through his eye.

"Gods, Cat!" Flynn breathes a sigh of relief. "That would've burned me alive."

"Good thing I'm here," I say saucily.

"And modest, as usual," Beta Sinta mutters even though he looks impressed.

"You're one to talk!"

"Go!" he growls.

I hold out my hand. "Give me my sword." My knives are somewhere in Flynn's bag.

He does. He thinks I'm going to run.

There's another bowman nocking an arrow. He's a little far away. I reach…reach… *Got it!* He lets fly, and the arrow spins crazily up and then back down again, splitting his skull. *Ha!*

The Fisans roar in fury.

That's right. I've learned new tricks.

They charge. Beta Sinta maneuvers his horse in front of

me, blocking the first attack and bellowing at me to leave. Weapons flash. The Sintans form a solid wall of horse and muscle between my enemies and me. They're fierce and thrilling to watch, and for a moment, I almost think the Fisans won't get through. But four against thirty never goes well, no matter who the four are.

At first, I'm the only one on my feet. Hooves grind the earth. Dust flies in my eyes. Metal clashes, sparking, heating the air and dulling my ears. I'm not sure how long it takes to unhorse the Sintans, but they eventually end up on the ground. Apart from the dead bowmen, no one has magic. Except Otis. I know what he's got, and I can't wait to give some back.

A hole forms in my line of defense. Kato is down and bleeding from a long gash in his thigh. He rolls to avoid a downward thrust, kicks his attacker in the head with his good leg, and holds off another with his mace.

I race toward him, reaching for a dagger that isn't there. "Talia!"

I skid to a stop to face Otis. Stupid, but it's not as if he doesn't know it's me. He leaps through the hole left by Kato, who's now grappling with three men on the ground. Beta Sinta roars something I can't make out over the clash of swords. He's probably still trying to get rid of me. He wants me gone *now*? He hasn't let me out of his sight for a bloody month!

"She's mine!" Otis snarls.

Oh, good. He wants me all to himself.

"You murdering little bitch," he spits. "You'll pay for what you did."

I scrunch up my face and make fake sobbing sounds. "He didn't have it coming at all. Let's all stop fighting and cry."

"Did you enjoy slicing him open?"

Not one bit. "Very satisfying. Really bloody. But you know all about that, don't you?"

Otis smiles viciously. "Weakness is never rewarded."

"Good thing I'm not weak."

He smirks, gathering red-hot power in his hand and holding it there just to try to intimidate me. "You know what I can do to you."

Yes.

"I've done it before."

Now I can do it back.

There's such maniacal glee in his eyes that it scares me. Not because I fear him, but because I could have *been* him.

The first lash comes too fast for me to defend myself. Long, thin, burning, the whip unfurls from his hand and strikes with the speed of a snake.

I cry out, a red welt rising across my neck and chest. With the pain and pulsing heat come a jolt of power as Otis's Fire Magic fuses with my blood. I float on the wave of unfamiliar magic, readjusting. Then I grin, rather maniacally I imagine, and strike back.

Otis yelps and touches his face. The slash runs diagonally across his right eye, scorching off the middle of his eyebrow. His magic-induced injury doesn't heal in a matter of seconds like mine does—another benefit of Poseidon's gift.

"Just giving you a scar to match Beta Sinta's." I cock my head. "I'm rather impressed with my aim."

Otis's eyebrows, or what's left of them, snap together. "Beta Sinta?" He didn't even know who he was fighting, or that attacking the people with me would constitute a major act of war. He didn't care. "Traitor!"

"Blah, blah, blah." I pretend to yawn.

"Cat!" Beta Sinta bellows. He throws off two men, plants a dagger in the sternum of another, and then sweeps his leg around to bring a fourth one crashing to the ground. He created an opening for me. "Run!"

Fierce, skilled, powerful—utterly commanding—right now, he's hard to ignore. Good thing I've had practice.

"He wears the scar better," I say, turning back to Otis. "It's much manlier on him. By the way, how's your mother?"

Otis bares his teeth, gathering magic in his palm again.

Are you stupid?

Now I remember. Yes.

My sword raised in my left hand, I catch the whip of flame with my right one and then send it back. Instead of letting go, I strike one, two, three times.

Otis screeches, red blossoming across his face, neck, and torso.

"Not much fun, is it?" I keep striking until his tunic hangs in shreds. The skin beneath is raw and blistered, oozing blood. When he attacks again, his fire doesn't faze me. It only strengthens what I've already claimed.

I laugh at the flicker of fear in his eyes. Using the same magic never means doing it with equal power. Otis knows I can skin him alive.

"This is for me!" I slam the whip down on his head before redirecting it into a burning cage. I've never done it before, but I've watched Aetos turn his fire into a living sphere hundreds of times. At first, it wobbles and is more egg-shaped than round. Then it encases Otis as I gradually draw it down toward his feet. He shouldn't be able to burst through. Only the creator of the sphere can break it. The magic originally came from him, though, so I'm not sure where that leaves us. In a gray area, to say the least.

I detach myself from the flames as soon as Otis is

contained and look around. Kato is up again and still fighting, but his mobility is undermined by the serious injury to his leg. Carver is next to him, his blade moving so fast that no one can get too close. He's intact, but tiring. Flynn is bloody, and his left arm is hanging uselessly at his side, but he's still swinging with his right.

I don't see Beta Sinta anywhere, and the way my stomach drops makes me ill.

Something crashes behind me, and I whirl. Beta Sinta is fighting like a madman and coming straight for me. Our eyes collide. He won't reach me, not before the Fisans do. There are more than a dozen of them left, and there isn't a spark of magic among them. Only swords, men, and muscle, and I don't have enough fire whip to overcome more than a few. I have three minutes, maybe four, before they massacre the Sintans and are on top of me.

Someone darts around Flynn's bad side and grabs my sword arm. I slam my other hand into his nose along with Otis's magic. I let too much out at once, and the last of the fire whip leaves me. The Fisan's face melts under my palm, leaving my hand hot with gore. I wipe the sludge on my pants and turn in uneasy circles, waiting for the next attack. My heart pounds as our situation sinks in. There are too many Fisans. The odds are impossible. The Sintans *can't* win.

An idea takes hold. If Beta Sinta dies, I can go back to the circus. There will be no binding vow. No one who knows about me. I don't have to fight. I could turn invisible. When it's all over, I could slip away.

The thought presses on my chest like a lead weight. Not stopping to question why, I push it aside and fall to my knees, raising my hands to Olympus.

"Cat!" Beta Sinta roars.

I glance over my shoulder, my eyes narrowed.

"Get up! Fight!" His eyes are wild. His face is stark and splattered with blood.

I squeeze my eyes shut and turn back around. I block him out. I block it all out—clashing metal, roaring men, the stench of fear and blood, and the feel of dust turned to thick, reddish muck sucking at my knees.

"Help me," I whisper, not knowing what will happen. If *anything* will happen. "Please."

The world drops away. My stomach heaves as I tumble down a long tunnel and then land with an icy splash, sinking deep into black water. My ears hurt and my lungs burn by the time I figure out which way is up and start kicking.

I break the surface and gulp down air, slapping water out of my eyes. I'm adrift on a vast ocean. It's a dusk of shadows and gloom. The water is gray and churning where a storm brews on the horizon. Waves roll in—powerful, angry, dark.

"Poseidon!" My God Father might not be listening. He might not care.

I swim, looking frantically around. The waves are monstrous, and there's no land in sight. I rise up on a swell and then plunge back down on a stomach-churning ride, salt spray stinging my eyes and nose.

The rough surf suddenly splits, the slippery back of a giant sea serpent slicing the water only an arm's length away. I gasp and flail back. Its tail thumps my leg, and I let out a shriek. I know exactly where I just landed, and Poseidon's Ocean Oracle isn't known for its tolerance. It's either going to help me or eat me. Right now, that's anyone's guess.

The creature circles me, closing in. I spin in the water, its long, sinewy body creating an eddy that whips me around. Red, serpentine eyes with tall, narrow pupils study me, unblinking. There's a nudge in my head, insistent. My instincts scream to shield myself, but I can't. Not now. Gritting my teeth, I force myself open and bare my mind to the Oracle's scrutiny. It filters through my thoughts and memories. My dark deeds. My sacrifices. My fears.

The long look it gives me reminds me of the Lake Oracle, taking its time to decide if I'm worthy. After what feels like an eternity, a forked tongue snakes out and licks my cheek. It's smooth and icy and leaves a trail of numbness across my face. I shiver, hoping I taste like mercy instead of dinner.

Giant reptilian jaws unhinge and open wide, revealing two enormous fangs dripping seawater, saliva, and venom. The Oracle's breath stinks like the bowels of the Underworld. My heart sinks, and I cringe. It's going to swallow me whole. I squeeze my eyes shut and wait for the inevitable. It was arrogant and stupid to call on Poseidon like this. I'm surprised the Gods even let me live this long, knowing what I'm destined to destroy.

"Taaaakkkke," the creature hisses.

My eyes fly open. I gape at the huge head swaying above me, razor-tipped fangs only a foot from my face, a pink, slippery gullet pulsing behind them.

Have I cheated death again? Hades must be allergic to me.

My heart hammering, dizzy from spiraling, I hesitate only a second before reaching up and grabbing a curved fang in each hand. They come loose with a soft, sucking pop.

Stunned by the magnitude of the gift, I start stammering my gratitude, but the Oracle whips the water into a frenzy, circling so fast that its huge body becomes a blur. The foaming ocean surges, roaring in my ears and pelting my skin. Water crashes over me, muffling my scream as the funnel drags me deeper into its narrow abyss. My stomach heaves again seconds before the world goes airless and black, and the whirlpool sucks me under.

I land hard on my hands and knees, hacking briny water out of the back of my throat. The ocean is gone. The storm raging in my ears is replaced by the jarring, metallic clang of battle. Soaked through, I stare at the venomous fangs heavy in each fist. *I'm alive!*

Adrenaline hits me like a lightning bolt and snaps me into action. I stand, face Otis's cage, and then smash through the fiery prison with one punch. My skin blisters to the elbow in a flash of searing pain before healing as my body claims the magic again.

Otis stares at me, wide-eyed, his mouth gaping.

"And this is for Eleni!" I plunge a fang into Otis's heart.

His face turns ashen. "You're worse than the rest of us." His voice is a death croak. "That makes two."

My eyes narrow. *Kill or be killed. Wouldn't Mother be proud?*

The light drains from his eyes. Green eyes. Fisan eyes.

I pull the fang from his chest. It comes free with another soft, sucking pop as he slumps to the ground.

I plunge into the battle, and a rhythm takes me, a rhythm driven by Poseidon, his Oracle, and the fangs. Strike, duck, whirl, kick, lunge, roll. Strike!

Beta Sinta and the others fight their way toward me. Sometimes, in the heat of battle, it's hard to distinguish friend from foe. I have no trouble with that today. Beta Sinta reaches me, and the moment we end up back to back, I don't worry about what's coming from my blind side anymore.

I lunge forward, slicing a fang across a Fisan's chest. Flynn's ax whistles over my head while I'm still ducked down, and there's a spray of blood. I straighten and keep fighting, using the fangs like daggers. They're sharp and poisonous, but I don't have much reach, and both my enemies and their swords come alarmingly close.

Someone hammers a kick into the side of my knee, and I gasp, buckling. From the ground, I see Carver and Kato furiously working their way through a tangle of men. Beta Sinta snarls something and gets in front of an enormous Fisan who springs at me from the left. He blocks a bone-jarring hit that would have cleaved me in two, but the blow is hard enough to knock Beta Sinta's sword from his hands.

His eyes widen. Mine do, too.

The Fisan's face twists in triumph. I pivot on my hip and whip a fang up, throwing it like a knife. It sticks in his eye. Before the man falls, Beta Sinta grabs the fang from the Fisan's face and then backhands it into the chest of an enemy I didn't even see coming at me from behind.

He just saved me. Twice.

"Get up!" Beta Sinta snaps.

I lurch to my feet, my knee aching. Our backs touch again, and we circle, each with a fang gripped tightly in one fist. But it's over. Flynn rips his ax from a crushed chest. Carver wipes his sword clean on someone's blue tunic. There's no one left to kill. Between Beta Sinta's men and us, we've won. They're all dead. Fisans lie at our feet, and I'm slippery with their blood.

I blink and recognize some of the dead.

I blink again and try to forget them.

Kill or be killed.

The fangs melt from our hands with a barely audible hiss, fading into nothingness. Poseidon's power seeps from me as well, leaving me limp and drained. Panting, I double over, bracing my hands on my thighs.

Kato groans and slumps against Carver, his face turning pallid now that the blood rush of battle is draining from it. Flynn's left arm is broken and needs to be set. Beta Sinta is dripping blood, but it's not gushing from anywhere vital, and a lot of it isn't even his.

I catch my breath, letting it sink in that I haven't lost anyone. I'm amazed—and far too relieved for my own good.

I stagger upright. "That was fun."

Sort of.

Not really.

They look at me like I'm a lunatic.

Maybe I am. "Days ago I said we should get out of here and hide!"

Flynn recovers first. "Who needs to run when you've got magic fangs? And fire cages." He waves his good arm in circles, imitating me, I guess.

Beta Sinta grabs my shoulders and glares at me. He looks like he's about to explode. He might want to shake me. Or kiss me again. I can't tell. Given the choice, I'd rather a good shake. *Definitely*, a good shake.

"When I tell you to run, you run!"

I roll my eyes, and he shakes me so hard my teeth clack together.

"If I'd run, you'd all be dead."

"That's beside the point!" he bellows.

"That *is* the point!"

His fingers dig into my shoulders. Growling a curse, he lets go and drags his bloody hands through his hair, slicking it back. "How?"

"How what?"

His eyes flash. A muscle bulges in his jaw. "How in the name of the Gods did you get magic fangs?" He flings a hand toward the fallen. I refuse to look.

I think what he's really asking is why I didn't do this before, why I didn't call on the Gods weeks ago and murder him and his men in their sleep. I suppose I could have, if the Gods were listening, and one in particular. But since Poseidon has taken Beta Sinta under his trident, I doubt he would give me the means to kill him. And I don't take murder lightly. Kill or be killed, okay, but so far, the Sintans haven't hurt me.

"Who cares?" I shrug. "The Kingmaker's alive and bound by an unbreakable vow. Hooray for you. Congratulations to the lucky tyrant."

"Cat. Be reasonable."

Reasonable? Reasonable! "Don't ask me about magic and Gods, and I won't ask you about warlord stuff." My tone lets him know just how insignificant "warlord stuff" is in comparison to magic and Gods.

Beta Sinta's gray eyes flicker with irritation. *Ha!*

Sort of.

Annoying him wasn't actually that satisfying.

His hard look turns even flatter than usual. "God Daughter? Or lover?"

I swallow. For a southern Sintan Hoi Polloi warlord who doesn't know magic from a goat, he sure knows how to hit a Cyclops in the eye every now and then. "Why do you care?"

Something primal flares in his gaze. "Either way, you're mine now."

Nervous laughter bubbles out of me. "Your arrogance never ceases to amaze me. You would defy a God for a Kingmaker?"

"He gave you to me."

My heart stops. *He did, didn't he?*

"God Father," I answer with a shrug. "No Olympian lovers for me."

That primal look turns wholly possessive, doing unacceptable things to my insides. Before I can think about anything, and especially that quick, rough kiss, power bites the edges of my awareness. I turn toward the source and see a bowman nocking an arrow.

Fisans always have three bowmen. I can't believe I forgot. He must have come up the back side of the rise, and he's sighting the biggest target. Always take down the strongest first.

He lets fly, and the arrow zooms toward us with unnatural speed, glowing Chimera's Fire in its wake. I reach, but the fight and the fangs have left me drained, and I can't grab the magic.

"Griffin!" I twist and jump in front of him. Pain lances my back as the arrow slams me into Beta Sinta's chest. I clamp down on a cry and push off as hard as I can before I burst into flames. He stubbornly holds on, his face blank with shock. I cuff him in the ear, startling him into letting me go seconds before the inferno engulfs me.

My scream splinters the air. Crimson heat swallows me whole. My back bows in agony. My skin blisters instantly. The blaze deafens me to my own howl as my world narrows to pain—intense, searing pain. Then the flames suddenly implode, sucked inside for later.

I stagger and draw in a shuddering breath. My whole body shakes. My clothes are mostly gone, and my skin is revolting—an angry, charred mix of red and black. A violent tremor runs through me, excruciating, and then the healing process takes hold.

The bowman is frantically chanting fire into another arrow. I can't let him get away after what he just saw, or let him kill someone. Somehow, I force a thread of Chimera's Fire from my depths and will it toward the Fisan.

The magic is fast, a bright smear in the air. The Fisan burns, but unlike me, he doesn't rise from the ashes. And that's all that's left. His scream still rings in my ears, but I don't even see a bone.

The tension keeping me upright disappears along with the bowman, and my knees turn to liquid. My breath comes in short, painful pants. My eyes are doing their best to roll back in my head.

I blink rapidly, halfway to the ground when Beta Sinta grabs my restored arms, stopping my fall. I swivel like a puppet, trying to regain my footing.

His eyes are huge. "Of all the stupid, idiotic, imbecilic, reckless—"

"I get it," I moan.

"—things to do!" His fingers tighten painfully. "Don't ever do something like that again!"

Anger makes me see red again. "Why not? If I want to save someone, I will! What good is the Kingmaker without a king!"

He stumbles back, clearly as shocked as I am. I hadn't meant to, but I think I just pledged him my loyalty.

"I'm not Alpha," he says roughly.

"You should be!" My yell is more of a gurgle. Frowning, I wipe the back of my hand across my mouth, and it comes away bloody. I'm suddenly aware of a hot pulse of pain in my back and remember the arrow. Is that why it's so hard to breathe?

"Griffin?" I sway forward, and he catches me against his chest. It's like a rock. A bloody, sweaty, dirty rock. It feels good. I breathe shallowly, catching the faint scent of citrus through all the blood and dust before my legs give out.

"Cat?"

I grimace, my back throbbing. "Can't... Can't breathe right."

He sits and drapes me across his lap, his powerful hands moving incredibly gently over my back.

"It must have pierced a lung," Carver says, crouching next to us.

Beta Sinta curses, breaks the arrow shaft but doesn't pull out the head, and then curses some more. "You shouldn't have done that."

"Chimera's Fire," I wheeze. "Kills. Really hurts." Not to mention the arrow heading straight for his heart.

Beta Sinta turns me in his arms. My eyes flutter closed, but not before I glimpse the haunted look on his face.

I must have blacked out because he's suddenly on his horse, and Carver is lifting me up to him. One of Beta Sinta's tunics covers me from neck to knees. He must have sliced a hole in it for the broken arrow shaft because I don't feel it pulling.

"Burn the Fisan leader," I whisper. "Dilute my blood."

He gives the order without questioning me, splashing water over my mouth, hands, and back while Carver and Flynn do as I said. Kato is slumped over his horse, barely holding on to consciousness.

"Griffin?"

He leans down, putting his ear close to my mouth.

"The circus. In Kaplos again." We're closer to Velos, but the two cities are neighbors, and Kaplos can't be more than an hour from here. "Selena. Healer."

"You'll want to stay with them." His bloodstained fingers curl into the material covering my hip. The look on his face makes my heart twist.

Actually, if I survive, I kind of want to stay with him. I really am an idiot. "No choice," I rasp.

His mouth flattens. His eyes flick up as he spurs his horse, heading west. The shock of sudden movement sends a burst of pain through my back, and I moan. Beta Sinta's arm tightens around my waist, and I burrow into his chest, holding on. Maybe I'll trust him to fight my monsters while I sleep. Maybe I don't have a choice.

His voice is fierce in my ear. "You're mine now, Cat. Don't you dare die on me."

CHAPTER 11

I WAKE UP IN A FAMILIAR TENT. IT SMELLS LIKE home. "Selena?"

She leans over me, smiling. Her blonde braid slips forward and brushes my arm. It's glossy and sleek and so thick it's the size of a man's wrist. Her face is flawless. Ageless. She could be thirty, she could be two hundred, and her eyes are the color of a northern lake on a clear, windless day—dark blue and so deep that when I look into them, I sometimes think I'm seeing another world.

She gently brushes the hair back from my face, and I burst into tears.

Selena arches delicate eyebrows a shade darker than her braid. "That's a first."

"I missed you." I hiccup, embarrassed.

"I'm flattered. I didn't think you cried."

"I don't," I say, swiping at my tears.

She sits back, bringing her thumb and index finger nearly together. "I'm *this* close to perishing from curiosity."

I blink, surprised. Selena always seems to know everything, at least before anyone else does. "That would not please Hades."

She smiles a secret, satisfied smile that makes me wonder what it's like to be loved by a God, even one who already has a wife.

"The warlord isn't talking, I think out of a misguided effort to protect you. Information on my end has been scarce lately, so tell me, who is the man that carried you into my circus, roaring for me to save you?" Her grin turns impish. "'*Fix her! Now! Or I swear to the Gods that the Furies will rain death and destruction upon you, and there will be lightning bolts to pay!*'"

I gasp. "He didn't!"

"He did." Her extraordinary eyes dance with mirth, and I cough up an involuntary smile. It takes a certain dimension of balls to threaten Selena. She can be really scary in a mother-hen-meets-warrior-queen kind of way. The magic around her is palpable, awing, and, frankly, a little disturbing it's so intense. It's a good thing their goals converged—protecting me—or Beta Sinta might have been in trouble.

"How long have I been here?" I ask.

"Two days. You had to sleep it off. Me too."

Selena hardly sleeps unless she does something incredibly taxing. If she needs rest, Hades brings her to the Underworld, although I can't imagine she does much sleeping there.

Troubled, I ask, "It was that close?"

"*Minutes* close, and you still need your rest."

Tiny goose bumps rise on my arms. I've always been aware of my own mortality. That doesn't make almost dying any easier. I cheated death again. Hades must *really* not want me. He's probably afraid I'll cause as much trouble in the Underworld as I will in Thalyria.

I frown, rubbing the chill from my skin. "He hasn't told you who he is?"

Selena shakes her head.

"Beta Sinta—the new and improved." I mean to sound sarcastic, but it doesn't really come out that way.

Something flickers in her eyes, maybe a flash of annoyance. It's gone so fast I might have imagined it.

"Definitely improved," she says. "Especially after I got through with him."

Worry slams through me. "Was he badly hurt?"

"Do you care?"

I hesitate, alarmed by the intensity of my reaction. "I'm...not sure?"

Selena lets out an elegant snort. "You're not very convincing. And, no, he wasn't badly hurt. Cuts and slashes. Some blood loss. Nothing irreparable."

Relief floods me, but the feeling is short-lived. "Did I bleed?"

"Yes, but I burned the tunic and diluted everything else. Nothing traceable was here for more than a few minutes."

Selena's never asked who I'm hiding from or why. She protects me regardless. "Thank you."

She inclines her head so regally I feel like I should kneel, or bow.

"And the others?" I ask.

"The lanky, dark one was weary but fine. Carver, I believe? And the jolly ax-wielder needed his arm fixed, but he wasn't too damaged otherwise, a bit like your Beta Sinta."

My heart has a miniature seizure. "He's not *my* Beta Sinta."

She continues like I haven't spoken. "And the very handsome Kato nearly lost his leg. It took everything I had left in me after finishing with you to save it."

Kato of the smiling blue eyes and sunny hair. Of Athena. Of wisdom and war. I can't believe he almost lost a leg.

"They're all okay, then?" I grin like an idiot. What is *wrong* with me?

She rises from her chair, fluid and vaguely shimmering. Her grace is legendary. I'm agile and strong, but I'd rather move like sunbeams on water, like Selena.

"In good health and arguing incessantly with Desma and Aetos. Those two are under the impression the Sintans abducted you."

She's asking a question. I owe her an answer. "They did. Sort of."

Her sculpted lips purse. "Help me understand a 'sort of' abduction," Selena says, pouring me a cup of water.

Well, it sounds stupid when you say it like that.

My throat is parched, so I drink before answering. "He's Beta Sinta. He said he'd have you all arrested if I didn't come."

"And you believed him?"

It's a loaded question coming from Selena. I nod. After nearly a month with him, I also know he would have done it because he felt he had to, not because he wanted to.

"He needs a powerful Magoi to help him and his precious Alpha sister, Egeria." Egeria is no Alpha. She sounds more like a buttercup. Beta Sinta on the other hand, he's Alpha material. Fierce on the battlefield, bloody, focused, ruthless...*fair?*

"Plus, he had a magic rope."

Selena laughs, and the sound is like wind chimes on a spring breeze. "You? Caught by a magic rope?"

I flush. "Don't remind me."

She clears her throat, taming more laughter, and asks, "Will you help him?"

Selena may not know *who* I am, but I'm certain she knows *what* I am—the Kingmaker—even if we've never discussed it. "My abilities can be valuable in diplomatic situations," I say carefully.

"He came here to save you. He looked like he cared."

I shrug, glancing down. "I'm a weapon he doesn't want to lose."

"I think there's more."

My eyes snap back up. "Don't infer something that isn't there. We're both monsters."

Her dark-blue gaze flicks over me, unnerving. "Monsters still mate."

I choke on my own spit and then cough.

A faint smile curves her lips. "Why didn't you just escape?"

"The rope." That stupid, infuriating enchanted rope that led me to make a binding vow to stay with Beta Sinta until his—or my, if it comes first—dying day.

She looks incredulous. "You couldn't find a way out?"

"It was a bloody good rope!"

Sighing, she drops the subject and reaches for my hand. "Of all the monsters chasing you, Cat, you could have been caught by worse."

I look away from her. Colorful fabrics hang from the domed ceiling of Selena's tent. I stare at them, thinking she's right. I don't usually like to be touched, but I leave my hand where it is. No one has held my hand in years. Except Beta Sinta. But that was different; he was dragging me around.

"Is that your pearl of wisdom for the day?" I ask.

"No, this is. Listen to your heart. You think it's black. I don't know everything you've been through, but I know enough to understand that your past filled you with hostility and hate. But you still laugh. You still love, and you protect the people you care about. You're not who you think you are. You're better, and you're *more*." Her powerful, fathomless gaze holds mine, and a prickly feeling crawls up my nose toward my eyes. "No matter what you think, your heart is still red and beating." She squeezes my fingers. "Listen to it."

I nod, resisting the urge to sniff.

As soon as Selena leaves, Desma and Aetos burst into the tent.

"Cat! You're awake!" Desma falls on top of me, hugging me, the cot—everything. It would hurt if she didn't weigh less than I do.

Aetos looms over us, huge and blue.

"Don't *you* try that," I warn.

He grins, and I reach up, drawing him down for a quick hug. Happiness bubbles inside me at seeing these two again.

"How are you?" I ask, smiling.

He pats my hand. "Better, now that you're back."

My smile falls, landing somewhere near my toes. "I can't stay."

"You have to!" Color erupts from Desma. Without thinking, I gather the magic she released. I let part of it go, and it shimmers around the tent, turning the warm air the color of jewels in the sun.

"You're not leaving with *him*," Aetos growls.

I think we all know who *him* is. "I have to. I gave my binding word."

"That son of a Cyclops!" Aetos pounds his massive fist down on Selena's vacated chair. It shatters like a toy made of twigs. "He made you promise before he brought you to Selena."

I shake my head. "I promised before I got hurt."

His mouth snaps shut. I've left Aetos speechless. Definitely a first.

"Why?" Desma asks.

"There was about to be a battle. I was magically tied up. Actually, I was tied to him. Neither of us could fight like that."

"So if he untied you, you promised to stay with him?"

I nod, and Desma looks appalled by my stupidity. "You traded one shackle for another, much stronger one."

"I know," I say, disgusted. "I had a better chance of escaping the enchanted rope than my own binding word. But we're alive, right?"

"*We?*" Desma asks pointedly.

My face heats. "They're not that bad. And they might be better for the realm." Unless having a Hoi Polloi Alpha makes Tarva and Fisa rain years of fire and monsters down on us.

"What do they have to do with Sinta?" Aetos asks.

As I explain who the Sintans are, my two best friends turn an interesting shade of yellow. Aetos looks a bit green, actually, given his blue tattoos.

"So, a strapping warlord, who is actually Beta Sinta, takes one look at you and decides he *has* to have you?" Desma asks.

"Strapping?" Aetos grumbles.

"Not as strapping as you, darling." Desma smiles sweetly, and Aetos looks mollified, lowering his head to kiss her soundly on the lips.

My jaw goes slack. I've been waiting years for this. I go away for a month, and it happens without me? Life is *not* fair!

I clear my throat, and Desma breaks the kiss, blushing.

"Apparently," I answer, my eyes bouncing back and forth between the two of them so fast it gives me vertigo.

"But why? Why you?" Desma asks, still pink.

"Because I'm cute and funny?"

They stare at me.

"No, really," Desma insists. "Why *you*?"

I sigh. "He needs a Magoi with my skills. He thinks I can be helpful in diplomatic situations. Alliances and treaties. Things like that."

Aetos chokes on something. "You? Diplomatic?"

"I know!" I throw my hands up. "I guess he thinks insult first and kill after will be good for the realm."

We all laugh, but it feels forced.

"There's more to it," Desma prods.

I shake my head. "He's Hoi Polloi. He needs Magoi. I'm a soothsayer."

"You're more than that." Aetos doesn't ask. He states a fact.

When I don't say anything, Desma asks, "How does Beta Sinta know you're more than that? Why work so hard to save you when he could just abduct himself another soothsayer?" She frowns, obviously hurt. "You didn't just tell him whatever else you are, did you?"

"Of course not!" I say hotly. "It was an *oracular dream*." I roll my eyes. "Thanks a bunch, Poseidon."

Silence. It lasts so long I get sleepy. Magical healing saps my energy like nothing else.

"Poseidon?" Aetos eventually echoes.

I yawn. "Because of him, Beta Sinta watched me, put two and two together, and found some old scroll confirming it all."

Silence again. Then Desma asks, "Will you ever tell us, Cat?"

It's getting hard to focus. Fatigue turns the multicolored tent into a kaleidoscope. "I don't know. It's not what I want to do with my life. It's what I ran away from."

Blue lines pull tight around Aetos's mouth. "But you'll do it for him?"

I don't answer, and my eyelids sag.

I wake up sometime late in the afternoon and then eat like a person three times my size. An embarrassing amount of roast chicken and an entire tray of spice cakes, which I'm guessing Desma left by my bedside, disappear in less than an hour. I feel stronger but stickier than the cakes I just inhaled.

A parade of visitors keeps me from leaving the tent for a bath. Dozens of circus residents pop their heads in to see if I'm awake and to check on me. I get tired again fast, but I'm too happy to see everyone to say so. Tadd and Alyssa bring me a pot of honey from the beehive they carry around with them everywhere the circus goes, and Zosimo and Yannis tell me about the performances I missed while I was gone. Vasili and his wife give me a new knife, clearly under the impression I need more blades.

"In case you lose one in the warlord's gut," Vasili says with no expression whatsoever.

Who me? Do I look violent and prone to slaughter?

Finally alone, I get up to tuck the knife into my satchel and discover just how weak I still am. I groan, taking baby steps across the tent. My legs wobble, feeling like dough that's been rolled out but not baked hard.

Kato, Carver, and Flynn show up just as I'm crawling back onto the cot. Instead of collapsing like I want to, I sit, greeting them with a sour expression. "Didn't you all die?"

Flynn smiles, his brown eyes alight with humor. "Almost."

I grimace. "Maybe next time."

Carver looks more serious. "You didn't let us die."

I glance down and pluck at the sheet, uncomfortable with his gratitude. "You didn't let me die, either."

"That was mostly Griffin," he says. "He rode like a bat out of the Underworld to get you here. We showed up with Kato while Selena was finishing with you."

"Well," I say, ignoring the warmth spreading through my middle, "Kingmakers only come around every two hundred years or so. When you've got one, it's best to keep her alive."

Kato shakes his head, giving me a look that says I'm as stubborn as a Cyclops. "It's not just that. You gave your word. You're part of Beta Team now. Griffin will keep you alive, or die trying."

I roll my eyes. "This again?" Beta Sinta wouldn't die for me. Sacrificing himself would defeat the purpose of, well, *everything*. He was overconfident outside of Velos, even though I told him to run. He won't take a risk like that again.

"This *always*." Flynn's tone is reproachful. "What's more important—"

"—than loyalty?" I finish acerbically.

All three men look at me like I'm a strange creature they have no idea what to do with.

"Griffin will change your mind," Flynn announces.

I snort. "He could try."

Suddenly, we're all laughing, and it's not at all forced, which makes some part of me feel horribly guilty.

"Thirty to five." Carver shakes his head, smiling in disbelief. "Too bad no one was betting on those odds."

The high, cloud-capped peak of Mount Olympus rushes to my mind's eye. "Maybe the Gods were."

"And that's why they intervened?" Kato swirls around the tent, imitating me fighting the Fisans with a venomous fang in each fist. He's a whirlwind of blond hair, blue eyes, and hard muscle. He's fast, every movement coiled with strength and power even though I can tell his leg is still bothering him.

"Where'd you learn to swing a fang like that?" he asks, grinning.

I wave a hand in the air. "Here and there."

"No, really." Kato sinks into a chair, his color high for such simple exertion. "How'd you do it?"

I arch a superior brow. "Didn't you hear? I'm amazing."

"And modest, too." Flynn snickers.

I grin. "I've been taking lessons from His O So Scary, Arrogant Highness."

Manly laughter fills the tent. I laugh, too, hoping Beta Sinta's ears are burning.

Sitting next to me, Carver asks, "Most people are scared enough of Griffin. Why aren't you?"

I motion everyone forward by crooking my finger. They lean in, anticipation on their handsome faces. Performing is an art, and I've picked up a few tricks. I make them wait and then whisper, "Because I'm scarier."

They burst out laughing. They think I'm kidding.

"You're arrogant and hotheaded," Flynn says.

"So?"

"Griffin is arrogant and levelheaded. He'll beat you every time."

I scowl. He's also bigger, stronger, and faster. He's not stupid, either, even if our knowledge backgrounds aren't the same. Worse, magic bounces off him. I saw it in Velos even though I was too high on euphoria to care.

"Oh my Gods!" I smack my forehead with the palm of my hand. "The Chimera's Fire wouldn't have burned him. I am *such* an idiot."

No wonder he ate my magic salamander without a twitch of doubt. Selena healed him. I healed him. But harmful magic must simply not work on him.

I frown. I've never heard of that.

Carver shakes his head, confirming my thoughts. "But an arrow will still put a hole in him, just like you."

"That's how he got into the castle and cut down the

Sintan royals? Their magic couldn't touch him, and he was just plain better than any of them with a sword?"

Carver nods, and my mouth pinches into a disgusted pucker. The realization is hard to swallow. Beta Sinta would best me in a fight, no matter what magic I had stored up.

I blow out a long breath and try to look on the bright side—he can best a lot of my enemies, too.

As if my thoughts conjured him, Beta Sinta pushes the tent flap aside and storms in, eyeing the four of us with a hard glint in his eyes. Seeing him is like a really strange punch in the gut, winding me, but not entirely unpleasant, either.

His chin dips. "I heard you were awake, *Talia*."

I mutter a curse that makes Flynn blush.

Kato, Carver, and Flynn leave so fast I practically feel a breeze. *So much for having my back.* At least they leave the tent flap tied back and the door wide open.

Beta Sinta arches dark eyebrows, looking expectant.

Not wanting to have this conversation sitting down, I stand too quickly, and bright spots streak across my vision.

"I'm awake," I confirm, although it's kind of obvious. "So?"

Beta Sinta crosses his arms. "So tell me what's going on. Talk to me, like you did in Velos."

"I wasn't myself," I say stiffly.

"True. You were fun."

My face contorts into a scowl of epic proportions. I take an angry step toward him and stumble, completely off balance.

He's there in an instant, his hands on my waist, the heat of his skin blazing between us. My pulse surges.

"You're weak." His tone sharpens. "I thought she fixed you."

I wiggle away from the hands scorching holes through the sides of my tunic. "You don't have to sound so mad about it. Selena did what she could."

He frowns. "Talk to me, Cat. Why Talia? Who were they?"

I shake my head. "I can't."

Magnetic gray eyes capture mine. "You can trust me."

I scoff. "So says the kidnapper."

He just stares at me like he fully expects me to start talking. *Gods! He's infuriating!* "It'll be a cold day in the Underworld before I trust you." *Or a moderately cool one. Well, a day with a stiff breeze anyway. Gah!*

I back up until my legs bump against my cot, oddly chilled after being so close to him.

"How are you feeling, *Talia*?"

I glare at him. "That's not my name."

"According to the Fisan it is. You know, the one yelling 'She's mine!' with bloody murder in his eyes."

My heart slams hard against my ribs. "He must have mistaken me for someone else."

Beta Sinta's stare turns flat with disbelief. "For days, you told me they were coming for *you*."

Oh, right... I shrug.

His eyes flash silver. "Who was he?"

"I don't know! Fisans are insane. Get used to it." I grin maniacally, but it fails to have any effect on him.

"The two of you had a chat while the rest of us were fighting to the death. You don't do that with someone you don't know."

Beta Sinta couldn't have heard what we were saying. There was too much noise and confusion for that. "I always get to know people before I kill them. It's much more satisfying that way." There. That sounded sufficiently insane.

His eyebrows slam down. "Don't make me ask again," he says, sounding like he's grinding stones between his teeth.

I turn and fold my blanket, just in case my eye really does twitch when I lie. "My ex-lover. It didn't end well. He's been out to kill me ever since."

Beta Sinta's hands land on my shoulders, heavy and hot. I jolt and then stiffen. He turns me around, making my head spin. I barely keep my feet from tangling up in each other.

"I thought you were done lying to me." He drops his arms but stays disturbingly close. "You know when people lie to you. They can't get away with the smallest falsehood. You, on the other hand, can lie all you want."

"So?"

"So I can't protect you if you won't tell me the truth!" He actually growls at me. Loud. "I want to protect you, Cat."

I blink. *Want.* Not need. The word strikes me hard, like a dagger trying to pierce the tight knot of muscle beating far too rapidly in my chest.

My lips part and then press together again. I can't deal with this. I'm woozy, my stomach feels like lead, and it's all too much.

A sudden, horrible thought occurs to me. "Can you see me when I'm invisible?"

He shakes his head, seamlessly reining in his temper to answer me. "I only reject magic that harms."

Thank the Gods! My eyes narrow. "That's convenient."

"It is," he agrees.

"I should've let you take the arrow."

"You should have." His eyes bore into mine, demanding answers. "Why didn't you?"

Good question. An evening breeze comes through the open doorway, tossing his longish hair around. His eyes are the color of thunderclouds, both luminous and dark, striking against his sun-bronzed skin. There's steadiness in them, and my nerves settle. For some reason, the strength and deadliness he keeps so easily leashed make him the most compelling man I've ever met. I envy his self-control.

"Temporary insanity." I shrug. "A moment of complete idiocy. I must have forgotten who you are."

He looks disappointed, and something tugs inside of me. His eyes stray to the scars on my arms, lingering on the fresh one Selena had to make to keep me alive. "Regardless, don't ever do something like that again. Now answer the questions, *Talia.*"

I turn mute on him. I'm good at that.

Beta Sinta waits for what must seem like a reasonable amount of time to him and then grates out, "He hurt you, and you won't even tell me who he was!"

"Hurt me?" I laugh, the maniacal in it a little too real. My filters snap. Or maybe some deeper part of me does. Secrecy isn't the only reason I don't talk about my past. I don't talk about the things that have happened to me because acknowledging them plunges me into nightmares and sucks the light from the world. "Hurting me is keeping me in a cage for eight months. Not a single change of clothes. Not a bath. Not a pillow. Not a bloody second of privacy. Only enough bread and water to survive, and spitting fire and lies at me just to see me writhe."

Beta Sinta's face turns thunderous. "The Fisan did that to you?"

"The Fisan royals!" An edge of hysteria is creeping into my voice. I hear it. I hate it. I can't do anything about it. "They're the ones who call me Talia. It was Beta Fisa I killed." Gamma, actually, but that hardly matters now. "Don't ever call me that. *Ever!*"

Big, warm hands rise to my cheeks. Long fingers curl around the nape of my neck, their hold on me light yet firm. He tilts my face up, saying in a low, calming voice, "I won't. It's all right. You're Cat. Just Cat."

"It's not all right!" I explode, grabbing his wrists. I don't know if it's to hold on to him, or to push him away. I do a little of both. "They won't rest until I'm theirs again. Or dead." My legs start to shake, making the rest of me tremble. "They'll never take me alive. Never!"

A note of frantic conviction hangs in the air between us. It's thick, like fear.

Beta Sinta makes a soothing sound and slides his fingers into my hair, smoothing them over the back of my head and sending all sorts of misguided sensations spiraling around my body.

Leaning down, he lightly drops his forehead against mine. "I won't let anything happen to you."

He sounds so sure. I resist the temptation to lean into him, to find shelter in his arms, my internal battle complicated by the knowledge that he wouldn't push me away. He's still cradling my head, gently massaging. We're breathing each other's air.

Awareness rushes through me. Heat swirls in my veins, and my stomach tumbles wildly. My eyes close, and my hands slip from his wrists. The left one drops, limp. The right one hovers and then presses against his chest. Under it, his heart thumps hard and then beats faster. I open my eyes and stare at my fingers, wondering what they're doing there, touching him, absorbing his warmth.

"Never promise things you can't deliver," I whisper.

"I can try," he whispers back, and I hate myself because I smile. Tension drains from me, leaving me far too aware of his height and strength, of his subtle scent, and of the fact that this man kissed me.

He lifts his head and strokes my jaw, the touch feather-light despite the power in his hands and the calluses on his fingers. "Tell me about the Fisan royals. The more I know, the better I can defend you."

"I can defend myself."

He smiles. It's lopsided, and more heart-stopping than I care to admit. "Is that how you got caught by a warlord with a magic rope?" he teases.

Scowling, I shove hard against his chest where my hand is still resting.

"Tell me about the Fisans," he says again, voluntarily stepping back.

I shiver. "Later." I glance around Selena's tent. "There are names I don't want lingering in the air."

He nods in understanding. "Soon, then."

I nod back. There's no escaping it. He's too damn stubborn.

Watching me, Beta Sinta backs toward the tent opening. I can still feel his fingers on my skin, rough and masculine, and I have to quell the urge to touch where he touched. It's unsettling. I bite my lip.

"Cat?" There's enough warmth in his voice to send my heartbeat into dangerous territory.

"Yes?"

"You do a good job of defending yourself."

I nod. "I've been taught well. I'm the favored child."

"Of Poseidon?"

Not answering, I turn and swirl my fingertips in the basin of water by my bedside, watching the pattern I make form and fade. *Yes, well, of him, too.*

CHAPTER 12

WE SPEND THREE MORE DAYS RECOVERING. THE SINTANS camp outside the circus grounds, but I sleep in my old tent. Temporary homecomings are bittersweet. Sometimes it's better not to go back at all than to have to leave again. I don't have a choice, though, binding vow or not. Otis may have failed, but Alpha Fisa won't give up. Andromeda knows I'm in Sinta now. She's still coming for me, and next time, she'll send something worse.

My friends gather behind us as we prepare to leave, throwing dirty looks at my Sintan companions. Only Selena's brow remains unruffled, as if she knows something the rest of us don't. Before we ride out, she breaks rank and strides toward me.

"This is for you. From Hades." She drops a small charm into the palm of my hand. It's a gold figurine of Cerberus. The hound has six ruby eyes, a set for each of its three heads.

I can't hide my astonishment. "Why is Hades interested in me?"

"Only use it if you have to." She closes my fingers around the warm metal, not answering my question.

"How does it work?"

"He didn't say."

I look at her, incredulous. "You didn't ask?"

"I was busy doing other things."

I snort. "That's helpful."

Her blue eyes sparkle. "It was for me."

I shut down my imagination before it paints too vivid a picture. "Do you at least know what it does?"

Selena shakes her head.

"Really? Nothing?" I ask.

She pats my cheek. End of discussion.

Beta Sinta reaches down for me and helps me clamber up the side of his gigantic horse. I take a deep breath as we then turn to leave. I don't look back. I don't want to see a huge, blue man with his arm around a weeping rainbow and a woman who shimmers like the sun. I don't want to see dozens of people I care about or Cerberus's terrifying, ugly, furry heads because if I do, the already painful ache inside me might turn into something I can't bear.

Beta Sinta tries to talk to me, but I stay silent, afraid words won't make it past the thickness in my throat. After thirty minutes of riding in silence, we turn west, skirting the farms outside the city instead of heading north.

"We're staying in Kaplos?" I ask, confused.

He shakes his head, his midnight hair sliding along his neck and curling slightly around his ears. I find myself looking a little too hard at the back of his tanned neck. The spray of freckles across it is...kind of appealing.

"We're going to a horse breeder I know."

Oh? The horses all seem fine to me. "Why?"

"Don't you want a horse?"

Actually, it never even occurred to me. "Now that you mention it, it would be fabulous to get away from you and... What's your horse's name? All this time, and I never thought to ask."

"Horse."

I roll my eyes. "That's original."

"Brown Horse," he amends.

It's hard not to laugh. "Much better, but I can't afford a horse."

"I'll take it out of your wage."

"Then I can't afford to eat."

"Don't worry about it, Cat."

"I don't want you buying me a horse!" My voice comes out sharper than intended, but I don't want to be dependent, or beholden, or anything really.

"Then ride with me."

I weigh my options. "I'd rather starve and have a horse."

He doesn't argue. Maybe he saw how many spice cakes I consumed over the last few days and thinks cutting back would do me good.

The farm we stop at is only a midsized affair, but I can tell just from the upkeep of the fences that we'll find high-quality animals here.

"Take your pick," Beta Sinta says after the breeder gives us a demonstration of five horses he thinks would suit me.

I glance at him, surprised. I thought he'd choose for me. "I don't know anything about horses. The last time I had a choice, I was too young to care about anything other than pretty or not pretty."

He slides me a long look. I never volunteer information about my past, so I'm surprised when he doesn't press for more. He points to a chestnut whose reddish coat gleams in the sun. "He's the right size and fairly placid."

"Why do I need placid?"

He hits me with his hard stare. "Because then at least one of you will stay calm."

"Calm is boring," I retort.

His white teeth flash, and his gray eyes crinkle at the corners. "Absolutely," he agrees, looking at me with undisguised heat in his eyes.

My stomach flips over in a way that makes me want to throw up for a variety of reasons, but significantly lessens the urge to argue.

I take a deep breath. "The chestnut, then?"

"Or that gray." He nods to a horse the color of dirty snow with four black socks and a dark muzzle. "He's fast."

"Faster than the chestnut?"

Beta Sinta nods. "But the chestnut can run, too. He's powerful enough."

"He. He. What about a girl horse?"

He shakes his head. "You don't want a mare."

"Why not?"

He angles his head toward mine, his eyes still smiling. I don't think my eyes are even capable of smiling. "Females are temperamental," he says with a roguish grin.

My eyes narrow, and I give him a hearty shove. Playfully, he shoves me back. I land on my ass.

"For the Gods' sakes," I mutter.

Beta Sinta looks surprised. "You fall over too easily."

"Excuse me for being half your size!"

"Next time, I'll remember that," he says, extending his hand to me.

Next time? Next time! I pop up and launch myself at him. I'm not quite sure why.

Flynn, who's on my other side, catches me in midair. "We're a team, Cat, remember? No fighting." Roped with muscle, Flynn's arm covers my entire midsection. I go limp, blowing sweat-dampened curls out of my eyes. *All these stupid rules of camaraderie! Gag!*

Beta Sinta grins at me. Flynn sets me down.

"So which horse do you want?" Beta Sinta asks as if I hadn't just tried to get into a brawl with him for no apparent reason. He's just... He's just so... *Argh!*

"The chestnut," I answer sourly. "At least one of us will stay calm."

I like having my own horse, and traveling with the Sintans without being tied up is actually kind of fun—something I would die a thousand horrific deaths before ever admitting to them. Carver thinks my sword technique could use work, so he offers to spar with me. Having seen him wield a blade, I can't say no.

We circle, weapons raised. Kato is off hunting, Flynn is on watch, and Beta Sinta is polishing his sword, keeping an eye on us. My attacks are child's play for Carver. He's so fluid with a blade that I start to wonder if there's something magical about his ability, some magic I can't steal, or even feel. After an hour of practicing, I'm tired and sweaty, and I haven't landed a single hit.

Frustrated, I spin out of a deadlock before Carver disarms me or pushes me to the ground again. Before I can turn back around, he spanks me with the flat of his sword. It stings, and I howl.

Rubbing my backside, I demand, "Do all men have a thing for spanking?"

Carver wiggles his eyebrows. "Most women, too."

I huff, *although I have heard...*

"Ever been spanked before?" he asks.

"Don't be cheeky." For some reason, a conjured up image of Beta Sinta trying to smack my naked bottom while I half-heartedly scramble away flits through my much too active imagination. Warmth billows up inside me, singeing my face.

"You have!" Carver grins.

"Not. Answering." *Nope.* Out of the corner of my eye, I see Beta Sinta look up.

"There are different kinds of spanking," Carver goes on, his tone getting friskier by the second.

I press my lips together to keep from smiling. "Enlighten me."

He shakes his head, looking as if I've just confessed to a colossal tragedy. "That must mean you haven't been spanked enough."

I'm pretty sure spanking is a metaphor now. "No," I agree sadly, playing along. "Not nearly enough."

Before I know it, he's on my other side, slapping my ass with his sword again. I let out a screech that would make a Harpy proud, swing, and slice air.

Laughing, Carver dances to my right and feints, tricking me into stepping the wrong way, and then hits me again. "I could help you with that. Just say the word."

He's flirting again. What a pest. My rear end is a strange mix of numbness and heat. I refuse to be smacked again, so I drop my guard, lower my eyelashes enough to distract, and turn my voice a shade breathy, stepping right into Carver. "With an offer like that, how can I refuse?"

He gapes at me. Clearly, my reciprocating was the last thing he expected. I whip a dagger from my belt and plant it at his groin, pricking just enough to make him yelp. Carver freezes.

I cant my head, saying coolly, "I haven't been spanked much because I do the spanking."

Beta Sinta laughs, startling the birds in the branches above. "Carver," he says. "She just handed you your balls."

Carver grins. "That's all right, as long as I get to keep them."

I can't help it. I laugh. Carver takes advantage of my distraction and sweeps my feet out from under me. I land on my side, a rock digging into my hip. He leans over, maybe to help me up, but I twist and kick him in the jaw. Not too hard, but hard enough. He reels back, and I jump to my feet, raising my sword. We spar again until he disarms me, sending my weapon spiraling across the clearing. In a blink, his blade is at my heart. I leap away with a series of backflips and then pick up my sword again, ready.

Carver's eyebrows fly up. "Where'd you learn that?"

"The circus. When Alyssa was pregnant, I used to fill in for her on the tumbling routines."

Instead of trying to engage me again, Carver sheathes his blade, signaling an end to our practice. He approaches, giving me a bold once-over. "I like a woman of many talents."

"I think you just like women."

He gets an odd look on his face, a flash of vulnerability, gone so fast I might have imagined it. "All shapes and sizes," he magnanimously admits.

I roll my eyes, and he throws a sinewy arm across my shoulders, hauling me against his sweaty side. "You use a sword well enough, but that'll only get you so far, especially because you're tiny and weak."

Frowning, I pinch him really hard.

"Stick to knives," he says, twisting out of my grip. "Do some magic. Only engage in one-on-one combat if you're sure you can win."

In other words, my sword is for show. Sheathing it, I throw his arm off me. "I want to get better with a blade."

He shrugs. "You have other skills."

"Men don't understand discretion. My goal is to survive on my weakest abilities. That saves other talents for when I really need them and doesn't reveal important skills to any idiot who might be watching."

Carver laughs. "You and 'discreet' don't belong in the same sentence."

I pinch him again. His response is to grab me and wrestle me to the ground. I'm pinned in five seconds flat. I know because he counts.

A shadow looms over us. "Go for your swim, Cat." Beta Sinta doesn't look amused anymore now that Carver is lying on top of me. "Then I have questions."

I scowl. He gave me three days, which is actually more than I expected. My mood souring, I toss him a dirty look, wiggle out from under an extremely uncooperative Carver, and then head for the stream. At least I get to bathe alone.

Dry and dressed, I amble back to the clearing, in no hurry to answer Beta Sinta's questions. Kato came back with two rabbits, and I caught a fish. It kept bumping into my legs, so I snagged it, thinking it must be a gift from Poseidon.

Kato guts the fish and skins the rabbits and then whittles something with his knife while Flynn does the cooking. Carver patrols the perimeter, staying relatively close. I look through my satchel, taking inventory of my possessions and trying to hit Carver with kalaberries from the bush next to me every time he comes near. Beta Sinta must get tired of waiting because he finally pins me with an impatient look and motions for me to join him near the fire.

"It's time," he says when I reluctantly plop down next to him. "I want to know about the Fisan royals."

I lean back on my elbows to get away from the heat, glimpsing the first of the night's stars overhead. "And I want a lamb steak slathered in butter oregano sauce with tiny red potatoes fried until they're crispy."

The look he gives me is flat and devoid of humor. "And I want one bloody night when you answer the damn question and finally realize there are bigger issues here than your obvious love of sarcasm, evasion, and sullen silence."

I purse my lips, suddenly extremely uncomfortable.

Something stirs inside me. *Guilt?* "We can't always have what we want."

"Clearly," he growls.

I glance at him, frowning. Not that he's wrong—I am sarcastic, sullen, and evasive—but he's always in a bad mood after I spend time with Carver. Or Flynn. Or Kato.

Is he jealous? That's ridiculous.

An achy tightness clamps around my heart at the idea, though, squeezing hard. Heat unfurls in my belly and then crawls up my neck. "I thought you cared about your team."

His eyes turn tempest gray. "Have you decided to be part of the team?"

I thought that was obvious. I shrug.

He stares at me until I almost squirm. "Then you can start by telling me what you know about the Fisan royals."

I know a lot. The question is what to tell Beta Sinta. There's a dark look in his eyes tonight, making me wonder how much bending of the truth I can get away with.

I stretch my legs out and cross them at the ankles, hoping I look more relaxed than I feel. "The Queen, Andromeda, had eight children."

"Andromeda. Ruler of men."

"Ruler of men, women, children, large monsters... She controls everything and everyone. The King Consort, Dimitri, is useless. He sits around looking pretty and donating seed for her womb."

"Eight children and Alpha Fisa. A busy woman."

He mentions children first, which intrigues me. "What with terrorizing everyone, especially her own kids, I imagine she hardly has a second to spare."

"Why have eight children only to terrorize them?"

I sigh, throwing my head back. "Sinta's going to get squashed."

"What makes you say that?" The sidelong look he slants me is heavy with warning.

Here's something I never thought I'd say... "You're too nice."

Beta Sinta's eyes spark dangerously. "I'm fairly certain the Magoi royals weren't thinking I was nice the night I plowed through them with my sword, and you'd do well to remember what I'm capable of, too. Don't cross me, Cat. Ever."

I mock shudder. "I'm so scared."

He ignores my sarcasm, his hard stare hitting me even harder than usual. "I'm just as capable of making people miserable as other royals. I don't do it for fun. That doesn't mean I won't."

Did he just threaten me? "Fine. I like to provoke. Warning ingested." *And spit back out.* "You're big and bad. I'll try to remember."

He arches a dark eyebrow. I think his lips twitch. "So. Eight children." He pokes a stick into the fire, sending sparks spiraling into the gathering gloom.

I actually respect the way Beta Sinta can end an awkward situation and move on as if nothing happened. We brawl? So what. Everyone gets up, and it's done. I swim around naked high on euphoria? It's forgotten. Pretty much. I think... I insult him and insinuate that he can't protect his realm? He tells me he's as mean as the next guy when he wants to be, and it's over, back to the eight children.

"Eight children should be enough to ensure the bloodline even with all the fighting among them. Andromeda is Alpha. Like most royals, to avoid coming under constant attack from her own children, she spent their childhoods teaching them to fear her and to hate each other. To them, she's terrifying. Untouchable. They fight to become Beta, to inherit the throne. It's suicidal to even think about trying to eliminate an Alpha like her."

"But Betas challenge Alphas," he argues.

"Not Alphas like Andromeda. But yes, otherwise, if the Alpha's power dwindles, and when other threats, like siblings, are taken care of."

"It's not natural. Why not raise her family to be loyal to her? And to one another? They'd be stronger that way. A unit."

"Because royals, and especially Andromeda, don't think like you. Power is their ultimate goal. They challenge each other for it. They kill to get it, and they kill to keep it. Everything else is secondary, including emotional and family ties."

"And you gleaned all this while spending eight months in a cage?"

Eh... "It was an instructive period in my life." I hesitate and then add, "But I was in the castle for a lot longer than that."

He studies me, his eyes dark and metallic in the firelight. Reflecting the flames, they glint a burnished bronze. "How old were you?"

"You mean in the cage?" That's not the question I was expecting.

He nods.

My lungs constrict in a familiar way, making it hard to breathe through the memory of lies, sneering grins, tempting food just out of reach, fists, flames, and blades, all snaking their way through the bars, and Andromeda's face, a cold, marble mask, watching it all. "Nine."

"Nine!"

"Don't look so horrified. I'm lucky none of them killed me. Andromeda had guards on me day and night to avoid it coming to that." I huff a bitter laugh. "The guards didn't stop much else, though." Only Thanos did. For brief, blissful moments I could sleep, and he kept everyone at bay.

Beta Sinta's voice turns gruff with anger. "She caged you for your magic."

I'm tempted to say "like you," but things have changed too much for that. It wouldn't be fair, and he's nothing like Andromeda.

"Yes." It wasn't really a question, and I don't elaborate. I don't tell him how she encouraged the royal children to lie to me, or how she hid me behind screens during gatherings and made Ajax record my every twitch so she'd know who was lying to her.

"How did you get out of the cage?"

I stare at the tips of my boots, itching in my own skin, sick with the knowledge that Andromeda made me an accomplice to cavalier murder a hundred times over. "When I found out she was eviscerating people for utterly insignificant falsehoods, I learned to control my reactions. She knew I still felt the lies, but when she couldn't beat the truths out of me, she let me out of the cage."

"Odd she didn't just kill you."

I glance over at him. He could just as easily have said, "Odd she didn't serve pheasant at dinner." Sinta might survive after all.

"I'm too valuable to kill. Kingmakers are rare, and useful. She bribed me. More guards, food, clothing, beautiful accommodations. It worked for a while. I was only nine, and I'd just been tortured and deprived of all comfort for eight months."

A mixture of fury and disgust contorts his features. "How did you get away? People don't just let a weapon like you go."

I give him the evil eye. "You should know. But you asked about the royals. Let's talk about the royals."

He starts to say something, but I cut him off. "Of the eight children, four were left. I killed Otis. That leaves Laertes, Priam, and Ianthe. They're probably busy trying to kill each other off now that they've each moved up a rank."

Ianthe had only just turned nine when I escaped Fisa City. Priam was eleven, Laertes thirteen. Andromeda was already hard at work turning them into monsters. Otis was fourteen. Now he's dead.

"Are they all Magoi?" Beta Sinta asks.

I snort. "Andromeda's line would produce nothing less. If by some fluke of nature it did, she'd probably drown the child at birth, like the unwanted runt of the litter."

He grunts. "She sounds like a treat."

I almost smile. That was funny. It would have been funnier if she hadn't terrorized me for years.

"They mostly have Fire Magic. It's common among Fisan royals, but they can all do different things with it. Needles of fire, Chimera's Fire, fire whips, fire balls, flaming attack birds… You know, that kind of thing."

"No," he says broodingly. "I know very little of that kind of thing."

I stare into the fire. Rabbit fat drips from the spit, making it spark and hiss. "Use your imagination. None of it's fun."

He's silent for a while, using his imagination, I guess. "Did they attack you with fire in the cage?"

I sit up, drawing my knees under my chin. "Among other things. Torture is a favorite pastime in Castle Fisa."

He looks at me strangely, a crease settling between his eyebrows. Compassion? Pity? I can't tell. I don't want either.

"But you absorbed it and sent it back?"

I shake my head. "Not then. I couldn't do that then."

I see the exact moment he puts the pieces together. It doesn't take long. "The Oracle. The gift."

I don't deny or confirm, and I don't tell him I was granted two gifts, or that I've felt Poseidon's presence close to me ever since.

"The Fisan royals are abominations," Beta Sinta announces.

I nod. I couldn't agree more.

"What do you say we kill every last one of them?"

I turn, and my eyes crash into his. *For me?* "I'd say our goals have common ground," I answer cautiously, a little breathless.

His gaze turns even more intense than usual, and heat swamps my insides. "Tell me about the others. The first four."

"Why? They're dead." *Mostly, anyway.*

"Humor me."

It's not in my nature to humor people. I start talking anyway. "Thaddeus killed Ajax. Lukia killed Thaddeus. Otis killed Eleni. And Lukia is missing."

"The Lost Princess?"

I smile vaguely. "Heard of her?"

He nods. "I didn't know her name, but I think everyone has heard of the Lost Princess of Fisa. Do you know why she disappeared?"

"The ambiance in Castle Fisa wasn't exactly homey," I answer tartly.

He grins. It's wide and unexpected and sends a sudden thrill through me.

Shifting uncomfortably, I push the feeling aside. "Andromeda trapped Lukia and Eleni and then forced them into an arena, intending them to fight to the death." I use words Beta Sinta will understand. "They were a team. They worked together to stay alive. The two girls actually liked each other, and Andromeda couldn't have that. They were growing up, becoming more powerful, *thinking*. Their popularity was reaching dangerous levels, especially since Andromeda had none."

"So she found a way to tear them apart?"

I shake my head. "They refused to fight. She deprived them of food, then water. When that didn't work, she got in their heads. Compulsion," I explain. "Planting ideas. Controlling actions. Making things seem…not what they are. They resisted. It took seven days and a lot of weakening for the princesses to come to blows. They were both half-dead by then. Eleni was older, stronger, and Lukia's magic wasn't useful in combat. But Eleni wouldn't kill her sister, no matter what Andromeda did."

"What happened?" he asks when I fall silent.

"Eleni could hardly walk. The pressure in her head must have been unbearable. She was bleeding from her ears, her nose, her eyes… She still put herself between her mother and Lukia. Andromeda grabbed her by the hair, said, 'Weakness does not go unpunished,' dragged her over to Otis, and handed him a knife. He stabbed Eleni through the heart."

"Gods!" Beta Sinta breathes a curse. "That's barbaric."

For once, we agree.

"Were you still at the castle? What happened to Lukia?"

"A few days later she was gone, never to be seen again."

"What did Andromeda do?"

"She went crazy. Lukia was her favorite."

"She had favorites?" He says that like I just spouted gibberish.

"Didn't your parents?"

"No. Never."

I frown, trying to imagine a life like that.

"Why was Lukia her favorite?"

I've always wondered the same thing. I give him the truth, as far as I know. "Lukia was the only one without fire, like her mother. Their magic was different, more... internal. I guess Andromeda thought that made her special."

"Didn't it just make her weaker?" Beta Sinta asks.

The ghost of a smile haunts my lips. "Maybe it made her stronger. She had to fight harder to survive."

"Makes sense." He pulls out a long knife, the blade flashing in the corner of my vision. He lifts it, startling me, and my legs punch out on instinct, kicking the knife from his hand. People talk about fight or flight? That's nonsense. It's fight *and* flight. I twist and take off.

"Umph!" The air leaves my lungs as my chest hits the ground.

One second Beta Sinta is next to me, and the next he's on top of me, heavy and volcanically hot. He flips me over and pins my wrists to the ground on either side of my head.

I blink. *What just happened?* He looks like he's wondering the same thing.

"What are you doing?" he grates out.

My eyes widen. *I don't know!* "I saw a knife."

"And you assumed I was going to attack you?" Surprise colors his tone, and maybe some anger. His expression seems to question my sanity. "I was going to cut you a slice of rabbit for dinner."

He was going to feed me? I swallow, my throat suddenly dry. Of course he wasn't attacking me. It's this conversation putting me on edge. I didn't think. I just reacted. Fear and aggression are always so close to the surface. I was raised to fight, fight, fight. "I'm violent by nature."

His grip eases on my wrists. He shakes his head, looking bewildered. "Save it for your enemies, Cat. That's not me."

I scoff and start thrashing.

His body presses me down. "You can't fight me, so you might as well stop trying."

Gah! It's true. I get nowhere. Beta Sinta doesn't let me up, and he's so close that I can see the dark-silver rims around his irises, and smell the sunshine and wind still clinging to his hair after the bright, breezy afternoon. His warm breath fans my lips, and my traitorous body turns pliant, some parts of me softening while others heat up, thrumming with tension. My lips part, and his eyes drop to my mouth, lingering there before flicking back up, softer now, heavier lidded.

Heat swirls through me, and something more potent, like need. I beat it down and glare daggers. "Get off! You weigh more than a Dragon." I thrash again, moving about half an inch.

His arms tense as he lowers his head, inhaling long and deep in the curve of my neck. When he speaks, his lips brush the sensitive skin below my ear, and a shiver races from my head to my toes. In a low rasp, he says, "I like the way you feel."

What!

He lifts his head, and his raised eyebrows tell me I didn't just shriek that in my head.

"And you won't admit it," he says quietly, "but you like the way I feel, too."

My eyes shoot wide open as shock ripples through me. *Do I like how he feels?* He feels hot and heavy and hard, and there's more hardness growing against my thigh. My cheeks burn while something dangerously close to excitement flutters in my belly. Between my legs, the sudden emptiness throbs, muscles tensing in anticipation. *Stupid muscles.*

"See how well we fit?" Beta Sinta's question is like a toe-curling caress, soft yet urgent. "You have no idea how much I want to touch you."

I gasp. I thought we had boundaries. Apparently not.

He takes advantage of my surprise to settle more firmly against me, rocking once. The movement is barely there, but it's enough to send sensation crashing through me. He dips his head again, his cheek brushing mine. His tongue flicks the shell of my ear, and I inhale sharply, a jolt of desire thundering through me. His lips skim down my throat, his warm, suddenly ragged breath curling around my neck and captivating my senses. He nips softly at my hammering pulse. My whole body jerks under him. I stifle a moan.

Smoothing his thumbs over the insides of my wrists, he rises above me, his eyes never leaving mine. The sensual touch makes me tremble. So does the earthy roughness in his voice. "I never know what to expect with you. Worldly cynicism or blushing innocence. It's enough to drive a man insane."

I stop breathing, going perfectly still while my heart throws itself against my ribs. I fight the urge to draw up my knees and cradle him between my thighs. For one charged moment, I'm not sure what will win: common sense, or instinct. It seems wrong for them to be at war.

My lungs start to burn. At my shuddering breath, Beta Sinta smiles, the raw hunger in his expression fading into amusement.

I narrow my eyes and jerk my forehead up, but he dodges, lifting off me in one powerful, fluid twist.

Dazed, I sit up and glance around. Kato, Carver, and Flynn are busy looking anywhere but at us, and I feel my face flame kalaberry red.

"Why would Andromeda send her favorite child into an arena for a fight to the death?" Beta Sinta asks.

Seriously? It's over, just like that. No more tussle. No more hard, heavy body on top of mine. No more hot breath in my ear. No more tongue.

Thank the Gods. Gag!

Sort of.

Except not at all.

Gah! I'm going insane!

That fluttering is happening again, almost like feathers whispering over the insides of my ribs. I press my palm to my chest, pushing back while Beta Sinta picks up a twig and holds it to the flames. I watch it burn. There's too much fire in my life, and I hate the heat.

"Probably because she thought Lukia could win." I'm surprised my voice comes out steady. I don't feel steady.

"But she couldn't."

I pull my legs to my chest again, locking my arms around my knees. "Maybe she couldn't. Maybe she didn't even try."

He turns to me, his gaze intent, his eyes deep and turbulent like Poseidon's seas. "Where'd she go?"

I roll my eyes. "How in the Underworld should I know? I'm not an Oracle, and it doesn't matter. You're asking the wrong questions, Beta Sinta."

"My name is Griffin."

"Your name is Beta Sinta."

"That's *what* I am, not *who* I am."

I groan and bury my face in my hands. "You're hopeless!"

"Call me Griffin, and I'll ask the right questions."

"Fine. Griffin. Are you happy now?"

"Yes."

He also just proved it's possible for one word to hit me like wine—potent, and a little intoxicating.

"What's the right question?" He winks. "Cat."

I huff, clamping down on the need to claw and bite. I haven't felt this savage in years. It's his fault. He brings it out in me. "What does it mean if the Lost Princess is still alive?" I prompt.

"What does it mean? ...Cat."

I glare at him. He's teasing me, and it's getting to me, making me feel hot, and annoyed, and...happy. Everything about this is dangerous. Worst case—it'll get one of us killed, and it probably won't be me.

"It means no Fisan royals after Andromeda can be secure in their reigns. The current Beta, Gamma, and Delta will always be wondering if Lukia is alive—if she'll come back to challenge them. Fisans will always be wondering if they're bowing down to the wrong ruler, especially when they'd probably prefer Lukia to anyone who's left. When people start asking questions like that, of themselves, of others, that's when realms explode." I look at Beta Sinta. *Griffin.* "That's when warlords from the south sweep in and massacre royal families."

His eyes sharpen. "Are you saying there are people who would challenge Andromeda?"

Adrenaline floods my system, setting my heart suddenly to galloping. "Not without Lukia, or someone else to rally them. But Tarva and Fisa are just like Sinta. The royals here were too busy fighting each other to realize how powerful you had become. You surprised them all. You gathered Sintans behind you with the simple promise of being different. The royal family was left with their magic and their army. How hard did their army fight for them?"

He frowns, considering. "Surprisingly few soldiers were willing to sacrifice their lives once it looked like I might win."

"Of course not. Who wants to die for selfish, cruel people no one likes to begin with? Eleni and Lukia were different. Fisans liked them, especially Eleni. She's dead, and Lukia's gone. If Andromeda falters or dies, it won't take much for Fisans to rebel if they think there's a real chance of winning instead of getting massacred. Fisa's army won't fight any harder than Sinta's did. Royals keep their power through fear. Plant a seed of doubt and vines spread. Until Fisans see the Lost Princess's dead body, or she returns to rule, they'll never truly accept one of the others as Alpha. They bow down mostly out of terror, but partly out of sheer tradition. Tradition breaks without the true Alpha."

He's quiet for a while. When he says my name, something in his tone makes me look up. There's admiration in his eyes, and it gives me a warm feeling I don't like at all.

"You're more than just the Kingmaker. You're a strategist. You understand how people think and can predict their moves. You'd make a capable ruler."

His words strike fear into my heart. His next words rattle me like the gong of a death toll.

"It sounds like Fisa's ripe for a takeover."

"You have Sinta," I say, swallowing stronger protests I can't explain.

"Egeria has Sinta."

I don't say anything. I'm not about to encourage him to take over Fisa now that I'm tied to him for life. His life, anyway.

"So why was Otis so bent on killing you rather than bringing you back to Fisa?"

I shrug. "I don't know if he wanted to kill me or capture me. It didn't get that far."

His eyes meet mine, challenging. "He *looked* like he wanted to kill you."

He did, didn't he? "Andromeda wants me alive. I'm certain of that. Maybe he wanted to thwart his mother. Or make sure someone else didn't get me instead."

"Your eye is twitching."

Damn eye! "Dust."

He snorts.

Fine. I didn't believe me, either. "Otis knew it was him or me. It was Andromeda's mistake for sending him instead of someone else. She doesn't understand human emotion, or attachment, so it didn't factor into her decision, but Otis knew I'd kill him for what he did to Eleni. She was good to me. We were…close, and she did her best to protect her sister. I only got away thanks to her. She died, Lukia took off, and with all the confusion in the castle, I was able to slip away. I owe Eleni my freedom. I owe her my life."

He nods, believing me this time. "You must have enjoyed killing Otis, then."

My lips twist in a smile Mother would be proud of. "You have no idea."

CHAPTER 13

Beta Sinta wakes me up, darting back to avoid my fist. "You're whimpering and all curled up in a ball."

Lovely. He's on watch. I only have nightmares now when Beta Sinta—*Griffin*—isn't snoring a few feet from me. Well, he doesn't really snore, at least not much, but he got me used to sleeping next to him with that bloody rope, and now I don't sleep nearly as well without him.

Knowing that makes me want to kick him. I resist. I don't want to end up with his tongue in my ear like I did earlier.

Not really.

Really, no.

No.

I clear my throat.

"Watch with me," he invites.

I regard him warily. "Why?"

"So you can tell me about the Tarvans."

Oh. I get up, my blood still pounding hot and cold. I shudder, rubbing my arms until I see Griffin watching me with a frown.

"Do you dream?" I ask.

"Doesn't everyone?"

"I guess, but are your dreams just scenes your mind conjures up, or are they real?"

He rubs his hand back and forth over his jaw, his fingers rasping on thick stubble. "Real as in memories?"

I nod.

"No, they're just normal dreams."

"Huh." *Must be nice.*

"And yours?"

"Memories." *And sometimes premonitions.*

While we walk the perimeter of the camp, I force the nightmare aside by concentrating on a dream from earlier in the night. Not all my memories are bad.

Eleni and I are running up a hill, about to crest the rise and tear down the other side. I'm pushing hard, my seven-year-old legs straining to keep up with her longer, stronger, nine-year-old ones. I'm only a few feet behind, and her laughter whips back to me on the wind. My heart soars. We escaped. It won't last long, but we escaped them all.

We hurtle over the top of the hill and run smack into a shepherd boy and his flock. Eleni and he crash to the ground in a tangle. I stumble, too, scraping my knee and knocking over a lamb. It makes a pathetic bleating sound, hops to its feet, and scampers away. All three of us stare at each other, stunned, and then the boy's father is there, picking everyone up.

The color leaches from his face when he sees the Fisan royal crest on Eleni's shoulder clasps. Stammering apologies, he falls to the ground, prostrate, dragging his son down with him until both their foreheads are flat against the grass. Eleni commands them to stand, but they're too scared to rise farther than their knees, keeping their eyes downcast.

I barrel around a few sheep with my usual finesse and then shove a half-wilted posy of flowers I'm clutching in my hand at the boy. He's about my age. I don't want him to be scared.

The wind tosses my dark hair. It's loose, and I know I look like a wildcat, with dirt and bruises and scrapes all over me. The boy's eyes widen. He hesitates, but when I try giving him the flowers again, frowning and huffing, he takes the drooping blooms from my grubby hand.

The shepherd murmurs endless apologies, begging for Eleni's mercy. Begging for their lives. She smiles sweetly and kneels in front of him, taking a jeweled clip from her hair. Her blonde locks lift on the breeze, pale dawn sunbeams framing her shining face. The clip is entirely encrusted with sapphires, tiny Fisan pearls forming a row of delicate sea stars across the center. Blue and white. Ocean and ice.

She places the treasure in his hand and gently wraps his work-worn fingers around it. "To feed a village," she whispers.

My breath shudders, and Griffin slides me a sidelong glance. "You all right?"

"I'm fine," I answer, wondering how the sun still rises every day without Eleni in the world.

"You can talk to me, Cat."

I shake my head, but the same sudden, overwhelming warmth that kept hitting me all evening curls through my body again, heating me up. It's been harder to act indifferent to him since the moment he stretched out on top of me, pressed his body into mine, and told me he wanted to touch me.

I manage—more or less—and we move farther from the others, sitting where we won't wake them with our talk. I tell him about the Tarvan royals, but my information is mostly common knowledge, a lot of which he already knows. I supply names, which are meaningless since royals are always referred to by rank, but I humor him since he seems to think they're important.

"Galen is only Alpha because his father came down with a mysterious illness and died before his reign should have been over. Everyone suspects poison—and Galen—but no one can prove it. For all their cruelty, royals don't usually stoop to poison. An Alpha is Alpha by magic and might. Anything else leaves people antsy, and the door open for challenges. Galen's two children will pay the price. They've already lost their mother, Galen isn't strong enough to last, and they're too young to defend themselves. Acantha, Delta Tarva, is the one to watch. She's Galen's sister, and she already killed off two of her brothers. Galen and his kids are next. She's just biding her time since we're already on the cusp of a Power Bid."

He nods, and I know I don't have to explain. It happens every forty years or so, sometimes less, sometimes more. Current rulers pass their primes. Their children reach theirs. Alphas shift. Realms burn.

I glance at Griffin, wondering if he started it all. Wondering about my role. The prophecy rolls through my head, sending ice down my spine.

"What makes her so powerful?" he asks, drawing me out of dark musings.

"Acantha is a Drakon charmer. It helps having giant serpents, usually with multiple heads and deadly venom, hanging on your every word."

His mouth lifts in that lopsided smile that never fails to make my heart skip a beat. His lower lip is fuller, but the top one has a decadent curve that's distracting. It's hard not to think about how it would feel if I touched it—or if it touched me.

"That does sound useful," he agrees. "Got anything like that up your sleeve?"

"Not currently," I reply cryptically.

His smile broadens, making my stomach dip in the most annoying way.

"Appoline is next, but with little magic and even less intelligence, no one has bothered killing her off yet. I don't know much about Bellanca and Lystra, the two youngest sisters. They might have significant power; they might not. Their magic hadn't fully matured when I left Fisa, and I haven't been privy to the same information since."

"Why were you privy then?"

His question is so deceptively casual that I speak without thinking and then don't see any reason to stop. "I had tutors. Andromeda wanted me to know all about her nobles, her rivals, Gods, creatures, the other realms, their royals and elite..." I shrug. "I had to know what was important, so I could filter the lies."

"Learn anything useful?"

I gaze into the darkness. "All the time."

"And what happened?"

Besides burning up inside and being in constant pain? "If I told Andromeda about it, people usually died."

"And did you always tell her?"

I arch an eyebrow. "What do you think?"

We stop talking. I don't know what Griffin is thinking— probably about how often I might lie to him, or withhold the truth.

"Did she know when you lied?" he asks after a while.

Andromeda always knew when I was lying. Kind of like Griffin. I nod.

"And what did she do?" His tone turns cautious, as if he doesn't really want to hear the answer.

I roll up my sleeve and bare my upper arm to the moon-light. Long, thin scars shine like silver threads, marring my skin from elbow to shoulder. The other arm looks the same. I don't bother showing him. He's already seen it. "Do you know what these are?"

"Death Marks. There's the new one here." He softly touches my arm, his finger warm against my skin.

"Selena did that. It's what healers do when you're so close to death they have to enchant your blood to get it flowing again. They draw it out on a knife, chant over it while you lie there struggling for your final breaths, and then smear it back on and hope for the best."

"There must be a dozen," he says grimly, counting both arms. "Andromeda caused this?"

"She tried beating the truth out of me several times. Unsuccessfully."

His lips flatten into a tight seam, eliminating that distracting curve. "You're not one to break under torture."

There's respect in his voice, which I choose to ignore. I roll my sleeve back down. "I'd rather die, so don't bother trying."

Griffin's eyebrows slam down. "Cat—"

I pop up, brush myself off, and return to my bedroll without letting him finish. My blanket is cold. Oddly, so am I.

Griffin shakes Kato awake, and Kato takes over watch while Griffin spreads his bedding on the ground about ten feet from mine. In a matter of minutes, he appears to be asleep. I argue with myself for a while and then drag my things closer to his, stopping four feet away.

Perfect. Just like with the rope.

Something flashes, and I realize it's Kato's teeth. He's grinning at me. I make a rude hand gesture and roll over, turning my back before he can retaliate.

"You could come closer." Griffin's gravelly voice rumbles over me in the dark, teasing.

My pulse leaps, and I flush with embarrassment. "I don't think so."

"Suit yourself."

"I hate you."

He's silent for a moment and then very deliberately says, "I hate you, too."

His lie rips through me along with the truth, searing my bones and charring my organs, especially my heart.

CHAPTER 14

"HADES, HERA, AND HESTIA!" FLYNN CURSES, POINTING UP. "What in the Underworld is that?"

I squint into the sun. *Oh my Gods!* "A She-Dragon."

Everyone turns to me, and as much as I love having four handsome men gape at me in stupefaction, right now, I could do without.

"What do we do?" Griffin asks urgently.

Magical creatures rarely stray from the Ice Plains. To southerners, they're almost mythological. "Scurry like mice."

"Be serious!"

"I am serious! Run!"

There's a lake in the distance, maybe two miles away. I press my heels to my horse's sides, spurring him into a gallop.

"Cat!" Griffin shouts, chasing after me. "Where are you going?"

"The lake!" I yell over my shoulder.

"There's no cover!"

"There's no cover anywhere!"

Racing alongside me, he reaches over in a move worthy of a circus acrobat and draws on my reins, pulling hard. "There's no cover there. Here, there are..." He glances around. "Rocks."

"Rocks won't help us against a Dragon!"

"And water will?"

"I don't know! Maybe."

His eyes flick to the sky. "We'll never make it. She's moving too fast."

I'm afraid to look up, almost cringing when I do. Her features are recognizable now. There's no doubt the monster is Sybaris, which means Alpha Fisa is driving her telepathically. When this moment came, *if* it came, I always thought I'd scream, or run, or panic, but the closer she gets, the more dazed and numb I become. My thoughts grind to a halt. I feel rooted in place, blank. I think I've discovered the true measure of terror.

"My Gods," Griffin says on an exhale, his tone part horror, part awe. I can't blame him. Sybaris's upper body is that of a beautiful woman, albeit huge. Silky blonde hair trails behind her in a long wave. Inhuman, her lower body is covered in reptilian scales that run the spectrum from sea green to shiny black. Her dark wings are sinew-veined and talon-tipped, smacking the air with a sinister pounding. Powerful hind legs end in massive feet with sharp, hooked claws, each one the size of my entire foot. I've seen her pop a man Griffin's size. To her, it was like crushing a bug.

"Alpha Fisa sent Sybaris for me." I sound scared, which scares me even more. "She wants me alive. Separate from me, and there's a chance she won't kill you." I jerk my reins out of Griffin's hand. "Go!" I yell.

I don't want my horse to die, either. He's strong and steady and seems to like me. I was just getting around to naming him. I was going to call him Panotii because of his freakishly large ears, just like those elusive tribesmen in the north. I slip off his back and start running.

Griffin curses and gallops after me.

I stop and turn, drawing my sword. "Back off, idiot!"

"I won't leave you!" he thunders.

"Neither will we," Kato says, skidding to a halt on my other side.

Oh Gods! They're all going to die.

Sybaris shrieks, and I shake my head, trying to dislodge the more disturbing sound overlapping her eerie call, an echo of triumphant laughter only I can hear.

"Can we fight her?" Griffin asks.

I push Andromeda out of my head with a brutal mental shove, hoping I make her ears bleed. "Sybaris is enormous. She breathes fire. She devours people." I shake my head, my eyes as huge as throwing discs. "No."

"Can you control her?"

Does he have that much faith in me? "I said I *might* be able to drive a Dragon. I've never done it, and Andromeda's magic is stronger than mine. She's had years of practice. There's no way I can break her hold on Sybaris."

He looks up, his jaw clenching. Sybaris's wings flap, immense and leathery, two ominous shadows stretching across the cerulean sky. His gaze drops back to mine. "You could try."

My heart tumbles in my chest. "I will. But only if you four *back off*. I mean it. If you come anywhere near me, I swear to the Gods I'll jump on her back and tell her to take me home."

Did I just say home? I feel sick.

Griffin looks like he's about to leap off Brown Horse and tackle me. "I thought you weren't part of the team! That it's idiotic to sacrifice yourself for someone else."

"It is!" I snap, looking at each man in turn. It's probably the last time I'll see them.

"Cat—" Flynn starts.

"Shut up!" I say. "And...don't die."

I run. I leave them and the horses, and I run faster than

I've ever run in my life. Sybaris swerves, adjusting her course to follow me. I lead her as far from the Sintans as I can before she cuts me off in an explosion of dust and fire. I skid to a stop and draw on the power inside me. Desma's colors burst over the Dragon's scales along with Otis's fire whip and a scorching blast of Chimera's Fire.

Sybaris dances away from the flames, unscathed, but her eyes turn wary, and she halts her progress in my direction. A voice with Andromeda's inflection floats from her gargantuan mouth. "Child of Fisa, I have found you."

"I won't go back!"

"Who are your companions?"

Trust Alpha Fisa to go straight for the jugular. Andromeda can't see us. She connects to Sybaris's thoughts, not her eyes. All she knows is that Sybaris sees a woman who is me, four men, and five horses.

"Sintans," I say, watching them inch closer out of the corner of my eye. "No one."

Andromeda has always believed that Fisans are the gift of the Gods, Tarvans are tolerable, and Sintans are pond scum. Apart from the ex-royals and a few select nobles, they don't have enough magic.

"Sintans. Expendable, then."

My eyes widen as Sybaris opens her mouth. Her gaping maw ignites and flames pour forth, scorching the ground at the Sintans' feet. The horses rear, scrambling back, and the men shout in alarm. A shower of sparks erupts from the Dragon's nostrils, catching a low-lying bush on fire. One lands on my hand, singeing my skin before my body absorbs the magic and heals.

I gawk at my unmarred skin. *I can absorb the magic of creatures? I can absorb the magic of creatures!*

Sybaris opens her mouth again, no doubt for the kill.

Before I even realize what I'm doing, I jump in front of the flames. The torrent condenses, tightening on me as my blood pulses to seize the magic.

Dragon's Breath slams into me. It lifts me off my feet and sweeps me along its flaming path. My clothing ignites. My braid unravels, my hair whipping around my head in a savage dance of fire and sparks. My skin blisters, and I scream, burning alive for the second time in a matter of weeks. Like a rag doll, I tumble through the surge, the pain so fierce my body starts shutting down, overwhelmed.

Through a haze of red and black and agony, I hear Andromeda's bellow garble with Sybaris's roaring breath. The Dragon chokes back her fire, and the inferno cuts off before reaching the Sintans. I drop, skidding and rolling until the momentum dies.

My moan is pathetic. I can't move. I can hardly breathe. This kind of torment has no words. It's indescribable. Darkness beckons me, the kind of endless night where peace might actually find me on the other side. The lure is so strong I reach for it, desperate for the pain to end.

Griffin drags my failing consciousness back to the surface, shouting my name. I can't have him running over to me. Dragon's Breath might not harm him, but Sybaris could still kill him in a hundred different ways. I roll to my knees, shaking and panting. I thank the Gods when healing begins. Under my ruined clothing, my skin restores itself in a rush, my body finding strength and balance again. I stand as the last of the pain fades, a slow smile stretching my lips.

Power like I've never known before settles deep within my frame. I stretch out my arms and flex my hands, feeling ancient, terrifying magic surge through my veins and leap to my bidding. For a stunning, magnificent second, I feel my heritage like never before. I feel *invincible*.

With a laugh that sounds a lot like Andromeda's creepy mirth, I throw my shoulders back, look Sybaris straight in the eye, and then release a cascade of flames from my wide-open mouth.

Sybaris dives to the right. Too late. A raw scorch mark mars her face and shoulder, leaving the left side of her scalp charred to the bone. A hunk of hair slides to the ground, sizzling.

"Ha!" I shout, and *by Gods* do I ever mean it.

Sybaris's eyes roll in her head. She snarls and bucks, beating her gigantic wings against the earth and creating a maelstrom of dust and heat. I duck, shielding my face from the pelting grit.

Andromeda's words slide out of Sybaris's singed mouth, cool as ever. "You've learned new tricks."

I have other tricks, too, but the second I disappear, she'll take it out on Griffin and the others. Besides, Sybaris can track me by scent, so unless I fried her nose, I can't take the risk. I don't want Andromeda knowing I can disappear anyway. It would explain too much, and I can't stomach giving her the satisfaction.

Sybaris's magic makes me stronger than I've ever been before. I run at her and leap as high as I can, striking with my sword. I can't reach her head, or even her neck, so I slash at her bare chest from underneath.

Sybaris shrieks and swipes at me with her claws, overcoming Andromeda's control in her pain and rage. I drop and roll, springing back up as she thunders toward me.

"Enough!" Alpha Fisa's command holds such absolute authority that I almost cower like I used to.

Sybaris changes course with stupefying suddenness.

She leaps over me and charges the Sintans, reaching them in two flaps of her enormous wings. Her mouth opens wide, igniting.

"Wait!" I cry.

She stops, fire rolling between her jaws. I throw my sword down and hold up my hands. They shake, and my heart pounds, pumping dread. At least I have the satisfaction of knowing Mother failed. I don't hate everyone. I won't sacrifice anyone.

Sybaris turns to me, and I think back to what Mother tried to teach me about creature driving. I never did it—not once—just to spite her, and for the first time I regret my stubbornness.

Focusing, I probe Sybaris's mind, encountering first darkness and then a sheet of ice—Andromeda's hold on the Dragon. I dig deeper, but my mental push slips, sliding off a barrier of powerful magic. Sybaris shakes her head, flicking off my untrained effort at compulsion as easily as she would a pesky fly. It takes mere seconds for me to know this isn't going to work.

My stomach drops, and my eyes meet Griffin's. His widen, and then in a flash of glistening scales and blistered skin, Sybaris grabs me and throws me on her back. Powerful hindquarters propel us high into the air. Within seconds, the whistle of the wind and the leathery thump of wings drown out Griffin's heart-wrenching roar.

I squeeze my eyes shut against a shattering sense of loss. Eight years of freedom wasn't nearly enough. I haven't even begun to live. Tears sting my eyes, only partially from the thin air and biting wind. I feel hard, brittle things inside me begin to crack, and I almost look back. The need to see Griffin one last time is both overwhelming and terrifying, proving just how much of a fool I am. I keep my eyes closed so I won't look down. I can't bear to see what I'm leaving behind.

When I open my eyes again, we're over the lake. I can't help imagining us on the bank, Panotii, Brown Horse, and the others drinking their fill, me diving deep, Griffin thinking about who knows what, Kato whittling, Carver being an ass, and Flynn cooking a meal for everyone, all of them sitting too close to the fire.

My vision is so compelling that I start slipping off Sybaris's back. She tilts, shifting me back into place, and I almost regret not falling. From this height, I'd die the second I hit the lake.

What was the point of all this, anyway? Why did Poseidon even want me with Griffin? I guess I'll never know. I'll never escape again. Andromeda will make sure of that.

I shudder, imagining the methods she might use, and for the first time in my life, I wish I hadn't survived.

Chilled to the marrow by the knowledge of what my future holds, my eyes lock on the lake again with sudden clarity. Every muscle in my body tenses, and my breath stalls in my lungs. I can't go back. I can't let *her* have me. I'd rather die in the deep.

Not leaving myself time to second-guess, I twist and leap off Sybaris's back. Andromeda's screech splits my ears. Ragged clothes flap. Air pounds my skin. Wind whips at my hair. My heart breaks and explodes.

The water glows like the inside of an oyster shell, iridescent and bright. Fear, regret, relief—I feel it all as I throw my arms wide with no choice left but to embrace the end.

The water below me churns, changing shape in a rush of eddies and waves. An enormous hand rises from the lake. A living waterfall, the cascade surges up, rushing skyward in a tumble of foaming crests. Liquid fingers form, cushioning my fall, cradling me, wonderfully cool, infinitely protective.

"Daughter of my heart."

"Poseidon!" I almost weep from joy.

"You are brave, but foolish."

My heart pounds against my ribs so hard I think they'll break. *"What was I supposed to do?"*

A deep, hearty laugh resonates in my head. *"The Gods give you gifts, and you do not think to use them?"*

"If I'd turned invisible she would have killed them."

"Do you care?"

"Shouldn't I? You sent Beta Sinta to me."

"Gave him to you," Poseidon corrects.

What's that supposed to mean? "Why?"

"Healing." Poseidon's voice increases in volume and echoes in my head, the word overlapping dozens of times in a way that makes my brain hurt.

"I don't understand!"

The hand gently sweeps me toward the shore and then disappears from under me, dissolving into the lake along with any answers I might have gotten. I swim five strokes and then crawl up the bank, limp from an overload of emotion. I start shaking and can't stop.

A high-pitched cry rends the air. I drag my gaze toward the noise and see Sybaris spiral into a dive, heading straight for me.

I pull myself together. Sort of. I manage to stand up.

What gift did Poseidon mean? Sybaris won't breathe fire at me now that she knows I can breathe it back, and I won't turn invisible and run away when Griffin and the others can still be used against me. I rack my brain. There must be something.

Hades! The Cerberus figurine!

I plunge my hand into what's left of my pocket. My fingers close around cool metal, and I draw out the figurine. Three golden heads swivel in my direction, ruby eyes glinting, and bark.

Mighty Gods on Olympus!

Sybaris crashes down in front of me, spitting mad. So is Andromeda. "You could have died!" she explodes.

"So? How many times did you almost kill me yourself?"

"You are protected by Gods." There's an undertone of stunned interest in her voice. I ignore how that makes me feel and hurl the Cerberus figurine at Sybaris's head, praying to Poseidon, Hades, and anyone else who might be listening that something useful will happen.

The tiny gold statue hits the Dragon and explodes into the real Cerberus. He snarls, his gargantuan jaws snapping once before latching onto her neck in three places. Canines the size of my forearms puncture her flesh and start the gory process of ripping out her throat. Cerberus's hind claws shred her stomach scales, tearing through them to expose the blood and muscle underneath. He's strong and ferocious and completely unexpected. Sybaris's eyes go wide and then blank. It happens fast, without even a gurgle. Dragon blood stains the bank and drains into the lake, its power stinging my skin. I absorb the magic, feeling layer upon layer of it coil deep inside my body.

Cerberus keeps chomping and maiming, apparently just for fun. Finally satisfied, he turns six burning eyes on me, growling deep in his throats. He's horrifying. Ugly. Vicious. I've always liked him.

"Easy, Cerberus." I keep my voice low.

He bays, a long, eerie howl that makes my skin crawl. It goes on and on, his three heads taking turns so that it never stops. It's all I can do not to cover my ears and cringe. The lake smokes and hisses where his saliva splatters the surface, and I back deeper into the water to avoid the venomous drops.

He eventually quiets and stares at me, his upper lips still curled and twitching.

I ease a hand in his direction. "Thank you."

Cerberus snuffs noisily in response and then disappears in a shudder of fur and fangs, leaving his carnage behind.

I sink into the lake, utterly spent despite the power I just absorbed. Breathing for the first time in what feels like years, I look up to see Griffin, Flynn, Carver, and Kato galloping toward the shore, leading Panotii behind them.

I wait, only my head above water, watching as Griffin leaps down from Brown Horse and splashes toward me. The closer he gets, the harder my heart hammers in my chest, beating some life back into me.

He grabs my shoulders and pulls me to my feet. "Are you insane?" he thunders.

"Marginally." I cough because he managed to slosh water up my nose.

"You. Dragon. Falling. Giant…water hand. Cerberus. *Gods, Cat!*"

"That about sums it up."

Griffin glares at me like he wants to throttle me. Instead, he hauls me up against his chest and kisses me. There's heat and urgency and relief in his touch. My lips part in surprise, and he deepens the kiss, sweeping his arms around me and lifting me to my toes.

Wings unfold inside my chest, the feathers pulsing lightly against my ribs. I'm achingly aware of every point of contact—Griffin's warm, firm lips moving over mine, his solid chest flush against me, his big hands splayed across my back. Before I can question the strange wings, he angles his head, and his tongue touches mine, scattering my thoughts completely.

Sensation roars through me. One of Griffin's hands slides up my back, delving into my wet hair to cradle my head. The raw, almost desperate sound that rises in his throat makes me feel powerful in a way that has nothing to do with magic, or knives, or knowledge. Heat sizzles through me, desire scorching me from my head to my toes.

Griffin's mouth leaves mine, gliding across my cheek and jaw, stopping where my pulse pounds in a wild rhythm. Gathering me tightly against him, he places a searing kiss just below my ear. I feel the hot press of his lips like a brand and wonder if it's permanent.

His voice drops to a low, ardent growl. "I would have come for you." His strong arms are a fierce pressure around me. His ragged exhale warms my neck, making me want to curl into him. "When you jumped, I thought I'd lost you."

I blink. *Does he think he has me?*

The desire blazing inside me falters. I ruthlessly shake off the passion making me weak and push out of his arms, splashing back a few steps. Stumbling, really. My lips burn. My body is on fire.

I somehow dredge up the scowl to end all scowls and wipe my entire forearm across my mouth, glaring at him.

He grins.

I disappear.

Trembling and breathing hard for reasons I refuse to examine, I climb the bank, grab my bag from Panotii's back, and then rummage for a change of clothing. Decently covered *and* invisible, I sit on a rock, compulsively touching my lips. I had no idea a kiss could feel like that. *No. Idea.*

Flynn scans the area, his hands on his hips. "Where is she?"

"Not far," Carver says.

How does he know? *Smug bastard.*

"Cat?" Kato calls. "There's no need to hide. We're just glad you're all right." He chuckles. "I would have settled for a pat on the back, but you know Griffin. He's overemotional."

I snort. "I'll stay invisible until Beta Sinta learns to control his urges."

They laugh. Except Griffin. He's not laughing at all.

I shiver even though I'm the exact opposite of cold.

Carver ambles over and sits on my rock. On me.

"Get off!" I grumble, kicking him.

He gets up. "So this is *your* rock?"

"They're all my rocks! Go away."

Carver clasps his hands over his heart. "And leave our loyal soldier? The one who slays Dragons?"

I roll my eyes. Too bad no one can see. "Cerberus killed the Dragon."

"You had Cerberus."

"Not anymore," I say sullenly.

Carver frowns. "How did you have Cerberus?"

"Hades." Which explains everything, and nothing at all.

"Cat's better than loyal."

My heart jolts at the sound of Griffin's voice. Things tug in my chest, and tiny, winged creatures swarm my belly, dive-bombing left and right. I hate him. Hate, hate, *hate* him!

"What's better than loyal?" Flynn asks.

"Loyal and self-sacrificing," Griffin announces.

I feel myself blanch. *Me? Self-sacrificing? Gag!*

CHAPTER 15

I CAN'T BEAR TO FACE GRIFFIN AFTER THAT KISS. MY maturity level is apparently that of a five-year-old because I stay invisible for two whole days, until Panotii starts to protest. I'm there, but I'm not, and it starts making even my calm, reliable mount nervous. Steadiness only goes so far, and you can only ask so much of a horse.

His blue eyes twinkling, Kato heaves a sigh of relief when I finally reappear. "That was the strangest two days of my life. It was like talking to a realm-walking spirit."

"With an attitude," Flynn remarks.

"You could have just pretended I wasn't there. That's the point of invisibility." Instead, they'd hammered me with questions. Royals, realms, Magoi, magical creatures, the Ice Plains, the Lake Oracles. My voice is hoarse from talking when all I'd wanted was to be left alone. I need to think about Andromeda, what might come next, what I've gotten myself into with the Sintans, and not at all about Griffin's kiss.

Not. At. All.

No.

At least all this talking has filled me in on a thing or two concerning the new Sintan royals. It turns out Carver isn't Gamma Sinta like I'd assumed. He's Delta Sinta. There's a brother, Piers, between Griffin and Carver who's in charge of the army when Griffin isn't there. After Carver, there are two younger sisters, Jocasta and Kaia. Their parents, Anatole and Nerissa, are still alive. Anatole led their tribe for forty years, making it one of the most powerful in the realms, before passing the reins to Griffin.

The idea of buttercup Egeria being Alpha while her father is still alive and she has strong, warrior brothers shocks me to the core. It doesn't *work* that way. How could a warlord from the south sweep in and shake up everything so thoroughly, including me?

Panotii tosses his head, protesting my death grip on the reins.

"Sorry," I mutter, patting his neck and trying to relax.

"I'm happy to see you," Griffin says, his unhurried gaze roaming over me and snagging on places that make my temperature rise. "I didn't fancy introducing my family to a person they couldn't see."

We're two days from Sinta City and a future that promises to be sheer torture. "I have conditions."

Griffin smiles with just enough resigned humor to make me want to kick him in the teeth. "Why am I not surprised?" he asks.

I open my mouth and sparks fly out.

"Steal that from the Dragon?" He doesn't even look impressed. He's relaxed, in a good mood. They all are. Carver is even whistling. They forced me out of hiding after eight years. We fought off thirty men and survived. We killed a She-Dragon driven by Alpha Fisa, by far the most powerful mortal in Thalyria. We could be attacked at any time by only the Gods know what. What is *wrong* with these people?

"Your fire won't work on me," Griffin says. "You'd end up frying Brown Horse, and then I'd have to ride the chestnut."

"Panotii. At least my horse has a real name."

"Panotii? Because of his ears?" He studies Panotii's

head for a few seconds and then chuckles. "Maybe he's part donkey."

"Shhh! Don't say that. You might hurt his feelings."

"He's a horse."

"He's *my* horse. Any attack on him is an attack on me," I say frostily.

"You're the one who named him after people who are supposed to have ears down to their feet." Griffin's mouth tips up at the corners, drawing my eyes to the distracting curve of his lips. Full lips. Warm lips. Firm, demanding, possessive—

Gah! Get a grip!

"Panotii." His oversized ears swivel in my direction. "Let's ditch these southerners and find some people who understand us."

Flynn pulls up on my left, so tall and broad he shadows me from the afternoon sun. "You like us too much for that," he says, his cheerful smile threatening to infect me with something awful, like a good mood. "And everything's going great."

"*Great?* You almost died. Twice! We all did."

He shrugs, grinning. "But we didn't. And you're funny."

Funny? Funny! I grin back. I can't help it. I'm such an idiot.

"So what are your conditions?" Griffin asks.

My smile dies as I turn back to him. "First, no one outside of this group ever knows I'm the Kingmaker. Most people don't even know what that is, but I can't take the risk. Tell them I'm a soothsayer and can read people. That's it."

"I'll have to tell Egeria."

"I mean it, Griffin. No one. If one day I decide to trust Egeria, *I'll* tell her. But you won't. None of you will."

"Or?"

"Or I won't help you. You won't enjoy trying to get the truth out of me, and I won't break under torture."

"Are you sure?" he asks.

"Am I sure I won't break? I thought we covered this."

"Are you sure I won't enjoy getting the truth out of you," he clarifies. His eyes brighten with mischief, and I'm pretty sure his mind is somewhere it shouldn't be. *Definitely* shouldn't be.

A flush crawls up my neck, and he laughs. The warm, teasing sound seems to take up residence inside me, lightening my bones.

"Stop flashing your teeth," I grumble. "They're blinding me."

"I don't like it, but I'll agree," Griffin says, still smiling. "You'll report directly to me on any lies you hear and the truths they reveal."

I look around the group. Carver is staring straight ahead, but he hasn't missed a word. Flynn appears unconcerned, huge ax slung over one shoulder. Kato grins at me, looking like Adonis—too handsome for his own good.

"Don't worry," Kato says. "Your secret is safe with us."

"*All* of you?"

Flynn and Carver give their consent.

Okay then. "Second, no one knows the Fisans are after me, not even your family."

Griffin frowns. "Why not? We can protect you."

My heart trips a little at his gruff tone. "I'll protect myself."

His midnight eyebrows slam down, so I wave an ungracious hand in the air. "You can help, if I need you."

He grunts. "How generous."

"If no one knows Alpha Fisa wants me, no one will be tempted to sell me out. It's simple. It's human nature.

People with knowledge betray that knowledge, sometimes out of greed, sometimes out of malice, sometimes out of necessity. It happens every time. That's why I never told anyone at the circus who I am."

"Who are you?" Griffin asks.

"*What* I am," I amend.

He gives me a look that says he wasn't born yesterday. *So what? Neither was I.*

"Third, no one mentions Poseidon, oracular dreams, or any of my abilities. Turning invisible, absorbing magic, possible creature driving, calling on a God—these are *not* things we casually talk about."

"Why?" Flynn looks genuinely perplexed. "Our people will fall at your feet. They'll worship you."

I chuckle. "Like you all?"

Flynn grins. "Exactly."

"Magic is a weapon. It's always better when you can spring something no one's expecting."

He nods. "That's smart."

"Of course it is. I do have experience with this kind of thing."

Griffin chokes on a laugh. "Astounding modesty, as usual."

"You're one to talk, Your Arrogant Highness."

Griffin leans closer, his voice dropping to a low, suggestive rumble only I can hear. "There *are* things I could boast about, but I'd rather show than tell."

My head jerks around, and our eyes collide. He winks, and my jaw goes slack. I thought that moment of insanity was over, left behind at the lake. What exactly is he referring to anyway? *Oh Gods!* Now I'm thinking about it. Him. Us. Together. *Stop!*

"You'll be waiting a long time," I say coolly, burning from the chest up.

His eyes dip to my mouth, lingering there. "We'll see."

It's all I can do not to wet my lips.

I nudge Panotii so I'm ahead. *Eat my dust, Warlord.* "Fourth, I won't live on the castle grounds."

"Absolutely not," Griffin says, pushing Brown Horse alongside me again. "You'll stay behind the castle walls, and that's final." His storm-cloud eyes flash until I think I'll hear thunder.

"Calm the lightning bolts. There's no reason I can't stay in the city."

"No reason?" He starts ticking off so-called reasons on his fingers. It takes both hands. "At the castle, I can keep an eye on you. I'll know where you are. Carver can keep an eye on you. I won't have to waste time looking for you. Flynn can keep an eye on you. When I need you, you'll already be there. Kato can keep an eye on you. You won't get dragged off without anyone even knowing about it. And, especially, *I can keep an eye on you!*"

"You already said that. It was point number one in a long list of inanity."

His jaw muscles bulge. "I'll give you your other conditions, but not this. You'll have access to the castle and two hundred and sixty acres of training grounds, gardens, and woods. There are baths and an entire army barracks to explore if you want to, but you will *not* leave the castle grounds without one of us. Is that understood?"

"No."

"Promise, Cat."

I snort. "I hope that's a joke."

His nostrils flare when he realizes the enormity of what he just asked me. "No vow, then. Just agree. It's better for everyone."

"Better for you."

"And you."

"Not really."

He growls deep in his throat. "Zeus's *bollocks*, you drive me insane!" His eyes darken. He looks ready to wring my neck.

"The feeling is mutual," I assure him.

With a sudden snarl, Griffin snatches me out of my saddle so fast I shriek, landing facedown across his legs.

I twist, glaring up at him. "What are you doing?"

"I'm not sure yet," he grates out.

In that case... I knee him in the ribs. He grunts and slaps a heavy hand down on my rear end, pinning me. I bite his thigh.

"Gods damn it, Cat!" He kicks Brown Horse into a gallop and heads for a rock formation up ahead. The horizontal ride is so jarring that my teeth hurt by the time he reins in, lets me slide to the ground, and jumps down after me.

Griffin grabs my wrist and drags me toward a cavern entrance. There's no way I'm going into a dark cave with a seething male. Life has taught me *something*.

I swing at him with my free hand, landing a punch on his jaw. *Son of a Cyclops!* My fist feels like it hit a wall.

"Hit me again and you'll regret it."

There's no lie. He definitely means it. Outwardly at least, he's mastered his temper, calm again, like he's the eye, and I'm the storm. He makes me crazy! Why am I always the one to explode?

I tear my arm out of his grip, pivot, and kick him with everything I've got, catching him squarely in the chest. Thrown only slightly off balance, he narrows his eyes and tackles me. I land hard, going half-numb from the impact.

Griffin grabs my wrists, pins them above my head, and

then lowers his forehead to mine. Our mouths are suddenly even. His breath fans my lips, a warm, seductive caress across my mouth. Heat floods me, and my anger flies like a bird from a cage.

"What are you doing?" I gasp.

"Making sure you don't head butt me, you little Harpy."

Oh. I'm not disappointed. *Definitely* not disappointed.

He rolls off, then heaves me up and flops me over his shoulder. Not liking that at all, I slap his backside as hard as I can. I smack him again, just in case he didn't feel it the first time.

Griffin hits my ass back, making it sting. "Control yourself! You're not a bloody animal."

He doesn't hit me again, but he strings together a long, colorful sentence detailing just why my ass deserves his hand. *Infuriating*, *reckless*, and *hot-tempered* pop up, peppered with a few choice curses I haven't heard often, despite living in a circus.

His diatribe leaves me momentarily speechless, my ears ringing from the unfortunate truth in it.

The cave is cool and dark compared to outside. He sets me down hard, and I blink, adjusting my eyes to the gloom. "What are you planning? To beat on me where no one can see?"

Griffin looks at me like I've gone mad and doesn't bother answering. His jaw flexes, and he glares at me, silently fuming. Then he throws back his head and howls. It's a sound of utter frustration, and I feel a moment of sharp anxiety when both his hands clench into fists. Maybe I shouldn't have wanted him to crack. His tanned skin and dark hair blend into the shadows. Only his eyes stand out, and they're feral.

He drags both hands over his scalp, raking his hair back

and tugging hard. "You get shot. You nearly burn to death. Twice. You think a good escape plan is to jump off a flying Dragon. You disappear for two days and then come back griping as usual. You make selfish, impossible demands."

His tone is scathing, and I feel my face flame. I should scream at him. I should knock him over the head. Who is he, to scold me like this? He should be in awe of me, not slinging me around like he has every right to do as he pleases.

Griffin kicks a rock, sending it flying into the darkness. His barely controlled fury feels like a third person in the cave. I can't take my eyes off him. I'm not sure I should.

"You're rash, willful, and hostile. You have no self-control." He whirls on me. "Do you even think before you act?"

I stare at him, my eyes wide, my heart in a knot. He's listing my worst traits, everything I fear and wish I could change—things that make me like *her*—and it *hurts*.

My eyes sting. I try to breathe.

"Impetuous, obstinate—" The flat of his hand rockets into a stalactite, sending it flying with a crack. His nostrils flare, and he swings his burning gaze back on me. "If I ever see you throw yourself in front of a Dragon...or off a Dragon..." His voice trails off in favor of an ominous growl. "I swear to the Gods I'll lock you up for the rest of your life."

My mouth opens, but no sound comes out. My chest tightens painfully. He's...worried about me?

"Don't you have any sense of self-preservation?" Griffin thunders. "Don't you fear?"

"Fear?" The word echoes eerily, louder and more high-pitched than I intended. "I have nothing *but* a sense of self-preservation, and there's only one thing I fear."

A tiny muscle contracts under Griffin's eye. "Alpha Fisa."

I nod, watching him carefully. He exhales with a curse and starts walking. He paces the cavern for a long time, his jaw grinding, his fists tight, glancing furiously at me every now and then. Minutes pass, and I eventually see the smoke settle.

Inhaling a deep breath, he stops in front of me, his hands on his hips. "Don't leave the castle grounds without one of us," he finally says. "Please. I'll worry if you do."

Everything in me stills. *Did he just ask nicely?*

I swallow, my throat suddenly thick. My voice comes out raw. "Why? I'll always come back. I can't leave you unless you release me from my vow." Or I'm abducted, so he kind of has a point.

"I have enough to worry about. I don't want to worry about you, too."

I press my lips together and look away, escaping something in his eyes I don't want to face, or even acknowledge. I stall by brushing myself off and then pushing disheveled hair out of my face. My braid is a mess, my clothes are dusty, and I'm pretty sure I have a scrape on my hip. It stings, but it's not bleeding. If I could use magic on him, Griffin wouldn't dare toss me around, and I wouldn't end up the loser at the end of every fight. I hate him. I really do.

Sort of.

Not really.

Gods! I'm such a mess!

"Fine."

"Fine?" He looks surprised.

"Do I have to repeat it?" I snap.

He flashes a lopsided grin. "Or say it in sign language?"

My insides dip, going cavernous and light. There's a flutter deep in my belly. "Why don't I ever think of stabbing you?" I ask, sliding my fingers over the knife in my belt.

Griffin chuckles, and before I can frown, or curse, or say something cutting, he closes the gap between us, sweeps me into his arms, and kisses me.

I must be demented because I don't even put up a fight. A long rumble of thunder vibrates through my body. Lightning races under my skin. Stunned by the strange and startling rush of power, I open my mouth, and Griffin invades it, his hot tongue rolling over mine. Desire instantly surges on a wild, irrepressible storm. I've never been kissed like this before—part passion, part possession, part need. All heat.

Temporarily insane, I slip my hands around Griffin's neck and touch my tongue to his. I taste his husky groan as he spears his fingers into my hair, gripping the nape of my neck to tilt my head back and deepen the kiss. His other hand tightens on my waist, pulling our bodies together. He's intense, hungry, and yet surprisingly gentle. No one has ever been careful with me before. I don't need careful, but something inside me still cracks, a fissure created by this earthquake of a man.

I should fight him. I really should, but my fingers curl into his hair, and my tongue tangles more urgently with his. He smooths his hand up my back and then back down again to the curve of my bottom, squeezing. With us pressed together, I can feel all of him, making me intimately aware of his coiled strength, of the tension rising in his powerful frame. His lips cover mine, brushing, seeking, drowning me in sensation. Unable to stop myself, I lean into him, and my body ignites. Wings beat, fanning the flames, and I hear a moan that couldn't possibly be mine. *Definitely* not mine.

I should really do something about this.

Soon.

Very soon.

My leg skims up his thigh to hook around his hip.

With a ragged sound, Griffin grabs my leg and tears his mouth from mine, trailing his lips along my jaw and down my neck. He's probably getting a mouthful of dust. *Ha!*

Sort of.

Hmm...

His tongue swirls against my skin, and I gasp. His voice rough with passion, he rasps, "You're living fire. I burn."

I open my eyes. Actually, I'm the Fisan without fire.

His lips mold to mine again with alarming perfection, but I twist, breaking his hold on me and stepping back. It's one of the hardest things I've ever done.

"Don't kiss me." My legs are unsteady. My voice comes out hoarse. We're both panting.

Griffin stares at me, his eyes dark, his chest rising and falling. "Why not?"

A fist squeezes my heart, crushing it. "You abducted me. You kept me tied up. You coerced me into working for you. I don't want to be with you."

"You're lying."

That fissure gapes wider. I press my lips together, as if that small act of cohesion will keep the rest of me from falling apart.

Griffin blows out a long exhale and then touches my cheek in a way that makes my breath stutter. "What's scaring you?"

Everything. Her. I feel like crying. "Don't kiss me again. Vow it."

His fingers fall from my cheek, and he scrubs his hand down his face, looking tired all of a sudden. "Is that really what you want?"

I nod, too scared to open my mouth. Something unexpected and dangerous might pop out.

Carver enters the cavern just when it looks like Griffin might speak. "I was the unfortunate chosen to come in here and make sure you two haven't killed each other off," he announces cheerfully.

"We haven't," Griffin replies evenly.

"Yet," I mutter.

Griffin throws me a somber look and then strides out of the cave. It doesn't escape me that he never gave his word. And as I stare in shock and confusion at the charred footprints branching out like lightning bolts in the dust where I just stood, it doesn't escape me that I'm relieved he didn't.

CHAPTER 16

GRIFFIN DISCUSSES PROJECTS AND POLITICS WITH CARVER for the rest of the journey. With Flynn and Kato riding as a pair, I spend our final two days on the road trailing behind. There's no sparring, no teasing, no being hounded with questions. There are no jokes, at least not for me, and being on the outside suddenly tastes like sour lemons.

I pull up alongside Flynn. "Why is everyone ignoring me?"

His big shoulders roll in a shrug. "We're not. We just don't understand. Griffin agreed to your conditions. He asked *one* thing in return, and you went berserk."

His disappointment jars me. "I said I wouldn't leave the castle alone."

"Under duress. And we'd all like to know what Griffin did to make you agree."

"He asked nicely," I answer tartly. *And nothing else I'm talking about. Or thinking about. Or acknowledging. Ever.*

Flynn turns to me with round eyes. "Is that all? If being nice to you is all it takes to make you less prickly, why do I always feel like I'm talking to a hedgehog?"

Feeling more than a little chastised, I urge Panotii ahead and only drop back again when we reach the walls of Sinta City. I can't believe Griffin hasn't sent someone ahead to prepare an escort, or at least get some kind of fanfare going. This is Beta and Delta Sinta returning to the royal seat after weeks away. There should be a ceremony.

Instead, we amble toward the castle largely unrecognized. Taking quiet back roads through the city, Griffin and Carver talk over what their guards said at the gate. Apparently, nothing is happening. People are satisfied, settled. Trade is healthy. Crops are good. A Magoi royal family gets butchered. A Hoi Polloi family moves in. All in a day's work. I feel like I should dust off my hands and shrug. If you ask me, it's weird.

Entering Sinta City feels a little like coming home. The circus's main venue lies just outside the walls, and we'd all come here for shopping, worship, and entertainment. It's a bright, open place full of marble statues, clear, cool fountains, soaring temples, and symmetrical architecture. The main bathhouse is almost as grand as the one in Fisa City, and the market is the biggest I've seen—a true agora, where people shop, talk, and scheme. The castle sits on a rise to the northwest, dominating the city. Since I avoid royals like the plague, I always steered clear of it. I guess that strategy got tossed out the window along with my freedom.

There's a somewhat more satisfying commotion at the castle gate. A loud horn blasts two and then four times, for Beta and Delta Sinta. A moment later, people spill out of the barracks, cheering, grinning, and shaking fists.

The courtyard is enormous, as big as two city blocks, and paved entirely in white marble. A high, fortified wall with an imposing gatehouse rises behind us, its spiked portcullis slamming shut with a definitive clang. To our left lies a block of sandstone barracks. In front and to our right sits the castle itself. It's huge—five levels high with thick marble walls and tall, arching windows, deep set to combat the heat. Decorated columns and domed arcades band the entire building. On the side overlooking a large wooded area beyond the castle, the arcades extend into tiered terraces gurgling with fountains and shaded by potted citrus and cypress trees.

The ornate structure glows in the evening sun, the slanted, orange-tinged light turning the white palace into a pearlescent, peach-colored jewel. It's breathtakingly beautiful—and nothing like Castle Fisa. There's warmth here. Castle Fisa is as cold as the Ice Plains lurking behind it.

A statue of Athena dominates the courtyard. She's a different-colored marble, streaked with the rosy tones of the south. She must have been brought here. The soldiers filling the courtyard kiss their fingers and then touch her sandaled feet as they pass.

Wisdom and war. They could do worse.

We're halfway across the courtyard when the castle's main doors burst open. Four women run toward us, hiking up their skirts. There's no mistaking Egeria, Jocasta, Kaia, and Nerissa—Griffin's sisters and mother. The family resemblance is striking.

Griffin slides off Brown Horse and opens his arms. All four women jump on him at once, babbling like excited geese. They attack Carver next, and he stumbles under the onslaught. They greet Flynn and Kato with barely less enthusiasm before flying at Griffin and Carver again.

These people actually like each other? What kind of family is this? I turn away, a tight, prickly feeling spreading across my chest.

Egeria, Alpha Sinta, approaches me, her dark head cocked to one side, her soft-gray eyes inquisitive. I know it's her because she's at least thirty-five while the other sisters are both much younger. Then there's Nerissa. She's just plain old.

"Is this who you've found for us, Griffin?" Egeria asks, shading her dove-like eyes from the setting sun.

"*This* has a name," I say frostily. "It's Cat."

"And she has claws," Griffin supplies, winking at his sister. "So don't provoke her."

"It was not my intention to provoke," Egeria says, smiling at me. "Welcome, Cat."

I try to smile back but feel my expression twist into a dash of murderous, a pinch of maniacal, and a sprinkle of watch your back. *Oops.*

Egeria swallows hard enough for me to see her throat move. "Griffin set out to find Magoi to employ. What do you do, Cat?"

"Stay alive," I answer. "I'm good at it. Are you?"

Her already-huge eyes get even bigger. I see her throat move again.

"Toughen up, Alpha," I say sharply. Turning to Griffin, I ask, "This is your plan? Benign queen, implacable warlord?" I roll my eyes. "I can hardly contain my cynicism."

Egeria responds first, surprising me. "Please do. At least until we're inside."

"Where's Basil?" one of the girls asks. Kaia, I think—the youngest. "Did he confess?"

"Cat figured him out," Griffin says. "She reads people. That's why she's here."

Understanding flickers to life on their faces. It's like watching the stars come out one by one at night. These people are so open it's frightening.

"Where's Father?" Griffin asks.

"Sleeping," his mother responds. Nerissa has salt-and-pepper hair and a plump, matronly figure. Her arms look welcoming and soft. If I'd seen her as a little girl, I'd have wanted to crawl into her lap.

"And Piers?"

"Patrolling with Gamma Team. They'll be back tonight."

After a few more questions, Griffin sends the women

back to the coolness of the castle. Before leaving, they dip down awkwardly in my direction, I think as a sign of respect. For Magoi? For me? Officially, I'm a nobody. Don't they know I'm supposed to be the one bowing to them? I can't help shaking my head as they disappear into the castle.

Griffin turns to me, his gray eyes flinty. "What?"

My heart flips over. It's the first time he's really looked at me or talked to me in two days. He wasn't being cold, or even unpleasant. I don't think it's in him to be that childish. He just busied himself with other people and other things until there was no room left for me.

My pulse abnormally quick, I answer, "You're clearly in charge no matter who's Alpha. And they need to work on their curtsies—and who to give them to. People will laugh when they see them wobbling like that."

"Who cares what people think?"

"You care. The second people laugh at you, it's over. You took this on, now you all have to play the parts. Flawlessly. Or else…" I make a throat-slitting motion.

"Can you teach them court etiquette?"

"Seriously? Now I have to play nursemaid as well?"

"Can you?" he repeats evenly.

I hesitate. Becoming a personal princess trainer could work to my advantage. "For a price."

Griffin's tone hardens. "What price?"

"If Fisan or Tarvan royalty come here, I stay hidden. Same thing for their top advisors."

"Invisible hidden? Or not-in-the-room hidden?"

I look at him like he's left his only bucket at the well. "Invisible hidden. I won't be much use detecting lies if I can't hear them."

He studies me for a moment, as if assessing my motives, and then agrees.

Huh. That was easy. "Is that a promise?"

He nods. "It's a promise."

In the waning light, his gray eyes are darker, softer, but still magnetic. I tear my gaze away before I give in to any ridiculous urges, like being nice to him. "Can I have a bath now? I need to wash off that cave."

I don't mean the dust, and Griffin knows it. His expression flattens in an instant, and the sinking, hollow feeling in my stomach feels a lot like regret.

We stable the horses behind the barracks and then make our way across a second, smaller courtyard. "You're welcome to use the royal bathhouse." Griffin points toward an arched entryway, his voice unbearably neutral.

I scan the buildings. "Where's the women's pool?" A quarter of the soldiers spilling out of the barracks were women. Unusual, but not unheard of.

He points to our left. "It'll be crowded. There are over a hundred women in the barracks. You'll have more privacy in the royal bathhouse."

True, but the idea of sharing his family's personal space is just too awkward.

"Cat?" Flynn calls.

I turn, and he grabs me, his big arms squashing my ribs.

"Ow! You big oaf! What are you doing?"

Kato snatches my ankles and swings them up. Carver leads the way, whistling a marching tune, and they start toward the royal bathhouse, Griffin trailing behind.

"What's going on?" I curse, wiggling helplessly. Well, not exactly helplessly with all the Fire Magic I have stored up, but I don't want to maim or kill anyone, either.

"Initiation," Griffin says tersely. "Don't bother struggling."

Ten seconds later, Kato and Flynn toss me into the water, boots and all. Fuming, I sink to the bottom of the pool and stay there until my lungs nearly burst, watching the smug looks on their faces veer toward concern.

"Gods, Cat!" Kato says when I finally surface. "You're the last person I thought we'd drown."

I spit an enormous mouthful of water at him. Kato uses his dusty forearm to wipe off his face, leaving it streaked with mud, and I can't help laughing when he gives me a huge grin from behind whiskers and grime.

"Don't take long. We're next," Griffin says in clipped tones.

"At least you didn't all strip naked and jump in with me," I joke.

Kato chuckles. "Maybe next time."

"Out!" Griffin barks.

"Did you leave your sense of humor somewhere?" I ask, treading water and trying to take my boots off at the same time.

Granite eyes flash to mine. "It must be in the cave."

I can live in the castle or the barracks. I choose the barracks, but instead of being housed in the women's wing, I'm given the room between Kato and Flynn. I guess Griffin wasn't bluffing about everyone keeping an eye on me.

Griffin lives in the castle, and as I settle into my new room, I feel annoyingly dejected. I was getting used to his solid presence, hearing him breathe in the dark. I'll miss sleeping through the night.

Alone and bored, I take a nap because it's impossible to resist the bed. Later, Griffin arrives, cleaned up, shaved, and looking striking in much finer clothes than I've seen him in before. He informs me that I'm having dinner in the castle and then shepherds me across the courtyard with a firm hand on my lower back, nudging when I balk at the entrance to the formal dining room.

"I'm not dressed enough," I mutter, digging in my heels.

He looks me over. "You look dressed to me. I recall a lot more skin when you're not."

The blush that instantly hits my face sparks a teasing gleam in his eyes. Once it's back, I realize how much I missed it.

"And a few freckles over here," he adds, trailing his fingertips up my ribs and coming dangerously close to the swell of my breast.

A wave of pure heat crashes over me, and I jerk away from his hand. "I'm about to dine with Sintan royalty. Not that I take any of you seriously, but there is such a thing as tradition."

He shrugs. "I'm wearing pants."

"Are the *women*?"

His expression turns resigned. "I'll take you shopping tomorrow."

"I can go shopping by myself. I've been to Sinta City before."

He shakes his head. "You're not leaving the castle without me."

"You have other things to do. Send Kato. Or Flynn."

"No."

"What do you mean, *no*?"

He goes from resigned to belligerent in a heartbeat. "Do you need me to say it in—"

"Sign language won't be necessary," I interrupt, scowling. Disgruntled, I straighten my shoulders and lift my chin. I'll show these people how a curtsy is done, even if I am wearing soggy boots and a bloody pair of pants. Literally. There's blood on them, and I can't get it out, no matter how hard I scrub. At least it's not mine.

I take a step forward only to get jerked back.

"Are there things men need to know about court etiquette? Things *I* need to know?"

I huff. "Men just stand around looking ferocious, frowning, and flexing their muscles. It's very unfair."

Griffin chuckles and raises his hand. I flinch—old habits die hard—and he frowns at my reaction. He smooths his hand down my braid, his calluses snagging on strands of hair. The tips of his fingers brush the side of my neck, and their roughness makes me shiver.

"You should really stop resisting me," he murmurs.

I swallow, fighting the urge to step away. Or step closer. *Gods! What is* wrong *with me?* I hardly recognize my own voice when I speak. "Why?"

He leans down to whisper in my ear. "Because you don't want to." He slips his hand around my waist, and his lips graze my cheek, soft and warm.

I freeze, disturbingly aware of how my body tries to gravitate toward his. When he lifts his head, his gray eyes are stormy and full of things I can't have, or even think about. My heart starts thumping, the wild, erratic pounding leaving me breathless. I step back, grumble something about arrogant warlords, and straighten my clothes, which were straight to begin with. Looking smug, Griffin offers me his arm. I ignore it and step into the room first, breaking etiquette just to get away from him.

Still hot and flushed, I dip into a court curtsy. It's less pretty without the flowing folds of a dress around me, but it'll have to do. I hold the pose. And hold. My thighs start to burn. "Alpha Sinta is supposed to tell me to get up!" I hiss to Griffin.

"Egeria!" He mimes something I see out of the corner of my eye.

"Cat!" she cries. "Please stand."

I do, suppressing a groan of relief.

"That was a lovely curtsy." Kaia beams, clapping. Definitely the youngest. So enthusiastic, and completely inappropriate. "Can you teach me?"

Griffin gives one of her loose curls an affectionate tug before taking an intricately woven hellipses grass crown from the leather pouch at his side. Kaia looks delighted, and there's an odd pang inside me when I realize he must have made it for her. "That's part of Cat's job," he says, positioning the circlet on his sister's head with exaggerated care and concentration. "She'll teach us all about court etiquette, especially you ladies."

Egeria smiles warmly. "Where did you learn court etiquette, Cat?"

"In Castle Fisa."

"What were you doing there?" She sounds genuinely interested, and a little awed.

"Mostly getting tortured," I answer. "*Loads* of fun."

Everyone gapes while I look over Piers and Anatole. *Gods!* I thought Nerissa was old. Griffin's father looks like he can't even stand up. Piers resembles Griffin except he's not as solid or weathered, and there are ink stains on his fingers even though he was out patrolling today.

"Tortured!" Jocasta finally breaks the silence. "How awful!" She's close to me in age. Like all the siblings, she has dark hair. It's braided and pinned up. Brilliant azure eyes set her apart from the varying gray tones of the rest of the family.

"Never happened to you?" I ask as if getting tortured were as common as lamb stew.

Her jaw drops before clacking shut again. "Griffin would never allow us to be tortured."

Something twists in my chest. I wonder what it's like to feel that secure.

"Please sit." Egeria indicates a chair between Griffin and Piers, ranking me above everyone except for Griffin and herself. I don't say anything. Griffin is still standing and pulls out the chair for me.

Servants dressed in traditional tribal clothing begin piling my plate with dolmades, fat green olives, and glazed dove breasts. I stop them. Etiquette lessons begin now—for everyone. "Alpha Sinta is served first, then Beta, and so on. I'm last."

"But you're our guest!" Egeria protests.

I almost snort. "Is that what we're calling it?"

"Isn't she?" Egeria looks at Griffin, apparently confused.

He shrugs, and I grit my teeth. "You're the royals," I say. "You're first."

"I fail to see how being royal changes the rules of hospitality," Egeria huffs.

Hopeless. They're all hopeless. "Is that how things are done in the tribes?" It occurs to me that I know as little about their way of life as they know about mine.

Egeria nods, her eyes wide.

I sigh. "You've already shaken up everything else. What's one more thing?" Besides, the idea of being served last rankles, and I'm not even sure where to fit the parents in. They're usually first, or dead.

Egeria beams and motions for the servants to continue.

"What else have my children shaken up?"

The question comes from Anatole. I'm surprised his voice doesn't wobble like the rest of him. He's a big man with bushy white hair and craggy skin, but his body, which was obviously powerful at one point, is passing into frailty now. His mind seems intact, though. There's a definite twinkle in his eyes, telling me he knows exactly what his family has shaken up.

"In a traditional royal family, one parent is Alpha until he or she weakens and is eventually killed off, usually by the next in line wanting to *be* Alpha. So, Anatole—may I call you Anatole?"

He nods, and I continue. "Egeria might have murdered you in your sleep a long time ago. But since Griffin is clearly stronger and more ruthless than Egeria, it's probably Griffin who would have eliminated both you and Egeria to take over the realm." I turn to the lovely, round woman at Anatole's side. "Nerissa, you're just the Consort. You don't matter."

Griffin's mother lifts one eyebrow. Slowly. I could probably have phrased that differently.

"Piers, while likely a capable warrior, doesn't strike me as the type to care about ruling." I glance at the other brother again. He looks fit enough, but he's not part of Griffin's essential team like Carver is, and those ink stains on his fingers make me think he lives for learning, not conquering. "However, Carver might have slit Piers's throat anyway just to move up a rank. Then Carver and Griffin would be at odds, waiting for one or the other to make a move."

I turn to the younger sisters. "Jocasta and Kaia aren't nearly brutal enough to get involved, so they would be married off to royals or nobles from Tarva or Fisa to form alliances that never last. The realms aren't attacking one another at the moment, but that doesn't mean they won't. The girls would be miserable but probably not dead, which is always a good thing. Their children, though, like all of yours"—I sweep a hand around the table, indicating the six siblings—"would get caught in the race for power and start trying to kill each other off as soon as they could walk.

Royals call it the nursery bloodbath. It's why they have so many kids. It's like throwing vicious puppies together and waiting to see which ones live."

As the whole family stares at me in shocked silence, I raise my glass in a mock toast. "Here's to court life!"

Anatole's slate-colored eyes turn bright with humor. "So, Cat—may I call you Cat?"

I nod, my mouth twitching.

"I'm heartily glad we prefer shaking up tradition to killing each other off."

"You never know. Griffin might still murder you all in your sleep," I joke, setting my glass to my lips.

"He could try," Anatole says with a chuckle, and I nearly spit out my wine.

The servants clear away the first course and bring in the next, once again serving me first. I stare at the lamb steak slathered in butter oregano sauce with tiny red potatoes fried until they're crispy. I look at Griffin, realize my jaw has come unhinged, and snap it shut. He winks, and I kick him under the table.

"Everyone knows Magoi royals are bloodthirsty," Nerissa says. "Among themselves and their people. We'll give a new example to the realms."

"Good luck," I say. It comes out less sarcastically than I planned.

"Griffin says you're a soothsayer." Kaia smiles at me from across the table. She's pretty and fresh. Too bad she's been dragged into this mess. "Can you see my future?"

I shake my head. "It doesn't work that way, at least not for me. I do more of a character reading. It helps determine who can be trusted."

"That sounds useful," Piers says, looking interested for the first time.

"Yes, well, that's why Griffin abducted me. To be *useful*."

Silence. Egeria clears her throat. "Griffin says you're very knowledgeable, and that your magic is vast. What else can you do?"

Do I need *something else?* Against my own better judgment, I say, "At the moment, I can breathe fire and burn you all to a crisp."

Kaia giggles.

"You think I'm joking?"

She giggles some more.

"Why at the moment?" Egeria asks, perhaps shrewder than I gave her credit for.

I try to look apologetic. "I can't explain unless the stars align just right and Zeus makes me his wife."

Griffin chokes on a bite of lamb. Carver coughs into his fist. Everyone else looks like they're trying to decide if I'm serious.

"Breathe fire for us," Kaia begs, bouncing in her seat.

I shake my head. "That would break etiquette. No fire breathing at the dinner table."

"Why Zeus?" Jocasta frowns. "He's so…mercurial."

Yes, well, so am I. "I'm forgetting to eat." I pick through my plate for the crispiest potato and combine it with a big bite of lamb, chewing slowly to get out of talking.

Kaia bounces again. She can't be more than fifteen, probably an unexpected last gasp from her mother's womb. She's so different from me at that age that I find myself oddly fascinated by her. "Show us. *Please*. I've never met anyone with real magic before."

"Real magic?" *Is there any other kind?*

"I wish I had magic," Jocasta says. "You can do anything."

Eh… no. "I can't fly," I offer.

Griffin isn't even trying not to laugh anymore. I put my

knife down before I slip and stab him. "Do you have something to add, Your Highness?"

"Good effort at discretion," he whispers, still laughing.

I give him the evil eye.

Kaia pops a potato into her mouth. "You were gone for ages. What have you been *doing* all this time?"

When no one answers, she plasters a truly pathetic look on her face. "Breathe fire for us, Cat. *Pleeeease.*"

Anatole, Nerissa, and Jocasta beg, too. Egeria looks like she's using all of her self-control not to join the chorus. Piers couldn't care less. He finished his dinner and clearly wants to go back to the library. As it is, he's reading a scroll at the table. Carver is grinning like an idiot, and Griffin... I'm not looking at him.

"It's really not done," I hedge.

Griffin leans close, heating my entire left side. "Stage fright?" he rumbles in my ear.

Me? Ha! I flick my wrist, smacking his chin as he draws back. "Sorry. Gnats."

The ladies gasp. Griffin's eyes spark, I'm not sure with what.

"Learning court etiquette is one thing. Knowing when to apply it is another," Nerissa says primly. "Right now, it's just family."

How in the Underworld do I qualify as just family? I look around the table and almost groan. "You're all so spontaneous. And innocent. Court etiquette is awful. I'm not sure I want to change you."

Griffin snorts, and I scowl at him.

"Except *you*. You could definitely use improvement."

"Innocent?" he asks, arching a dark eyebrow.

I roll my eyes. "Hardly."

"Spontaneous?"

I shrug, noncommittal.

Carver clears his throat, his dark eyes laughing. "What about me?"

"You're an incorrigible flirt and a pain in everyone's backside."

Kaia claps her hands, beaming. "Cat's wonderful, Griffin! I'm so glad you found her."

I put my elbows on the table and bury my head in my hands. To the Underworld with etiquette. No one else has any, so why should I? "You're hopeless! All of you."

"Why are we hopeless?" Egeria asks, reaching for more potatoes.

"Because you're all so *nice*." I'm pretty sure they can't mistake that for a compliment. "The Power Bid is about to happen. You're going to get annihilated." I glare at Griffin. "Except for you."

"I'm not nice, or I'm not going to get annihilated?" he asks, casually taking a bite of lamb. He's completely unconcerned about the enormity of having obliterated an impossibly old system of ruling. And no one seems at all worried that every forty years or so—now—a new generation of Alphas and would-be Alphas decide they just have to go to war with one another and burn down the realms in the process. What's wrong with these people? I feel like I'm at the circus.

No, wait—the circus was saner than this. "I doubt you'll get annihilated," I answer him. "You're impervious to magic, and it's bloody annoying."

"Is that appropriate language for the dinner table, Cat?" Nerissa scolds.

I blink at her. *Good Gods! I already have one mother, and she's more than enough.*

I rise from my chair, kicking it back with a flourish. "Forget etiquette. Let's see some fire!"

They cheer. The Sintan royals cheer.

Wasting any of the power I've gathered, or even revealing it, is stupid. But I'm arrogant and a show-off, and self-control has never been my strong suit. Otis's fire whip is gone. There's still a tiny seed of Desma's colors in me, a large dose of Chimera's Fire, and everything I could possibly absorb from Sybaris's blood.

I separate the currents of magic slumbering in my veins and call upon what I want. A ball of Chimera's Fire blazes to life in my hand. I take the top and stretch it into a thin line, throwing it up and out. It forms an arc, which I call back toward me, connecting it to the original flame. A sphere.

I turn the circle so it's parallel to the floor, step inside, and then draw it up, stretching it until I'm encased in a cocoon. The flaming cyclone crackles around me. It's searing and loud, and I can barely stand the heat. The royals stare at me, entranced, their awestruck faces vacillating behind the burning wall. They remind me of that spellbound audience at the last circus in southern Sinta, and a knot forms in my chest. I miss my friends.

"Friends and lovers make you weak."

"But what about Father?" I'm barefoot and wearing a shredded dress that barely reaches my knees. It used to be white. I'm dirty and starving, and she's eating a spice cake dripping with cinnamon honey right in front of my cage.

Mother laughs, but there's no joy in the sound. It's cruel. "You think I care if he lives or dies?"

I stare at her, frightened. I don't think she cares if anyone lives or dies. Except perhaps me.

Mentally stomping on my memories, I punch through the burning cocoon. The explosion blasts through the room, rattling the dishes on the table. Sparks flash off the bright lapis and gold of the ceiling frescoes. I consider roaring like Aetos, but that would probably be ridiculous. Instead, I release a puff of Dragon's Breath and launch into a series of back flips while my nostrils still glow, leaving orange streaks in the air. When I straighten, it's in a shimmering haze of more colors than even the Gods can name.

The family stares at me, speechless. Even Griffin looks surprised.

The colors fade as I saunter back to the table, wondering how long it takes Desma to stop glowing after her dance now that I'm not there to absorb her magic.

"Well," Nerissa says, "I'm impressed."

Anatole starts clapping, grinning from ear to ear, and everyone launches into applause. Griffin's eyes never leave my face, his expression a little too warm for my peace of mind.

My cheeks heat as I drop back into the seat next to him. "Did you think I spent eight years at the circus and didn't learn how to perform?"

His wide mouth curves into a smile that does alarming things to my insides.

Egeria looks thrilled. "With your abilities, you'll certainly be a valued ally."

My eyebrows creep up. "Is that what I am?" It keeps changing. Captive. Beta Team. Guest. Ally.

Egeria seems surprised, too. "What else would you be?"

"A prisoner."

"No! You mustn't think that!"

I turn to Griffin. "So I'm free? I can leave whenever I want?"

His shoulders stiffen. His jaw hardens.

His silence is answer enough. I turn back to Egeria. She's Alpha, after all. "I'd like to return to my room now."

She frowns. "But you haven't finished. And there's still dessert."

"Thank you for your hospitality." I rise, dip into a curtsy, and leave without permission.

I may know how to perform, but I also know how to make an exit.

CHAPTER 17

ALL THAT FIRE MADE ME SWEAT. THE WOMEN'S bathhouse is small, half the size of the royal one, but the water is clean, and it's late enough to be mostly empty. Three women occupy the far end, but the rest of the pool is deserted. I slip into the water, wash quickly, and then wrap myself in my outrageously flamboyant drying cloth. I'd stay longer, but the Sintan women keep throwing me dirty looks.

As I'm tying off the end of my braid, the women emerge from the pool and pad toward me, naked.

"Nice cloth," a tall blonde says.

I ignore her. Ignoring her sarcasm is harder.

"You're the new member of Beta Team?" another one asks.

When I nod, she looks incredulous. "How did you get invited to dinner?"

Before I can answer—or not answer—the first one spits out, "She's obviously spreading her legs."

I narrow my eyes. Snarky gets my temper up.

One of the other women lays her hand on the blonde's arm. "Griffin will get tired of her. You'll see."

A thorny sensation spreads through me. I study the woman with chiseled features, legs about eight inches longer than mine, and long, sleek hair the color of honey in the sun. My hair is unruly, wavy, and dark, and I'm smaller and curvier despite the weight I've lost since leaving the circus. Like mine, her eyes are green, but the shades are nothing alike. Hers are dark with flecks of brown. Mine are elongated, and the light, clear green of magic and the north. I hate that I'm even comparing us, but since I can't seem to stop... In spite of my unusual eyes and decent looks, I just feel short.

I turn to leave, consoling myself with the knowledge that I can kill her with one breath.

She stops me with a question. "What's your name?"

I only half turn back. "Cat. What's yours?"

"Daphne. Watch your back, Cat."

"Why?" I'm actually curious.

"Because I've got my eye on you."

I can't help it. I laugh. "I'll let you know when I'm scared."

Her eyes flash with anger a second before she lashes out. I duck on reflex, and her punch sails over my head. I come up, landing an uppercut to her gut. She grunts, her exhale warming my face. I would keep going, but the other women grab the blonde's arms, and I don't hit people who are tied down.

"Watch *your* back, Daphne." I trace a finger down her cheek, leaving a thin red welt from the corner of her left eye to the curve of her chin. I rein in the hottest part of the Chimera's Fire so it won't scar, but when I smile, I don't hold back on the maniacal. "I just love the way burns sting for days."

The other two women pale, but Daphne just looks spitting mad. My first enemy in Castle Sinta. *Great.*

"Griffin will punish you for that."

She sounds so sure that something sour unfurls in my stomach. "No, he won't." I am the Kingmaker. I am a thousand times more important to him than Daphne, even if I'm not spreading my legs. Clearly, that's her job.

I refuse to think about that, or how awful it makes me feel, as I make my way across the Athena courtyard toward the barracks. Kato and Flynn show up as soon as they hear me moving around in my room.

"How was dinner?" Kato asks.

"Enlightening."

He grins. "Did you like the family?"

I shrug, not willing to admit I found them entertaining. "I can't believe how old Anatole is."

Flynn shuts the door with his boot. He's wearing a new tunic, and his auburn hair is combed for once and neatly tied back, showing off the clean lines of his broad cheekbones and freshly shaved jaw. "Old but sharp. He unified most of the southwest before passing the reins to Griffin."

And Griffin took over Sinta. Not bad. "How have the girls stayed so innocent? Even Egeria, and she's not exactly young."

Kato flops across my bed, linking his hands behind his head. The casual position stretches his tunic across his chest and over his biceps. I can't help noticing. I'm not interested, but I still have eyes. "They've been sheltered by all of us," he says. "Maybe too much."

His affectionate, brotherly tone sends an immediate spike of envy through me. *Gods! I'm the most irrational person ever!* "Can they handle being royals?"

Kato's mouth pulls into a frown. "They expect the best from others. They won't believe people are out to use them now, or harm them. They think everyone is a potential friend."

I shake my head. "Not for long."

Flynn looks stricken. "I hate to see them disillusioned."

Oddly enough, me too. "Griffin did this. The girls could have been happy, high-ranking tribal daughters, comfortable and secure in a place they understood. Everything is different now."

"But you'll help them, won't you, Cat?" Flynn asks, his brown eyes wide and pleading.

Damn it. I really am the new nursemaid. "What makes you think I can do anything?"

He spreads his hands wide. "You know everything."

I grin and flip my damp braid over my shoulder. "I do, don't I?"

Kato's cobalt eyes flash with humor. "Saucy *and* bossy." He chuckles, somehow making two insults sound like a compliment.

I like hearing the deep rumble of their voices, so I don't kick them out for a while even though I'm exhausted and looking forward to sleeping in a real bed. Eventually alone—and not liking it one bit—I fall into the arms of Morpheus, one God who's rarely kind to me.

Needles burn deep into my skin, a stabbing pain in the night. Sudden. Searing. I shoot upright, keening into the dark.

Can't see! Where is he?

My shoulder brushes something. I whirl and hit it.

The impact wakes me up, and I howl, clutching the fist I just drove into the wall. The next thing I know, Kato and Flynn burst through the door along with a flicker of torch-light from the corridor.

Flynn tackles me, pinning me to the bed. "It's all right. It's just us." His voice is a soothing monotone. "You're not there."

I gulp down a scream. I can't breathe. I'm not used to this anymore. It's even worse when I'm not used to it!

"Shhh." Kato drops to his knees next to my bed and pats my hair. His hand is so big it covers most of my head.

I try, but I can't calm down. I keep feeling that final attack, seeing the end I chose. It unfolds over and over again in my head, and the worst part is, even if I could change the outcome now, I don't think I would.

The second he stops burning me to draw more power from the Ice Plains, I slip the blade from under my pillow and plunge it into his throat. I don't hesitate. He's had too many second chances already.

I'm faster, even though he's bigger and stronger. His eyes shoot wide as he collapses on me, gurgling. I push him back with a muffled scream, instinct making me shove him right off the bed. He crumples, twitching, not quite limp.

Pounding starts on my door. Fighting nausea, I swing my legs around to sit on the edge of the mattress, my blistered fingers digging into the sheets. I don't feel much pain. I'm numb despite the burns, watching a boy only a little older than I am bleed to death on my bedroom floor.

Our eyes meet, and I consider giving the blade a vicious twist, knowing he would do it to me.

With this, I hesitate. I hesitate so long he dies.

Aching, shaking, I lie back on the bloody bedding, waiting for Thanos to break down the door my brother barred and help me clean up the mess.

Shaking now almost as hard as I did eleven years ago, I glance at my fingers. For a heartbeat, they still look crimson—death on twelve-year-old hands.

As soon as I can take a breath without choking on it, I shove Flynn off me. Not easy, considering he's huge. "Taking advantage?"

Standing up, Flynn grins. "Not interested."

The shaky laugh that rattles from me sounds more like a sob. Why didn't I have brothers like Kato and Flynn? My life would have been so different.

I sit up, rubbing my face and brushing hair out of my

eyes. "Get out of here. Shoo! Before everyone thinks I'm sleeping with you two as well."

Flynn frowns, making his forehead wrinkle. His eyes narrow ominously. "What are you talking about?"

"Apparently, the women soldiers think I made Beta Team in exchange for being Griffin's personal whore."

Both their faces blank with shock, then Kato's lips draw back in a snarl. "What daughter of a Cyclops said that?" he demands.

The protective fury in his voice goes a long way toward making me feel better. "I don't know names," I lie. I'll handle Daphne on my own.

"When you do, you let me know," he growls fiercely.

"So you can do what?" He's not the type for cold-blooded murder. Despite Mother's calculated efforts, even *I'm* not the type for cold-blooded murder.

Kato scowls, his blue eyes shadowed and hard. "I don't know. Something."

I laugh, the sound chasing away the past.

"*I* know," Flynn says, pounding his right fist into his left palm and looking very mean.

I roll my eyes. I don't believe for a second either of them would beat up a woman over a few insults. "It's nothing I can't handle. I killed a Dragon, remember?"

"Cerberus killed the Dragon," Flynn corrects.

"But I had Cerberus. It's all the same in the end."

He shakes his head, his auburn hair loose and wild again. "You're comparing grapes and olives. Sometimes they look alike, but they're really not."

I snort. "Thank you, O Wise One. I'm anxiously awaiting your next lesson."

"I'll bet you are." Flynn ruffles my hair. "Sleep better now."

Kato pats my head.

"I'm not a bloody dog!" I mutter, slapping at his hands.

After they're gone, I light a lamp in my windowless room and stare at the shadows flickering on the wall, not willing to close my eyes again.

I have no idea what I'm supposed to do with myself the next morning, but I'm bored and hungry, so I head for the refectory as soon as I hear the barracks stirring, looking around for Kato and Flynn. They wave me over, and I sit with them, a plate of fruit and a buttered roll in my hands.

Kato unfolds a napkin and hands me a spice cake. "Cook likes me," he says, brushing away the crumbs sticking to his fingers.

I'll bet she does. My mouth instantly starts watering. "I love these!"

Kato grins, making most of the women in the refectory stop talking and sigh. "One every morning for Beta Team," he says, completely unaware of his effect on the surrounding tables.

I groan, ignoring the dirty looks coming my way just for being next to him. "I can't. I won't fit into my pants."

"Those leather ones from the circus?" Flynn chuckles. "Griffin couldn't take his eyes off your ass."

I choke on what's left of my spice cake, and Flynn pounds me on the back. "What are we doing today?" I croak, my face absurdly hot.

Kato shrugs, leaning back in his chair. Feminine eyes follow his every move. "Griffin and Carver will be busy going over whatever happened while we were gone, and any messages they received. I doubt we'll see them."

A ridiculous and rather terrifying amount of

disappointment pangs through me. Was I really looking forward to seeing a certain warlord turned royal *that* much?

"We could set up knife throwing," Flynn suggests.

I nod. "The Gods know you two need the practice. And I'm always happiest with a knife in my hand."

We finish breakfast in quiet conversation and then agree to meet in front of the Athena statue in one hour. Back in my room, I sort through my meager belongings, putting things away. There's not much left between all the blood and fire of late. I'm just slipping my knives into my rather charred belt when there's a tap on the door. I draw a blade before cracking it open.

Jocasta looks at me and then at my knife. I stick it in my belt, and she extends her arms, holding out an enormous pile of dresses. "Griffin said he promised to take you shopping, but I know he won't have time. These were in the castle. I think they're about your size."

Surprised by her thoughtfulness, I push the door open wider. "Thank you."

"Your room is very small," she says, stepping inside. "You should live in the castle."

"I haven't been invited," I lie.

She glances at me. "I just invited you."

It's not Epsilon Sinta who has the authority to invite people to live in the castle, but she was being kind, and I have good manners when I choose to use them. They were beaten into me. "I'd rather not, but thank you for the offer."

She shrugs, the movement slight and naturally graceful. "I'll ask again. Maybe you'll change your mind."

Something about the way she says that reminds me of Griffin. Jocasta looks harmless, and she's more subtle, but I have a feeling she's as obstinate as her brother.

"Let's see what fits," she says, picking through the dresses.

I spend the next half hour trying on gowns that were custom-made for royalty. Jocasta gives her honest opinion about each, and I feel uncomfortable, like Eleni is in the room with us, a ghost of companionship that has no place in my life anymore. We end up with four dresses that fit and a few others that simply need shortening. They're all similar in cut, with deeply scooped necklines, cinched waists, and long, flowing skirts that float around my ankles. Some have geometric patterns bordering the hems or gold cording crisscrossing the front from under the bust to low on the hips. All the dresses are held up by thin gold chains that buckle at the shoulders or behind the neck.

I look down, swishing my skirts. White and ivory flatter my complexion, but I prefer bold colors, and vanity makes me like this sea-green dress best. It's a good match for my eyes. The draping is soft and light, flattering my curves. I haven't been in linen this fine in years, and I can't tell if my shiver as it tickles my legs is from pleasure or unease.

"This one suits you," Jocasta says, echoing my thoughts. "Wear it tonight."

"Tonight?"

"For dinner."

"I don't have to dress like this for the refectory."

"But you're dining with us."

My stomach dips at the thought of seeing Griffin, especially dressed like this. "Why?"

She looks at me strangely. "Because we want you to."

"Beta Team doesn't eat with the royals."

Jocasta laughs. The sound is light and full of joy. I wonder what my laughter would be like if I'd had a life like hers. "Half of Beta Team *is* royal. Besides, you're more than just Beta Team."

Whoa. What? "What do you mean?" I keep my voice even and airy. It doesn't reflect years of wariness.

Jocasta takes a green ribbon from the pile of accessories on my bed. It matches the gown. "Griffin is ten years older than I am. All my life, I've seen women watch him, *want* him." She presses the ribbon into my hand. "He looks at you the way they look at him."

Adrenaline floods me until it feels like my heart is about to explode.

"You're coming to dinner," she says firmly, her azure eyes steady on mine.

I shake my head, fighting a rising sense of panic. "It'll never happen."

She gathers discarded gowns, the ones that didn't fit. "Dinner or Griffin?"

"Griffin. He'll get over it."

She smiles at me like she pities me. "He's very persistent."

"I'm stubborn."

"*He's* stubborn."

I swallow, thinking I might pity myself a little bit right now, too. "He abducted me. He threatened my friends. He kept me tied to him with a magic rope. I couldn't even pee by myself. He's awful."

"You'll get over it." Jocasta cheerfully throws my own words back at me. "See you at dinner."

I gape at her as she leaves. It's strange not having the last word.

We lose ourselves in the trees and throw knives until our hands are raw. Flynn and Kato are hitting the target more often than not. I never miss, which leaves me arrogant and gleeful and them looking for a way to take me down. Wrestling does the trick.

"Gods! What do they feed you in the south? Minotaur meat?" I kick Flynn off me with a groan.

He grins, springing nimbly to his feet. "Another go?"

I shake my head, declining another squashing. "Why don't we train with the others?" Everyone else from the barracks is in the blazing heat of the Athena courtyard with Piers, undergoing traditional drills.

Kato winks at me. "Because we're better."

"True." I glance at the sky.

Kato squints up with me. "What are we looking for?"

"Lightning bolts. Punishment for our overwhelming arrogance."

"Do you think the Gods are listening?" he asks, scratching his blond-stubbled jaw.

I shrug. "Do you think they're not?"

"They're listening to you, anyway," Flynn says.

"One is." *Maybe two. Possibly three...*

"Come on." Wrapping his big hand around my elbow, Flynn tugs on my arm. "Let's run so you can eat your spice cake tomorrow."

Taking the long way, we jog back to the barracks and then go our separate ways. I visit Panotii with an apple, making him share since Kato, Flynn, and I skipped lunch while we were out in the woods. I brush Panotii until his chestnut coat shines and then sit on a barrel, stroking one of his enormous ears and stewing about dinner.

I use the women's bathhouse again and spot Daphne and her two friends giving me the evil eye. The burn on her cheek is still red and puckered. I have no idea if she bothered Griffin about it, or if she's even seen him. Or how *much* she might have seen of him.

My stomach hollows at the thought of them together. I know myself well, and I could list my own flaws until I pass out from lack of air. I'm not beyond jealousy, or spite, or completely illogical behavior, and seeing Daphne helps me decide—I'll go to dinner at the castle.

Back in my room, I dress in the green gown and silently thank Jocasta for tucking a pair of high-heeled sandals under the foot of my bed. I can't do anything elaborate with my hair without a maid, so I take simplicity to a new level and tie it at the nape of my neck with a simple bow. I probably look Kaia's age, but I don't really care.

Delicate sandals. A long, flowing dress. Gold shoulder clasps. A green ribbon.

This should feel comfortable. Familiar. Instead, it feels like the past is creeping up on me without giving me any choice.

Anxiety churns in my stomach as I knock on Flynn's door. Kato is with him. They're playing cards, and it smarts that I wasn't invited.

Squaring my shoulders, I ask, "Do I look all right? I don't have a mirror."

They whistle enthusiastically, and I can't help blushing.

"Pretty as a posy. Spin for us," Flynn says.

I twirl, throwing them a saucy look over my shoulder.

"Come sit on my knee," Kato says, patting his thigh. "So I can inspect."

I laugh. "I'm not falling for that."

Griffin erupts into the room, filling the entire doorway. "What are you doing in here?" He looks me up and down, his tone a mix of disgruntlement and accusation.

Heat floods me at the sight of him. Irritation overrides it. "I was having fun ten seconds ago. Now I'm annoyed."

"Answer the question," he grates out.

My hands land on my hips. "Having a wild orgy. You're not invited."

His eyes narrow dangerously. He turns to leave, and I *know* I'm supposed to follow.

"Wait!" I cry in mock alarm. "Where are my underclothes?"

"Gods, Cat!" Flynn visibly pales.

Kato barks a laugh.

Griffin spins back to me. His large hand lands on the nape of my neck with a firm grip, and a jolt of awareness rampages down my spine. I back up when he starts pulling but grab both sides of the doorframe on the way out, hanging on.

"See what I have to put up with?" I ask.

Flynn and Kato exchange a look before returning to their card game.

"Not helpful!" I grind out as Griffin drags me back to my room and tosses me inside.

"What about dinner?" I ask, rubbing my neck.

He closes the door and stalks in after me, caging me against the wall with a muscular arm on either side of my head. "Jocasta said she wasn't sure."

I shove his shoulders, which does nothing. "I didn't dress like this for the refectory."

His eyes flick down, taking in my appearance. "What were you doing with them?"

His blatant jealousy sends a pulse of heat through me that ends in a completely inappropriate place between my legs. "Talking. They're my friends."

"Your team?"

"Yes! Isn't that what you want?"

An expression I can't read crosses his face. "Does that mean you'll stay with us if I release you from your vow?"

My heart thumps an awkward beat. I don't answer. I don't know.

He leans toward me, and suddenly all I can think about is his height, his strength, his scent. I go impossibly still, afraid to move because I know I'll step closer.

"I thought about you all day," he gruffly admits. "Now, seeing you like this…" He inhales between parted lips, his gaze turning ravenous as it drops to the exposed hollow between my breasts. When he exhales, his breath shudders on the way out.

My reaction is immediate, intense. Some things ignite. Others melt. A deep, almost irresistible pull nearly rocks me toward him. I dread this power he holds over me. It makes me want to tell him all my secrets and see if he still wants me.

I swallow, banishing the thought. "Let me go."

Griffin's smoldering eyes lift to meet mine. "I'm not holding you."

Oh.

Right.

Quite.

I could easily duck under his arm. I wet my lips instead. It's impossible not to.

The rumble in his chest sets me alight. It's predatory. *Hungry.* Griffin lowers his head until his mouth hovers over the curve of my neck. His warm breath curls lazily over my bare shoulder, and a spray of gooseflesh travels down my arm. Anticipation shivers through me, turning my heartbeat wild as a slow burn spreads through my middle, as languid and intoxicating as mulled wine.

His lips brush my shoulder and then skim lower, teasing

the sensitive skin along the scooped neckline of my gown. The feathery touch makes me quiver. I plant my hands on the wall behind me, palms flat against the cool stone to keep from reaching for him. My nipples harden, straining against the thin material of my dress. He growls something low and fierce, and then his tongue flicks out.

I gasp, surprise and desire thundering through me. I know exactly where he licked. There's a freckle high on the inside of my right breast. My breathing turns shallow, almost painful. Griffin's hands slide down the wall to land on my hips, anchoring me as his mouth moves lower and his lips graze the concealed peak of one breast.

I draw in a sharp breath, feeling both crests stiffen even more. The mounting throb in my core echoes my galloping pulse. The beat of blood and want. My hands ache to touch him, to slip into his hair, to hold him to me for another hot, shocking touch. A moan rises in my throat, and I bite my lip to stifle it, shifting against the growing pressure, against the restless need to press my body into his.

Griffin's tongue slides over the freckle again, and my knees nearly buckle. His husky voice vibrates against my skin. "I've been wanting to taste that for weeks."

"What does it taste like?" The breathy murmur sounds nothing like me.

"Like a snowflake on my tongue. So cold it burns." He lifts his head, his eyes searing. "It tastes like magic. And you."

His hands rise to cup my jaw. Wings unfurl inside my rib cage, bigger and stronger than ever before.

"Don't kiss me," I whisper, and the wings stretch in protest.

His thumbs glide over my cheeks in a tender, sweeping caress that makes my chest ache. "Give me one good reason not to."

When he looks at me like this, touches me, it's hard to think at all. Part of me doesn't even want to. But there are some things even I can't ignore. "Alpha Fisa. She'll kill anyone who gets in her way."

"I'll fight her with you."

"You can't. You'll die."

He shakes his head. "I won't let her take you from me."

I close my eyes, so tired of the fight. Unable to stop myself, I lean my forehead against Griffin's solid chest. His arms come around me, and just for a moment, I let my body mold to his. "You don't get it," I say, my voice muffled by his tunic. "She won't let anyone take me from *her.*"

"*You* don't get it." He sets me back enough to look me in the eyes. "You're mine. Not Cat the Soothsayer. Not Cat the Kingmaker. Just Cat."

I shiver at his words, the chills running both hot and cold.

"It's inevitable," Griffin says softly. His gray eyes are like anchors, weighing down my heart.

I shake my head. "It's not."

"You were made for me. I know it."

I stare at him in stark fear. He believes that. I feel the crushing weight of his truth in my bones.

"You need time." He reluctantly steps back, opening the space around me again. "In time, you'll see. For now, just come with me." Griffin takes my hand and doesn't let go until we're in the dining room. I skip the curtsy and sit in the chair he pulls out for me, too preoccupied to think about etiquette, especially when no one here cares.

"You're pale," Nerissa says, reaching over to pat my hand. "Are you all right?"

I stare at her plump fingers, resisting the urge to snatch my hand away. "I'm fine." I look around. "Where's Anatole?"

She sits back, worry creasing her brow. "Feeling poorly. He stayed upstairs."

"Why don't you call for a healer?"

Awkward tension fills the room. "We're having trouble getting healers to cooperate," Egeria eventually says.

Of course. Like most Magoi, they look down on Hoi Polloi, more often than not refusing to help them. "Choose one at random," I suggest. "If he or she won't help, hang the healer from the castle gate. The next one won't refuse."

Nerissa's face reflects her shock. "That's cruel, dear."

That's life. "How did your tribe deal with dissenters?"

"Combat with Griffin," she answers warily.

"That'll work." I take a bite of something wrapped in phyllo. *Goat cheese. Yuck!* I put what's left back on my plate and force myself to swallow. The women stare at me, obviously scandalized. I think Piers is, too.

"I'm not advocating random murder," I say somewhat defensively. "Ask first. But if a healer refuses to obey for no apparent reason other than snobbery..."

"A lesson must be learned?" Nerissa supplies.

I nod.

"Egeria is Alpha," Griffin says. "The order would have to come from her."

Everyone turns to Egeria—Alpha Sinta. Her soft-gray eyes go wide with alarm, and it's all I can do not to gag, especially after that goat cheese.

"I think we'll keep negotiating for now," she says softly. "I'm trying to give them incentive to work with us by opening a healing center in Skathos."

"Skathos?" I shake my head. "It's too far south. Healers won't want to live that far from the Ice Plains. They're weaker the farther south they go. Not only will they be weaker, and unhappy because of it, but they won't be able to help as many people because their magic won't be as strong. Skathos is a terrible idea." Egeria looks crestfallen, so I quickly add, "Build your healing center farther north. Ios could work."

"But what about the south? We don't want the tribes thinking we've abandoned them."

I sip my wine, thinking. "If Ios works, you'll probably get other healers to go south, even if it's not their preference. Healers are vain and attention hungry. Once Ios gets recognition, and its healers along with it, the ones who initially refused to help will start trying to get their names attached to it. At that point, you can be magnanimous and give them their own healing center—in Skathos."

Jocasta smiles at me. "That's an excellent plan."

I smile back. It's actually not that hard.

"Griffin also advocated starting in the north," Egeria says. "He mentioned Ios as well. You two are so well matched. You even think alike."

Heat floods my face, and my heart starts pounding like a herd of Centaurs. I don't look at Griffin. I *will not* look at Griffin.

"I would still have to begin construction of both healing centers at the same time," Egeria continues as if she hadn't just splattered the issue of Griffin and me across the dinner table. "I don't want to offend southerners."

I try to focus, which is really difficult when the man next to me makes my entire body hum with awareness. "Then build faster in Ios and establish it first. It'll go faster anyway. Everything is more efficient closer to the magic."

"Including you?" Griffin asks.

"I'm efficient everywhere."

"And modest, as usual," Carver says, tipping his full wineglass in my direction. He sets it down again without drinking.

I incline my head in acknowledgment. "Lovely to see you again, Carver. Your existence had completely slipped my mind."

Kaia chokes on something, probably goat cheese.

Carver grins. "I'll remind you tomorrow when I spank you in a sword fight."

"Spank me? I doubt you're immune to magic like your brother is." A ball of Chimera's Fire crackles to life in my palm.

"Cat!" Nerissa says sharply. "Manners, please. And don't threaten Carver at the dinner table."

"He said 'spank' first!"

"You're the lady. Rise above."

"That's not fair," I say, sounding suspiciously like a four-year-old.

Nerissa looks at me like she's been scolding me since before I could walk. "Who told you life was fair?"

Good point. I scowl and reabsorb the flames. As soon as she looks away, I glare at Carver and mouth *tomorrow*.

Griffin does his best not to laugh—fails—and I kick him under the table.

Kaia bounces in her seat. "Tell us about the Lost Princess of Fisa."

We just started the main course, and I nearly spit out my moussaka. I swallow and clear my throat. "There's not much to tell. She's gone, and unless she's found, or killed, the Fisan royal line after the current Alpha can always be called into question."

"But how can she just disappear?" Kaia asks.

I shrug. "Maybe she went to the Ice Plains."

"Then isn't it likely she's already dead?" Piers asks.

"Not everyone who goes to the Ice Plains dies there. I have a friend, Aetos, who survived."

"She could have gone to the Lake Oracles," Griffin says.

My heart kicks me in the ribs even as I shake my head. "I don't think so."

"Why not? An Oracle could help her escape."

"That's assuming she needed help."

He swirls the wine in his glass, frowning. "Doesn't everyone?"

"Do you?" The question pops out before I realize I've trapped myself.

"Yes." Griffin faces me, his one softly spoken word settling deep inside me. But I see more than need in his eyes. I see desire, and care, and possessiveness, and a whole mess of things I refuse to deal with.

I swallow the lump rising in my throat. "I don't." Denial works. Always has.

Sort of.

"What about fangs?" he asks. "And giant hands?"

Eh...

"What about fangs and giant hands?" Kaia asks.

"Nothing!" Carver and I say at once.

"Well, that's intriguing." Egeria eyes us in a way that makes her look exactly like her mother.

"We'll start curtsy lessons after dinner," I announce.

"Subtle," Griffin whispers in my ear.

I swivel my head to give him the evil eye, find us so close our breath mingles, and can't quite manage it.

"Excellent idea," Egeria says. "Especially with the nobles coming soon."

What? "When?"

Her hands flutter nervously above her plate. "In a month's time. Invitations have already gone out for our first realm dinner."

It's a smart move. Fast. "That will be an important evening."

Egeria and Griffin exchange a glance. "It will likely determine whether Sintan Magoi back us, leave us alone, or plot to overthrow us," she says.

I nod. "If you really want change, you're going to have to strike a delicate balance no one has tried before. You've got the Hoi Polloi heart of the realm, but Magoi nobles are still the blood, pumping all over the northern half of Sinta to their little fiefdoms where they rule, just like warlords do in the south. Gain their respect, and they may turn into valuable tools. At the very least, gain their indifference to keep them from actively thwarting you. Anything else, and they'll all be wondering why they aren't on the throne."

"There's so much to learn," Egeria frets. "Who they are. What they can do... And then there's court etiquette. How to greet. How to bow. Who can talk to whom. Everything's so different in the north and among Magoi." Her eyes widen in her pale face, and she looks at Griffin like he has all the answers. "What if we're not ready?"

"A month is plenty of time to get ready," he says reassuringly.

I attempt an encouraging smile. "It's true. And I can't wait for you to prove to them that southern Hoi Polloi aren't complete heathens after all. Half the nobles will probably die of apoplexy on the spot."

Egeria turns to me, two splotches of pink washing across her cheeks. My stomach drops. My version of supportive clearly needs work.

"I'll make study scrolls about the nobles and their magic," I offer. "All you'll have to do is memorize them, and by the party, your court manners will be the best in the realms. I promise."

Magic zings through me with the vow. I look at Griffin. "A lot will be riding on you, on your welcoming the nobles with a wolf's smile. They need to know you'll rip their throats out if they cross you." I can't help adding, "It shouldn't be too hard. Just act like usual."

"Like this?" He gives me a ferocious grin that's all teeth.

I roll my eyes. "Yes, exactly like that."

Everyone laughs, and I realize what he just did. He put his entire family at ease when they were on the verge of panicking. Mother would have reveled in the fear and fanned the flames of panic until we were all crashing into each other like frightened goats.

I turn to Egeria. "You're *Alpha*. You rule everyone and everything, from the highest noble down to the last speck of dust in this realm. Remember that, but still do that smile of yours—the one for widows and orphans. It's what makes you different."

Egeria blinks at me, nodding automatically.

Nerissa studies me over the rim of her wineglass. "Your bluntness is refreshing, Cat. Life is always so much simpler when people say what they really think."

My heartbeat falters before accelerating. I'm pretty sure something about Griffin and me—especially me—was just thrown across the table again.

"What about you?" Griffin asks.

For a second, I have no idea what he's talking about. "What about me?"

"You'll be there to read people." He waves his hands around. "Soothsayer, remember?"

I almost laugh. *Almost.* "I'll pose as a servant."

His eyebrows slam down. "No."

"What do you mean, *no*? It doesn't matter wh—"

"You'll be Jocasta's friend," Griffin decides, cutting me off. "Her companion. You live at the castle."

I chew my lip. "That sounds reasonable. What do you think?" I ask, turning to Jocasta.

"I think it would be lovely to have you as a friend," she answers.

Warmth spreads through me. *Gah!* When did I turn so emotional?

"Won't people wonder why Jocasta has a Fisan friend?" Carver asks. "She's from the south. You're from the north. Your eyes give you away."

I give him a flat stare. "Let's just say she picked me up at the circus."

Egeria clears her throat and glances at the ceiling frescoes. Everyone else decides it's a good time to eat.

After a while, Nerissa breaks the silence with a story about how Griffin got chased by a bull when he was young, and that's when he got serious about swords. "He was determined always to have something longer, pointier, and sharper than that bull's horns."

"It was the Minotaur," Griffin rumbles. "As big as a house."

Nerissa's lips twitch. "It was old Cosmo from the field across the river."

I smile, my mind filling with the image of a black-haired scamp running from a crotchety old bull, the boy's legs pinwheeling.

"Speaking of creatures," Egeria says, "the other advisors were just telling me about Dragons. Apparently, I need one."

"It's not urgent," I tell her.

She looks surprised. "But we're the only realm without."

"Fisa doesn't have one, either."

Egeria frowns. "What happened to Sybaris?"

"She's dead," I say. No further explanation necessary.

"Cat killed her," Carver announces, earning my death glare.

"That's not *exactly* true," Griffin says.

"Fine. Cerberus killed her, but Cat had Cerberus," Carver clarifies.

"Oh, that's helpful!" I cry.

Carver shrugs. "They're family. You can trust them."

"Like I can trust you?" I fume.

"You had Cerberus?" Piers is looking at me. He even set down his scroll. "How?"

So much for secrets. "Hades gave him to me. In case of emergency."

Nearly every face around the table turns a shade paler. *Huh.* That stunned everyone into silence.

"You converse with Gods?" Egeria finally chokes out.

"Not usually." I stand. "Ladies, let's curtsy."

CHAPTER 18

IN A SWORD FIGHT THE NEXT MORNING, CARVER SPANKS me in every way imaginable. Since I don't actually want to hurt him, there's not much I can do except get better with a blade. After, he leaves with Piers, who has concocted some scheme to get urchins off the streets by recruiting them for building projects. In exchange for food, clothing, and shoes, they've started repairing weak spots in the city's south wall.

Griffin is busy with Egeria on healing center plans and realm dinner preparations, so that leaves Kato, Flynn, and me to occupy ourselves. We throw knives in the woods, wrestle—which never works out well for me—run, exercise the horses, and bathe in our respective bathhouses. At dinner that evening, the royal family bickers and laughs; I kick Griffin as often as possible; Nerissa scolds me; Anatole eats like the Minotaur now that he's feeling better; and Egeria asks questions I don't want to answer. After dessert, I show the ladies how to stretch their necks to look down their noses at people who are taller than they are. Later, I collapse in my bed, exhausted, and wake up screaming, tangled up with Kato and Flynn. Grown men whisper "Shhh" in my ear and pat my head. I feel like an idiot, but I don't want them to stop.

The next day—repeat.

Little changes over the next week except that Daphne gets bolder. I catch her lurking outside my door, and she threatens me twice in the bathhouse.

"I had Griffin until you showed up." If she bit me, I swear I'd feel venom.

A weight settles in my chest. "Take him back. I don't want him."

"It's about what *he* wants!" Her look is scathing, as if she can't fathom what he sees in me.

"Then I guess you're out of luck." If there's one thing Griffin has made clear, it's what he wants.

She strikes, claws bared. I mostly avoid her fingernails, but one still gouges my chin. I dive underwater to dilute the blood. While I'm under, I drag Daphne down with me and hold her there until she almost drowns.

"Really?" I taunt. "You're a soldier, and the best you can do is scratch?"

She recovers faster than I thought she would and punches me in the eye. I guess I asked for that. I punch her back hard enough to make her nose bleed.

"Now you've ruined the bath." I grab her hair, dunk her, and give her a good shake before letting her back up. She wrenches out of my hold and attacks with practiced, forceful moves, but I'm like a fish in the water, slippery, and nothing connects.

Daphne finally gives up and pokes at her nose. "You're nothing to him. A passing fancy. And now you're whoring for the rest of Beta Team, too."

"Is that so?" I ask frostily.

"I see you going into their rooms. At night, I see them going into yours."

That also means she knows I'm screaming my head off at the time. "Don't you have anything better to do than to watch me?"

"Oh, I'm watching you."

My eyes narrow. Threats bring out my natural instincts.

"I have no mercy," I say, shoving her away from me. "Touch me again and you'll regret it."

Griffin comes to collect me for dinner and finds me with Kato and Flynn. He doesn't look happy about it and steers me back to my room with a possessive hand on the small of my back. Except for a few advisory moments here and there, some of them contrived just to get me into the castle, I think, I hardly see him except in the evenings. It's obvious he doesn't like my spending most of my day without him, especially in the company of other men.

"What happened to your chin?" he asks, his concern tinged with jealous aggression.

I touch the scratch. "Nothing. Just a cut."

"Is there anything to worry about?"

I shake my head, but his eyes narrow, and he takes my arm to pull me closer. His warm, strong fingers make my pulse race.

"You're not planning on mauling me again, are you?" I try to pull away, but my effort feels disgustingly halfhearted.

He doesn't respond, brushing his fingertips just under my eye. It must be turning colors. Tomorrow, it'll be hideous.

"What's this?" he demands. He's close enough that his masculine scent teases my senses—sun, citrus, and something uniquely Griffin's that's increasingly hard to resist.

"Nothing." I turn my head from him.

He turns it back, his tone sharpening to a dangerous edge. "Who hit you?"

Not answering, I fold my arms across my chest, creating a barrier between us. He unfolds them and takes my hands in his, holding on to them. His are steady and warm and so large that mine feel lost in them.

"You don't have to handle everything on your own, Cat. And I need to know what's going on. Egeria may be Alpha, but I'm king of this army. You're part of my team. An attack on you can't go unpunished."

A warm feeling I don't like at all spreads through me. I can't afford to depend on anyone for protection. My life doesn't work that way. "The guys and I get into scuffles all the time. I probably just ran into one of their elbows with my face."

"Don't lie to me."

Argh! He always knows! "What if I don't tell?"

He backs me against the wall, a wolfish smile spreading across his face. My heart kicks into a faster rhythm, and a nervous thrill flutters in my belly. I've seen how creative people can get with a wall.

His voice a low rumble, he angles his head toward mine. "Then you'll be punished, too."

My breathing turns shallow. Tingles skim down my spine. "How?" *Good Gods! Was that* my *voice?*

He takes his time answering, all the while devouring me with his eyes. Apparently only satisfied when my skin catches fire, he finally dips his head and murmurs in my ear, "Spanking?"

Traitorous anticipation streaks through me on a flash of white-hot desire. Faster than I can blink, he pulls me against him, fitting our bodies together like two pieces of a sizzling puzzle. I gasp, wondering if spanking is a metaphor again.

"Don't even think about it," I say sternly, tilting my head back to look at him. I shouldn't have. His eyes are dark, intense, and full of things I can't have, but can't help thinking about. Thinking about in detail. *Explicit* detail.

Stop.

Stop now.

Stop!

Griffin looks down at me, his smoldering gaze making me want to dive headlong into disaster. His big hand circles my thigh, lifting it to hook my leg around his hip. I'm forced to grab his shoulders for balance. There's not a whisper of air between us. His swelling hardness presses against my lower abdomen. Fear and excitement whirl through me in a wild dance. I'm catching fire, burning up. I feel like Icarus too close to the sun—and we all know how *that* turned out.

Griffin's free hand settles on my waist before sliding a light, fiery caress along my ribs to the outer swell of my breast. Sensation ripples through me, and I shiver.

His eyes turn hooded. "Or I could kiss the information out of you," he says, leaning in.

I panic and jerk back, hitting my head on the wall. "It was some blonde woman. She doesn't like me. It's not important."

He straightens, frowning. "Who?"

If he can't guess, it just shows how insignificant Daphne is to him, despite what she obviously thinks. The knot that unwinds inside me is proof of everything I keep refusing to admit. The realization makes my stomach cramp.

"Don't worry about it. She looks worse than I do. She won't bother me again."

Griffin hovers a moment longer and then retreats. Goose bumps spread the length of my body. The only time I'm ever cold is after being too close to his heat.

His expression turns rock-hard. "Whoever she is, if she touches you again, she'll be punished."

His voice is flat and deceptively casual, reminding me of the ruthless warlord I met at the circus fair. Strange how he's become just Griffin to me, smiling often, the keystone of his family, jealous, overbearing, fun to torment, strong, with an amazing mouth that turns me into a hot, molten volcano about to explode...

I clear my throat. "She'll be punished? Not by spanking, I assume."

I realize I just flirted, or teased, or something equally awful, and my face flames kalaberry red.

Humor brightens Griffin's eyes, and I blurt, "I'm still seriously considering stabbing you in your sleep."

He smiles. "You don't want to."

"I'll take that bet."

"You'd miss me," he says confidently.

I roll my eyes, letting him know what I think of that bit of arrogant absurdity.

"You'd miss this." He swoops down and kisses me, his lips softly urgent. Incredibly enticing. It's all I can do not to open for him, to let him invade me, and to conquer him in return. I want to throw my arms around his neck, press myself against him, and tangle my tongue with his so much it hurts.

Need unfurls inside me—a deep ache coupled with a deeper longing. The wings in my chest beat, confined and unsatisfied. I fight them. Fight him. Fight myself.

I nearly melt under the warm pressure of Griffin's mouth as he tries coaxing me into kissing him back. I don't. I *won't*. I do my best to ignore the hot throb between my legs and the restless tension coiling inside me, and cage a scream of yearning and frustration and rage. He sets me ablaze. He makes me *want*. If it were only physical, I might just give in. I wouldn't care what happens to him because of me, or what he'll think of me once he *knows*.

After another scalding brush of his lips over mine,

Griffin lifts his head. His rough thumbs stroke a burning path along my jaw, and his glittering silver eyes nearly make me reach out with both hands to take what he's offering. Instead, I steel myself and scrape the back of my hand across my mouth. "That was worse than goat cheese."

Not really.

Not at all.

Gods, I hate my life.

Griffin laughs, grabs my hand, and drags me out of the barracks.

"Not easily discouraged, are you?" I mutter.

He shepherds me across the courtyard, Athena watching with flat eyes. "Do you think I could have conquered Sinta if I were easily discouraged?"

I glare at him. *I guess not.*

He deposits me at the table before stalking back to the doors for a word with the guards. One leaves immediately.

My eye must get worse over dinner. By the end of the meal, the women are fawning over me like a flock of incredibly irritating mother hens. I flap my hands to keep them back. "Shoo! Or I'll give all of *you* black eyes."

Kaia frowns. "Are you supposed to threaten us?" She turns to Griffin, flouncing prettily in her seat. "Is Cat supposed to threaten us?"

He nods. "It means she likes you."

"That doesn't make any sense." Kaia smiles brightly anyway. "I like you too, Cat."

Griffin grins, obviously pleased with himself.

"You'll pay for that," I whisper so Nerissa won't hear.

Griffin arches an eyebrow and discreetly mimes spanking between our two chairs. I seriously consider bolting, binding vow or not.

"I have an herbal remedy for that," Nerissa says,

grabbing my chin and forcing my face toward the lamp-light. "Stay in the castle tonight, and I'll make it up for you," she offers.

"There's no reason to return to the barracks every night," Jocasta says. "You'd be much more comfortable here."

"That would be lovely." Kaia joins the campaign with an enthusiastic bounce. "And I have an excess of night garments positively loitering in my dressing room. You *must* come look at them."

Kaia has a tutor now. She's starting to sound like a real princess. It's annoying.

I scowl at Griffin. I don't, in fact, have any nightclothes. "You were supposed to take me shopping."

He looks surprised. "I thought Jocasta took care of everything."

"I only brought Cat dinner clothes." Jocasta turns to me. "I didn't know you needed anything else."

Griffin frowns. "It'll have to wait. I'm going away."

"Fantastic!" I force an exaggerated smile, my stomach suddenly off-kilter.

"Cat…" A growl starts deep in his throat.

"We have everything Cat needs here," Nerissa cuts in, putting a stop to what would likely become a thundering argument. "The previous royals had enough clothing to last a lifetime."

I'm sure that's true, but I need real clothes, like pants, which I'm pretty sure the former princesses never wore. But that's an argument for another day. "I'll stay at the barracks," I say, coming back to the original point. "But thank you for the offer."

"I'll still set aside some nightclothes for you," Kaia promises cheerfully.

I'm surprised when Kato and Flynn enter the dining

room before I leave. "Take Cat back with you," Griffin orders. "And, Cat, lock your door."

There's no chance of that. If I do, Kato and Flynn can't get in, and I've gotten used to them tackling me in the middle of the night and patting my head. "I don't need an escort. This is ridiculous."

"Follow your orders." Griffin's tone is brusque, his attention on Kato and Flynn. "Be ready at dawn. We leave for Ios in the morning."

We do? "Good. Panotii needs the exercise. And why didn't anyone tell me we were leaving for the healing center site?"

Griffin glances my way. "Not you. You're staying here."

"What? Why?"

"You'll be safer."

"No!" Something close to panic rises in me. I don't understand it. I don't know where it's coming from. And I *don't* like it.

Irritation flashes in his eyes. "Stop arguing about everything. It's infuriating."

I blink, surprised. How dare he order me around? *Me!* "You can't—"

"I can, and I will," he cuts me off.

"You arrogant son of a Cy—"

Griffin latches his hand around my wrist and jerks me toward him. "You were saying?" he asks coolly.

Sparks erupt from my nostrils, singeing his tunic. My eyes follow a glowing ember to his throat with its hard, lean lines, corded muscles, and masculine hollow. Flush against him, it's hard to hold on to my anger. Awareness flares at every point of contact, kindling a foolish, fevered craving.

There's a subtle increase in the pressure around my

wrist. I jerk my eyes up. "I was saying I'll enjoy feeding your eyeballs to Cerberus one of these days."

Griffin's mouth twitches. He lets me go.

I don't rub my wrist. I *refuse* to rub my wrist.

"Do you need us both?" Kato asks.

Slowly, deliberately, Griffin turns to him. "Why do you ask?"

"Someone should stay with Cat."

Griffin's eyes spark dangerously. "She can handle whoever hit her."

"Someone should still stay," Kato insists.

Griffin sweeps me behind him, his voice dropping to a low growl. "Why? Do you want it to be you?"

Kato glances at me. I shake my head. Our exchange is subtle, but Griffin still notices. His hands ball into fists. He looks ready to use them.

Flynn mutters something unintelligible and steps between them. "Because she screams bloody murder every night and is terrified of being alone."

My jaw drops. "Flynn!"

Griffin gives me a sharp look. "Why haven't I heard about this?"

"You saw for yourself," Kato says. "Before we got here."

Griffin frowns, shaking his head. "It happened a few times. Not more."

Flynn sighs. "That's because she was almost always with y—"

I dart around Griffin and punch Flynn in the kidney. He grunts and stops talking, but it's too late. Everyone knows what he was going to say. Griffin looks nauseatingly gleeful, and every member of his family suddenly has a hideous gleam in their eyes. I hate them all.

Well, maybe not the girls.

Or the parents.

Or anyone, really.

Gods! What is wrong *with me?*

Piers, who rarely speaks or pays attention to the usual bickering says, "She can stay in the castle."

I groan. "We just had this conversation."

"If you have nightmares, you can stay with me," Jocasta offers. "My bed is big enough for at least four Flynns." She glances at the auburn-haired warrior and then blushes kalaberry red.

"No." I shake my head, turning to Griffin. "I could kill her before I even woke up."

"Stay in my room."

"What? No!"

His generous mouth lifts in a sly smile. "See if it helps."

"Absolutely not!"

"It wasn't a request."

"You don't own me!"

His voice deepens, making me shiver. "Ownership isn't what I'm after."

"It's useless," I croak. "Give up."

Griffin pins me with a steady gaze. "Never."

My insides somersault, drop, and combust. *Never give up on me? Does he mean that?* "Why? I'm not that pretty, I'm a huge pain in the ass, and people around me usually die."

Griffin laughs, and right then he's so compelling, so utterly unafraid of all the things that terrify me, that I want to jump on him and kiss him until my lips bruise.

"You think I'm kidding?" I demand. "You. Will. Die."

"Worried about me?" He winks, and I see red. "And Cat? Modesty doesn't suit you. You're the most beautiful woman I've ever seen."

My jaw goes slack. My whole body does. Did he really just say that? In front of everyone? "Y-You're delusional," I sputter. "And I'm staying in the barracks!"

Griffin turns to his brother. "Piers! If Cat hasn't moved into my room by tomorrow night, you will forcibly remove her from the barracks and bring her to the castle. Is that understood?"

Piers nods and then goes back to the scroll he couldn't put down long enough to finish his dinner.

I'm stunned. Discussion over. *Again.* "How do you know I won't incinerate him if he touches me?"

"I trust you," Griffin says.

Those three words squeeze all the air from my lungs. I don't deserve his trust. "Why?"

"Because I want to."

"That's idiotic!" I cry, ready to pull my hair out and wail. Protecting this family is going to be like trying to stop a Cyclops with nothing but a stick.

"Don't leave the castle grounds while we're gone," Griffin says.

"Where do you even think I'd go? I'm bound to you for the rest of your life!"

"Just while we're away." His hands circle my upper arms, his eyes darkening with concern. "Promise, Cat. Please."

Something in his tone annihilates my need to be stubborn. This time, anyway. "Fine. I promise I won't leave unless there's a dire emergency."

"At all," he grates, giving me a little shake. "I won't leave the castle *at all.*"

"*Unless* there's a dire emergency. If everything is burning down around us, or we're under attack, do you really want me physically incapable of leaving this place?"

I can tell by the way his mouth flattens that he hadn't

thought of that. "Unless there's a dire emergency," Griffin concedes, giving me his hard look as the vow jolts through me, brutally taking hold. "And our definitions of 'dire' had better be the same."

CHAPTER 19

I GET UP BEFORE DAWN AND STUMBLE INTO FLYNN'S room, rubbing my eyes. "Don't do anything stupid," I mumble sleepily. "Like die."

He nods gravely, tying the straps on his leather bag. "I'll scratch that off the list, then."

I grunt. "How long will you be gone?"

"Not more than a week, probably less. Ios isn't far, and Griffin and Egeria have to concentrate on the realm dinner next."

Queasiness slithers around my insides at the thought of all those nobles here. I've been describing their magic and lineage for the family. I know of many of the people we'll see, even though they're Sintans and I've never met them in person. "I can't believe you told Griffin I don't have nightmares with him."

Flynn shrugs. "It's true."

"He just snores so loudly you couldn't hear me screaming."

"Nice try," Kato says, coming in behind me. He musses my loose hair, and I bite my lip, feeling empty and sad. The circus made me soft. Being here is making me something even worse—emotional.

Unable to shake the ache in my chest, I lay my head on Kato's arm, feeling his biceps roll under my ear.

"What's wrong with you?" Flynn peers at me with a frown. "Are you sick?"

I sigh. "I'm being left behind."

"Plan something unpleasant for Daphne," Kato suggests. "It'll keep you busy."

Of course they badgered her name out of me. "I think I'll destroy Griffin's room with the sword he bought me, make him regret forcing me in there."

"Maybe you should hold off on the fits of martial irony," Flynn suggests. "You're only staying there while we're away."

I'm not sure any of us fully believes that. I'm scared to death Griffin is going to come back from Ios and somehow convince me to stay. Andromeda would merrily dismantle him piece by piece if she ever thought I needed him. She'd move Mount Olympus to get her hands on him, carve him up, and serve him to me for dinner. She'd probably call him Sintan Steak and present a slab of meat on Fisan pottery with a sprig of rosemary and my favorite crispy potatoes. I don't think she'd expect me to eat. She'd smile like a knife's blade and tell me the fun was in the cooking.

We make our way to the stables. I help Kato and Flynn saddle their mounts, my job mostly consisting of patting noses and sneaking apples to the horses from a barrel across from the stalls. Griffin shows up for Brown Horse and readies Egeria's mare as well. Carver appears last but makes up for lost time by being efficient. Panotii looks as grumpy as I do about being left out.

"We'll have our revenge," I whisper into one of his donkey ears. He nudges my shoulder like he understands. Then again, he might just want another apple.

A few minutes later, I find myself staring in confusion at the empty courtyard. The only thing out here besides us is the statue of Athena glowing in the first rays of the morning sun, her toes polished to shining by the adoration of men. "Where's Egeria's entourage?"

Griffin leads Brown Horse behind him, the stallion's shoe irons clip-clopping on the marble, his hot breath chuffing as he senses a run. "We're her entourage."

I groan. Apparently, I need to be more proactive in my role as advisor, but I thought this was common knowledge, or at least common sense. "She's *Alpha*. She shouldn't travel without part of the army, at least ten attendants, and a few maids."

Griffin's expression turns mulish. "She doesn't need attendants and maids. That'll only slow us down."

"It's not a question of need. It's a question of appearance. You want healers to take you seriously. They won't listen to Egeria unless they think she's a force to be reckoned with. They respect power."

"Power isn't about being ostentatious. It's about results."

I shake my head. "Not only. Not for them."

"Egeria will convince them."

He either has too much faith in Egeria, or too much faith in human nature. Probably both. "They're not reasonable. They're attention-hungry sycophants. If they don't think Egeria will last, they won't give her the time of day. They'll look for someone else to flatter and fawn over and get rewards from. You'll have a mass exodus of healers on your hands. They might all just pack up and go to the other realms, back to royals they understand."

"Capricious rulers who would as soon kill them as reward them?"

"Yes."

His eyebrows lift doubtfully.

"You have limited experience with healers because they shun Hoi Polloi and the south. But you have to understand, the ways of millennia aren't easily changed."

The hand resting on Brown Horse's muscled neck balls into a fist. "How can people be so blind?"

I shrug. "Don't overestimate the masses. They love you until they hate you. They hate you until they love you."

"Healers aren't the masses. There aren't even that many of them."

"It doesn't matter. The principles are the same."

Griffin slowly exhales, uncurling his fist. "How do healers function in Fisa?"

"They need Andromeda's permission to lift a hand, let alone heal someone. They're all confined to Fisa City."

"And how many people needlessly die because of that?"

Brown Horse flaps his lips against my palm, searching for an apple. I give him the last one I have with me. "A lot. People send requests by dove all the time, but they're rarely answered, even for powerful nobles."

Griffin looks incredulous. "And you see merit in that system?"

"I never said that. Just don't expect people to change overnight. It takes more than a few months to unravel the traditions of the realms."

"I don't want to unravel the traditions of the realms. Only the asinine ones."

"Good luck with that." There's no sarcasm in my voice.

Kato and Flynn pat my head before they mount, Carver promises me a sword fight when they get back, and Griffin sweeps me into his arms and kisses me in front of all three of them. He lifts me to my toes, and I forget to kick or punch or scratch, or even breathe. When he lets go, I come to my senses enough to cough out a "Yuck!"

He grins. "Keep telling yourself that."

Egeria flutters into the courtyard, looking unused to traveling. I don't do anything ridiculous like wave good-bye, but I watch them go, not liking what I see. Four men and a woman. No escort. The majority of the population is firmly on their side, but we're in the northern half of Sinta now, and there are more Magoi around. They might try to cause trouble. And danger can come from anywhere, even accidents. If something happens to them, Sinta loses Alpha, Beta, and Delta. There's a good chance the realm would fall to pieces. Without Griffin holding things together, I doubt there would be anything left.

Feeling anxious, I return to my room, pack, and wait for breakfast. Cook still gives me a spice cake, but it's tasteless without anyone to share it with. I have nothing to do—not today, not tomorrow, not for days. Since there are already dozens of children waiting at the castle gate, hoping for their chance at clothing and food, I find Piers and manipulate him into asking me to oversee street urchins for another building project. I reluctantly agree to his request, casually suggesting something that's been on my mind for days. Since I can't leave the castle grounds, I'll have them shore up the north wall on the far side of the woods. One good hit with a battering ram and a whole section would fall to bits.

Ordering starving, homeless kids around isn't nearly as much fun as I thought it would be. They can't work properly until they're stronger, so I arrange for a picnic instead. Nerissa, Jocasta, and Kaia come out of the castle despite the heat. We stuff the children until their bellies are round and then coax them into playing blindman's bluff in the shade. In the meantime, soldiers bring in rocks from the quarry. Daphne is with them. Her nose is still swollen, and she's sweaty and dusty and hauling rocks she can barely lift while I play court games with the royals. I feel her loathing like a beetle crawling on my skin.

She doesn't understand. This is my place in life, and for the first time, I don't hate it.

I lie down in Griffin's bed for the third time. His crisp, masculine scent still lingers on the sheets. The shallow dip in the mattress is the imprint from his body, fitting around me like an embrace. I haven't had a nightmare once.

I hate this.

I hate needing him.

I squeeze my eyes shut. *She'll kill him.*

They're in Ios without me, a full day's ride to the east. Today, they probably discussed strategies, scribbled building plans on scrolls, and argued about how to recruit healers. The healers probably watched from nearby, wondering and gossiping about the new royals, and deciding not to help them. Until one of them does. Then the rest will follow. They're fickle but predictable.

I'm staring at some clothes Griffin left over the back of a chair when there's a knock on the door. I get out of bed, pull on a lightweight wrap because the former princesses' nightgowns are so sheer they're practically see-through—scratch that, they *are* see-through—and answer the door with a knife in my hand.

Jocasta doesn't even blink. She's getting used to me. I set down the knife and motion her inside.

"Am I bothering you?" she asks.

"Not at all." In fact, she just saved me. I was about to wrap myself in Griffin's tunic. It still smells like him, like salt, citrus, and sunshine. I know because I stuck my nose in it once already.

"I wanted to ask you something." She shifts, hesitant, her bare feet sinking into the flokati rug, and then shivers.

I climb back onto the bed. Jocasta follows, and we curl our legs up under us. I drag the blanket over our laps for her sake, because I can tell she's cold.

"Is it about Flynn?" I ask.

Her head jerks up, and she blushes uncontrollably.

I knew it! A girl doesn't know her bed is big enough for four Flynns without having thought about him in it.

She worries her bottom lip, her cheeks an alarming shade of pink. "Do you think he's noticed me? I mean, I know he *knows* me. But has he *noticed* me?"

I don't really know. I've only seen them in the same place twice. They probably had a lot more interaction before, when they were both just part of a tribe.

"I think for the moment, he notices weapons, and war, and women he doesn't intend to marry," I answer honestly.

Jocasta sighs, and her eyes drop.

"He'll help me with the north wall when he gets back. Keep coming for picnics. He can't miss you then."

She looks back up. "All right. But do you think it's even possible? Before, I was just a warlord's daughter. Or a warlord's sister. Now I'm Epsilon Sinta, and he's a soldier."

"He's not just any soldier. He's Beta Team."

"Like you." She looks hopeful, and I understand why. Griffin's made no secret of his interest in me.

"If I were really Beta Team, I'd be in Ios."

"It's not like that," Jocasta says. "Griffin just wants you to be safe."

"I'm either part of the team, or I'm not."

Her eyes widen. I sound like a wasp, only I'm the one who's stung.

"Maybe he thinks you're more useful here. It's not just about what you want. It's about what's good for the realm."

I snort. "You're all so idealistic. It's nauseating."

She frowns. "Do you really think that?"

"No," I reluctantly admit. "It's actually kind of nice, as long as there's strength behind it. If there isn't a driving force, there's chaos. The realm dinner will be the test of that. Everything could go to the Underworld in one night."

"Griffin is strong enough to keep Sinta together."

Jocasta's confidence doesn't bother me. Maybe because I agree. "Does he always get what he wants?"

If she's surprised by my question, it doesn't show. "Griffin is very persistent. Relentless, even."

Since there's no point in beating around the Harpy's nest, I ask, "Why does he want *me*?"

She looks genuinely puzzled. "Why wouldn't he?"

Something tightens in my chest. Such blind loyalty, and she doesn't even know me.

"Why don't you want *him*?" She looks genuinely puzzled about that, too.

I press my lips together, not answering. "Has he been serious about anyone before?" I try to sound casual and fail miserably.

She shrugs. "Women have come and gone. I've never seen him fixated before, or really even care one way or the other. You're different."

I flush as hot as Jocasta did before, a mix of jealousy and triumph. I want to kick myself because I have no right to either emotion. "It's probably just because I said no."

A delicate crease forms between her eyebrows. "Why did you say no?"

I pluck at the blanket, accidentally pulling a thread loose. I try to stuff it back down before a whole section of embroidery unravels, but it doesn't work. That's me— destruction. "I have a complicated past."

"Past lover?"

I snort. "Past mother."

She looks confused. "Why does that matter if she's dead?"

"Oh, she's not dead."

Jocasta shakes her head. "I still don't understand what that has to do with Griffin and you."

There is no Griffin and me. There can't be. "My mother has a tendency to destroy anything I might get attached to."

Comprehension dawns in her blue eyes. "You won't let Griffin claim you because you're afraid your mother will harm him?"

Claim me? Southerners have such a different way of putting things. So basic. Primal. Deep inside me, excitement flutters to life, and something needy clenches in anticipation. I ignore it. Whatever irrational part of me craves claiming will have to learn to live without. "Friends and lovers make you weak."

"That's not true."

Instant denial. But she's never watched people she loves murdered before her eyes.

"It is. They make you vulnerable because you want to protect them, and weakness never goes unpunished." Eleni paid with her life, and at this rate, I'll end up just like her.

"Love isn't weakness," Jocasta argues. "What in the Underworld did your mother do to you?"

My laugh is brittle. "It would probably go faster to list the things she *didn't* do."

She looks at me warily. "An example, then."

I don't know why I'm talking like this, revealing things. Maybe the more secrets get out, the less important the remaining ones seem. "I had a puppy. It was the only living thing to ever show me affection besides my sister and my nurse. I loved them. I hated everyone else." *Except Thanos. Not that he was exactly lovable. And Ianthe wasn't so bad.*

"Mother knew I loved it. It was white with big brown spots, floppy ears, and huge round eyes, black like slabs of jet. Not quite a year after giving me the dog, she tore it from my arms, snapped its neck, and dumped it at my feet. She told me, 'Love nothing and no one can hurt you.' I couldn't have been more than eight. I cried, and she beat me unconscious. When I woke up, I had one of these." I pull up my sleeve to show her the long, silver scars.

Jocasta pales. "I saw them before but... She almost beat you to death?"

I tug my sleeve back down. "It wasn't the first time. Or the last."

"What happened to your nurse?"

A lump lodges in my throat. "Dead."

"And your sister?" she asks quietly.

The lump starts choking me. A burn hits the back of my eyes.

I don't have to answer. Jocasta's eyes fill with tears, and she reaches out to squeeze my hand. "I'm so sorry."

Sitting here with Griffin's sister, I find myself teetering on a precipice—down one slope a hard shell, down the other an emotional swamp. The swamp is rising up to meet me when Kaia pushes the unlatched door open, sticking her head through the crack and saving me from getting sucked down into it.

"I thought I heard voices." Yawning, she slips inside and closes the door behind her. She stumbles over to the bed and climbs into the middle, pulling the blanket up to her chin. "You can't have a party without me."

"You're half-asleep!" Jocasta chides. "Why did you get out of bed?"

"More fun here," she mumbles, closing her eyes.

Not really. Kaia is sound asleep in seconds. I hand Jocasta a pillow and settle back down on the opposite side of the bed.

Jocasta lies down, too, her thick black hair unbound and

covering most of the pillow. "Not worried about killing us?" she asks softly.

"Griffin was right," I mutter, annoyed. "I don't have nightmares in his bed."

Across Kaia's sleeping form, I see Jocasta smile. She looks maddeningly like her older brother—smug.

"Don't tell him!" I whisper-shout. "Swear you won't."

She grins and burrows under the covers. "Your secret is safe with me."

I blow out the lamp, getting the feeling she's talking about more than just the nightmares.

CHAPTER 20

GRIFFIN, CARVER, AND EGERIA ARE HUDDLED OVER THE HEALING center plans. There's dust on their fingers. A breeze stirs the air. I peer around Kato's shoulder, listening to the crackle of scrolls while the afternoon sun scorches the back of my neck. Flynn is taking a drink, and I wonder why he doesn't offer me any water while he's at it. He knows how hot I get. Healers and other curious Magoi watch us from under the shade of a thick ivory cloth draped over a wooden trellis. It's crowded under their makeshift tent, and workers are busy constructing a second one.

The men already laid out stones marking the four corners of the future building. The site is flat and open, visible, yet close to woods that provide water and herbs for cases that don't require magic for healing. Placing the healing center outside the city walls declares its neutrality and availability to all. It's risky, though, and leaves the establishment vulnerable. Not that Ios offers much protection. Like too many Sintan cities, it's barely fortified.

I turn to the woods, squinting into the shadows while Griffin argues with Egeria. She wants another wing. He says they'll add it if necessary.

He looks up sharply, following my gaze. I heard it, too. A rustling. He shoves Egeria toward the healers and draws his sword. Tarvans with blue tribal swirls erupt from the trees. Southern Tarvans in northern Sinta? It doesn't make any sense. There are at least sixty of them, their swords drawn, their rhythmic battle chant pounding the air like drums of war.

I feel no fear. I have powerful, deadly magic simmering in my veins. I breathe; they die. In a moment, I'll show them. I'll give them a chance to change their minds.

The adrenaline of imminent combat surges through my body. I reach for my knives and don't feel anything—not even myself.

Horror fills me.

"Griffin!" He doesn't hear my shout. He doesn't hear me yelling at him to run, to get behind the walls. He doesn't hear me because I'm not there!

He stands firm, buying the fleeing people time. They all do. Kato, Flynn, Carver. Griffin.

They watch the Tarvans come, their legs braced for attack, bellows on their lips, and my heart plummets. They don't stand a chance.

My eyes snap open, and my whole world implodes.

"Wake up!" I sit up. Kaia is next to me, Jocasta on her right. "Get Piers. Now!"

Jocasta jumps off the bed, hastily throws a wrap around her shoulders, and then runs from the room. In less than a minute, I'm dressed. Then Piers is in front of me. Nerissa and Anatole, too.

"A Tarvan tribe is going to attack the building site. Sixty men. It hasn't happened yet, but it will by sometime this afternoon. We have to get to Ios, or they're all dead."

They stay rooted to the spot, pale, with too-wide eyes. Only Anatole holds himself together. "To Ios!" he barks. "Now!"

His voice is like a whip. Everyone flies into action. I'm the first one out, sword strapped on, four daggers in my belt. I raise the alarm at the barracks. Soldiers tumble out of their rooms and into the dawn-cool courtyard, the white marble pearlescent in first light.

Piers jogs over. The hilt of a full-sized sword pokes up over his shoulder, and there's a shorter blade attached to his belt. He's wearing leather armor. "We have forty horses in the stable," he says, stopping next to me.

Forty is a decent number. Armies travel mostly on foot. "Have fifteen horses carry women, and they double up. The twenty-five others carry your best men. Sixty more follow on foot. And they *run*. I've run for a day. So can they."

I finish adjusting Panotii's saddle and then reach for the stirrup. He's prancing, reacting to the stress in the air.

Piers lays a hand on my arm. "You're not supposed to leave."

I shake him off. "This is a dire emergency."

"Griffin won't want you in danger."

"I don't give an Olympian damn what Griffin wants!"

"You've made that abundantly clear," Piers snaps, grabbing Panotii's reins. "But I do."

"Let go," I snarl.

"Why? From what I've seen, you'd abandon him in a heartbeat if you could."

It's all I can do not to kick Piers in the face. I hold up my hands instead, backing off. "You're right. Go get killed."

Piers throws me a contemptuous look before turning to the gathering soldiers and calling out orders as they form ranks.

With a running leap, I land on Panotii's back, grab his mane for balance, and throw my right leg over his other side. Before I'm even upright, we're thundering across the courtyard, under the raised portcullis, and out into the sleeping streets of Sinta City.

Urgency explodes inside me. Panotii feels it and stretches his legs. Waiting for the army doesn't occur to me. I have no food and no water. I don't even have a bloody sense of direction, and I have to slow down at the east gate, shouting to the guards for the road to Ios.

As the sun climbs the sky in front of me, I'm forced to stop in two villages so Panotii can drink and rest. It'll kill him to run flat out in the heat. I drink, too, and then ask him to carry me again. When he's lathered with sweat and breathing impossibly hard, I get off and jog beside him, telling him how brave and strong he is while I scream inside with the need to gallop.

Hours pass. I'm so hot I get a decent idea of what it must feel like in Hades's dungeon and so thirsty that my mouth feels like the dried-out basin of an evaporated puddle. Steam rises from Panotii's drenched hide. I slow him to a walk so he can breathe and then reach down to stroke his burning neck. His sides heaving, he shudders beneath me.

"I'm sorry. I'm so sorry, but we can't let them die." I dismount again, and we run together until my whole body aches.

Finally—*finally*—Ios looms in the distance, but Apollo has already driven his chariot of fire more than halfway across the sky, and I'm still on the wrong side of the city.

I glance over my shoulder, squinting against the sun. Where's Piers? I don't see any sign of the army, and the terrain behind me is flat and clear.

I haul myself back into the saddle and push Panotii into a canter, dreading hearing the sounds of battle. Will there even be any battle noise? How long can it take sixty men to slaughter four?

My heart knows the answer to that. *Just long enough to get Egeria to safety, along with a bunch of healers who despise them and everything they stand for.*

Anxiety cramps my stomach as we skirt the city's east side, following the shade of the wall so that Panotii can pick up speed again. At last, the building site comes into view, and I go limp with relief. People are working and standing around. The healers' tent is still overflowing with gawkers and casting a long shadow across the parched ground.

My eyes find Griffin among the crowd. He's talking to Egeria when his head snaps up, and he looks toward the woods. Panic wraps icy fingers around my heart, squeezing out a painful, punishing beat. I'm too late.

I shout a warning cry, too far away to be heard. "Go. Go. Go!" I beg Panotii for one last gallop, wincing at the sickening sound that rattles in his chest.

Healers race toward us, running for the city. I see Egeria among them, white-faced and panicked. I tumble off Panotii and grab her.

She shrieks, then recognizes me and falls into my arms. "Cat! Oh my Gods, Cat!"

I push her off me and then shove her onto Panotii's back, turning him back toward Ios. I send him off with a slap on his rear, yelling hoarsely, "Close the gates! Give my horse food and water!"

"Cat!" Egeria cries, twisting in the saddle.

I run toward the Tarvan tribesmen, snagging a healer by the dress and dragging her with me in case I need her later. Healing magic works on a curve, limited when young and old, and at its peak near middle age. Women are universally stronger. The woman is about forty years old, potentially the most powerful of the fleeing group. She jerks and stumbles at the sudden change in direction, but I keep her with me, either with my momentum, or by sheer force of will. I hardly feel her pushing on my arm, trying to break free.

The Tarvans have maneuvered tactically, coming

around Griffin and the others to cut off any chance of their retreating into the city. It doesn't take a strategic genius to know they're after the royals, and Griffin in particular. Carver's an added bonus, and they probably figure they'll have Egeria soon. Sixty armed men have a good chance of taking an unprepared, weakly fortified city like Ios, and I'm guessing they know it.

What the Tarvans don't know is that their position now puts them between Beta Team and me, and every last one of them is about to comprehend something vital—that's the *wrong* place to be.

I draw in a deep breath and let Sybaris's deadly magic out on a scorching exhale. Dragon's Breath surges from my mouth and melts the thirty men closest to me. There isn't time for them to scream before the skin sloughs from their bones and there's nothing left but smoking, stinking puddles of melted men, metal, and leather.

For a moment, everything stops. The clanking of arms ceases, and all eyes turn to me. I see only Griffin, and the endless chaotic wrath inside me focuses, turning sharp as a blade. Powerful magic explodes from previously dormant places. My loose hair lifts on a sudden gale. Lightning bursts from my body, splitting the air with cracks of thunder. I advance, my footsteps charring the ground as bolts radiate from my feet, long, jagged, and intensely hot. There's a tearing pain in my back, along each shoulder blade. I don't stop to question it, or the lightning, or the wind. I don't question anything. I am *mighty*, and I will kill anyone who gets in my way.

"Run." The command is deep and echoes eerily. It doesn't sound like me. It hammers my enemies like a storm from Olympus.

Half the remaining Tarvans sprint for the woods. The

rest make a stand. Griffin shouts my name, the sound of his voice reaching me through layers and layers of sound-dulling power. My vision wavers like a mirage, everything coated in fiery orange. I'm too close to indiscriminately blast Dragon's Breath from my mouth without endangering the people I'm here to protect, so I throw a ball of Chimera's Fire at the Tarvan closest to me instead. He goes up in flames, screaming. I repeat until the Chimera's Fire wanes—five more fire balls, and then it's gone.

I still have the healer in my left hand. Her face is stark with fear and shock, but she's looking at me, not at the Tarvans, or the battle, or the gore. I draw a dagger and throw it at the man charging us. It sticks in his eye, and he crumples without a sound.

Across from me, Beta Team slices through the remaining Tarvans with ferocious efficiency. Two stumble back from their onslaught, trapped between Beta Team and me. The younger one turns my way, cocking back a small throwing ax. Griffin's knife lands in his kidney before the man can complete the throw.

I stare across the bloody space at Griffin, my eyes telling him I could have handled the tribesman myself.

He stares back, his brilliant, battle-bright eyes telling me he knows.

The last Tarvan sloshes through the liquefied remains of his companions. His frantic eyes dart between us, me on one side, Beta Team on the other. He knows it's over, the defeat total. Making a placating motion, he goes to lay down his sword. As the leader, Griffin steps forward to accept his surrender, but the man abruptly twists and throws his blade with a quick, powerful snap of muscle. It flies end over end and buries itself in Griffin's chest.

My scream snuffs out the storm. Silence crashes down

as magic collapses back into me. Confusion, disbelief, and the rawest pain I've ever felt make me stumble. I lose my grip on the healer, and she runs. I'm slow to move and then waste time chasing her down. I grab her by the hair and jerk her back while Carver sprints toward the fleeing Tarvan, ruthlessly taking his revenge.

Griffin drops to his knees, shock etched across his rapidly paling features. Tarvan swords are short. A skilled warrior can throw one with relative accuracy. It's not a technique used in Sinta, and no one was expecting it. Griffin grips the hilt and pulls out the blade, his face turning ashen. Blood washes down his front, shiny and dark. Kato and Flynn ease him to the ground while I scramble to his side, dragging the healer down with me. My shadow falls across Griffin's face.

"You saved us. Again." He reaches up to touch my cheek. I try to turn into his hand, but his fingers fall too soon.

"You should have taken me with you!"

The anguish in my voice makes him frown. "How did you know?"

"Soothsayer. Remember?"

He smiles faintly and then coughs. Blood bubbles in his mouth, drips from his lips. "...thought that was a front."

"Usually. Not always."

His eyes lock on mine. They lack their usual piercing clarity. "My kingdom's treasure. My treasure. So glad I found you."

My eyes sting, and my heart aches, and I want to rip someone apart with my bare hands. He coughs, and there's more blood. Too much blood.

"Merciless, merciless Cat." He sounds proud of me. His voice is weakening. There's blood everywhere. I'm kneeling in it. It's on my hand, which is pressed to his wound. It's in the air, damp and metallic in the dry heat.

I yank the healer's hand down and hold it to Griffin's chest. "Heal him."

Her eyes are huge. "Not him. Not Hoi Polloi southern warlord scum."

Everything in me flattens. My anger is surprisingly cold, a torrent of emotion frozen solid in an instant. I shove her hand away from Griffin and blow on it. The softest breath melts the entire appendage, leaving the charred stump of a wrist bone and mangled, blistered skin.

Her breath starts coming in short bursts. Her eyes turn unfocused. I'm afraid she'll lose consciousness, so I give her a shake. "Heal. Him."

She spits on me. "I'd rather die."

There's no searing pain, no roasted organs to tell me that she's lying. Why would she do this? Do idiocy and prejudice run this deep? Griffin is a thousand times better than any royal Sinta has ever seen. She should be falling on her knees to kiss his feet.

I don't have time to teach her a lesson in humanity, or to show her how little I have myself. I grab her head and squeeze. She screams as magic rips from her and jumps to me. I've never absorbed a healer's power before. I've never actually taken any magic that wasn't either given to me or directed at me, except that euphoria in Velos. There's something liquid about healing magic, but it's not a soft current. It's a raging tide, and it hits me so hard it knocks me over.

My back hits the ground. Carver sits me up, holding me steady while I grab the healer again. Like a swamp leech, I take everything she's got. I drain her until her skin turns gray. I drain her until she'll regret denying me until her dying day. I drain her until she slumps to the side, limp and vacant.

Jittery with power, I bring trembling hands back to Griffin's chest and send magic into his wound. It tears from me like layers of skin peeling off one by one. I cry out, and Griffin pales, fighting to stay conscious. Magic seeps into him, agonizing for us both. I grit my teeth and keep going until I realize he's not getting better fast enough. He's too far gone.

"Get me a knife!" I yell.

Griffin focuses on me one last time before his eyes close.

"No! No! No!" I shriek, shattering on the inside.

I don't know who hands me the knife. I grab it and make a long, shallow incision from Griffin's shoulder to his elbow. Flesh splits, and crimson wells up. I flip the flat sides of the knife in his blood, coating both surfaces. No one taught me to make a Death Mark or say the chant. Most of the times it happened to me, I was unconscious. The few times I wasn't… It's not something a person forgets.

I raise the knife to Olympus and pour healing magic into the blood, chanting fast and low. I say the incantation ten times. It's either six or ten. Anything else invites chaos, and more is always better, right?

With the last words, I smear the blood back onto Griffin's arm. Tossing the knife aside, I put one hand on his chest and the other on his arm and drain myself of the healer's power. I empty every last drop of it into him. When it's gone, I pour in some of myself. My magic doesn't knit wounds, but I have power I don't understand, that I didn't even know existed before today.

Once I start, I can't stop. I was never any good at self-control. My magic begins to shred. It's startling and painful to feel it ripping free. Disjointed threads collide and splinter, latching on to parts of me that I then dump into Griffin with the single-minded focus of a person on the verge of unbearable loss.

Time is irrelevant. I have no idea how much passes. The flow of magic ebbs as I weaken, leaving me numb. I'm only dimly aware of the first part of the army arriving. Dust swirls, catching in my nostrils and sneaking grit into my mouth. People talk. It's indistinct, but I think they're stunned by what they see. The carnage—my carnage— seems far away now. Over. It doesn't concern me.

Piers falls to his knees across from me, his face washed of all color. Griffin's face is even paler, and frighteningly still. I want to shove Piers away, but I can't move. My vision is dulling, my senses cloaked in an ever-thickening fog. Low voices sometimes penetrate it. I hear Kato and wish he would pat my head while Flynn says "shhh" in my ear. This is a nightmare, and I need them to wake me up.

My eyes close and won't open again. I wage a fierce battle against fatigue. It wins, and I collapse across Griffin's chest. His tunic is wet and sticky with blood. I want it to be cool like a Fisan lake, but it's hot. He's hot. I force my lips to move, to continue a chant I've heard healers use, but after a few mumbled words, they stop. I'm heavy on the outside, empty on the inside. I probably did something wrong. I don't feel my magic anymore. I can't feel my blood or my breath or my thundering hate. I can't even tell if Griffin is alive, and I want him to live so much I'd make dark bargains with shadows in the night.

"Poseidon! I'll do anything!" I silently beg.

An unfamiliar voice invades my head. *"Daughter of Fisa, turn to me!"* The booming echo between my ears is so frighteningly powerful that I use the last of my strength to cringe. A white light flashes, bright enough to sear unseeing eyes. The accompanying crack of thunder is terrifying. Deafening. I taste Griffin's blood on my lips before darkness crashes over me like a wave.

CHAPTER 21

I'M NOT SURE WHERE I AM. I RATTLE DOORS THAT WON'T open, pound on windows with no view. If this is the Underworld, it's not what I expected. It's endless, timeless. Crushingly eternal. I thought there would be peace here. I thought it would finally be over. Haven't I proved my warrior's heart?

Trapped in this unsettling, empty gloom, my only regret is leaving Griffin.

But then his familiar voice comes to me from somewhere beyond the shadowy veil. Relief sweeps through me, only to be crushed by a devastating thought. Is he alive, or are we both dead? He's talking, but I can't hear. The words are garbled and faint, like he's above the surface, and I'm below.

I kick, trying to reach the light, to hear, but I sink farther under, wondering how I can breathe down here in the dark.

CHAPTER 22

I WAKE WITH A MOAN. THE STRONG ARMS CIRCLING MY waist tense, and a long exhale warms the top of my head. I'm instantly aware of the hard, bare chest against my bare back, skin on skin.

"Cat?"

At the sound of Griffin's deep voice, my heart thumps hard against my ribs, proving it still works. "You're alive," I murmur.

"You don't sound disappointed," he gently teases. "I must be moving up in your esteem."

I feel his body behind mine, and water lapping at my skin. I want to turn in his arms, but my limbs won't obey. "Where are we?"

"Ios's bathhouse."

"What's wrong with me? I can't move, or see."

He doesn't answer right away, and worry starts like an itch, spreading. "I think you gave too much to save me. I woke up to a great clap of thunder, perfectly healed. Even my old scars were gone."

Really? I'll miss the one over his eye. "I thought you needed improvement."

His soft chuckle rumbles through me. His arms tighten, sliding me up his chest.

"Am I naked?" I don't feel any clothes.

"Yes."

"Are you naked?"

"Yes."

I try to turn invisible. "Am I invisible?"

"Save your energy, Cat. It's your turn to heal."

I guess that means no. I'm so empty, completely drained. My arms float, weightless in the water. "What if I can't?"

"Of course you can. Just rest." His lips brush my hair, his gruff tenderness making my heart turn over. Then he shifts, and something thick and hard presses against my bottom.

I feel my cheeks heat despite my pitiful state. "Don't get any ideas," I mutter.

"Oh, I have ideas. But I'd prefer you to be conscious."

Warmth blossoms low in my belly, radiating throughout me.

"Trust me," Griffin whispers in my ear.

"Don't...trust...anyone."

"You could try."

I smile on the inside since that's all I can manage.

CHAPTER 23

DARKNESS RECEDES, SLOW AND THICK LIKE OIL. "Griffin?"

"I'm here." His grip around me tightens. I like lying on his chest, rising and falling when he breathes.

"How long did I sleep?"

"Hours. It's the next day. The water woke you up yesterday, so I brought you back."

That sounds...worrisome. "Have we been here long?"

"Hours," he repeats. "We're as wrinkled as my parents."

I laugh. Sort of. Not being able to see makes my sense of touch come alive. His body cradles mine—hard thighs sprinkled with crisp hair, ridged abdomen flat against my back, strong arms circling my waist, holding me a shade closer than necessary. "Thank you for bringing me to the water."

He presses a scalding kiss to my shoulder. "Thank you for being insane enough to think you could save us. Save me."

"I told you not to go alone."

"I should have listened to you."

"I told you to bring an army."

I feel him smile against the curve of my neck. My skin tingles under his mouth. "Turns out, all I needed was you."

His words make me feel like honey that's been left out in the afternoon sun. It's hard to be ruthless when I'm slowly melting. "Release me from my vow."

He goes utterly still. I don't even think he breathes.

Then his lips draw a searing path along my shoulder while his thumb moves in slow, sensual circles just below my breasts. I'm suddenly glad I can't move. It gives me an excuse to stay where I am.

Low and gravelly, he finally says, "I release you from all vows to me."

Hints of magic flare inside me and then extinguish, my binding vows dissolving. Freedom doesn't feel any different.

"Don't go, Cat." Griffin's mouth never leaves my skin, his breath a warm whisper. "Please."

My heart splits wide open, finally finishing off the crack he started that hot night at the circus fair.

CHAPTER 24

THERE'S A COOL HAND ON MY FOREHEAD. THE FINGERS are light and smooth. "Selena?"

"Egeria."

Disappointment washes through me like a tepid wave. She lifts my head and puts a cup to my lips. Cool water slips down my throat. Some does, anyway. The rest dribbles down my neck.

"How's my horse?" I ask.

"He's fine. Stabled with the others and eating his weight in oats."

"He deserves it. He saved you all."

There's a lengthy pause. "I think you did that."

"I wouldn't have gotten far without Panotii."

"Panotii? Like the mythical tribe?"

Who says they're mythical? "He has big ears."

A cool sponge touches my chest. She moves to my arms next, first the right, then the left, and then does my hands, carefully washing each finger. My eyes won't open. I'm powerless, unable to see or move. Utterly vulnerable.

"Who are you, Cat? Really?"

"Where's Griffin?" I ask.

Water sloshes, and then the sponge slides over my legs and feet. "Resting. He hasn't slept in three days."

My immediate impulse is to shake my head. It doesn't work. "That's impossible. People always sleep after healing."

"Whatever you did to him had the opposite effect."

Egeria trails the sponge over my lower stomach. My brain tells me to jump because I'm ticklish there, but nothing happens. "He's hardly left your side. He thinks you did something harmful to yourself in order to save him."

If I've been mostly unconscious for three days, I probably did.

A chill spreads through me, icing my blood. I've known all sorts of fear—fear of pain, fear of discovery, fear of capture. This is new. This is the kind of fear that teaches me the difference between trying to stay alive, and wanting to *live*.

"Did you?" she asks. "Why aren't you getting better?"

"I am. I can talk." Sort of. My words are already slurring.

The door opens on creaking hinges, and Egeria throws a sheet over me, scolding, "Don't you knock?"

"We heard talking. Is she awake?" Kato's voice helps thaw the frost settling in my veins.

"More or less," I answer for Egeria.

"Time to get up," Flynn says brusquely. "We're all waiting for you to give us that know-it-all look of yours so we can kneel down and kiss your feet."

Kiss my feet like a Goddess. Like Athena. Wisdom and war.

Well, war anyway.

"And present our arses for spanking," Carver adds.

A smile tugs at my lips. "Don't...tempt me."

"Out," Egeria says. "Cat needs to rest."

No! "Stay."

There's a scraping of chair legs. They surround me. Beta Team. My team. A big hand covers mine, engulfing it. "What did you do to yourself?" Flynn asks.

"Wish I knew."

He squeezes my hand, but I can't squeeze back.

"Sleepy," I mumble.

Kato pats my head, and Flynn holds my hand. Carver whistles a tribal tune, and with them close by, I'm not as afraid of the dark.

CHAPTER 25

"WHY WOULD A TRIBE OF SOUTHERN TARVANS ATTACK this far north? Or even attack in Sinta at all?"

Slogging through fog, it takes me a moment to place the voice. Piers.

"Why would they even care about stopping a healing center?" Egeria asks.

"They didn't care about the healing center." Griffin's response is edgy and gruff. It still soothes me to hear his voice. "There's no reason for them to care, or to even know about it. Someone else was behind this, someone with knowledge of our plans and gold to buy mercenaries."

"Someone Tarvan or someone Fisan?" Carver asks. "Or both, creating an alliance against us?"

"Or Sintan," Piers suggests. "Nobles are used to having a certain amount of influence with the royal family. It's in their best interest to replace us with one of their own."

Egeria sighs. "I wish Cat would wake up. She'd have ideas about all this, I'm sure."

"I just wish Cat would wake up," Griffin says dully.

Emotion swells in my chest. Warm fingers brush my forehead. The touch is gentle, the skin rough. I want to turn into Griffin's hand. The irony isn't lost on me. I spent weeks rejecting him, and now that I don't want to anymore, I can't even move.

"Do you have any idea who she is?" Piers asks. "She's the perfect match for a Fisan noble—northern coloring, light-green eyes, a terrifying amount of magic, and the arrogance to match it. She could practically be a Magoi royal in terms of power."

"Except she's not a bloodthirsty tyrant," Griffin says.

They're all silent. I'm not sure anyone agrees.

"The realm dinner is coming up," Egeria says nervously. "What if a Sintan noble was behind the attack?"

"Cat will figure it out," Carver says. I can't help thinking his confidence is optimistic considering my current state.

"How?" Egeria asks.

I imagine him shrugging, his lean, muscled shoulders rolling with the effortless grace of an expert swordsman. "That's what she does. Reads people."

"What if she doesn't get better?" Egeria voices the question everyone is thinking, especially me.

Griffin strokes my hair. "She will."

"But what if she doesn't?" Egeria insists.

Boots stomp, and the door creaks open. "Kato! Flynn! Get a healer in here!"

Egeria's muttering tells me this ground has already been covered. Repeatedly. "They can't do anything, Griffin."

"They're not trying!" he snaps.

"I think they are."

He curses. "I need to be sure." He comes back to the bed and picks up my hand. "Otherwise, I'll take her to Selena."

Yes, please.

"You shouldn't move her," Egeria frets. "It might disturb her."

"I don't care if it disturbs her! She's not eating or drinking. She's skin and bones."

Me? Skin and bones? Ha!

There's a commotion to my left. The door opens, feet shuffle, and the door closes again.

"No more games, Healer. Fix her." Griffin is either pointing imperiously at me or he's got his legs braced apart, his arms crossed over his chest, and a ferocious scowl on his face. I can't decide.

"My colleagues and I have already tried," a man responds stiffly.

"Try *again*," Griffin orders.

"There's nothing we can do."

An ominous sound rises in Griffin's throat. "She's northern. She's Magoi. She's like you. She saved all of your sorry lives. While you were running away, she was defending this place. It doesn't matter what you think of me. Fix. Her."

"She killed Belinda."

Who? The healer I drained flashes in my mind, limp and vacant. Dead, apparently.

"Belinda should have cooperated." Griffin's voice levels out dangerously. The healer would be stupid not to heed the threat.

"I would help her if I could, but I can't. None of us can. This is what happens to healers who give too much. She drained her life force, and now she's not strong enough to get it back."

"Explain yourself," Griffin says sharply.

"She gave it to you, Beta Sinta. She needs it back."

Alarm hits me like a lightning bolt. Griffin must realize the same thing. With him, I can only give.

"What if that's not possible?" Griffin asks.

The healer's answer is dispassionate. "She'll die. Look at her. She's already fading away."

He's telling the truth. I'd know even without my gift.

The conversation grows faint, and I feel feverish. I've heard the Underworld is hot. Is Hades stoking his furnaces?

Will he let me see Selena? I guess prophecies don't always come true...

The voices around me fade, and a dark wave rolls over me, followed by endless gray. *Where's Eleni?*

No! Not yet!

I fight my way back, trudging, clawing, and force my mouth to move. "Griffin?"

His weight instantly buckles the mattress, making me roll toward him. "Take it back!" He lifts my hands to his face. His jaw is prickly, and I wish I could see him—strong, determined features, black stubble, gray eyes that never fail to unmask me. His voice is rough with emotion, and I wonder what I did to earn his affection. I'm not even nice to him.

"Take your life force back!" His grip is urgent, his face close enough for his breath to stir my hair.

I try to find what I've lost, but he's impenetrable. My feeble attempts slide right off. After a while, Griffin must understand that nothing is happening because he snarls in frustration and lays my hands back down.

"She can take ours. Some from each of us," Kato says on my other side. A moment later, three heavy sets of hands land on me, one by one, followed by a smaller, feminine pair that joins the others.

My heart squeezes painfully in my chest. I don't take anything from them. I won't risk taking too much.

"Well?" Griffin asks impatiently.

"Nothing," Flynn answers. "Either nothing's happening, or she's not trying."

Griffin unleashes a string of curses that likely teach Egeria a thing or two. "Out!" he eventually barks.

Muttering under his breath about how stubborn I am, he lies down next to me, tucking me against his side. I wish

I'd kissed him back. I should have thanked him for the lamb steak.

"Can you hear me?" he asks.

I manage to push a sound from my throat.

"Did you even try?"

I don't respond, and he quietly curses. "I didn't think so. You don't always have to have the last word, you know."

I wish I could laugh. I haven't won a single fight with Griffin. Right now, I can't even talk, but he thinks I'm always getting the last word?

He shifts, sitting me upright and propping me against him. My head flops to the side, and he pushes it back, bracing it under his chin. "I have an idea. I don't want to hurt you, but I don't know what else to do." He picks up my hand, rubbing my palm with his callused thumb. "What is life force? Mind? Body? Spirit? All of it combined? Is it in our blood? I can give you my blood. I'm going to cut myself."

That's never a good idea.

"Your turn."

Wait! What?

A blade stings the palm of my hand. Blood seeps out, along with my perpetual fear of discovery. He pulls me onto his lap. My panicked breathing gradually calms as Griffin holds me against him, our fingers laced together. It tingles where our blood mixes, frighteningly intimate.

I listen to his steady heartbeat under my ear and fight exhaustion, terrified that the next time I fall asleep, I won't wake up.

CHAPTER 26

INSTINCTIVELY, I CURL INTO THE LARGE, SOLID BODY next to mine, sighing when I detect Griffin's familiar scent.

"Cat?"

I wiggle closer, sliding my cheek along his bare chest.

"It's working!" He sits up, and I grumble a protest. "Easy, *kardia mou*. I'm just cutting deeper."

My breath hitches. *His sweetheart?* Most people have forgotten the ancient language of the Gods. The tribes must have retained some endearments. No one's ever called me anything special before, except Thanos, and I'm not sure "little monster" counts.

Griffin must cut himself first. I force my eyes open just as he's coming at me with the knife. Everything's blurry, but my heart still flips over at the sight of him—midnight hair, sculpted features, wide, sensual mouth, magnetic gray eyes. I could stare at him for hours.

His blade draws a line of fire across my hand. "She'll find me," I croak. I have no idea how long my blood's been exposed.

"Alpha Fisa?"

I nod. Almost. You'd think I'd be used to pain by now. I still grit my teeth when he presses our hands together.

Frowning, Griffin settles me on his lap again, like he did earlier. Blood stains the front of my tunic. The shirt is Griffin's, and it reaches my knees. He's bare from the waist up, his skin hot and hard like sun-warmed marble. He moves his free hand up and down my spine in a slow, soothing stroke that makes me want to rub against him and purr. His hand is rough from a lifetime with a sword, powerful, and spanning half of my back. It makes me think about the times we brawled, about the restraint he must have shown to keep from snapping me in two, especially when I deserved it.

His mouth brushes the top of my head, sending warm tingles across my scalp. "We'll leave here soon. I promise."

"Is that a binding vow?" I'm only half joking. We have to go.

Griffin tilts my chin up until our eyes meet. "I love you, Cat. I would do anything to keep you safe. That is my binding vow."

My heart twists so violently it hurts. "Don't say that."

His hand returns to its steady glide up and down my back, exploring lower with each stroke. Pleasure ripples over my skin, shivers along my spine. I melt against him, heat pooling in my abdomen and warming me from the inside out.

"Why not?" His tone is casual, but his body feels tense under mine.

I swallow, wishing I could sound as calm and sure as Griffin always does. "It makes you a target."

His hand stills on my back, then he rolls us so that he's on top. My eyes widen, and my heart beats faster, pumping our mixed blood to my waking limbs.

"I don't care," he says flatly. His storm-cloud eyes drink in my face like he's memorizing every detail. "You're everything to me."

The truth of his words resonates through me like a thunderclap, and I gasp. Griffin swallows the sound with his mouth, his lips an intoxicating mix of hard strength and subtle pressure. They move over mine, seductively insistent, coaxing me to open for him. His tongue slides along the seam of my lips, and desire awakens with a hot pulse that hollows me out and makes me desperate with want.

I unlace our fingers, throw my arms around his neck, and kiss him back, pouring all the jumbled-up, foolish, crazy, confusing emotions he brings out in me into the kiss. An Olympian-powered jolt arcs through me, rousing the wings in my chest. They unfurl inside of me, and I arch off the bed, propelled into Griffin's body.

He groans low at the contact. Wrapping his arms around me, he sweeps his tongue over mine, claiming my mouth and so much more. Passion ignites, and I forget about wings and Gods and the thunder hidden in my veins. I lose myself in his fiery embrace. Sheltered by his big body, feeling him move above me, surround me, hold me, need coils deep within. I moan at the intensity of it, and Griffin pulls back, concern darkening his eyes.

"More," I urge breathlessly. I use what little strength I've gathered to pull him back, wildly seeking his lips again.

With a sound of raw desire, Griffin molds his lips to mine for another scorching kiss, cradling my head in his hands like I'm something fragile and precious. "Why did you save me?" he rasps against my lips, kissing me again. He kisses me like he can't stop.

I take his face in my hands, smearing blood down one scruffy cheek. We stare into each other's eyes. His are the color of a turbulent sea. I see tempests with silver linings, their deadly force raging for me. Looking at him, I feel recast, melted down and formed anew, and realize this is how lives change, how reasons for existing shift. "Because I wanted to."

Heartbreakingly gentle, he brushes messy hair back from my face. "I thought you hated me."

The feelings I've finally unleashed swell, becoming

poignant to the point of pain. "I tried to hate you. It turned out to be harder than I expected."

His sudden grin makes my heart clench. I lightly trace the crinkles at the corners of his eyes, marveling at how his gaze darkens and then heats, turning smoky and swirling with intent. Drawn by an irresistible force, I close the space between us, lifting my mouth to his, my kiss raw and open and truthful.

I started the kiss, but Griffin dominates every inch of my mouth, his fierce tenderness setting off explosions of excitement deep in my belly. I move against him, caught between restlessness and hunger, clinging to his shoulders and grinding my hips. My knees come up, giving me more of the contact I crave. My hands glide over his broad back, exploring his masculine strength.

Griffin rakes his lips down my throat to where my pulse pounds in my neck, sucking lightly on the thundering beat. My breath turns unsteady. I sink my fingers into his hair and hold him close. He grips my thigh and lifts me into him so that his hard, thick length presses against my core. I'm naked under his tunic, and the sudden, intimate contact makes me dizzy with arousal. Dampness floods the space between my legs.

Breathing raggedly, Griffin dips his head into the curve of my neck. He shifts to the side, bracing himself on one forearm and smoothing his large hand down my body. His fingers skim back up my ribs, taking my tunic with them and leaving sizzling anticipation in their wake. He slides the material off me inch by inch, baring my body to his avid gaze.

"You're everything I've ever wanted." He cups one breast, gently squeezing. The desire in his glittering gray eyes is too potent for me to feel self-conscious. His thumb brushes my nipple, and the sensitive bud tightens. He lightly rolls the dark peak until I squirm, pleasure cascading through me.

"The feel of you," he says, lowering his head. "The taste."

I gasp when his tongue slides over the stiff crest, teasing it with hot, wet lashes. Sensation thrums along every nerve, races over my skin. His tongue swirls, deliciously relentless, while his hand moves to the other side. His knuckles graze the sensitive underside of my breast, and I tremble. My hands curl into his hair, gripping harder as his fingers and lips roam, learning my shape and feel. Griffin closes his scalding mouth around my nipple, sucking with a husky sound that reverberates against my chest.

I buck under him, pulsing with desire. At the same time, my sense of self-preservation jumps to alert along with a desperate need to keep Griffin safe. My eyes fly open as his fingers feather down my belly, seeking the curls between my legs. I almost don't have the will to stop him. I wait a second longer than I should, and his wide palm curves around me, a finger sliding between my slick folds.

Panting, I reach for his wrist, halting him with a limp touch.

Griffin stills. A few heartbeats later, he presses the heel of his palm down, putting pressure on a place that sends an exquisite jolt through me. Deep inside, I start to throb.

"Cat." My name is a tortured plea. His breath comes in warm, erratic puffs against my breast. His finger dips deeper into my wetness, teasing my opening.

My body aches. Violently. Desperately. I'm unbearably empty and need to be filled. I exhale with a shudder and shake my head, biting my lip to keep from saying something I shouldn't. I deny him. I deny us both.

Griffin's hoarse groan intensifies the ache inside me. I shift restlessly against his hand, unconsciously lifting my hips.

His whole body tenses. "That's not helping," he mutters, dropping his forehead to my shoulder.

"Sorry," I mutter back, breathless.

It takes a long time for his breathing to settle. He stretches out on his side, absently smoothing his hand over my hip, the warm weight of it making me aware of how slight I am. Not just slight. *Concave.*

I glance down. I'm used to a certain amount of roundness, and the sight of tight skin over bones reminds me of things best left in the past.

Griffin eases onto his back, lacing our fingers again even though we've stopped bleeding. I turn into him without thinking.

"Should I reopen the cuts?" he asks. His free arm comes around me.

I touch the hard ridges of his abdomen, warm skin over steel. "We should go."

"Can you walk?"

I take a deep breath, not wanting to move. "There's only one way to find out."

Griffin scrubs his hand down his face and then rises, reaching out to help me up. I stay upright but feel like a ripple on water—ready to collapse. I groan, which seems to worry him. Then my stomach growls, and his eyes brighten.

"Food. Then we leave."

I shake my head, gripping the bedpost for balance. "No time."

His gray eyes turn flinty. "You need to eat."

"I'll eat while we ride. Andromeda could have spies anywhere. She might already know I'm here."

The muscles in his jaw flex, but he nods, turning from me to find a washbasin and sponge. He wipes the dried blood off us both. My immediate protest fades with his unwavering stare and gruff insistence on taking care of me. I bite my tongue and stand still for him because I understand his need. He watched me dying for days. I watched him dying for minutes, and it was beyond awful.

Heated shivers follow the path of the cool sponge and Griffin's smoldering gaze. Goose bumps sweep my body, and my nipples tighten again, causing his eyes to snag on my breasts and turn heavy-lidded. Unfulfilled desire molds his striking features into stark, hard lines as he washes me with a focus that makes my pulse pound and my knees weak. Warmth gathers between my legs again. My limbs feel languid. I can't catch my breath.

Griffin drops a lingering kiss on my bare shoulder before tugging a clean, white tunic over my head. He drags another one over his own head before throwing open the door and bellowing for the others.

Kato and Flynn rush out of the room next door. They see me, and their faces split into wide grins. We almost hug but hold back because Griffin is hovering like an overprotective Centaur. That, and I'm not wearing any pants.

Griffin hands Kato the basin of bloody water. "Dilute this." To Flynn he says, "Burn the tunic and the bedding. Make sure there isn't a drop of blood anywhere."

I turn to him, wide-eyed, and Griffin spreads his hands. "You think I'm not learning?"

I smile. No comment.

Egeria arrives next. She gets teary and launches herself at me, nearly bowling me over and squeezing me so hard I start to reevaluate her buttercup status. She's strong. Or maybe I'm just really weak. I awkwardly pat her back until she lets go.

"We need food for the road," Griffin tells her. "Fruit. Bread. And cheese."

I open my mouth, but he beats me to it. "Not goat cheese."

I grin. How did I ever not like him?

Carver pounds up the stairs, breathing hard. "Cat!" He picks me up and twirls me around. When he sets me down, I lose my balance, and Griffin has to catch me before I fall. He circles an arm around my waist and hauls me against his side, planting a kiss on the top of my head. His possessive display of affection has me blushing kalaberry red.

"Help Flynn with the bedding," he grumbles. "Get the horses ready, and tell Piers we're moving out."

Carver glances at me with concern, ignoring his brother's surly tone. "The sun's still high."

Griffin looks out the window, frowning. "We can't wait."

I clear my throat. "Can I please have some pants?"

Everyone's eyes drop to my legs, and Griffin pushes me behind him as if no one's seen knees before. Egeria hurries from the room, returning with a pale-yellow tunic and a pair of dark-brown pants.

"What happened to my clothes?" I see only my boots, tucked neatly under the bed.

"Ruined," she answers. "We burned them along with Griffin's."

That means I'm down to one tunic and my leather pants, and they're not even here. At least they'll fit. Actually, they'll probably fall off.

"I need to go to the agora when we get back. Not that I have any money." I scowl at Griffin. "When *is* payday, anyway?"

He laughs and kisses me in front of everyone. I'm too weak to shove him away, and the second his lips touch mine, I forget to protest anyway.

"You deserve a raise. You all do. Now move!"

CHAPTER 27

EVERYONE FLIES INTO ACTION. GRIFFIN STAYS WITH ME, coaxing me to drink water while I get dressed. Egeria's clothes are too big for me and much softer than what I'm used to. Wearing them is like walking through a cloud.

Just when I'm starting to think it would be great to sit down again, Carver opens the door and pokes his head into the room. "Everything's ready."

Griffin watches me take two steps and then swings me into his arms.

"That's not necessary," I protest, ignoring the white spots streaking across my vision.

"I'm Beta Sinta," he replies gruffly. "I'll decide what's necessary."

I have an excellent comeback to that. I just don't use it. Instead, I say, "Just wait until I have the strength to fight you again, Your High-Handedness."

Griffin grins like he can't wait. He juggles me in his arms to fit us through the narrow doorway and then carries me downstairs and across a shady courtyard, the floor entirely covered in colorful mosaics portraying the Olympians conquering the Titans in the War of Gods.

"Did you get Panotii for me?" I ask Carver.

He nods. "That horse is a legend. No one can understand how he got here over an hour before the army did. They were out of the castle five minutes after you."

I blink at him in surprise. I was pouring the healer's

magic and then my own life force into Griffin for *that* long? No wonder I almost killed myself.

We cross under a domed archway and into a second courtyard that's too big to be shaded. The sun hurts my eyes, and I turn into the shadow of Griffin's neck, the heat hitting me like a wall.

Beta Team and Egeria are waiting by the horses. "Where's Piers?" I ask, yawning.

"Heading the army," Griffin says. "They'll meet us at the west gate."

Panotii sees me and nickers. I slip out of Griffin's arms and go to my horse, stroking his neck. He nudges my chest with his velvety nose, nearly knocking me over.

"You're a hero, you know."

His enormous ears twitch. Of course he knows.

I try unsuccessfully to get my foot in the stirrup. Flynn offers me a leg up, but Griffin muscles him out of the way and lifts me up himself. Flynn grins in a way I don't like at all, and he and Kato keep poking each other in the ribs, looking back and forth between Griffin and me.

I make a face. "How old are you? Five?"

Flynn pats my thigh, giving it a hearty squeeze despite Griffin's dark look. "That's the Cat we missed."

Exchanging a look with Carver, the two of them then rummage around in Flynn's bag. It's Kato who hands me the flask they pull out.

"What's this?" I unscrew the top and sniff suspiciously.

He refuses to answer, his cobalt eyes merry, so I make a show of being wary before putting the flask to my lips. The familiar taste that washes over my tongue fills me with delight. "Fisan clover water!"

Kato grins, nearly blinding me with his good looks. "Flynn, Carver, and I thought you'd like it."

"I practically grew up on this stuff. My sister and I used to sneak into the kitchens and drink until our stomachs sloshed."

Griffin glances at me. "Sister?"

"Where did you get this?" I ask, tilting my head back for a longer sip.

Kato takes the flask back when I hand it to him, closes it, and then tucks it into Panotii's saddlebag. "Ios has a realms store. Fisan merchants arrived this morning with the clover water—and this." He turns to the others, and Flynn pulls a necklace from a leather pouch, gingerly holding the chain between his thumb and forefinger.

My heart skips a beat. Or maybe three. Tiny, hammered gold laurel leaves climb the pendant, protecting it and attaching it to a gold chain. Inside is a shard of glacier from the Ice Plains, encased in a magic vial to keep it from melting. The ice swirls with myriad shades of blue and pulses with so much magic that it must have been harvested near Olympus. There are probably only a handful of people who can make it that far onto the Ice Plains and back.

My hand trembles as I reach for the necklace. Both the chain and the pendant are bitingly cold. I can already feel the ice working for me, bolstering what little strength I have. I blink a few times before looking up. I can hardly breathe. "This must have cost a fortune."

All three men shrug, brushing off the colossal price that comes with this kind of treasure. "The merchant explained it to us," Flynn says. "Something about always being connected to the source of your power. A spell on the glass keeps it from melting. We thought it might help."

Carver grins like an idiot. "And it's pretty."

I choke on the lump in my throat, laughing and coughing at the same time. Looping the chain over my head,

I tuck the pendant under my tunic. It falls between my breasts, burning me with cold. "Thank you, *oikogeneia*." The ancient word for family rises unbidden, tumbling past my lips. I just claimed these people. Maybe someday they'll know.

I get my first real look at Ios as we ride out to meet the army at the west gate. The city is heavily marbled and overflowing with temples to the Gods. We pass more than one bathhouse, the agora is bustling, and the merchants look prosperous enough. I'm not surprised—the farther north in the realms, the wealthier the cities. What does surprise me is the train of people we collect.

Ionians line the streets in colorful clothing, dressed for a festival, watching us pass. Watching *me*. Women and children throw flowers along my path and then link arms with their husbands and fathers and fall into step behind us. Panotii's hooves click on the even cobbles, trampling the blooms and releasing heady scents into the afternoon heat. I hear my name on the fragrant breeze and thank the Gods the wind isn't blowing east.

Even though I'd much rather duck my head and hide my face, I manage to smile and wave here and there since it seems the appropriate thing to do. The residents of Ios cheer for me when we reach the gate. I wish they wouldn't. Saving them today doesn't mean I won't destroy them tomorrow. That's my fate, after all.

I swallow, finding my throat painfully dry.

I breathe more easily once we're outside the gates. Griffin and I fall into place at the head of the waiting soldiers, in front of Beta Team, Piers, and even Egeria. Taking the lead position feels both right and wrong at the same time.

"What about the healing center?" I ask.

Griffin glances over. "The plans haven't changed." Easing Brown Horse closer, he reaches out and gently brushes a loose curl off my temple. His fingertips graze the shell of my ear as he tucks it back, and I shiver despite the heat. Frowning, he asks, "Are you sure you can travel?"

The concern in his eyes nearly undoes me, but I nod anyway, which is a colossal lie. I'm not sure at all. "Won't the attack scare the healers away from here?" I ask. "They already don't want anything to do with it."

"The important thing is helping people. If they can't see that, they're idiots."

"They're idiots."

He shrugs. "Then we'll hire Hoi Polloi medics. They have skills even if they don't have magic."

Simple and yet so effective—archetypal Griffin. "That's brilliant. Healers will hate it. It'll push them into getting involved. Their egos won't stand for being passed over in their intended role."

Griffin nods.

We ride quietly for a while, but then I look over at him. "Thank you for saving me."

"We saved each other," he answers, and my chest squeezes tight when he reaches over again, like he can't stop touching me. His long fingers wrap around mine. "But don't ever sacrifice yourself for me, Cat. I can't live with that."

A knot of emotion tangles around my heart. His hand is so warm. Griffin's is the only heat I've ever been drawn to.

"How long was I out?" I ask.

He lets go of me in order to pick up both reins again when Brown Horse starts tossing his head. "Six days."

Six days! No wonder I'm emaciated. "But I only remember waking up a few times."

His eyes flick over to me, flinty and grim. "That's because you only woke up a few times."

I shudder a little. I've always tried hard to stay alive, but I was never truly afraid of death before.

A while later, Griffin says, "Those Tarvans were invading our territory, attacking Sintan royalty. That's an act of war."

"Welcome to the Power Bid," I mutter gloomily.

"Kill or be killed," he responds, apparently adopting my bitter philosophy.

A wry smile twists my lips. "You're as merciless as I am. You just hide it better."

"We're both ruthless when we have to be. It makes us a good match."

I shake my head. "There should always be someone humane in the mix, to keep the other one in line."

He chuckles a little. "We have Egeria for that."

I laugh and then cough. Griffin pulls out the clover water and makes me drink. He tries to give me more, but I shove it away, suddenly nauseated. "One more sip and I'll throw up."

His brow furrowing, he puts the flask away. "Unless they're utterly heartless, people put a certain value on human life. It keeps us from killing each other off for no reason. But for leaders like you and me, a moral high ground is too absolute. There are choices to be made."

"I'm not a leader."

A stubborn glint enters his eyes. "You are. I know how you handled Piers and everyone back at the castle. You make decisions. You execute them. You protect your people."

I snort. "My people aren't very numerous."

"Actually, they're more numerous than you think. The entire city of Ios worships you."

So that's what that was all about? Now I'm *really* nauseated. The water I drank pushes uncomfortably at the edges of my shrunken stomach. I don't want Ios worshipping me. I don't want anyone worshipping me. "I don't like people talking about me."

"It's too late for that. Everyone here knows you decimated those Tarvans almost single-handedly. The rest of Sinta will know soon enough, and the Ionians have already started building a shrine in your honor."

What? I look at him, stunned. "Shrines are for Gods." I blink, but nope, everything is still out of focus. That can't be good.

"Gods. Heroes." He gives me that lopsided smile that always makes me go into cardiac arrest. "A mysterious Fisan who gallops to the rescue on a donkey-horse and breathes fire…"

I try not to laugh. Or fall off my horse. "Panotii will kick you for that. And the Tarvans were after *you*, not Ios."

"They would have sacked the city. The place is virtually defenseless. There's a wall Brown Horse could jump over and a total of twenty guards. You saved Ios, and the people there know it."

I frown. "Sinta's in a weak position. It's the poorest realm with the driest climate and the least magic, and the ex-royals drove it half into the ground with their greed. The Power Bid is here, but everything is different this time because Alpha Fisa is still too dominant, Alpha Tarva took over before he should have, and you…" I glance at Griffin, an Alpha in Beta's clothing. "Well, I'm pretty sure you started it all."

He doesn't look repentant in the least. "And what happened at Ios was someone else's first move. A Tarvan royal?"

"That's my guess. But I think that Giant you fought after you abducted me was actually the first move. We just didn't know it then."

"The same person?" he asks.

Shrugging, I shake my head. "There's no way to know."

Griffin scans the horizon and then looks south, the bold angles of his jaw hardening as he takes in the arid vista. "I can give soldiers to Ios and Skathos to protect the healing centers, but I can't spread my army too thin. We have to protect Sinta City and the family. Mylos is safe, but I don't have enough people to cover Velos or Kaplos, and I barely have enough soldiers to keep the tribes peaceful in the south."

"Recruit. Sinta is poorer than it used to be, but that's only because all the wealth is at the castle. Redistribute. It's good for everyone."

He drags his hand through his hair, pushing it back. It's gotten longer, wilder—more warlord than Beta. "I don't trust soldiers who aren't my own."

"You don't have a choice, and they will be yours. Most people just want to eat, or feed their families. You'll have rotten fruit here and there, but so does everyone. The Fisan and Tarvan royals probably have a lot more than you do. Everyone hates them—the people because they're repressed and terrorized, the nobles because they're jealous and petty. There are constant plots to bring down the royal families. They just don't work. Well, except for you." I wave my hand in Griffin's direction.

His mouth twitches. He's still blurry, and my limbs are getting heavy. I struggle with the disturbing sensation while still trying to focus on the conversation.

"You'll have trouble with nobles and certain Magoi, like healers. Both are a minority. Most Sintans are happy with

Egeria. They even like *you*," I say with a *go figure* look that makes him chuckle outright. "Your family gives instead of takes. That's a huge change. It's unexpected."

"Are you finally warming up to Egeria?"

I shrug. "She's all right."

His eyes sparkle. "Such high praise."

"Recruit," I say, ignoring his sarcasm. "If that's not enough, we'll think of something else."

He cocks his head and looks at me with curiosity. "You have something in mind."

"I always have something in mind."

Griffin leans toward me, his voice deepening. "So do I."

His suggestive tone instantly heats me up. Despite my growing weakness, desire takes up a steady beat inside me.

"Don't tease," I admonish. "This is serious."

"Who's teasing?"

I give him a flat look. "Ipotane."

He gives me a flat look back. "Not what I had in mind."

I roll my eyes, trying to catch my breath, which takes a lot more effort than it should. "But you know what they are?"

"Magical creatures. Half-human, half-horse."

I nod, and his lips thin.

"Magical creatures aren't trustworthy," Griffin says.

"True, but there's always a way to ensnare them. It's their universal flaw."

"And you know how to ensnare a lot of Ipotane?" Griffin asks. "Enough to protect a half-dozen cities?"

"No, but I know someone who might. A Chaos Wizard in northern Fisa, just below the Frozen Lake."

A thunderstorm rolls into his eyes. "You would go back to Fisa?"

I swallow the anxiety welling in my chest. "Recruit first. We might not need the wizard or the Ipotane." I really hope not because I never want to set foot in Fisa again, and I *really* don't want that wizard spouting another prophecy at me. The first one was bad enough.

"We'll think about it," Griffin says. "Let's see how the recruiting goes first."

I would nod, but I don't seem to have the strength anymore.

The sun gets hotter and even more intense as we travel west. My dark braid absorbs the heat and burns a line down my spine. Weak and shaky and on fire, I grit my teeth and keep going. That's what I've always done. But strength and courage are in short supply, and I quickly stoop to silently begging Zeus for a storm. Nothing happens. Either he's not listening, or he doesn't think my being incredibly uncomfortable is an emergency.

Griffin hands me fruit and glowers at me until I eat, but I feel nauseous, and the heat is a constant, horrible plague. The only thing keeping me sane is the glacial shard around my neck. I push on the vial again and again, grinding it into my skin until its iciness brings some relief.

When it starts getting dark, I think Zeus heard me after all and sent a storm to cool us down. I don't realize it's my vision failing until Griffin's arm is around my waist and he's dragging me off Panotii's back.

"What are you doing?" I ask.

"You're about to fall off." He settles me onto his lap, tucking my head under his chin. "I've got you."

I know. And it scares me half to death. "Everyone will think I'm weak."

"They won't think you're weak. They know you're recovering." His deep voice sinks into me, soothing. His steady heartbeat thumps against my back. I feel like sighing, but that would be ridiculous. "My soldiers worship you. You saved me. You saved them."

"I didn't save them," I mumble. "They weren't even there."

"Under Piers's command, they would have fought to free Ios. How many lives did you spare?"

Sleepy, I scratch my forehead against his bristly jaw. "I didn't do it for them."

Griffin's arm tightens around my waist. It's almost too tight, but I don't have the energy to complain. Or maybe I just don't want to.

CHAPTER 28

"You can't trust her. She's northern. She's Fisan!" The voice is a woman's, and she's hissing like a snake.

My eyelids are so heavy I panic. I slowly slide them open, driving them up by sheer force of will. The glacial shard in my pendant pulses with magic, searing my skin with cold. It gives me the strength to turn my head enough to face the tent's wide-open door. Outside, there's a darkening sky and a canopy of leaves. Griffin is standing with a woman on the far side of a campfire.

His response is curt. "I trust her."

"You're blinded by... I don't know what. Lust? I don't understand."

He blows out a frustrated breath. "I'm not blinded by anything, Daphne."

Her. My stubbornness helps me focus enough to see them better. Daphne is much too close to Griffin, her blonde hair swaying down her back, her shapely height unmistakably a good match for his solid strength.

I want to kick her in the head. Unmistakably.

"We're good together. It's been too long." She reaches out and casually touches his arm in a way I wish I'd been doing for weeks. "I know just what you like."

Griffin immediately steps back, but my chest still feels like a Centaur kicked it. I'd love to breathe fire at her—just to scare her, not melt her or anything—but I know nothing would come out. I either lost my Dragon's Breath along with my life force, or I'm just too weak.

"She attacked me for no reason in the bathhouse," Daphne pursues, her lie igniting a fire in me that's even worse in my weakened state. "I've watched her. She's violent and unstable. With the amount of power she obviously has, she's a danger to everyone."

"Cat's…lively," Griffin says, his eyes narrowing.

Daphne snorts before scoffing, "She's insane." She closes the space he put between them. "A few months ago, I was fighting for the realm with you, battling with you during the day, staying with you at night. Every night."

Gods, it's hard to breathe. *Son of a Cyclops!* We're in the bloody outdoors, and there's no *air*!

Irritation sharpens Griffin's tone. "You were battling for the realm because that's your job. As for the rest, ambition is clouding your memory. I wasn't your first lover, and I won't be your last. No promises were spoken."

Daphne leans into him, undeterred—and apparently delusional.

Griffin grips her shoulders, stopping her. She turns partway. Even in profile, Daphne's come-hither look is a work of art, something I couldn't master in a thousand years.

He sets her away from him. "It's over, Daphne. Go back to your fire." He lets her go with a soft shove, stepping back to drive his point home. "If you bother Cat again, you won't be a part of this army anymore. Ever." Infinitely calm. Infinitely threatening. *Griffin.*

Daphne's hands curl into fists. When she speaks, her voice is so low I have to strain to hear her. "Why are you doing this? What does that dark little Fisan have that I don't?"

Griffin looks at me. He sees me watching them and doesn't look away. "My heart."

At his words, my chest contracts with a sharp spasm, squeezing the air from my lungs.

I guess Daphne can't argue with that. She leaves without another word, never once glancing at me. I wish she'd stormed away. Exploding and stomping off I can deal with. Cold, controlled rage reminds me too much of Mother.

Griffin doesn't spare her a second glance. Our eyes stay locked, and he looks so…*happy* to see me awake that I start to melt inside. Or maybe it's just that he's so handsome—tall, hard, and broad, with humor and warmth and stability in his eyes. I've never known anyone like him.

He approaches swiftly, his focus entirely on me. I shiver, anticipation making my pulse quicken.

He ducks into the tent and then crouches next to me, resting his elbows on his knees. His easy smile makes my heart skip a beat. "You're awake."

"You jilted Daphne for me?"

His smile fades. Griffin sits on the edge of the blanket I'm on, laying my head in his lap and stroking his long fingers over my scalp. The massage feels foreign, and nice, and I tingle from head to toe when he unravels my braid and spreads long strands of hair across his thighs, carefully arranging them. "She misunderstood, or wanted to see what wasn't there. I've never given a woman any indication of permanence. The day I saw you, I understood why."

Emotion roughens my voice, turning it husky and low. "Why?"

A smile pulls at the edges of his mouth. "Because you were made for me."

A thrill shoots through me. "Don't tell me you plan on keeping *me*?" I somehow manage to tease.

Goose bumps rise on my neck when Griffin winds a curl around his finger and gently tugs. His white teeth flash in the dim light. "I informed you I was keeping you shortly after we met."

"You didn't give me any choice. Stupid, bloody rope," I mutter.

His fingers stop moving in my hair. "You have a choice now. I freed you."

"You caught me," I huff. "It's very frustrating."

Griffin chuckles, sobering when I don't join in. "Why are you so limp?"

"I can't move." I pick up my hand as far as it will go— barely an inch off the ground.

He curses colorfully enough to impress even me. "Can we risk more blood?"

I shrug. Sort of. "We may have to."

Griffin carries me out of the tent and then sits me upright, propping me against his side while he slips his knife from his belt and burns it clean in the fire.

I glance at our surroundings. Campfires dot the area around us, none too close. I can't make out people in the shadows, or hear their conversations. I don't see Beta Team, Piers, or Egeria anywhere, although they can't be too far.

"Did you get my knives?" I ask. "And my sword?"

He nods, cooling the hot metal in the evening air. "Flynn has everything. I know how attached you are to your blades." Holding my arm, he rubs the sensitive skin on the inside of my wrist with the pad of his thumb. Warmth spreads through me until he replaces his thumb with the knife. "Ready?"

Not really, but Griffin doesn't wait. He cuts shallowly across the veins in my right wrist before doing the same to his left. I inhale sharply at the sting while Griffin doesn't appear to even feel it. He stacks our hands together, lacing our fingers in a way I don't think I'll ever get used to.

He looks around, frowning. "I need something to tie us together."

"Where's an enchanted rope when you need one?" I grumble.

Griffin barks a laugh. "Contrary to what you may think, I don't enjoy bondage."

I don't imagine I'd enjoy bondage much, either. So why is a place deep in my belly heating with something that feels suspiciously like interest?

Flushing, I clear my throat. "Then what do you enjoy? Apparently, Daphne knows."

Griffin's eyes glitter. "Jealous?"

"No!" I scoff.

He grins. "I'm glad I'm not the only one."

I roll my eyes. "You're delirious. From blood loss."

He squeezes my hand. "You have no reason to be jealous. I haven't touched her since the day I saw you—which was well before you saw me."

I feel my face flame. I have no idea why. If Griffin notices my awkwardness, he keeps it to himself. He unbuckles my belt one-handed, slips it from around my waist, and then circles our wrists with it, binding them closer together. The cuts are deep enough to bleed for a while, but not deep enough to be dangerous. They'll probably leave scars.

"As for what I enjoy..." Griffin leans close to finally answer, his scruffy jaw tickling my neck. "We could always give spanking a try."

I laugh. I can't help it. "I take it spanking is a metaphor again?"

"Maybe." He winks. "Maybe not."

Now I'm imagining both possibilities. Possibly both at once...

His teeth graze my earlobe, and I make a noise that sounds suspiciously like a yelp.

"Why so jumpy?" His lips press into my neck. He sucks gently on the sensitive skin below my ear before kissing the same spot.

My senses reel. Each brush of his lips is like a sip of decadent wine, turning me dizzy and light. "I'm...ah...not very experienced with all this."

He keeps nuzzling my neck, kindling a steady blaze low in my abdomen. "Ours clearly wasn't your first kiss."

I tilt my head to give him better access. Griffin's rumbling sound of approval vibrates against my throat. His splayed fingers feel like a brand on my hip. He squeezes, wringing a soft moan from me.

"Everyone kisses," I say breathlessly. "It's the rest I'm less sure about."

He abruptly straightens, looking agreeably surprised. "Never?"

I shake my head, my stomach flip-flopping.

His lips curve in an utterly male, utterly smug, utterly *possessive* smile. "I'll teach you."

My whole body clenches in anticipation. *Gods, yes! No!*

I panic and smack his chest with my unbound hand, grimacing at the ridiculously flirtatious tap. A month ago, I would have hit him hard—or at least tried to.

Griffin wraps his free hand around the back of my head and pulls me toward him for a scorching kiss. Our lips fuse, hotter than blood, and I forget all about ever wanting to hit him. Or kick him. Or even argue with him.

I'm such an idiot.

He fists his hand in my loose hair and tilts my head back until my back bows and my breasts press against his chest. Between fierce, deep kisses, he rasps, "If you had died..." He slowly shakes his head, his hot breath ragged on my fevered lips. The muscles in his shoulders tense, and a shudder runs through him. "Don't ever scare me like that again."

I draw back, stunned by the raw vulnerability in his voice. "I didn't think anything rattled you."

He skims the pad of his thumb over my bottom lip. My mouth tingles, almost too sensitive to be touched. "Not much does. Everything is different with you. I can't lose you."

His words douse the passion blazing inside me. I lower my eyes and turn away from him. *What in the Underworld am I doing?*

Griffin unbinds our wrists and reopens the cuts before strapping us back together again. I watch the red seep out and blend, wondering whose blood is tainting whose. I'm sure Mother would have an opinion about that.

I press our wrists tighter.

The more our blood mixes, the stronger I get. Griffin insists I eat, and he's almost comically happy when I swallow a few bites. My small appetite must inspire him because he forces bread and cheese on me until I nearly throw it all back up.

Raising his hands in surrender, he packs up the food. Efficient as usual, he unties us again, cleans and binds the cuts, and then dilutes any stray blood before lighting an oil lamp and putting out the campfire. He leads me back into the tent, closes the heavy flap, and then sits with his back against a sturdy wooden trunk. Setting the lamp aside, he looks at me intently. After a moment, he holds out his arm in invitation, and I go to him, hardly hesitating at all.

Once I'm settled, Griffin turns to me with a wolfish grin. "Do you think we'll need to exchange fluids every day?"

My eyes widen. *Yes!* "No!"

Oh my Gods! I'm going insane!

I clear my throat. "No. Uh…no."

"Funny," he says blandly. "I was hoping the opposite."

I shove him. "I'll bet you were."

He grins. "Still am."

Tucked up against him, I'm hotter than Hades, and my stomach is doing all kinds of somersaults. It's uncomfortable. And annoying. And exciting. "Men are strange. How can you go from fighting with me all the time to *this*?"

He looks at me with a mixture of indulgence and smugness that makes me want to sink my teeth into him somewhere that hurts. "You're the one who's always picking fights. Once I claim you, you'll see that fighting isn't the fun part."

The butterflies that colonized my belly the day I met Griffin take flight, spreading through me on burning wings. He gently pulls me onto his lap like it's the most normal thing in the realms and then trails his fingers from my throat to the tip of one breast, lightly circling my nipple through my tunic. It instantly hardens, pebbling under his fingertips.

A tremor runs through me, and I bat his hand away. "Confident, aren't you?"

He nods, completely arrogant and completely male.

I can't decide if I'm intrigued by his certainty, or disgusted by his ego. Where Griffin is concerned, I'm a mess. "And no one's claiming anyone."

"Call it what you want." He slides his hands around my waist and then down, playfully squeezing my bottom. "It doesn't change anything."

Whatever we call it, it changes everything. I wiggle in his grip, shaking my head. "*It* can't happen."

He laughs, the overconfident beast. His next kiss is both dominant and coaxing, long, deep, and completely intoxicating. "You'll change your mind."

My mind? I can't think. I can hardly breathe. "Is that a challenge?" I manage to ask. "Because I can be very stubborn."

Griffin's deft fingers find my breasts again, stroking, cupping, learning. He's not kissing me now. He's watching me with a smoldering intensity. Sizzling currents race beneath my skin. The low rumble of thunder in my veins makes my whole body quake. I lean into his touch, and he makes a noise that's gravelly and almost savage.

"This isn't a game, Cat. That's not how it works when it's real. When you want it to last." He lifts both hands to my face, keeping me from turning away from him. "When the other person means more to you than your own life."

I swallow hard as my stomach dips. Wholly unsettled, I press my lips together and don't say anything.

Griffin shifts me on his lap so I'm straddling him, my hands on his shoulders. "When I first saw you, I thought you were older, more experienced." His voice deepens, turning rougher. "I wanted to throw you over my shoulder, carry you out of the crowd, and make you mine behind the amphitheater. It would have been dark and hot, with only the sound of our panting echoing off the stones."

Heat crashes through me. I instantly see the starry sky, feel the rough stones…and Griffin's hard body.

His hands glide up my ribs, his wide palms brushing the outer swells of my breasts before sliding back down to my waist again. His glittering silver eyes turn heavy-lidded. "I wanted to push you against the wall, rip those tight pants off you, and bury myself in your heat."

My lips part as arousing, carnal, appealingly rough images flood my mind.

Griffin's fingers press into my sides. "I might have left the boots."

I suck in a quick, shallow breath as my imagination

supplies a vivid picture. The night cloaking us in darkness. My legs clinging to his waist. My back scraping the wall. Griffin's hands gripping my hips, grinding me down on him while he thrusts into me with powerful, driving strokes.

The tension inside me turns volcanic, growing molten, wanting to fracture, needing to explode. My whole body starts pulsing with a single-minded chant. *Take. Me. Take. Me. Take. Me.*

Ignoring the urgent call to join with Griffin is like cutting myself in half. "Was this before or after I turned poisonous?" I ask tartly, sounding only a little unsteady.

"*Weeks* before." He presses his lips to mine for a slow, seductive kiss. Then his mouth turns more insistent. Hungrier. "And every day after."

His words sink into me, working their way into my very foundation. Every time he kisses me, or touches me, or tells me something I secretly long to hear, I feel changed, irrevocably altered.

"And when you realized I was younger?"

Griffin's lips curve into that heart-stopping smile of his. "When you popped back into sight scrubbed clean and looking twenty years younger, I knew I'd found something special."

I grin like an idiot.

"And full of hot air."

Wait. What? I scowl, and he laughs, leaning in to capture my mouth again. He kisses me so deeply that I can't tell where he ends and I begin. Holding my hips, he rocks me forward and up, sliding me along the steely length of his arousal. I gasp, desire streaking through me. He guides me against him again, harder this time, and my blood simmers, my core muscles straining for more—more contact, more friction, more...*filling.*

My eyes drift shut. A torrent of sensation overwhelms me. "This is madness. How can madness feel so good?"

His response is guttural, unintelligible, and makes me tremble with need. I push up on my knees, sliding along his erection in an effort to ease the growing ache between my thighs. A tremor racks his solid frame. I do it again, and Griffin's fingers convulse on my hips. A groan tears from his throat.

His hands and mouth make me wild. I arch my back and press into him, hoping it'll relieve some of the mounting pressure, but my gut just tightens with longing, and the friction of our bodies makes me insatiable for more. Slick between my legs, pulsing with liquid heat, driven by a crescendo of unbridled want, I swirl my hips and scatter hot, open-mouthed kisses along his neck and jaw, flicking my tongue over his skin to taste him.

A harsh breath explodes from Griffin. He wrenches me down, grinding roughly. My breathing quickens. My knees spread until there's not a whisper of air between us, only scalding need and his burning arousal. My fingers spear into his hair. My thighs clench, clasping his hips as I rub against him, moaning his name.

Griffin shudders. Then his fingers sink into my backside, his iron grip putting an abrupt stop to my writhing. He holds me still, and I whimper a protest. Tightening nerves, spiraling sensations, throbbing heat, and a thrilling pressure low in my belly—something earth-shattering isn't far off. Thunder claps in my ears, and I get the nearly uncontrollable urge to tear off my pants.

Can't do that!

I jerk back so fast I nearly fall over. "We have to stop!"

With a low growl, Griffin grabs me and pulls me back. I land on his chest with a thud.

"Cat." His arms lock around me. He sounds tormented.

Panting, I push off his chest again and sit up, shoving hair out of my face. "Griffin!"

"Why?" he asks hoarsely. "Why do we have to stop?"

My eyes widen. "There are so many reasons I don't even know where to start!"

He rolls his hips, sending desire roaring through me. "You're sure?" he asks.

No! "Yes!"

He clasps the back of my head and kisses a searing path down my neck, each ragged breath accompanied by a rhythmic thrust of his hips. "This is what it could be like, *kardia mou.* We were made for each other. Just imagine it."

I am. I really am. My head falls back, and my whole body goes limp without ever consulting me. Just when I'm mindlessly following his tempo again, heady sensations coiling where our bodies meet, Griffin stops moving and drops his forehead to mine. He draws in a slow, labored breath, lifts me off his lap, and sets me on the ground next to him.

My jaw nearly unhinges. *What? Now?* I'm throbbing. It's delicious. It's excruciating. It's...*incomplete.* I almost crawl back on top of him and tell him to finish what he started. "You're meaner than a Cyclops."

His smile looks pained.

I scowl, making a sound of frustration.

"Was that a growl?" he asks. His chest rises and falls like he's been running for hours.

"Maybe." I throw him a dirty look.

Ignoring my crankiness, he decides that now is apparently a good time to unwrap my wrist and inspect the cut. He checks the fresh scab before binding it again with a clean cloth and then soaking the old one with water. My heart rate calming, I draw my legs up under me and sit there, fevered tension draining from me, annoyingly content to let Griffin take care of me.

"I'm going to check in with the others. I'll be back soon," he says, raising my knuckles to his lips. "Stay here and rest."

I nod, watching him dim the lamp and then leave the tent, my hand still tingling.

I miss him while he's gone, which is a rather terrifying thing to admit, even to myself. When he comes back, I'm more than ready for him to sit with me again and gather me close. He sees me still awake and waiting for him and doesn't disappoint.

"Earlier…" I clear my throat, leaning against him. "You stopped because I asked you to?"

Griffin's chin brushes the top of my head, slowly rubbing. "Yes. And because you were making enough noise to wake the entire camp."

"I was not!" I cry, outraged.

He chuckles. "That, and I was about three seconds from ripping your clothes off and sinking into you. I'm not sure you're ready for that."

Heat floods me. My heart slams against my ribs. I'm not sure I'll ever be ready for that.

"You should be stronger first."

"I told you, I can't." So I really need to stop imagining it.

"Don't delude yourself, Cat. Where do you think this is going to end up?"

His words knock the breath from my lungs. *Is he right? Are my only options to leave him or give in?*

I glance at his profile. Broad cheekbones, strong jaw, hawkish nose, everything shadowed in the faint light. He's so steady and sure, the exact opposite of me. For that alone, I never want to give him up. With every touch, every word, he shows me that life can be different from what I've always known, different enough to dull my past, and forget my future. Even the prophecy fades. Around him, I'm just a woman, not the woman who will destroy the world.

I pluck at my fresh bandage, and Griffin wraps his fingers around mine. "You'll unravel the knot," he says, keeping my hand in his.

Warmth travels from my hand straight to my heart. For Griffin, life isn't drawn in absolutes, but it's pretty black and white. He won't settle for less than what he thinks we should have, and I...I...

I don't know what to do.

He drags the flask of Fisan clover water over, opens it, and hands it to me. I drink and then hand it back.

"Good," he says, trying it for the first time. "Like cool spring mornings and sweetness."

Cool spring mornings and sweetness. *Eleni.* I take a deep breath. It shudders on the way out.

"You all right?" he asks, rubbing my back.

I nod, uncomfortable taking comfort from another human being, being cared for, sharing. Clearly, I've fallen off the deep end.

Can I go back to being alone?

I doubt Griffin would let me. He'd tie me up with his magic rope if he had to.

I smile, ducking my head to hide it. "You make me weak."

He stills. Even his breathing goes quiet. "What do you mean?"

"Don't bleed anymore. The Gods only know what my blood has done to yours."

"What's in your blood, Cat?"

I bite my lip. "Just be careful."

"You're not weak." He sounds confident. Calm. "You and me, we're strong. Together, we'll be unstoppable."

His breath stirs my hair. His chin is right there, so I scratch my forehead against the dark stubble and lay my hand on his knee. *What's one hand on the knee? Nothing, right?*

"I'll give myself up." The second I say it, I know it's true. I already did it once, with Sybaris, and that was before any of this.

His arm tenses around me so much it hurts. "What are you talking about?"

I tilt my head until our eyes meet. Even in the near darkness, Griffin's are like a storm. "Andromeda won't be coming for me anymore. If she figures this out, she'll be coming for you."

CHAPTER 29

BACK IN SINTA CITY, I'M FAWNED OVER TO A NAUSEATING extent by the women in Griffin's family. Egeria is suffocating and always trying to give me food. Nerissa wants to cure me with herbal concoctions that taste like goat cheese, and Kaia is too excitable, wanting to know every detail about everything, all the time, right away, bounce, bounce, bounce.

Anatole isn't much better. Every time he sees me he says, "Melted? You just *melted* them?"

"Like candle wax," I answer for the millionth time.

The old man looks gleeful. There's a familiar and alarming twinkle in his eyes. Ruthlessness must be hereditary—not that I had any doubt. "I wish I could have seen it."

Really? It was kind of gross.

My Dragon's Breath is hiding somewhere deep. I feel it, but I'm not strong enough to access it. Invisibility works most of the time. I'm too weak to run, ride, spar, or even throw knives, which means I'm irritable and bored. When I'm not sleeping, I test the family on their new knowledge of Sintan nobles, their backgrounds, and their magical abilities to help prepare everyone for the realm dinner. Arming them with information is crucial. Continued success can hinge on small things, or in this case, a big party.

Griffin thinks I need more blood. I won't do it. Not here. If I'm making Castle Sinta my home, I refuse to compromise it. He settles for exchanging saliva as often as possible, and his deep, hungry kisses must be working because

I'm getting better. Physically. Mentally, I'm a mess. I keep lurking in places Griffin might find me and then running away when I hear him coming. I want him more than I've ever wanted anything in my entire life, except possibly freedom from the miasma of plots, treachery, and revenge that make up court life. The problem is, I can't have both.

Thank the Gods there's Jocasta. She's normal, except when she's making me eat. Then, she's frightening. Despite Egeria's and her constant efforts, my stomach is still the size of a shriveled-up grape and tries to reject just about everything that goes in. After I almost throw up on her three times, Jocasta asks me if I'm pregnant.

My eyes pop wide open, feeling huge. "No!"

She shrugs. "I saw you kissing Griffin."

"And you think I just fell on my back?"

"He's very good-looking."

"That's no reason!"

"Don't tell me you haven't..." She waves her hands around.

Can't say it, huh? "No, we haven't..." I wave my hands around. *Can't say it either, I guess.*

"But things have changed. Anyone can see that. I don't think you've kicked Griffin at the dinner table once."

"I haven't," I say, just a little bit disgusted with myself.

"You should."

"Kick him?"

"Fall on your back."

She sounds very sure. Not that I'm planning on doing anything like that, but I'm sort of worried about the whole process, especially with someone Griffin's size. Just imagining the wall of muscle above me and his weight pressing me into the bed makes me shiver, and I'm not sure how much is anticipation and how much is trepidation. Not to mention that I've felt him hard and ready for the act. I desperately wanted him inside me at the time, but in retrospect, I'm not convinced he would fit.

"Do you just fall on your back?" I ask.

Jocasta laughs, but the sound isn't very merry. "With brothers like mine, no one comes near me."

In her case, "no one" means Flynn. "Does he know how you feel?"

She sighs, focusing on the wall. "I really don't know."

I squeeze her hand, feel weird about it, and pull my fingers back. "Marrying you would mean a different life for him. There are rules and obligations. Responsibilities."

"There are rules and obligations in any situation."

"Well, simple ones," I agree. "Right now, Flynn's are basic. Follow orders. Keep your weapons clean. Don't kill a man just because you don't like his face. Don't yank down your pants and scratch your ass."

Jocasta bursts out laughing.

I make a face. "Oh Gods. Now I'm picturing Flynn's ass."

"Me too." Her blue eyes sparkle, and I'm pretty sure she likes what her imagination has conjured up a lot more than I do.

"Flynn's a great warrior, but he's never had to be a leader. Suddenly being part of a ruling family can be intimidating." I nudge her arm. "As you know."

"And you," she answers, nudging me back.

I feel the blood wash from my face. "What do you mean?"

"Just that you're practically part of the family, and Griffin will make it official sooner or later."

My insides freeze solid. "I don't function well in families. And that's not his decision to make."

Jocasta laughs. "You fit in perfectly. We all love you, and Griffin has never been so focused, not even when he was taking over the realm. You're everything to him. More than any of this." She sweeps her hand out, indicating not just the castle, but the whole of Sinta, I think.

The ice inside me melts. Suddenly, I'm burning up and terrified, scared I'll be too weak to resist.

Scratch that—I'm petrified I've already given in.

As soon as I can cross the courtyard without my head spinning, I try to move back into the barracks. Griffin gave me his room and moved down the hall, but I can't help thinking he's planning on moving back in. Soon. With me still in the room. A few buildings between us would definitely help keep me sane.

He catches wind of my packing after dinner and arrives in my room with his eyebrows drawn down, his arms crossed, and only one word to say.

"*No?*" I repeat, incredulous.

"Do you need me to say it in sign language?"

I roll my eyes. "That won't be necessary."

"Obviously it is." He puts his hands on my hips, backs me against the wall, and then kisses me until I can't breathe. Or think. Or stand up, apparently, because I stumble when he lets go.

He steadies me, a satisfied smile curving his amazing lips.

"Don't look so smug," I say, panting. "I fall down all the time these days."

"Not when you're standing still." He drags his tunic over his head.

I stare, and he flexes.

"Show-off," I mutter.

He grins and drops the tunic over my head. "So you won't scream bloody murder," he says, backing out of the room.

His shirt falls to my knees. I punch my arms through the sleeves, make a rude hand gesture, and then slam the bedroom door.

Missing him already, I crawl into Griffin's big bed, curled up in Griffin's big shirt, and go to sleep wondering if it really matters what I do when no one can see.

With my continued guidance, the realm dinner preparations are well in hand and the royal family is irreproachable in their court etiquette and memorization of facts. As soon as I'm able, I also go back to supervising the rebuilding of the north wall. I get Flynn and Kato to help and Jocasta and Kaia to bring out picnics.

After we got back from Ios, I suggested employing some of the older children as servants in the castle. We need extra hands for the realm dinner, and in general. The castle servants from before mostly ran off during the takeover, and used to a simpler life, no one here felt the need to replace them until now. The children who were old enough jumped at the chance to make money for their families, and the Sintan royals now have adoring, loyal servants. A house full of children who love you eventually turns into a house full of adults who would defend you to the death. That's something Andromeda would never understand.

Jocasta and Kaia took them all, marching them back to the castle for a good scrubbing and their new uniforms. We replaced our missing wall builders the next day, starting again with food and fun. The new children still eat like they're starving even though their bones are no longer visible, and their faces don't look sunken or hollow. They work fast and well, always leaving us time to organize games after lunch so they won't have to work during the hottest part of the day.

Flynn doesn't interact with Jocasta beyond common courtesies, and I learn that he's known her since before she could walk, which isn't promising for what Jocasta has in mind. It's like she said, no one comes near her, and he and Kato seem more interested in impressing the children than impressing the princesses. They haul the heaviest rocks, tease the boys, show them fighting moves, and encourage them to join the army when they're older. They're strong, handsome, and fun, and the boys worship them.

If Jocasta almost never looks at Flynn, and Kaia looks too much at Kato, the men don't seem to notice. What *I* notice is that I end up the hub of this great big wheel, and without me, all the spokes would go flying. It's as bad inside the castle as it is out. If Griffin isn't around, everyone defers to me. *Me!* How in the Underworld did *that* happen? Now, I have to organize, direct, plan, and practically throw certain people together. *Gods! I hate responsibility.*

Two days before the realm dinner, the children march ahead of us on the way back to the main gate, singing a bawdy song Kato really shouldn't have taught them. Kaia is turning kalaberry red, and Jocasta is pretending not to hear.

I casually slide my foot to the side and trip her.

Jocasta lets out an oath I'm surprised she even knows and then glares up at me from the ground, her cheeks flushed pink and a dark curl bouncing over one eye. *Perfect.*

"Oh, no! You tripped on a root." I crouch down and poke her leg. "You twisted your ankle."

"No, I—"

"You can't walk," I cut her off. "Flynn, you'll have to carry her."

Jocasta snaps her mouth shut, her sapphire eyes shooting blue fire. Flynn bends down and scoops her up. She links her arms around his neck, blushing furiously.

Ha! That was easy enough. I grab Kato and pull him ahead.

"Don't hold hands with me. If Griffin sees, he'll have me dismembered."

I roll my eyes. "I'm not holding your hand. I'm dragging you away."

"Why?"

"I'll explain when you're older."

He grins. "Don't get your hopes up. She shouldn't, either."

"Why? She's beautiful."

"Beauty isn't the problem. It's rank."

"I'm a nobody from the circus, and Griffin still wants me."

Kato scoffs. "A nobody?"

"You look like Adonis," I say, rolling right over his skepticism. "I'm surprised it's not you she wants."

"I'm saving myself for Kaia," he answers with a perfectly straight face.

I snort a laugh.

"Jocasta is *good*," Kato says. "Flynn is *good*."

"And you're not?"

His broad shoulders lift in a shrug. "Flynn carried her home after she fell out of a tree when she was six or seven. There's no competing with that."

No, I suppose not.

"How's the sleeping?" he asks.

"I miss you patting my head." I mean to sound flippant, but I don't.

He glances at me, suddenly serious. "Nightmares?"

I shake my head.

"Because you're sleeping with Griffin?"

"I am *not* sleeping with Griffin! I'm sleeping in his room." In his tunic. In his bed… "It's completely different."

Kato's eyebrows creep up. "I see."

He drags the word out. It's annoying, so I shove him, but he doesn't even react. No playful tussle. No quick grappling. No *fun*.

Frustrated, I cry, "I'm not made of glass!"

His arm shoots out. He pushes me, and I careen off to the side, nearly falling over.

Kato gives me a significant look. "I'll wrestle you to the ground when you can handle it."

Scowling, I glance back at Flynn and Jocasta as I stumble onto the path again. She's stiff, and he's staring straight ahead. "What's wrong with those two? They could at least try."

"I'll pretend I didn't hear that," Kato says.

"Why?"

He gives my hair an affectionate ruffle. "Because I'm wondering the same thing about you."

I should have known Griffin wouldn't wait forever. After dinner, and a long time going over all our strategies to win support at the realm dinner, he doesn't leave me outside the bedroom as usual. He follows me in, shutting the door with a decisive click.

"What are you doing?" I back up, keeping an eye on him.

He takes two steps, cups my face in his hands, and kisses me ravenously. "I want you. I need you. For as many hours as possible, I don't want to think about anything but you."

My heart gives a desperate lurch. Griffin pulls me into his arms and kisses a scorching line along my jaw and down my neck, gently scraping his teeth over my hammering pulse.

"You need a lot of things," I say, already breathless. "Like a Dragon. That doesn't mean you'll get one."

"I don't give a Centaur's balls about a Dragon right now."

"Griffin! Language!"

"Are you trying to sound like my mother?" he growls against my neck.

"Is it like a bucket of ice?"

He picks me up and tosses me onto the bed. "What do you think?"

I land with an undignified grunt. I think not.

He crawls on top of me, pins my arms above my head, and plants his mouth on my breast, sucking my nipple right through my dress. I yelp and twist, pleasure exploding under his mouth. Desire arcs through me. I pull on my hands, wanting to touch him, but Griffin's grip tightens as he uses his teeth to pull down the neckline of my gown. My breasts pop out, pushed up like an offering. We both stare at the bare skin, at the dark peaks. Then he dips his head and licks one nipple. Heat rushes to my belly. He swirls his tongue over the taut bud before turning to the other side and sucking hard enough to lift me off the bed. I gasp, the drag of his mouth stirring an aching pull deep inside me.

I arch toward him, already damp with arousal. His erection presses against the most intimate part of me, sparking hot jolts of sensation every time he moves. He sucks, licks, and rocks while I writhe under him, my trapped hands curling into fists. Mindlessness sets in, feeling driving away thought.

Griffin lifts his head and lets go of my wrists. His callused fingers slide down my arms, adding a thrilling roughness to his unhurried touch. I tangle my fingers in his hair, powerless against the brewing storm and the heat and tension building between us. I wrap my legs around his hips because this fully clothed, grinding closeness isn't nearly close enough. I long for him. I want him filling the empty, throbbing place between my thighs.

His lips find mine again, kissing me deeply. "You want me," he rasps against my mouth. "I feel it in your body. Hear it in your breath."

Emotion overwhelms me. His words are so intimate. And true. His hips press down on mine. Most of his weight is on his forearms, his biceps a steely cage. I touch his shoulders, feeling tension there. "It doesn't matter what I want."

"This is right," he argues. "I know it."

His kisses turn feverish, his tongue demanding. His tunic drags over my sensitized nipples, and it's all I can do not to rip it off him in order to feel his bare skin on mine. I slip my hands under the fabric, smoothing my palms over his broad back. His skin is like sun-warmed marble, and there's a delectable dip in the muscle along his spine. I trace the indent with my fingertips, marveling at the sheer physical power above me.

Griffin drops his forehead to mine. "You're going to have to be a lot more convincing if you want me to stop."

I try to quiet my breathing. "I have to convince myself first."

"Don't," he urges. "We're fated. You must know that."

My throat tightens, starting to ache. "I can't do this."

"Why?" His question is a growl.

I have so many reasons, so many fears. "She'll come after our children."

He lifts his head. "I'll protect them. I'll protect you." He frowns. "*You'll* protect them, and I don't see much of anything getting past you."

A sudden sting hits the back of my eyes. "She'll use them to get to me. She'll use you." A fierce protectiveness surges through me. I don't even have kids, and I'm ready to sacrifice anything for them.

Griffin holds my face in his hands. His thumbs sweep across my cheeks. "I can take care of myself, and we don't even have children, at least not yet. And she doesn't need to know if we do. How would she even know?"

I laugh. It's a little shaky. "You think I won't bleed? It's already challenging enough just getting rid of—" I blush until even my ears burn. "Monthly…stuff."

His brow knits. At least he's taking me seriously. "If it comes to that, we'll go somewhere else and then come back with the baby." He kisses me quick and hard, trying to reassure me.

"But kids bleed all the time—scraped knees, busted lips. Their blood will be my blood. She'll know. She'll take them."

"Some people don't even have children," Griffin says. "It just doesn't happen."

I shake my head. "I can't count on that."

His mouth flattens, making his jaw muscles bulge. "There are methods. Herbs. Sheaths. I could pull out."

In my inexperience, those things hadn't occurred to me, but I know what Griffin means. Irrational disappointment washes through me. It's ridiculous, and dangerous, but I can already see little dark heads running around the castle, tiny Griffins with black hair, aquiline noses, wide mouths, and green, Fisan eyes. They're tugging on Egeria's skirts, playing games with Kaia, climbing all over Flynn and Kato, and getting medicated into stupors by Nerissa's herbs.

"Live your life," Griffin says. "For yourself. For me. We'll deal with Andromeda when we have to."

I look up at him, a battle raging between my heart and my head. I finally close my eyes against the heat in Griffin's gaze. I feel him sit up, kneeling between my thighs. He's going to leave me, and I desperately want to pull him back.

His fingers graze my exposed breasts, sending shivers through me. Then I hear a colossal rip, and my eyes fly open.

"That was my realm dinner dress!" I only wore it tonight to make sure it didn't need any final alterations before the party. I had it specifically made to fit my new stick figure, and he tore it clean in half!

"I'll take you to the agora tomorrow."

"You don't have time for that!"

"I'll make time." His voice rough, his eyes devour me as his fingers feather down my flat stomach and over the now-rather-bony flare of my hips. Disquiet and desire quiver in my belly in equal measures. My skin heats to his touch.

Griffin slowly and deliberately unhooks my shoulder straps, freeing my arms from the destroyed dress. I think he's waiting for me to protest. When I don't, he gets a fierce look on his face and pulls me up so that I'm kneeling in front of him. Every caress is like a lick of flame on my naked body—my shoulders, my back, my hips, and my bottom, which he squeezes hard, pulling me against him. His lips part on a low, hoarse sound, and then his hands move back up my front, palming my breasts and gently abrading my nipples.

"Harder," I moan, needing his hands to ease the growing turmoil inside me. I want him everywhere. I burn for him in places he hasn't even touched.

He rolls my nipples between his fingers and then pinches them with just enough force to spark a delicious ache. My breathing accelerates. My eyes flutter closed as he kisses my neck, lingering where I'm most sensitive. He nips and sucks, and the wings inside my chest unfold and beat to a familiar rhythm that's become a part of me. A part of us.

Griffin's mouth moves back to mine, hungry. I dive into the kiss, sliding my hands under his tunic and up the wide expanse of his chest, finally giving in to the need to touch him, to learn his body, to know every intimate dip and steely curve.

While I'm exploring, he breaks the kiss and slowly unravels my braid, spreading my hair around my shoulders. He rubs a dark curl between his fingertips, and my heart thuds against my ribs. He looks at me like he might not be able to breathe without me—like maybe he wouldn't even want to. I suddenly feel the weight of the world on my shoulders like never before.

It's too much.

When I ran, I didn't just run from my family; I ran from responsibility. The day Griffin came into my life, it came back—him, Beta Team, his family, the realm itself...

I don't want this.

I don't want this.

One more time and I might convince myself...

"Take off my tunic," Griffin orders gruffly.

My pulse surges in my ears, whooshing like a cyclone. *I'm so close. So close to...making myself more vulnerable than ever?*

Bitterness sweeps through me. I close my eyes. My hands fall to my sides. I can't do this. I can't dig Griffin's grave.

A stormy ocean rages to life behind my closed eyelids. Lightning bolts split the sky. Ragged, blinding trails of light reflect off chaotic waves as an enormous, dark trident rises from the depths, cascading foaming seawater and Olympian power.

I almost gasp out loud. *"Now? Really?"*

"You reject our gift!" Poseidon's voice is an angry tempest in my head.

"Griffin? A gift from the Gods? I'd better not tell him that, or I'll be hearing about it for the rest of my days."

"We gave him to you!" my God Father explodes. He's mighty and terrifying. He doesn't appreciate my humor.

"Why?"

Poseidon gives me the same answer he gave before. *"Healing."*

"I don't know what that means!"

The storm vanishes along with the trident, the lightning, and the waves.

The husky rumble of Griffin's voice brings me back to the room. *"Agapi mou?"*

His love. I open my eyes. The man before me fills my vision. He fills my heart.

Griffin's jaw is set sternly. He gives me that hard stare of his. "Stop questioning. Just take off my shirt."

If I undress him, am I giving my consent? I think so, and I'm petrified, but I do it anyway. Andromeda took my childhood. She took my dog. She took my nurse. She took my sister. She probably even took a chunk of my sanity. I won't let her deprive me of Griffin and a family of my own—a happy one, if I can help it. And for some reason, the Gods want us to join. Poseidon couldn't have been clearer. I've never gone against his wishes. It would be really stupid to start *now*.

I take a deep breath and pull off Griffin's tunic. He somehow manages to look relieved and alarmingly intense at the same time.

I swallow, nervous. "I might not live up to your expectations."

He takes my hands and puts them back on his chest, my palms flat. His skin is hot and smooth over chiseled muscle. "I doubt that."

I flush at his gravelly tone and slide my hands over his torso, my fingers bumping over the hard ridges of his abdomen. He groans even though I haven't really done anything, the sound a raw mix of need and strained control. My heartbeat turns erratic, pounding with fear, excitement, and want. I lean forward and kiss him. The tips of my breasts sway against his chest, and my nipples stiffen.

Griffin's hands clamp around my waist. He lifts me into him to deepen the kiss, and I wrap one hand around his neck and slip the other downward. My nails brush his erection through his clothes, and it jumps in response, surprising me. A nervous flutter ricochets around my belly. I want to touch him, please him. I tug open his pants, take him in my hand, and cautiously squeeze.

A harsh breath explodes across my cheek. Griffin goes still, seeming to forget he was kissing me. I glance down at his arousal. The skin is soft, but he's steely hard. It's a rather amazing contradiction. I carefully run my hand up and down his thick length, marveling at my discovery. I do it again, this time brushing my thumb over the blunt tip and feeling a bead of moisture there.

Griffin tenses. He backs away and then removes the rest of his clothing with his typical speed. When he's done, his enormous erection juts out at me. It's hard not to be intimidated by it. I can't stop staring.

I lick my suddenly dry lips. "I don't think this is going to work."

"It'll work."

His smoldering gaze travels over me. I'm kneeling naked on the bed, my hair loose, my skin flushed, and my nipples hard. I stop breathing as I look at him, taking in his trim waist, hard thighs, and crisp hair. I reach out and trace the ridge of muscle making an indent near his hip.

Griffin's eyes blaze, and he topples me over with a hearty push. I fall back, confused, and then squeak when he grabs me behind the knees and drags me to the edge of the bed. Before I have any idea what he's doing, he kneels on the floor and lowers his mouth between my legs.

"Griffin!" I jump, but his hands are on my hips, holding me down.

"Relax." His voice vibrates against me. Through me. His tongue sweeps up, parting my folds and hitting my sensitive nerve endings. My eyes go wide as the most incredible sensation spirals around my body. Then he sucks, sending a sharp burst of pleasure through me. Light flashes. Thunder rattles the bed. My mouth drops open, and my head falls back. I moan, my knees spreading wide.

"That's it, *agapi mou*. Just like that." He licks, flicks, and sucks, driving me wild. Tension coils under his mouth, tightening in my core. I pant and buck, curling my fingers into his dark hair, and then mindlessly gripping the rumpled sheets. While I thrash, Griffin slips a finger inside me, slowly stroking. I gasp, overwhelmed, and yet wanting more. A second finger joins the first, stretching me and sliding into a rhythm that threatens to undo me. Tingles and jolts rush up and down the length of my body, almost painfully intense. I writhe on his hand, under his mouth, trying to relieve the pressure.

"Griffin. Griffin! It's too much." He has to stop. I want. I ache. I'm unraveling, and I don't know what to do.

"Let go, *kardia mou*. It's all right."

With another long, swirling sweep of his tongue, I

shatter. The climax is explosive. It shakes me like an earthquake, throwing me off balance and straight into an abyss of pure pleasure. I tumble over the edge, shuddering with wave after wave of pulsing ecstasy. I don't do anything ridiculous like scream. It's worse. I mewl like a kitten and moan, "Oh my Gods" over and over again.

As the ripples subside, slowly fading, I open unfocused eyes, pretty sure that was the best natural disaster ever to hit the realms.

Still gripping my hips, Griffin sets his mouth on me again, sending an aftershock through me that makes my entire body curl in pleasure. I mewl—again—and he looks up, grinning.

My breath shudders. "Don't look so smug."

"Why not?" He stands up, towering over me.

My eyes automatically dip to his arousal. I scramble back, shaking off some of my stupor. "It wasn't *that* good," I lie through my teeth.

He laughs and crawls on top of me. "Then it's a good thing there's more to come."

He settles heavily between my thighs, his hips spreading my legs apart. Anxiety hits me again, and I push on my heels, scooting back.

Griffin's head jerks up. His hand lands on my stomach, pressing down. Holding my gaze, he moves forward again, repositioning himself without going farther. He waits. I could kick, punch, scream, bite, or just plain get up and walk away.

The strain in his face tells me how much he wants me. His restraint tells me how much he cares. I look into his storm-cloud eyes, and I can't resist. I angle my hips up until his hot tip presses against my core.

He slowly exhales. His eyes close and then open again.

He slides forward, pushing gradually inside. His thickness stretches me with an uncomfortable pressure. My nostrils flare, and I tense. The stretch turns into a burn.

Griffin stops, waiting for me to adjust. "Relax." He kisses me between labored breaths. "It'll get better."

He wants me to relax, but he doesn't sound relaxed at all. Perspiration dots his brow. It's one of the few times I've seen him sweat. He's right, though. It does get better—until he moves again.

Griffin braces his weight on his forearms, his muscles tense and bulging. Every so often, a tremor runs through him. His face is drawn in rigid lines. He doesn't look like he's enjoying this part any more than I am, so I turn my head and kiss the inside of his arm, inhaling his unique blend of salt, sunshine, and citrus.

He thrusts into me while I'm distracted, and I gasp, the last barrier between us broken.

Griffin drops his head into the curve of my neck. The sound that hisses between his teeth makes me wonder if he's in pain. I know I am.

He stays still, buried deep. Then his mouth finds mine again, kissing me until my body molds to his. I eventually find myself wiggling, relaying my renewed interest, and Griffin answers with a slow, controlled thrust that generates a breathtaking friction. When I moan, he presses deeper, stretching me farther. My knees come up as he rocks above me. The desire that faded with the discomfort ignites again in an instant.

Griffin's groan heats my lips. Our breath mingles, carrying short pants and sounds of pleasure. His steady rhythm and long, deep strokes drive me to the edge of reason. My body coils tight, straining for release. I wrap my arms around his neck and kiss him with all the passion of the

Furies. My hips rise to meet his, and he grinds down on me, hitting sensitized, throbbing nerves.

I cry out, tension gathering in my core. I pulse around him, on the verge of shattering again.

Just when I'm almost there, Griffin stops moving and traps my face between his hands, capturing my eyes with his. His voice drops to a low, fierce growl. "I claim you." He draws back and then thrusts hard, filling me completely. "I claim you."

Even as I burn for release, my heart nearly bursts. I understand this southern rite now. He's not so much declaring possession of me as asserting my right to *him*. Forever.

I nod and touch his cheek, accepting his gift of devotion and protection. Griffin's eyes flare a heated silver. He drops his mouth to mine for a bruising kiss before driving into me, faster, harder. The sensations inside me build to an unbearable level. I throw my legs around his waist and sink my fingers into his back, meeting his almost brutal thrusts with a wildness of my own.

Griffin slips a hand under me and slams me up at a new angle, pounding deep into my core. I convulse with a shout, mewling all over again. A bright light flashes from me, and thunder rolls through the room. Griffin stills, seeing and hearing it, too, and breathing hard while I pulse around him. Explosive pleasure radiates from my center in hot, throbbing beats. His splayed fingers tighten on my bottom, and he grinds our bodies together, his sudden roughness taking my climax to a devastating level. The orgasm spills through me again, agonizingly sweet.

Panting, dazed, deliciously fragmented, I slowly come back to myself and open my eyes. I feel deconstructed to my most basic components. Realigned.

Griffin cradles my head in his hands. "Should I pull out?"

I don't answer. I don't know.

"Cat! Tell me now."

I open my mouth to say yes. The exact opposite pops out. "No."

The sound he utters is rough and guttural—satisfaction on the most primal level. Griffin wraps his arms around me and pumps his hips rapidly, at last thrusting into me with a harsh groan. His release is a hot tide. His ragged breath warms my face as he holds himself rigidly above me. With a final shudder, his whole body relaxes, settling onto mine.

After a moment of absolute stillness, he trails his lips across my cheek to my mouth, kissing me and whispering gruff praise. I flush and grin like an idiot while his lips slide down my neck and chest. He rests his forehead on my shoulder, and I feel him smile against my skin.

I stroke his midnight hair, completely at ease for the first time in my life. I smile, too, until a strange, invigorating sensation sweeps through me. Griffin's liquid warmth doesn't stop at my core. It spreads to my limbs, my head, my fingers, and toes. I take a deep, surprised breath and feel like myself for the first time since Ios.

"You fixed me!" I say, laughing.

Griffin lifts his head. "Hmm?"

"I think you just gave me my life force back."

He grins, looking way too smug, as usual. "I knew we should have been doing this for days."

I'm not about to admit he's right. I groan, pushing on his shoulders. "You're as heavy as an ox."

He chuckles and lifts some of his weight off me. Instead of moving over, though, he strokes me again—inside. "Maybe you need more life force."

I roll my eyes. "Put a leash on your hips, Beta Sinta. I need to recover."

He stops moving instantly. "Was I too rough?"

I shake my head. "No. You were"—amazing, mind-blowing, better than anything I ever imagined—"fine."

He grins and kisses me. "High praise, coming from you. I'll let those high-pitched kitten noises speak for themselves."

"You do that," I mutter, shoving him off me.

Griffin rolls to the side, withdrawing from me and making me shiver. He gets up and goes to the washbasin to dampen a cloth in the cool water. Despite my rather violent protest, he washes between my thighs before wiping himself clean. There's some blood on us. Not much, but enough to concern us both. There's a spot on the sheet, too, along with a Cat-shaped scorch mark that neither of us comments on. I'm going to have to figure out this new thunder-and-lightning thing soon. Thank the Gods I can't hurt Griffin with magic since I don't seem to have any control over it, and he *definitely* brings it out in me.

After throwing his clothes back on, Griffin takes the sheet, the cloth, and the basin out of the room to burn my blood in the kitchen fires and dilute the water in the castle sewers.

While he's gone, I find a new sheet at the bottom of the bedroom wardrobe and put it on the bed. Ten minutes later, Griffin strips naked again and then sinks onto the mattress, pulling me against him, my back to his front. Within seconds, he's hard and ready again. He pushes my hair aside and starts nuzzling my neck, his breath coming faster and warming my skin.

"Tempting," I say, wiggling my bare bottom against him.

"You're playing with fire," he growls in my ear.

"Speaking of fire..." I face up and exhale Dragon's Breath, leaving the ceiling charred. "It's back!"

"Good." Griffin splays his big hand over my stomach. "You never know when you'll need to melt someone."

CHAPTER 30

I WAKE UP WAY TOO HOT. IT DOESN'T TAKE LONG TO figure out why. There's a naked warlord plastered to my back. I inch forward, trying to get away without waking him.

A steely arm bands around my waist, dragging me back. "Where do you think you're going?"

There's no trace of sleep in Griffin's voice. He's been awake for a while, holding me. My heart lurches, and I feel the intense need to run.

He rolls me to face him and looks at me like he wants me again, like all he wants is me. His eyes are shadowed pools I could lose myself in, completely and forever. My heart swells until a tangled mass of emotion clogs my throat, choking me.

I panic, turn invisible, and scramble off the bed.

"Cat?" Griffin grabs blindly at where I just was. Frowning, he sits up, throwing the sheet back.

I freeze, staring at him. I can't help it. He's naked and magnificent, every muscle hard and defined, lean and powerful. Heat sweeps through me, my insides tightening with the knowledge of what his body can do to mine. My mouth waters to taste his smooth, sun-kissed skin again. My fingers ache to touch him. Instead, I pad across the room on silent feet, ignoring the increasingly ferocious scowl on Griffin's face. Picking up some clothes I left lying around, I move quickly and as quietly as possible because he's stalking me now—him and his rampant erection. The second I have my boots in my hand, I throw open the door and run.

"Cat!" Griffin lunges at air, his bellow echoing off the marble walls. "I should put a bell on you!"

My heart hammering, I run to my old room in the barracks, dress, and then come out as if I'd been there all night. I try not to walk crooked. Maybe Griffin was a little rough? Or maybe this is how I'm supposed to feel—tender and a bit slippery. Regardless, as soon as the adrenaline of running away wears off, a dull soreness sets in.

I find Flynn and Kato in the refectory. They greet me with raised eyebrows since I haven't had breakfast with them in a while.

"No food in the castle?" Kato asks.

"Food's better here," I say, sitting gingerly.

Flynn hands me his juice, which he never drinks. "Fight with Griffin?"

I choke on the sip I was taking. "Not exactly."

"You've got rosy cheeks this morning." Flynn's forehead creases as he studies me a little too hard. He means I'm blushing kalaberry red.

"And a suck mark on your neck," Kato adds, leaning in for a better look.

I shove his chin, pushing him back. "Don't mess with me. I can punch again now, and it might actually hurt."

Kato looks intrigued. "How did that happen?"

"Don't ask. *Please*, don't ask."

He grins, and I'm pretty sure I turn even redder. I get hotter, anyway.

"How's Griffin?" Flynn asks.

I roll my eyes. "How should I know?"

They burst out laughing, and I scowl. "Fine. Smug and self-satisfied, as usual."

"Should he be?" Kato's still grinning. He's wiggling his

eyebrows now, too. I consider burning them off, but I don't want to accidentally blind him.

"That's none of your business. Who knew that men were such nosy gossips?" I press my pendant into my chest, glad I have a piece of the Ice Plains to keep me from spontaneously combusting.

Flynn holds out his spice cake. My stomach instantly growls loud enough to be heard three tables over. I'm hungry again!

"That's yours," I say, staring at it.

He shrugs. "I don't need it, and you need to fatten back up."

Fatten *back* up? I'm not sure how to feel about that. I take the cake, though.

"Since you probably can't ride today, or even walk, what should we do?" Kato asks.

Coughing, I blow spice cake crumbs all over the table. "Excuse me?"

"It's just that Griffin isn't, er…"

I narrow my eyes at him, and Kato actually turns pink. *Ha!*

"Known for his gentle nature," Flynn provides.

"And how many women know *that*?" The snap in my voice sends their eyebrows bouncing up.

Kato grins again, obviously enjoying my reaction. "Enough for him to know how to please the woman he wants to claim."

He's had plenty of practice, then. Lovely. But they're wrong. Griffin was careful with me. Or maybe I wouldn't know gentle if it bit me in the ass.

"So, can you walk?" Flynn asks.

I resist the urge to roast them both alive. "I got here, didn't I? We're not talking about this anymore. Ever. I have some unexpected last-minute shopping to do for the realm dinner, and you two are taking me to the agora." I look back and forth between them, giving them my frostiest stare. "And we'll walk, not ride." There's no way I'm getting on a horse today, even one as good-natured as Panotii.

They make noises that sound suspiciously like man giggles.

Griffin strides into the refectory, sword strapped on, boots clomping, and spitting mad. *Uh-oh.*

He marches straight to our table, hooks his foot around the leg of my chair, pulls it out with a screech of wood on stone, and then drags me up with a biting grip on my upper arms. My heart starts galloping like a herd of Centaurs. I have to tilt my head back to look at him.

"Don't disappear on me, Cat. *Don't.*" He drops me back into my chair, and I land on everything that's sore. "We're going to the agora. Now."

I take a slow breath through my nose, refusing to shift on my seat to find a more comfortable position. "The realm dinner is tomorrow. You have other things to do."

"I told you I'd take you."

"I'll go with Flynn and Kato. We'll take the girls."

A muscle feathers along his jaw. I look at him, my expression open and honest. Last night, I altered the course of my entire existence. Adjustments like this don't come easily for me. I need time. He must know I need time.

Griffin exhales loudly and then nods. "Be back in two hours, or I'm sending the army after you."

"Three," I say. "I'll need to be fitted for a dress, if you'll recall."

His nostrils flare. So do his eyes, but not with anger, and heat whips through me. He nods again and then drops a bag of coins onto the table.

Jocasta, Kaia, and I walk ahead. Flynn and Kato trail a few steps behind. We make our way through winding streets lined with whitewashed homes shaded by overhanging roofs, deep-set windows, and cypress and citrus trees. The cooler, rainy season is approaching, but for now the air is still sunny and dry. Sinta City glows on days like this, but now its radiance is reflected in the faces around us. There are practically no beggar children since most of them are employed at one or another of Piers's building projects, and the invalids and aging soldiers who used to line the streets sweating in the sun with their hands stretched out for coppers are now somewhere in the shade. Griffin started distributing pensions, even to the people who fought against him. *Go figure.*

I worried that between cutting taxes and giving away money, he might not have the funds to recruit soldiers, but he said the ex-royals had hoarded enough riches to stop all taxing for a generation if he wants to. I stopped arguing, wondering about the state of Fisa's finances for the first time in years.

Everywhere in Sinta City, faces are fuller, eyes friendlier. People have more coins in their purses, and the agora is bustling. We walk past the food stalls first, attracting a good deal of attention. The smells of baking bread and roasting meat make my stomach rumble, so I buy a honey-coated bun and eat it while we walk.

Everyone wants to touch the princesses, just a pat on the hand or a flutter of fingers across a shoulder. Just watching all the contact makes me want to crawl out of my skin, but the girls don't seem to mind. They find a gracious word for everyone. When an old woman with a rickety wagon wants to sell us lemons, I buy ten, not because I need ten lemons, but because she bows low and long to Jocasta and Kaia even though her joints look swollen.

The agora is a kaleidoscope of noises, scents, and colors. I've been here many times, but I've never seen it like this. Vendors smile and laugh, rush out to greet us, and press gifts into the princesses' hands. I buy all the new clothes I've been needing and two squares of yellow soap that smell like citrus. No one lets me pay full price for anything.

I was wary about taking the girls out with only Flynn, Kato, and me for protection. Not that the three of us are anything to scoff at, but still, it didn't seem entirely wise even with the new royals' overwhelming popularity among the Sintan majority. Street children have their fingers in a lot of pies, though, and what goes on at the north wall must have made the rounds of the city because it turns out we didn't need Kato and Flynn, except to carry packages. Jocasta, Kaia, and even I appear to be universally adored. After weaving through the outdoor marketplace at an agonizingly slow pace, it's clear that if anyone in Sinta City is stupid enough to even look at one of us wrong, they'll be shredded by an angry mob.

When we finally wind our way up the hill toward the more exclusive shops, it's with just enough time left before Griffin sends the army looking for me. I choose a discreet, intimate-looking establishment, and after a quick glance through the selection of ready-made dresses, I decide on an ivory gown with gold trim, finding high-heeled sandals, a geometric-patterned gold belt, and matching shoulder clasps to go with it. I try everything on, and while the seamstress is making final adjustments to the hem, the merchant, who's handsome and young and showing a particular interest in Jocasta, convinces me to buy a length of braided gold rope to dress my hair.

Satisfied with my purchases and once again in my tunic and pants, I emerge from the back room to find Jocasta having trouble unhooking a necklace she tried on. The merchant goes to her at once, eager to help, but the second his fingers touch her skin, Flynn shoots like a lightning bolt from the shadows where he and Kato were hiding from all the shopping. With a growl, he yanks the man back hard enough to toss him halfway across the room. Jovial Flynn suddenly looks rabid.

Kaia snorts and then sucks the sound back in, making for an interesting combination.

Jocasta's eyes jump to Flynn's, tense and grateful. I could swear Flynn's color rises. He tries to back away, but she holds her hair to one side, and he has little choice but to help her with the necklace himself.

It's a somewhat awkward walk home, mostly because Flynn and Jocasta act like they can't see each other even though they're never more than five feet apart. Griffin is in the Athena courtyard when we arrive. He looks at the sundial, turns on his heel, and goes back inside. Five minutes to spare.

"Let's meet back here in one hour," Flynn suggests. "We'll take lunch to the kids at the north wall." He's not looking at me. He's finally looking at Jocasta.

She nods, and we go our separate ways.

"That's a lot of lemons," Griffin says, following me into the bedroom after dinner.

I found a bowl earlier and put the lemons on the table, using them for decoration instead of handing them over to the kitchens. "The old lady selling them bowed to your sisters, so I bought her lemons."

"*All* of them?"

I throw him a dirty look. "No, not *all* of them."

He comes up behind me and wraps his arms around my waist, resting his chin on the top of my head. His earlier irritation seems to be forgotten. I feel more settled, too.

"You're not nearly as mean as you pretend to be," Griffin says.

"Oh, I'm mean," I assure him.

He chuckles. "My apologies. I believe you."

"Everyone loves them." I sigh. "They love you all."

"It seems so." He sounds pleased, and a little proud.

"It's revolting." We both know I don't mean it.

"Let's hope Magoi are as easy to win over as Hoi Polloi."

"Don't count on it, but if anyone is capable of conquering with charisma and ideas as well as force, it's you. You have the people. Get the nobles, and most Magoi will follow. Sinta will be locked down."

He rubs his jaw over my hair and then inhales deeply, as if enjoying the scent he stirs up. "With Sinta definitively stable, we can focus on the next step."

My gut tightens with worry. Is he talking about increasing Sinta's defenses and implementing the projects he and Egeria have cooked up, or something else? Something far more dangerous? I don't want to know. Not tonight. Maybe not ever.

Eager to change the subject, I wiggle out of his arms, sift through my purchases, and then shove the soap at him. "This is for you."

He looks surprised. "You got me something?"

I roll my eyes. "It's just soap. And you paid for it."

"No, you did. I keep forgetting to give you your wages, so I just gave you everything at once."

"Oh, well, we've been busy dying, and healing, and… everything else."

A smile tugs at his full mouth. "Everything else?" His voice turns gruff. He seems very interested in the *everything else* part. "Are you sore?"

A fiery blush paints me from top to bottom, but I shake my head. "It's better now."

"Good." Closing the small distance between us, he wraps his arms around my waist and lifts me up, kissing me deeply. "You know what they say about Ares and Aphrodite?"

I twine my arms around his neck. My feet dangle above the floor. He's strong and broad, and I cling willingly to his warmth. Our lips and tongues begin to dance, and the awareness I always feel around Griffin explodes into fierce, bone-deep desire.

"Cat?" he murmurs against my mouth.

"Hmm?"

"Ares and Aphrodite."

I'm more interested in kissing. Griffin lets my feet touch the ground again so he can slide his hands over the curve of my bottom and pull me tightly against him. His arousal presses into my belly, and an ache blossoms between my thighs.

"She's drawn to his violent nature," I finally say, breathless.

He chuckles, trailing kisses down my neck and unbuckling my belt at the same time. "That, too. But I was thinking of something else. She's so beautiful, so coveted, that she can have anyone, and yet she returns to him time and again, even though he's despised by the other Gods. He binds her to him. She can't live without his touch."

I frown. "You don't have to bind me to you with sex."

Griffin picks me up and carries me to the bed, lying down next to me. "I'll bind you to me in any way I can. Sex. Children. Love."

My heart jerks. My lungs suddenly feel too tight. "We're together. Isn't that enough?"

He shakes his head. He undresses me, and I let him. "You're bright like a star. You shine for me now, but the sky turns. Where will you shine tomorrow? Or the day after? I won't let you go, not without a fight that would make Gods tremble."

I shiver, rattled by his words. "You'll regret pledging yourself to me. It will cut your life short."

"You're my life now. We'll live together, or die trying."

I shiver again, the chills both hot and cold. "You've decided, then? For both of us?"

He nods, smoothing his hand down my naked body. His warm fingers come tantalizingly close to where I'm already slick with want.

I shift restlessly. "I should have a say."

He dips his head and teases my breast with his mouth while his hand inches toward the curls between my thighs. "Then tell me what you want."

I moan when his finger slides between my folds, gently rubbing. What I say now will have consequences. Words are binding, each one a promise, or a betrayal. He slips a finger inside me, his hot, wide palm putting pressure on my sensitive nub of nerves. I lift my hips and forget all about talking.

"*Agapi mou?*"

Tension builds quickly inside me. My pulse is a liquid beat, throbbing between my legs. One finger turns into two, thrusting firmly. I tilt my head back and grip the sheets. "I can't think when you're touching me."

Griffin stops and looks up from my damp nipple. "What do *you* want?"

I want him to go back to touching me so desperately

that I might say anything. Luckily, I'm not that stupid. Or rather, I was stupid before. "In case you missed it, I pledged myself to you last night when I accepted your claim and let you spill your life force inside me."

He doesn't rise to my baiting tone. "Live together, or die trying?"

It takes a moment to get the words out. I'm worried about Griffin, and the dying part. "Live together, or die trying."

Griffin's shoulders relax. He kisses me long and deep, his sword-toughened fingers wonderfully rough against the inside of my thigh. I slip my hands under his tunic and hold him close, pressing my face into his neck and inhaling his subtle, masculine scent.

I kiss his jaw. It's official—I am an idiot. At least there are two of us now. "Be my Ares and finish what you started. Otherwise, I might just kill you and all of this pledging will be irrelevant."

He grins. I think he's going to touch me again, but he doesn't. He drags his mouth down my body instead. I know where he's going, and I can't wait. He nips my hip and then my thigh, nudging my legs apart. Then his mouth begins a slow, delicious torture, his hands holding me steady while I come undone. He takes his time, tasting, teasing, exploring what makes me buck, and finally wringing a staggering release from me, leaving me panting, satiated, and stunned.

Griffin kisses his way back up my stomach and breasts. He stretches out next to me, leaving one heavy hand on my hip. My eyes lock on his fingers, dark against my pale skin. I wonder if I'll ever get used to the easy way he touches me.

"Your name suits you." His eyes are heavy-lidded, his thick, black lashes partially obscuring the molten silver beneath. "You sound just like a cat, purring and mewling."

"That's ridiculous," I say, throwing his hand off me.

Griffin looks mildly offended but gets over it when I tug him to the edge of the bed and then take off his shirt. I hop down near the foot of the bed, my feet sinking into the thick rug. I pull him up to standing next to me, undo his belt, and shove his pants down. He steps out of them, already barefoot, and kicks them aside.

My eyes widen at the size of him. His erection still surprises me. And it's still intimidating. It makes me wonder how wide my jaw opens.

I drop to my knees. I've heard men like this.

"Cat!" He pulls me back up. "You don't have to do anything."

"You did."

"That was only to give, and I enjoyed it. *A lot.* I don't expect this in return."

I'm getting more nervous by the second. "You're very giving. It's nauseating."

His lips kick up at the corners. He doesn't seem too perturbed by my pronouncement. "I don't need to be bad-tempered twenty-four hours a day to prove I'm strong."

I bite my lip. I probably deserved that. "Don't worry," I say, wiggling out of his grasp and sinking back down. "I have no idea what I'm doing. You might hate it."

There's a sharp intake of breath above me when I touch my tongue to his arousal. His voice already strained, he says, "There's no chance of that."

I lick him again, this time more boldly. I wasn't lying. I have no idea what I'm doing. I figure there aren't too many ways to mess this up, though, so I begin at the top. As I get used to his thickness and the taste of his liquid pearling on my tongue, I take him more fully into my mouth and suck a little on the way back up.

"Good Gods!" Griffin mutters, bracing one hand against the bedpost. The other touches the top of my head, curling into my hair. I move up and down, licking and swirling my tongue. I can't think of anything else to do, so I take the base of his shaft in my hand and squeeze. His hips buck, so I do it again. His breathing turns unsteady. His fingers tighten in my hair, guiding me into a faster rhythm.

Wanting to draw out the pleasure like he did for me, I rock back on my heels and look up. Griffin is watching me, his face rigid with need. There are other feelings there, too, and the stark emotion makes me want to do more than please him. I want him so delirious for me that he'll forgive me for anything, no matter what I do, or who I am. I understand what he meant now about Ares and Aphrodite. If I can make him want me enough, maybe he'll never give up on me.

I cup his balls and lick him from base to tip. Griffin follows my every move, and the way he watches me—the dark intensity, the longing in his eyes, how they blaze with raw desire—spreads through me like a drug. Heady pressure builds low in my abdomen. I grow wetter between my thighs.

I sink down again, taking his shaft far into my mouth. A groan rises in Griffin's throat. His breath comes faster, in harsh pants. I take him deeper, harder, and a shudder rolls through him.

He reaches for my shoulders and tries to pull me up. "If you keep up like this, I'll come in your mouth."

I don't let him move me. I'm not about to reject his life force. Maybe I'll end up twice as strong as I was before. I sink my nails into his sculpted backside and suck hard.

His breath rattles above me. "Cat..."

I don't stop despite his warning tone, trying to make up for what I might lack in skill with sheer enthusiasm.

Griffin throws his head back and roars. The rough sound

of his release whips up a storm inside me. Fevered need pulses between my legs. I want him inside me, thrusting hard and fast.

His liquid is warm and salty, and there's a surprising amount. The spasms stop just when I'm afraid I can't swallow any more without gagging.

Griffin yanks me up, clutching me against his chest, which rises and falls with labored breaths. "You can spit," he pants, crushing me against him. "Or throw up if you need to."

I laugh and then choke a little.

"That was amazing." He sinks his hands into my hair and rains kisses all over my face. "You're amazing. I love you."

My heart flips over, and I bury my nose in his chest. "The things men will say for sex," I mutter against his sweat-slicked skin.

"It's after the sex."

My head jerks up, and I frown. "Really? There's no more?"

The widest, most disarming grin I've ever seen spreads across his face, and I lose my heart entirely. Griffin grips my hips and tosses me back onto the bed. Following me, he kisses and touches and licks and nibbles until I'm thrashing and wild. When he finally comes to me, my whole body thrums with needing him. I moan at the fullness and revel in his firm strokes, meeting them with eager, raised hips as Griffin guides us toward a mutual climax that's even more intense and shattering than before.

After my storm quiets and our heartbeats calm, we lie together, tangled, sweaty, and spent. Griffin eventually gets up to blow out the lamps before coming back and tucking me against his side. I'm way too hot, but I don't move or push him away because I just don't want to.

Happiness is a strange, frightening, fragile feeling when you're not used to it. I turn into him, laying my hand across his chest and draping my bent leg over his thigh. I guess I can get used to the touching.

With a contented sound, Griffin puts his hand over mine. It engulfs mine, twice its size.

I stare at our joined hands for a long time, wondering what tomorrow will bring.

CHAPTER 31

THE NEXT EVENING, JOCASTA SENDS HER MAID TO DO MY hair. She styles it half up and half down, and I'm careful of the expertly braided coils interwoven with delicate gold rope as I finish dressing for the realm dinner, my nerves in a tangle. Griffin comes in just as I'm strapping on my sandals, and I find him devastatingly handsome in his new dark trousers and snowy white tunic with gold trim. He leans against the wall, folds his arms over his chest, and crosses his legs at the ankles, watching me. He looks relaxed, but his eyes burn, and my temperature rises.

Straightening, I walk to the mirror, feeling wraithlike under the gossamer folds of my new gown. They float around me like layers of soft mist. I'm much too slim, and in my olive-skinned reflection I see a ghost: dark hair, green eyes, hollow cheeks, and haunted eyes. I thought this girl was dead.

Griffin comes up behind me, sweeps my curls to the side, and kisses the back of my neck, making me shiver. "I've seen the others. They're the royals, but it's you who looks like a queen."

I shiver again. "I hate queens."

"You hate Alpha Fisa." He holds out a thin gold torque, stretches it open, and then pushes it closed around my neck.

I touch the cool, light metal, asking, "What's this?"

"Decoration."

He picks up my right hand and slips a ring onto my middle finger. It's gold with a large, square emerald, light green like my eyes.

My stomach dips wildly. "And this?"

Griffin presses my fingers to his lips. "A gift."

"From the coffers?"

"From the agora." He releases my hand. "I saw it and couldn't resist."

Emotion mushrooms in my throat, making it hard to breathe. "I don't have anything for you."

Griffin's smile turns wolfish. "We'll discuss that gigantic falsehood later tonight."

Heat swamps me, and I flush until it feels as though even my hair catches fire.

"Come greet the guests," he says, starting for the door.

I shake my head, resisting the urge to fan myself. "I'll come down later. I have no official place here. I can't be in the receiving line."

His expression hardens. "You're Beta Sinta's future wife. I think that's official enough."

My mind blanks in shock. Then I sputter, "E-excuse me? When did you decide *that*?"

His eyes turn wary. "What did you think I was going to do with you? Sully you and watch my illegitimate children run around the castle?"

The blood drains from my face so fast I get dizzy. My heart pounds, and my vision wavers. Suddenly seeing it as a betrothal gift, I drag off the jewelry Griffin gave me and toss it back to him. He makes no effort to catch anything, and the torque and the ring bounce off his chest and drop to the rug. "I can't marry you."

His tone turns disturbingly neutral. "Why not?"

I stare at him and can't answer. I'm terrified Andromeda will discover the extent of our relationship and sink her deranged claws into Griffin, but he'll never accept that, so I don't say anything.

In the face of my silence, he asks, "Then what are we doing? What are *you* doing? Live together, or die trying. Those weren't just idle words. I meant them." He reaches out and touches my chin, making me face him when I try to turn away. "Did you?"

Griffin towers over me. His eyes probe mine. I wish he were raging. Then I could rage, too.

Desperate, crazy, crushing emotion overwhelms me, and I suddenly can't believe how much he means to me. A sharp pain lances through me, regret and guilt. My eyes find the items on the floor. If he'd thrown gifts back at me, I'd be spitting mad, claws bared, fists flying, and possibly prepared for a lifelong grudge. Thank the Gods one of us is smart enough not to let me ruin the only good thing that's ever happened to me.

For once, I get over myself and bend down to pick up the jewels. I slide the ring back on my finger and then hold out the torque as a peace offering. Griffin helps me slip the gold band back around my neck without a word of reproach.

I take an unsteady breath. "My notion of right and wrong is mostly self-taught."

His eyes remain shadowed, his expression even.

I swallow. "It's clearly a work in progress."

Some of the tension drains from him, and his face softens.

My hand rises to his chest. I feel his heartbeat under my fingertips, aware of how lucky I am to have him, petrified of all the ways I could lose him. "I want to be with you. I don't want to be anywhere else."

Griffin cups my face in his hands. "I want you to be with me, too."

I feel ill. My heart is beating too fast. My stomach is in knots. "But I can't marry you."

His nostrils flare, and he tenses again, squeezing my head a little. "Why not?"

"You don't even know who I am!"

"So bloody tell me!" he growls, letting me go.

Daphne was right. He *is* blinded—blinded by love and trust I don't deserve. I've done awful things, caused awful things. My future is full of awful things, and Griffin is so *good*. "I'll never be free," I whisper.

His face slowly drains of color. "You're already married." He sounds strangled. He looks as though he's been struck.

I laugh. I can't help it. It sounds a bit off. "No. What did you think? That I was some kind of virgin bride?" I wrap my arms around him and lay my cheek against his chest. Griffin's hands slide down my back, drawing me closer. He smells like citrus and bright, sunny days, and I want to stay this way forever, never facing anyone, or anything.

"I wasn't thinking. I just want the truth." He hooks a knuckle under my chin and lifts my face. "You can trust me. You know that."

My eyes prick, and I blink. I do trust him, but is that enough? "I'm trying to leave the past where it belongs. I don't expect to live long. I never have. Can't we just take the time we have and not think about anything else?"

"No."

I frown up at him. "*No?*"

"You require an awful lot of sign language." Griffin lowers his head and kisses me so thoroughly that heat and need flood me in an instant. His lips mold to mine like we're two pieces of a whole, and my desire sizzles to life on a sudden storm, leaving a rumble of thunder in the air.

He breaks the kiss to speak, his lips still touching mine. "You're intelligent, brave, skilled, and lethal. You've got

Poseidon and Hades looking out for you. I don't believe you'll die young, and I don't believe they'd let you. And even if they're not paying attention, then I am. *I* won't let you. I told you I was keeping you. I meant it."

His declaration zings through me. I feel the promise in it, the utter, undeniable truth. "You have no idea what you're getting into," I warn.

"Then tell me," he says simply, lifting his head.

He makes it sound so easy. *I'm not who you think I am, and by the way, there's this prophecy...* Just thinking about that conversation makes me nauseous. "Later." *Maybe.* "Tonight is about Sinta. Go down. I'll come soon."

"Your eye is twitching."

Damn eye!

"This isn't over."

I'll bet.

Griffin gives me his hard stare. "Soon, or I'll come back for you."

I grimace, feeling burned to a crisp already. "I know I have a job to do."

"It's not about the lies," he says sternly. "I need you by my side."

I nod, pretending there's not a lump in my throat.

Invisible, I slip unseen into the crowd of snake-tongued nobles. My insides are about to fry. Melted bones. Roasted organs. *Fabulous.*

The guests are all staying in the castle, and unsurprisingly, most of them strut about as if they own the place—or think they should. Before even entering the vast reception room, I'd have bet my magic the more powerful families came here with just that in mind. An overthrow. They're

Magoi. They're better. They *have* to be. Nothing else could possibly be acceptable. But no matter their prancing and posturing, after two full turns around the brightly lit room, I realize there's not a single person seriously considering challenging Griffin and his family. They're all scared witless of him and what he's accomplished so far.

Sweating and prickly hot from what I've already heard, I start a third trip through the swarm of guests, weaving toward people I didn't come across on the first two circuits. Once again, I hear private conversations and nobles lying to one another for no good reason, providing me with an increasingly pounding headache and instant, indisputable truths.

"They have so little education," a woman sniffs. *Truth: Alpha Sinta and her sisters are more well-read than I am!*

"And all these healing centers everywhere. Can you imagine? It's unthinkable!" her companion replies with disdain. *Truth: If I'd thought of that, and actually done it, maybe the Hoi Polloi who live around me would have lifted a bucket to help me when my house burned down last summer.*

I move on.

An older woman scoffs. "Beta Sinta did *not* kill a Dragon?" *Truth: Beta Sinta killed a Dragon! He killed a Dragon!*

The man next to her turns to look at Griffin. "I heard Beta Sinta has a powerful Magoi woman working for him. Maybe she killed the Dragon." His face pinches. "He can't possibly be doing all this on his own. Not like *I* could." *Truth: I could never do this on my own. I need the woman. Can I take her? Buy her? Seduce her? Use her? What would I do with her?*

I snort. Silently, of course.

The woman, who must be his mother, grabs his arm. "I know you. Don't get any ideas. Beta Sinta. The Magoi woman. Whoever. They cut down the previous royal family. They killed a Dragon. You're no match for them." Truth.

The man looks irritated. "Of course I am. He's only Hoi Polloi." *Truth: What if Beta Sinta's not just Hoi Polloi? Who is this Magoi woman? Mother's right. I'm no match for them.*

I move toward people of more consequence and magic. People I recognize, if only from descriptions.

Calandra of Mylos catches my eye, not only because she's young and beautiful, but because of the way she's watching Griffin. She was watching him earlier, when he was prowling around the room looking ten feet tall and every inch the conqueror he is, and she's doing it again now while he speaks with a group of guests near an open window. Her eyes are as hot as the reception room. "It was the woman who melted the Tarvans. I heard it came from her mouth, so it must have been Dragon's Breath."

"But that's rare, and creature magic. How could she possibly have that?" the man by her side asks. He's her husband, but her magic is stronger. I know it, and I can also feel it.

Calandra shrugs. "Does it matter? She's working for Beta Sinta, which means Beta Sinta has Dragon's Breath."

"And who knows what else," the husband mutters.

Calandra answers, even though it wasn't much of a question. "He's impervious to magic. He walked right into the castle and seized it. No one could touch him, not with their power, and not with a sword."

Her tone matches her eyes, and her husband finally notices Calandra's patent fascination.

Scowling, the man snaps, "I don't know what everyone is talking about. Beta Sinta doesn't look that terrifying or impressive to me." *Truth: Gods! He's huge! If that man looks at me the wrong way, I'll wet myself.*

"No," Calandra agrees. *Truth: He's gorgeous. I want him in my bed. I wonder if he'd whip me? Chain me? Hold me down? Make me beg?*

I grimace, disgusted, annoyed, and irrationally jealous all at once.

"The Magoi woman might turn on him," the husband says. "Why would a Magoi even work for a Hoi Polloi?"

"No self-respecting Magoi would," Calandra replies haughtily. *Truth: If he looks at me the right way, I'll do anything for him.*

The need to publicly stake my claim to Griffin burning in my currently invisible chest, I continue circulating. A handsome middle-aged man draws my attention, and I follow him into a secluded alcove where he joins a private conversation. When I see who's talking there and recognize the people from physical descriptions, I wish I'd found them sooner.

These are people I know—or at least know of. Agatone and Urania are the parents, older, but still extremely powerful and without a doubt the most influential nobles in all of Sinta. Oreste, their only son, is clearly the man who just joined them. I had to brush up on a few Sintan nobles myself before the realm dinner. These Magoi weren't among them. You don't forget people who try to buy you for their adult son when you're only ten. They never saw me. It was all done by messenger, and Andromeda's response was to send the messenger back without any limbs.

I stare at Oreste, shocked by how healthy and attractive he is. He's a good deal older than I am, of course, but there's not even a mean downturn to his mouth, or a pinched look around his eyes. He looks perfectly normal and agreeable, and if Mother wasn't such a snob, he could have been my fate.

"Well?" Urania asks.

"She's fine," Oreste answers. "Resting. She'll be down later."

I don't know who Oreste is talking about. I don't know of any sister, so maybe he took a wife?

"I didn't expect to be, but I'm impressed," Urania says, glancing over her son's shoulder to take in the buzzing, crowded room. Truth.

Agatone arches a grizzled brow. "Sinta's in a weak position for the Power Bid with a Hoi Polloi family on the throne." Truth. At least in his opinion.

"I'm not sure..." his wife answers pensively. "If the rumors circulating are true, maybe we're better off." Truth.

"How so?" Oreste asks. He looks distracted. He's watching the stairs for someone.

"These are unpredictable times. Tarvan royals are obviously up to something. And even though no one has laid the blame for the attack at Ios at their feet, I'm certain it was them."

Definitely my top theory as well. I think they've been behind both attacks since I've been with Griffin. They have the money to buy mercenaries. And having Hoi Polloi on the throne next door is practically an invitation to invade. But we thwarted them when they sent the Giant after Griffin, and we beat them again at Ios. Unfortunately, officially blaming the Tarvan royals is also more or less a declaration of war, so it's best to avoid that—for now.

"A few men and one woman massacred every last Tarvan sent to Ios to kill the new Sintan royals," Urania continues. "That doesn't happen unless there's a lot more to them than we know."

"Makes me wonder what else they've got up their sleeves," Agatone says, looking to where Griffin, Piers, and Egeria seem to be regaling a group of people with a story we're too far away to hear. Agatone's voice conveys curiosity, and maybe even respect. The biting, jealous, condescending tones I've been hearing around the room are absent here in this corner where I imagined they'd be the worst.

"Everyone knows there was a great flash of lightning and then a deafening clap of thunder over Ios after the battle," Oreste adds. "What if Zeus got involved to keep Beta Sinta alive?"

My mouth drops open in shock. In the haze and fatigue, that flash, the boom, that great, terrible voice in my head that I'd never heard before and didn't recognize… It all got lost in the pleats of my memory, all those days without consciousness or thought. *Zeus. It was Zeus!*

Urania's almost-clear green eyes narrow. "Gods. Powerful magic. There are things at play here. Things we should land on the right side of if we value our lives."

Truth.

"But Gods backing Hoi Polloi?" Oreste asks, seeming more surprised and interested than inherently bothered by the notion.

"It's not impossible. Don't forget, they have the mysterious Magoi woman already," his father reminds him. "Fisan, I heard, which is something in itself. She must see something in them, or at least in Beta Sinta. And never underestimate Hoi Polloi when they decide to fight for something they want. They may be mongrels, but mongrels can be vicious."

Griffin? A mongrel? And I was starting to like these people. They didn't fry me once with lies to each other during their whole conversation.

"Sinta will be stronger with all these projects for new roads, schools, and healing centers. Not to mention a growing and loyal Hoi Polloi army, and royals who actually care about defending the realm and not just about themselves." Urania's eyes stray to Griffin. Everyone is looking at Griffin. All the time. He's that magnetic. "Just look at him. This Power Bid won't be like any other. Maybe Tarva should be worried about Sinta this time, and not the other way around."

I shift uncomfortably in my sandals. All this talk of invasion, whichever way around, makes me feel like I'm about to pop out with hives.

"And Fisa?" Oreste asks.

Both his parents shrug. Then Agatone says, "Alpha Fisa is a viper. She'll only strike if you get too close."

They've secluded themselves for too long already, and sensing curious looks from the other guests, the family moves back into the main part of the room. I very much doubt they'll say anything of interest to the other nobles, at least not tonight, so I leave and come back without turning invisible this time, having already heard enough.

Griffin spots me almost immediately and brings me to Jocasta, handing me a glass of chilled wine. As the three of us circulate, they introduce me as Jocasta's friend, but from the way Griffin keeps a possessive hand on my lower back, it's clear I'm more. At Griffin's side, I draw more attention than I've ever wanted, and whispers of "Fisan" and "Magoi" and "power" blanket the air, suffocating me.

After a while, Griffin maneuvers me into an alcove much like the one I was in earlier and leans close to my ear. "Have you picked up anything about Ios?"

I nod, accidentally sending shooting pains through my aching head. "Confirmation of what we already thought. It's probably the Tarvan royals who sent that tribe to attack."

Griffin looks back up. "Who thinks that?"

I shift my gaze to the right. "Most notably, the white-haired Water Mage over there, Agatone, and his wife, Urania. She's the snake charmer."

"And poison master."

I nod just a little this time. Griffin's studying is paying off.

"They're intrigued. And impressed. They didn't say it in so many words, but if the Power Bid heats up, I think you have their support."

"They'd fight with me?" Griffin asks, seeming surprised.

"Well, they wouldn't fight against you, and that's already something."

His eyes glint with satisfaction. "They're key players. Others will follow their lead."

"Cultivating their goodwill is important," I agree. "And they seem reasonable and intelligent, which is a good start."

"What else?" Griffin asks.

"Calandra of Mylos. Smile at her, say jump, and she'll ask how high," I say sourly.

Griffin lifts his eyebrows at my tone.

"She's the important one in her couple," I continue, "with both the money and the magic. Her husband married up. She has a weakness for pretty men and, apparently, strange and violent sexual encounters." I make a face, wishing I hadn't gotten a vivid taste of *that* truth. "He gives her what she wants, and he gets a high-ranking position in return." I glance at Griffin. "She took one look at you and decided everything was great. I guess she thinks you're pretty."

"Gods forbid," Griffin mutters.

I smile weakly. I have a headache the size of Zeus's ego, and I'm burning up. I touch my fingers to my forehead, finding it clammy. "She's not the most powerful Magoi here, but she's rich, and she's protected by her city's defenses."

"Mylos has the knowledge scrolls, and every temple containing them has its own company of guards. Altogether, there's practically an army there, and the commander listens to local nobles like Calandra. She'd make a strong ally, and a potentially difficult enemy. I'll have to make sure she stays on my side," Griffin says, finding the statuesque blonde with his eyes.

My voice sours further. "Yes, but without any weird sex."

The corners of his mouth twitch at my jealous tone. I could swear his chest puffs out. "Anything else?"

"Lots of things, but nothing to worry about. You have everyone thoroughly terrified and impressed with the way you so easily disposed of the previous royal family. The news has traveled from Fisa that someone in Sinta killed Sybaris, and they assume it was you, or at least something to do with you. Then there are the melted Tarvans." *And a possible intervention from Zeus.* "And, of course, there's also the mysterious and powerful Magoi working for you—the one drawing nearly as much attention as you are," I say unhappily.

"Or more," Griffin says, not helping my nerves. "What about the projects and responsibilities we announced earlier?" he asks.

I shrug. "More surprise than real resistance. Interest, really. Some people, like Agatone and Urania, seem to think the ideas are good and that Sinta will be stronger for them."

"And here you thought the nobles would all have internal fits when Egeria said they were to spearhead opening healing centers in their areas."

"They did. Sort of. They got over it faster than I thought they would."

"What about my requirement that they begin taking more responsibility for shoring up the defenses of their local towns and cities?"

"Same reaction. Mostly surprise. They've never been asked to do anything before except pay their taxes and sit around being superior." I worry my bottom lip, contemplating the possible outcomes we've been discussing for days. "I still think letting them build up their own forces is a risk. They might turn into rebellious city-states. They could become too powerful."

"And I told you, I'll give them incentives to stay loyal: gold, privileges, my ear so they'll know their voices matter." Griffin looks beyond me, surveying the crowd. "Everyone showed up tonight. No one has done anything offensive. You haven't uncovered any plots to murder or overthrow us. They just want to maintain their status. Otherwise they would have done something by now."

He's probably right. "At least Mylos doesn't need extra protection."

"No, but it needs a healing center." He winks. "I'll personally ask Calandra to be in charge of it."

I snort. "She'll love that."

"She'll love having a say and getting to push healers around. Most of these people are just bored. It's up to me to get them doing something useful rather than something destructive."

My temples are throbbing, but I find a smile for him. "And *that* is why you're a wise ruler."

Griffin draws me farther into the alcove, saying quietly, "But beyond all this, we can't just sit on our hands if Alpha

Tarva is preparing to move against us. We only delayed his plans at Ios. Galen Tarva won't give up that easily."

"What if it's not Alpha Tarva? What if it's his sister, Acantha? She might have planned it all."

"You have a theory?" he asks.

I always have a theory. "She eliminates all of you and then sets herself up as Alpha Sinta. That way, she doesn't have to kill her brother or her nephews, which could prove difficult, she ends up with allies next door, and she still gets her own throne, which is all she really wants."

Griffin frowns. "Alpha Fisa won't want two realms allied against her. Would she attack?"

I'm having trouble thinking over my excruciating headache. I take a deep breath, but it doesn't help. "She'd strengthen her border, but I don't think she'd attack. She'd probably think no one would dare invade Fisa, and not be too worried if they did. Fisans are pretty convinced of their own superiority."

"You don't say?" Griffin drawls.

I give him the evil eye. It doesn't feel very evil. "Magic is strongest in Fisa. It has the biggest chunk of the Ice Plains, and the Fisan royals are the only ones still blood-related to the Origin."

"The Origin? You mean the first king of Thalyria?"

"He was a God, remember. Zeus's son. Half-Olympian, half-Titan. A combination of the old Gods and the new. Zeus created Thalyria for him."

Griffin curses. "Does that mean Andromeda has God-like power?"

I shake my head. "She's very powerful, but the line is too diluted for that. It's been thousands of years. Gods are immortal, not unkillable. The Origin's demigod offspring, two sons and a daughter, turned on him. They beheaded him and then fell into war with each other, eventually splitting their father's kingdom into three realms: Sinta, Tarva, and Fisa."

"And Andromeda is the only living descendant of the Origin?"

"Andromeda...and her children."

His lip curls in distaste. I think I turn a shade whiter, but I was probably pretty pasty to begin with.

"Does she hold Zeus's favor?"

I swallow, my chest tightening with indefinable emotion, the echo of a booming voice swelling in my head. "I don't think so."

"Why not?" Griffin asks. "She's his blood relation."

She's not the only one...

Griffin is so capable that I sometimes forget we come from completely different backgrounds. In the south, people learn to fight and survive, farm and build, make and trade. Everything is like the climate, gritty and real. Ancient history is irrelevant, and Gods are worshipped, not studied. "Zeus hates infanticide because he was almost swallowed whole by his own father. In my opinion, Andromeda has brought about the death of too many of her own children to hold Zeus's favor," I explain.

Griffin looks out over the crowd, his eyes cool and assessing, his bearing confident and proud. People watch us curiously, but no one dares approach our private alcove. The guests here aren't stupid enough to bother the Alpha wolf in his den. "The Power Bid is in motion. There's no turning back." Griffin shifts his gaze back to me. "So let's do it our way."

"Do what?" I ask.

"Take over the realms."

I stop breathing. "Excuse me?"

"We'll bring things full circle. No more divided rulers. One kingdom, like the Origin's."

"Who? Where?" I sputter.

"Us. Wherever you want."

And I thought I felt sick *before*. This conversation is giving me a new appreciation for the dangers of tachycardia. "Ambitious, aren't you?" I ask, trying not to hyperventilate.

"You think I'd be here if I wasn't?"

"You already have a realm. We could all die in a war. We could destroy it all." *I* could destroy it all. "It's not worth it."

"It *is* worth it. We could change everything." His eyes suddenly blaze, turning a luminous gray. "That's what you told me in the oracular dream."

"I... But..."

"It's why Poseidon brought us together." Determination darkens his features, molding them into his conqueror's mask. "I understand now. It's what we're supposed to do."

"No." All I can do is shake my head, stubbornly denying what sounds too true. "No."

Turning to me, Griffin smooths his hands down my arms. "I know you're scared, but maybe we can avoid an all-out war."

"How?" I croak.

His fingers capture mine. "I have a secret weapon."

My eyes widen. "What?"

"You."

Good Gods! He has no idea how true that is. I kill one person, take my rightful place, declare the Origin's kingdom restored, crush Tarvan resistance, and... My stomach lurches, and I beat down nausea. "What happens when our children start fighting each other? Or our children's children? That's how we ended up like we are now."

Griffin shakes his head. "It won't happen like that. We'll bring peace to the realms. Healing."

Healing. That's exactly what Poseidon said, his voice thundering in my ears like a thousand storms rolling over the seas. What if we *are* supposed to unify the realms? But what about the prophecy? Why is my destiny written in destruction?

Griffin frowns. I must look as ill as I feel because his voice deepens with concern. "Cat?"

I shudder. "Plans like this... You have to talk to Egeria. She's Alpha."

A tiny muscle ticks under Griffin's eye. For the first time, I think he's annoyed he didn't put himself in charge. Then again, I guess he was saving himself for bigger things—like *everything*.

"We decide," he finally says. "You and me."

"*We* decide?" I snort softly. "I don't want to get married, and I *really* don't want to invade Fisa, but you appear to have decided on both without ever consulting me."

His expression flattens. "Give it time, and you'll see I'm right. On both counts." Griffin plants his hand on my lower back and propels me out of the alcove without another word.

Discussion over. *Argh!*

Seeing us available and circulating again, a boy, one of my first north wall workers, approaches with a tray of food. He grins, looking clean and boyishly handsome in his new uniform. Despite my pounding headache and the growing tension with Griffin, I can't help smiling back. I take a fruit kabob and ask him how he likes his new job.

"Actually, Your Highness, I prefer hauling rocks. It'll make me strong. I want to be a warrior like Beta Sinta." He glances shyly at Griffin.

I nearly choke on a kalaberry. "You don't need to call me 'Your Highness.'"

"He will soon," Griffin mutters.

The boy beams.

Fantastic. That news will be all over the castle by sunrise, and it's not even true. "We just talked about this!" I hiss after the boy leaves.

"You talked. I disagreed."

My jaw goes slack. "Unless you're planning on knocking me unconscious, dragging me to the temple, and practicing ventriloquy, I still have to say yes!"

Griffin's face shuts down entirely. "We'll discuss this later."

"Discuss? Is that what you're calling 'I decree, you obey'?"

Another tray of food passes in front of me, and I grab a phyllo triangle without really looking. Griffin plucks it from my fingers and tosses it back onto the tray. "Goat cheese."

Damn it! It's impossible to stay mad now.

Egeria signals that dinner is about to begin, and everyone moves into the formal dining room to find their predetermined places. Course upon course comes out of the kitchens, mostly northern fare with a few southern specialties thrown in. The dinner seems interminable, not only because I feel hot, achy, and sick, but because everyone keeps looking at me and noting my frankly conspicuous position among the royal family at Beta Sinta's right hand. On top of that, seated where I am, I can't learn anything of interest except that Piers, who is on my other side, is capable of disagreeing with absolutely everything I say, even when it's strictly a matter of personal opinion. By the end of dinner, I'm ready to stab Griffin's brother with a fork.

Before I can succumb to my baser urges, Egeria rises

and claps her hands. "Please proceed to the gardens for our post-dinner entertainment."

Fresh air, thank the Gods...

Along with a healthy supply of wine at every corner, musicians are peppered around the sprawling grounds. Usually, I like that kind of thing, especially in a torch-lined setting of terraced marble and vibrant green. Tonight, though, I think one pluck of a kithara string will make my head explode.

Gritting my teeth, I follow Griffin toward the gardens anyway, but I'm slow to move, and we end up trailing behind. The last of the nobles disappear from view as we cross the brightly lit reception room, the glare from the oil lamps like a fist in the eye. I glance longingly toward the stairs, wishing I could climb them straight up to bed.

A lone guest is lumbering down the main staircase. She looks up and sees me just as everything inside me freezes.

"Talia? Good Gods! Talia, is that you?"

I stop breathing and keep walking. There's a pause in Griffin's step, and I hope the woman bearing down on us from the side doesn't notice. My very pregnant cousin Helen waddles remarkably fast. She must have been in one of the bedrooms this whole time because she wasn't downstairs until now. I would have seen her.

"In Castle Sinta of all places!" she exclaims. "Just wait until I tell everyone I've found the—"

"I'm sorry," I interrupt, finally turning to her. "Do I know you?"

She looks taken aback and then laughs. "Very funny. We grew up together. Aarken tortured us both." She leans in and says confidentially, "Can't blame that fish for eating him."

I look confused, or at least I hope I do. "You're mistaking me for someone else."

She frowns. "It's me, Helen. I got away, too. I didn't cause *nearly* as much of a stir as you did, of course. I had to get married to do it." She grimaces, rubbing her enormous stomach. "My parents said it was a good enough alliance, and Uncle Dimitri seemed pleased, although we all know what *his* opinion counts for." She rolls her eyes. "You know, these Sintans really aren't that bad once you get to know them." She looks unapologetically at Griffin. "Pardon my saying so, Your Highness."

Griffin arches an eyebrow in a very successful expression of condescending astonishment, and if she weren't Helen Fisa, I think she might have fainted. As it is, she's very sure of her own worth and doesn't give a damn what Beta Sinta thinks. I always liked Helen.

"I'm afraid we've never met. Enjoy the party, and good luck with the baby." I walk away. It's too bad. Helen was one of the few people who didn't make me miserable, and we never tried to kill each other, which makes us allies of a sort.

Her voice echoes behind me, far too loud in my ears. "What's wrong with you? I know you! Talia, wait!"

I slowly turn back around, Griffin tense at my side and an unwanted audience for this charade. Helen followed. She's calling me out, and I see the exact moment she realizes she should have let me go. She pales, her eyes widening as she slides a protective hand over her swollen belly.

Mother is convinced that I'm just like she is, or that I'll at least end up that way. My greatest fear is that she's right, which is why I've never altered anyone's mind. If I take that small step, if I use compulsion to force Helen to back off to preserve my secrets and send her on her way, what's to stop me from taking the next step, and the next, until I'm slaughtering puppies, terrorizing children, and killing on a whim?

I stare at my cousin, hearing Mother's insidious whisper in my ear, *"It's nothing, Talia. Just this once..."*

Helen and I stare at each other. Her eyes grow more fearful, and her whole being seems to curl around her unborn child. I have no violent impulse. I feel compassion. I feel a need to reassure and protect, and in that moment, I finally understand that I will never be my mother.

Heaviness lifts from me. My heart feels weightless in my chest, and for the first time in my life, I am surrounded by air and by light.

I breathe again, not having realized I'd stopped. "Your husband must be looking for you." I look pointedly at Helen's midsection in what I hope is a nonthreatening way. "And worrying over your health."

The stress in her eyes eases, as does her protective stance. "Thank you, Your Highness." She curtsies— beautifully, of course, despite the state of her belly—and then doesn't waste a moment crossing the empty room and disappearing into the guest-filled garden.

My heart sinks. I glance fearfully at Griffin, but he doesn't seem to register anything amiss, at least not with that last part of the conversation, and I realize he already sees me as a princess—*his* princess. He doesn't know that Helen would never genuinely defer to anyone but Fisan royalty. In her mind, she can count on one hand the people that outrank her, and I'm one of them.

"How does she know you're the Kingmaker?" Griffin asks in a low voice.

"What?"

"You interrupted her before she could say 'the Kingmaker.' How does she know?"

That's not what Helen was going to say, and if it were in me right now to laugh hysterically, I would. "We were children together. It wasn't a secret in Castle Fisa."

"Who's Aarken?" he asks.

"Her brother."

"And the fish?" Griffin prods.

"Poseidon's three-tentacled trout. An Oracle in the Frozen Lake."

"Your Oracle?"

I nod, feeling increasingly numb.

"I'll piece your story together," Griffin vows. "Bit by bit if I have to."

My stomach plummets. "It's a terrible tale. I'd rather you didn't hear it."

He swipes a hand through his hair, clearly frustrated. "What am I missing, Cat? Why didn't your family come for you when you were a prisoner in Castle Fisa? I would never have left you there."

His words make my heart ache. As usual, my silence aggravates him.

"Should I ask Helen?" he growls.

"Please don't." My voice is rusty and catches in my throat. I'm unbearably hot, and my headache just started thumping to the beat of the pulse behind my eyes. Vomit crawls toward my mouth, and I swallow hard.

"Go enjoy the rest of the party. Enjoy your success," I urge. "My magic has been hard on me tonight. I-I need to rest now."

Griffin looks at me, seeming torn between concern over my well-being and wanting to interrogate me further. Then, his expression shuttering, he turns and steers me toward the stairs. I think he's going to leave me there, but my steps falter as I start to climb, so he grips my elbow and takes me back to our room. The second the door shuts, I wearily kick off my sandals and start sliding the pins from my hair.

I unravel a series of tight braids, groaning in relief. "I feel like a stampede of angry Centaurs tried to kick me to death."

Griffin watches me, his eyes dark. "There's too much I don't know about you. Too much you won't tell me." Closing the distance between us, he reaches out and runs strong fingers over my scalp, helping to shake out my thick curls. "You can trust me, Cat. I will never betray you."

Something heavy settles in my chest. "I do trust you."

His hands go still in my hair and then fall away. "Just not enough."

I feel the loss of his warmth so acutely that I throw myself against his chest. It takes longer than usual for his arms to close around me, and my heart feels that hesitation like the sharp end of a knife.

CHAPTER 32

Noise from the realm dinner continues well past dawn. The nobles who haven't retired to their rooms by now have apparently inebriated themselves into thinking that Griffin's plans came from them in the first place, and are bloody good ones at that.

"To the health of the realm!" someone still in the garden shouts. Griffin's new toast. Clever, really.

I can't sleep, partly because Griffin hasn't come back, and partly because I haven't been pounded this hard with lies and truths since I was a kid. I hadn't forgotten the toll it took. I just did it anyway. For Griffin. Now, I'm aware of every aching bone in my body. Even the tiny ones burn.

I give up on resting and climb out of bed. My arms and legs tremble as I force them into clothing that sticks to my clammy skin. Keeping my head down, I leave the castle using a discreet side door and then stumble past the royal bathhouse toward the women's pool adjacent to the barracks. I'd rather face early-rising soldiers than drunken nobles.

Morning sunshine slants through the high, arched windows, dappling the water with puddles of light. In a haze of pain and fatigue, I slip out of my clothes and sink into the deserted pool with a sigh. I should have done this hours ago instead of waiting—and hoping—for Griffin to return.

I spread out my arms and float in a patch of sunlight, half-asleep, my ears underwater. Naked. Relaxed. Healing.

A sharp pain splits my middle. I gasp, water spilling into my mouth as my eyes fly open, and my hands dart to my belly. I stare in shock at the knife sticking out of my stomach, blood billowing from me like a watery sunset.

Bare feet pad almost silently across the marble floor. My head whips around. *Daphne.*

She's always watching me. I guess her lurking finally paid off. "Throwing a knife from the shadows is something only a coward would do."

She shrugs. "It worked."

"Griffin will never forgive you." I use one hand to help me float. The other is pressed to my stomach, around the knife's blade.

"Griffin won't ever know I was here. There are hundreds of strangers in the castle tonight. Any one of them could have struck you down."

Air hisses between my teeth. My breathing turns harsh from the pain blistering my middle. "He doesn't love you."

"He will," she grates out, as if saying it makes it true. "Once you're out of the way."

Good Gods. Considering the powerful and horrible people that have tried to kill me, it would be enormously disappointing if *Daphne* were the one to manage it.

I open my mouth, but my Dragon's Breath fails me. I'm still too drained from last night. It doesn't matter. I have other ways to kill.

"I was doing my best to tolerate you," I growl, "but now I'm mad." I tear the knife from my stomach and send it back. My feet don't touch the bottom of the pool to steady me, and pain rips my insides as I throw. The knife is heavier than any of mine, but I'm used to working with different blades, and I've had plenty of practice adapting on the fly. I don't go for some ridiculous, slow-death stomach wound. I aim straight for the eye and hit it. Daphne goes over backward, her head cracking against the marble floor.

The satisfaction I ought to feel is absent. I feel...bleak. And light-headed. Panting, I struggle toward the shallow end of the pool. I shouldn't stay in the water, but it dilutes the blood.

A chill seeps into me, and I start shivering. My heart is heavy, my skin cold. It's getting harder to breathe. I didn't want to be right about dying young, and I never thought it would happen like this. The pool is turning pink with my blood, and that's all I can see.

That, and Griffin's face when he finds me.

Just hours ago, I was sure I'd never use compulsion on a person, but I start calling for Griffin in my head. I don't know what else to do, and summoning help isn't exactly altering minds. But it's always been those small, seemingly innocuous steps that terrified me, along with Mother's voice in my head.

He doesn't come. Maybe he's too far away. Maybe I'm too weak. More likely he's immune to compulsion, or maybe I'm just no good at it. The glacial shard around my neck starts turning the water around it to ice. It feels me fading and is working for me.

I'm not ready to give up yet. I never give up. Shadows creep into the edges of my vision, but I push Griffin from my mind and concentrate on sunny blond hair and cobalt eyes.

Kato! Kato! I need you!

I shout for him and picture myself in the bathhouse until everything goes distant and numb. No large, sturdy, dependable man bursts through the doors like I think he will, and I realize I've been incredibly stupid. I should have gotten out of the water while I still had the strength to find help.

Slowly, too slowly, I move toward the stairs, water still

up to my breasts and my hand gripping the edge of the pool. Blood pounds in my ears, and the steps never seem to get any closer. My legs give out, my hand slides off the edge, and my head slips underwater. Silence engulfs me. I'm going to drown. How utterly ironic.

In this soundless place, my eyes close, and I stop breathing until my body chooses for me. The first liquid lungful burns my chest, choking me. The second rushes in, filling me up. My neck suddenly stings, like someone's taken a blade and slashed the skin below my ears. The last bubbles of air leave my lungs just as strong hands grip my upper arms and drag me out of the water.

Someone lays me flat on the marble floor. "Don't be dead. Don't be dead."

Kato's voice shatters the darkness enfolding me.

"Breathe!" he bellows, slamming his hands down on either side of my head.

My chest convulses, and water spews from my throat, gagging me. I choke and cough and breathe, tearing at my wound. The stinging pain in my neck disappears as quickly as it came.

"Get Griffin!" Kato shouts.

Someone sprints out of the bathhouse, the heavy gait ringing like Flynn's.

"The blood..." I mumble, my lips numb.

"To the Underworld with the blood!" Kato presses his hand to my stomach. I gasp, my body jerking in response.

A few minutes must pass. It feels like seconds. Maybe I black out. Griffin's voice reaches me next, rough with panic. "Cat! My Gods, Cat!"

Griffin never panics. He's always infuriatingly calm. I raise my hand, groping for him, and he catches my fingers, squeezing them so hard it hurts.

"I'm sorry," I whisper, forcing my eyes to open. When he comes into focus, I wish I hadn't tried so hard to see. The look on his face terrifies me. I see my death in his harrowed gaze, in the stark lines and stricken planes.

"Don't die," he orders gruffly. "Don't you dare die."

Tears spill from my eyes and slide hotly down the sides of my face.

"Gods damn it!" Griffin explodes. He turns to his brothers. They must have arrived with him. "Piers! Get that healer."

There's only one healer among the guests, a solitary man who kept shooting Griffin and me dirty looks during dinner.

"I don't know which room he's in." Piers hesitates. "He didn't seem friendly."

"I don't care!" Griffin snarls. "Get him! Carver, go to the circus grounds. They're back. Bring Selena here."

They both leave immediately. If the circus is outside of Sinta City again, I know where Selena is. It'll take an hour to get there and back. I don't have that long. I'm surprisingly resistant to death, so I might have made it if I hadn't been so worried about the blood and Andromeda tracing me to here. I never thought it would take so long for someone to find me. It was stupid to stay in the water. I hate Mother more than ever. She's cost me everything. Again.

I shiver, my teeth rattling. "I'm cold."

Griffin visibly pales. He picks me up and cradles me against his chest. His heat feels like a balm, but it's not enough to warm me. Kato doesn't take his hand off my wound. He's up to his elbow in my blood and as white-faced as Griffin.

Flynn paces frantically before taking off at a run. "I think I know where a healer is!"

"Walk with me," Griffin orders Kato. They leave the bathhouse with me sheltered between them, taking the side entrance to the castle and climbing the stairs. "How did you find her?"

"She was shouting in my head. I thought it was a dream, but it didn't feel right, so I got Flynn up, and we went searching."

Griffin's arms tense around me. "You should have called *me*."

Jealous? Even now? "Tried. Didn't work."

He glances down, looking even more stricken. "I should have done something about Daphne. I never thought..."

"Not your fault." I wish I'd been more truthful with him, and not just about Daphne.

In our room, Griffin goes to lay me on the bed, but I rouse myself enough to protest. Whatever my blood touches will have to be destroyed. "Can't burn the bed." It's the only place I've ever felt happy, and safe.

Kato grabs a blanket with his free hand and throws it on the thick sheepskin rug. Griffin sets me down without Kato ever taking the pressure off my stomach. Tears keep spilling from my eyes, silently falling. There are too many people to leave behind. There's Griffin.

As I look at him, he moves to the side, and my gaze falls on the bowl of lemons. My eyes widen. *What if I live?* "Get the lemons. Wash the blood off with lemon juice."

Griffin swings a near-frantic look on me. "That's insane. That'll hurt like the fires of the Underworld."

I think we've already established that I'm not entirely sane, so I give him the best maniacal glare I can manage under the circumstances. "It'll corrupt the blood. Confuse her magic. More effective than water."

A muscle pounds in his jaw. His face turns thunderous.

He still cuts open all ten lemons and squeezes the juice over Kato's hand and my stomach. When the acid hits me, I scream like a child. I scream like the Minotaur is on my tail, and I just hit a dead-end in his maze. I scream for all I'm worth even after Griffin stops what he's doing and curses violently, hurling the lemon rinds against the wall.

Griffin's sisters and parents erupt into the room in their nightclothes, panicked.

"Cat!" Jocasta falls to her knees next to me. Trembling fingers brush wet hair off my neck and cheeks. She sniffs loudly and then bursts into tears. The second she starts crying, the other women do, too.

I blink leaden eyelids, wanting to keep looking at them. I have a family crying over me. What a strange idea. I hold on to that thought as I slip in and out of darkness. *Eleni emerges from the shadows to greet me, a smile on her lips, blonde hair glowing, green eyes merry, a bottle of Fisan clover water in her hand.* Has Hades sent her to collect me?

I guess not because she fades, and I wake up, limp and hurting. There's a sheet covering my nakedness. Griffin is on his knees next to me, his head bowed, his beautiful, wide mouth moving on silent words, praying. I read Poseidon's name on his lips.

Poseidon, I beg. *Please take care of him.*

Piers bursts through the doorway, two people in tow. "I found him! And another one! A girl."

Griffin jumps to his feet. He grabs the man and drags him down next to me. "Heal her!"

His eyes flicking over me, the healer smiles like he knows he's about to die and relishes it. "She killed my wife!" he snarls.

What?

"Belinda went to Ios." He turns burning, hate-filled eyes on me. "She wanted to stop that healing center garbage."

Ah, Gods. Talk about rotten luck. I had to grab this guy's wife and then accidentally kill her?

A storm roars to life in Griffin's eyes. *Idiot healer.* He's about to read some sign language.

"Can you drain him?" Griffin asks me, his expression murderous. "Heal yourself?"

I shake my head. My eyes say the rest. I'm already too weak, and it wouldn't matter anyway. Even healers can't heal themselves.

"Heal her. That's an order." There's steel in Griffin's voice.

"You can rot in the fires of the Underworld," the healer spits. "You and your Fisan whore."

With a snarl, Griffin grabs the man's head, snaps his neck, and then launches his body across the room. The healer thumps against the wall and then falls to the floor with the lemon rinds.

Kaia bleats like a frightened sheep and sits abruptly on the bed. Her face ashen, Nerissa wraps her arms around her daughter, but she doesn't scold Griffin like I half expect her to.

Piers shoves the girl at me. She can't be more than twelve, which means I'm as good as dead.

"I-I'm just an apprentice. I'm here with my parents. I've n-never fully healed anyone before."

Griffin takes her by the shoulders, doing his best to appear calm and nonthreatening despite having just killed a man and tossed him across the room. "Just help her hold on until someone else gets here. Please. I know you can do it."

She nods jerkily, shaking all over. "I'm strong. They always tell me I'm strong."

"Good." Griffin nudges her toward me. "We need you to be strong."

With his next breath, Griffin sends Piers to the bath-house. "Wash the blood off the floor. Drain the pool. Refill and drain again."

Piers nods and leaves the room but not before I see a shadow flit through his eyes, making me wonder what he's read in his scrolls about magic and blood.

The girl kneels next to me. She peels the blanket to my waist and then lays her hands on my stomach. I feel a tingle of magic, pure and strong, and hiss a breath through my teeth. The pain intensifies as torn things begin the slow, agonizing process of repairing themselves. When I can't stand it anymore, I moan.

"What are you doing?" Griffin jerks the child off me.

She gasps. "I-I'm doing what you said."

"You're hurting her!"

"I know!" the girl cries.

"Keep going," I croak. "You're doing fine."

She looks at me, wide brown eyes in a pale, oval face. I clench my fists until my nails sting my palms and nod in encouragement.

I suffer through the bite of magic and the misery of heal-ing, so drained of blood I think my skin will collapse and mold to my bones, leaving bumps and hollows and sunken flesh. After a while, the feel of the girl's magic changes. She's drained her healing power. This is her life force.

"Stop," I order sharply. "You're giving too much."

She pulls back, trembling with exhaustion.

I flop my head toward Egeria. "Wash her hands. She's done everything she can without hurting herself."

Egeria hurries over and half carries the healer child from the room.

I shift, wincing in pain but amazed I can move. The girl made a start at repairing the damage, although the gash is still open and oozing. "Rub the lemon rinds over it," I say to anyone who's listening.

Griffin leans over me, glowering. "There's been too much blood already. Don't hurt yourself for no reason."

No reason? I'd cut off my own arm to keep Andromeda from finding me. I was going to be happy here. With Griffin. "Do it!" I grind out.

"No!"

I'm cursing at him when Flynn barrels through the door along with a stranger. "Met him at a tavern. Found him again," he pants. "Not like the others. Supports the healing centers."

Griffin sizes up the healer with a glance. So do I. His chest is heaving, and he's so out of breath he looks like he's about to throw up, but otherwise he doesn't seem unwilling. He's about thirty, so fully trained but not yet at the peak of his power. He has unpretentious eyes.

"Save her and you can have the new healing center in Ios," Griffin says. "It's yours."

The healer's gaze darts to his dead colleague, easily recognizable from the symbol of Asklepios tattooed on his mangled neck. He doesn't hesitate. He drops down next to me and places his hands over my wound. "You've lost a lot of blood." He presses firmly, and I suck in a sharp breath. "I'm surprised you're still alive."

"Strong constitution," Kato says.

"Stubborn as a Cyclops," Griffin mutters at the same time.

"Get on with it." I grit my teeth. This is going to hurt.

Magic ignites, incinerating my insides as skin, muscle, and organs start knitting back together again, much faster than before. My back bows, and I scream, suddenly hating the healer girl for fixing me just enough to keep me conscious.

Griffin whirls and punches the wall. The marble wins that fight, and his hand comes away bloody.

"Don't bleed!" I shout at him and then scream some more.

He strings together an impressive number of obscenities, grinding his bloody knuckles into an emptied-out lemon rind. When he's done with that, he picks up a massive chair and pounds it against the wall until there's nothing left. He glares in disgust at the shattered chunk of wood left in his hand and then hurls it out the window with a bellow.

His family stares at him in shock. Only Anatole looks like he understands and would do the same.

"If you don't like it," Griffin rages, "get out!"

No one moves. Jocasta goes back to stroking my hair.

The healer rocks back on his heels, lifting his hands from me and using his forearm to wipe the sweat from his brow.

Griffin pounces on him. "What are you doing? You're not done yet!"

The healer tries not to cringe in the face of Griffin's wrath, and succeeds—for the most part. "I have to rest, gather more magic. It's impossible to keep going until it's done. Using that much healing power that fast can have dire results."

We're well placed to know *that's* true. With a frustrated curse, Griffin drops to my side.

I scowl at him. "I liked that chair."

His lips jump up in surprise. "I'll get you a new one."

"I liked *that* one."

Light returns to his eyes. He lifts my hand to his mouth, pressing my palm to his lips for a scorching kiss. "You must be feeling better. You're arguing."

Heat kindles where his breath whispers over my skin. I'm still cold, and there's only one thing I'm certain of in my life. Only he can warm me.

"Cat's not dying anymore, is she?" Kaia asks.

Griffin shakes his head, his eyes focused solely on me. "Everyone go back to bed. Cat needs quiet. And rest."

Griffin's family shuffles out, reluctantly, I think. Flynn and Kato plant themselves near the door, clearly with no intention of leaving.

I turn to the healer and ask his name.

"Eneas," he answers.

"When can you finish?"

"Soon." His face is pallid, his voice lacking vigor.

Eneas finishes the job as soon as he's able. It doesn't hurt like before, but it isn't easy. Griffin paces furiously and looks like he wants to destroy anything within reach. I moan nonstop, sounding a lot like a coward.

When it's done, Griffin bends over me, his eyebrows drawn together in dark, foreboding slashes. "Why is there a scar?" he demands.

Eneas frowns. "It may have something to do with the lemon juice." He studies me with a sidelong glance that tells me he knows something about location spells. He very thoroughly washes my blood from his hands. Smart man.

Egeria pokes her head into the room, the healer child in tow. "Do you need Calla again?"

I shake my head, but Griffin motions the girl forward. Kneeling so they're roughly the same height, he asks, "How would you like to be the personal and primary apprentice of the healer in charge of Ios?" He nods toward Eneas.

Calla blushes and dips into a respectable curtsy. "Very much, Your Highness."

Griffin stands. "Now that that's settled, everyone out. Cat needs to sleep." He herds everyone out of the room, asking Kato and Flynn to stay close. He uncovers me and washes the blood off while I lie there, tired and sore. Once I'm clean, he carries me to the bed and wraps me in one of his tunics before tucking the sheet up under my chin.

I watch from under sagging eyelids as he removes all traces of blood from the room, rolling stained clothing and blood-ied cloths into the soiled rug. Griffin, Kato, and Flynn take everything from the room, promising me a bonfire behind the barracks that'll make me complain about the heat soon.

When he comes back, Griffin strips out of his boots and lies down next to me, gathering me close. "Still cold?" he asks.

I shake my head even though I am still chilled. Curling into him helps.

Gruffly, he says, "You scared me to death."

"Me too," I mumble drowsily. I sink deeper into my cocoon of safety and warmth, knowing Griffin will keep my monsters at bay.

"Sleep," he says, his arms tightening around me. "When you wake up, I'll make love to you and give you as much life force as you can take."

I grin against his chest. I can't wait. "How smug do you look right now?"

"Very," he admits.

"Feed me first."

He chuckles. "If I have to." After a slight pause, he adds, "And then you and I are having a conversation. No more mysteries, Cat."

I stop smiling. For *that*, I can wait.

A whispered argument wakes me up. "Eight years with me and *one* broken arm because she was overambitious with the acrobats. A few months with you and she almost dies! Repeatedly! What in the Underworld is wrong with you?"

Selena.

"She's fine," Griffin grumbles.

"Because you found a healer who doesn't hate you! And you're not even keeping him at the castle. You're sending him to Ios!"

"We'll find one for the castle."

Selena snorts. "Most healers don't give a Cyclops's eye about healing Hoi Polloi."

Griffin's voice turns deceptively casual. "I could always keep you."

My eyes fly open. I've never seen perfectly groomed, perfectly poised Selena lose her temper, and I don't want to miss it. What I see is startling. Her long braid is a mess. Her ageless face is flushed with anger, and her blue eyes flash with that otherworldly light I can never quite nail down or see the other side of. She looks as vengeful as the Furies, and just as ready to light Griffin's hide on fire.

"I wouldn't have gotten here in time. This is *over!*" She slices her hand through the air with finality. "I'm taking her back."

"Over my dead body." Griffin steps in front of me, crossing his arms.

Selena stares him down. "That can be arranged."

My heart jumps into my throat. She's not bluffing. "No one's killing anyone," I say, my voice hoarse from sleep. "And it's a sorry day for the realms when *I'm* the peace-keeper. The world must be about to implode."

Actually, that's not funny.

"Cat!" Selena flies to my side like she has wings. She lands next to me, taking my hand in hers. Her eyes are unnaturally bright.

"Thank you for coming," I murmur.

She throws a dark look over her shoulder at Griffin. "I didn't do anything. I would have been too late."

I squeeze her hand. "You would have found a way."

She turns back to me, her face etched with worry. "Even I can't bring back the dead."

"Then it's a good thing I'm not dead." My attempt at a joke is shaky, and no one laughs.

"Tell me truthfully, Cat. Are you happy here?" It's not a simple question, but there's a simple answer.

"Yes." My eyes find Griffin's. My voice softens. My whole body does.

"I see." Selena's lips purse. "Aetos and Desma will be disappointed. Vasili, too. Everyone misses you, especially Cerberus."

I grin. Cerberus couldn't care less. "I'll visit soon."

"When you're stronger," Selena says briskly, her expression smoothing into its usual cool lines.

"I miss you," I tell her. "I miss everyone."

"And we miss you." She leans close and whispers the ancient word for family in my ear. Its power electrifies me like a lightning bolt, and magic whooshes through my veins. I gape at Selena as my body settles. She's hiding more power than I ever imagined.

"Real family works both ways," she says with an enigmatic smile. Then her eyes narrow on my willowy frame. "What happened to your curves? You look like you did when I found you."

Funny. I thought I'd found her. "They'll be back. I'll be struggling with certain pants again soon enough. Some people are just made that way, and spice cakes don't help."

She sits back, straightening her rumpled clothing. "Do you want me to stay?"

I shrug. "Yes. But you have a circus to run, and I'll just be sleeping for days."

"Sleeping and eating," Selena says firmly, bending down to kiss my forehead. She smells like blossoms and budding leaves, and I wonder if this is what it feels like to have a mother who loves you.

"How's Hades?" I ask before she goes.

She gives me a significant look. "Virile. As always."

I smile. I get it now. "Give Cerberus a pat."

She arches one sculpted eyebrow. No one pats Cerberus. Selena and I are the only ones who even go near him. He terrifies everyone else.

She squeezes my fingers before rising. "Cerberus didn't guard the circus until you came. He hasn't been around since you left."

It takes a moment for her words to sink in. Hades may be her lover, but Cerberus is my watchdog. My eyes blur, and my nose stings, and I'm not really sure why. I press my lips together, holding a flood of emotion at bay.

Selena leaves with Carver after delivering a series of grisly threats to Griffin. I don't hear everything, but I hear enough to know he'd better not let anything happen to me.

Taking a slow breath, I turn to the man I love. He's been standing off to one side, hovering, protective and extremely male. "She won't carry through."

He looks dubious. Selena must have been pretty convincing. "You mean she won't personally rip my beating heart from my chest and string my innards from one end of the Underworld to the other?"

I make a face.

"Or lop off my head and give it to Cerberus for a chew toy?"

I mash my lips together to keep from smiling. "That would be a terrible waste of a handsome head."

"Or have a Cyclops pummel me with its meaty fists until my bones are splinters and my organs ooze out?"

I grimace. "Ack!"

Griffin grunts. "More like ouch."

I laugh, clutching my aching middle, and in that moment, I don't care that Griffin has all but vowed to uncover everything I can't bear to confide in him, that he wants to take over the realms, that Andromeda is coming for me, that I have thunder and lightning in my veins, or that I am destined to end the world as we know it. But when my smile dies, I close my eyes for the briefest of seconds and see war and crumbling kingdoms and me in the middle of it all, and I can't help wondering how fleeting my happiness will be, and how many people will suffer along with me.

I open my eyes and meet Griffin's steady gaze. "I love you, and I'm so glad you love me, too."

His eyes widen at my admission. He stops mid-breath, his whole body going utterly still. "Live together, or die trying?" he asks, his voice a deep rasp.

I nod. "Us. Together. Forever." I speak instinctively, trustingly, and this time magic whips through me, acknowledging the unbreakable promise even as fate whispers in my ear that my forever might not last long.

I hold out my hand. "Make love to me."

His gray eyes ignite. "Are you sure?"

"I want you. In me. Around me. Always."

He's by my side in an instant, achingly fierce, terrifyingly gentle, afraid that I might break. With each caress, each softly spoken endearment or sensual drag of his lips over my skin, Griffin heals me in a way no magic ever could. And when he rises above me, filling me completely, he's a rock and a wall—my shelter, my home. He wraps his arms tightly around me, thrusting slowly to drive my pleasure to new heights. He kisses my shoulder when I shudder beneath him and then joins me in completion, offering me his strength as his head drops to my neck and his powerful body quakes and trembles. When he shifts to the side, he cups my jaw and feathers his lips over mine, murmuring words of adoration and praise that sweep aside my fear of the confrontation between us I know is yet to come.

I kiss him back and touch every part of him that I can reach. And when he makes love to me again, I don't cry at his tenderness even though I feel like I might, and I don't tell him that if I were going to break, it would have happened a long time ago.

HERE'S A SNEAK PEEK AT BOOK TWO IN AMANDA BOUCHET'S RIVETING KINGMAKER CHRONICLES TRILOGY

ᏣᎶ *BREATH OF FIRE* ᎧᏍ

DAWN BREAKS OVER THE ICE PLAINS, TURNING THE icicles lining the mouth of the cave into fiery daggers. Around us, a landscape of white, gray, and glacial blue slowly emerges from the night like a cautious beast leaving the shadows—still, monumental, treacherous. In the silence of daybreak, Griffin takes steel to flint, lights one of our two torches, and then hands it to Kato.

I peer to my right. The glacial tunnel leading into the labyrinth is as dark as a Cyclops's heart. Griffin hands me the second, unlit torch, and I slip it into a loosened dagger loop in my belt.

In turn, I hand Griffin Ariadne's Thread. He holds the silvery ball of twine while Carver ties the loose end around my wrist, tugging hard on the knot to make sure it's secure.

Griffin rechecks it, twice, his expression grim. "Remember what the wizard said."

"Only Kato and I go in. Beware Atalanta's bow. Find the lyre before the three-headed beast. Heed the Goddess's needs."

His eyes bore into mine, dark and troubled. "I don't like being separated."

My chest contracts painfully as I lean into him. "I know."

"Don't you dare cut this thread." Griffin's arms clamp around me, hard as rocks. "If you do, I swear to the Gods I'll come in there, find you, and give you a spanking you'll never forget."

A shaky laugh explodes from my lungs. "I find that a lot more tempting than I probably should."

Griffin squeezes me. "Come back to me. Don't do anything foolish."

Me? "I'm never foolish."

He grips me until my bones creak.

"I'll be careful," I promise.

Griffin eases his hold, pressing his lips to the top of my head and inhaling deeply. When he lets me go and offers his hand to Kato, the other man shakes it, absorbing Griffin's long, hard look with a solemn nod. The silent communication has "protect her with your life and then some" written all over it. A few weeks ago, I would have dismissed it as a lot of overprotective male posturing. Now, I only wish I could convince them that dying for me is *not* an option.

As Kato and I enter the labyrinth, I have to convince myself to put one foot in front of the other. About thirty feet in, just before the tunnel curves to the right, I stop and look back even though every instinct tells me not to.

My heart seizes, tumbling painfully at the sight of Griffin. Ariadne's Thread trails from his tightly fisted hand. His big frame is taut and still with the kind of coiled tension that hovers on the brink of explosion, as if he's barely restraining himself from coming in after me.

Our eyes collide across the frost-blanketed entrance of the cave. "I swear I'll cut this thread, drop it, and leave it behind me if any one of you steps past this point in the tunnel before we're back." The vow jolts through me, sealing itself in my skin, my blood, and my bones.

Griffin's face twists. He curses violently.

Fighting the burning rawness inside of me, I say, "You can take shelter in the cave's entrance, but if you come after us, I'll be physically compelled to cut the rope and not pick it up again." The magical chain reaction will hit me no matter where I am, not leaving me any choice.

"I release you from your vow," Griffin says.

"It's not a vow to you, it's a vow to myself. You can't release me."

"Cat. Be reasonable. What if—"

"Just wait for us," I call. "We'll be back."

My pulse thuds wildly as I back away under Griffin's livid stare. A muscle jerks in his cheek, ticking hard enough to send a ripple through his beard. His eyes blaze, and my heart wrenches as I turn away.

"Cat!" he roars.

I turn the corner without looking back. My eyes burn, and every shallow, quick breath shudders in my throat.

Kato waits until the light from the cave's entrance fades entirely before asking gruffly, "Are you all right?"

I sniff and press my chilled fingertips to my stinging eyes, stemming the hot prickle of tears. "No."

He doesn't try to talk to me again, which is for the best.

With only the light of the torch and the dim glow from our cloaks, we wind our way deeper into the labyrinth, ducking pointy icicles and slipping on mirror-smooth patches of ice. When the tunnel splits into three branches, we peer into the darkness. Which reveals nothing. Because it's dark.

"What do you think?" I ask, my voice rough from disuse and swallowing tears.

Kato lowers the torch, scanning the tunnel floor for footprints or signs of passage. There are none. The ice is even and unmarked underfoot, and so cold that the chill is already seeping through my thick-soled boots.

He shrugs. "Straight?"

After that, there are so many offshoots that we simply

take turns deciding which way to go. Twice, we stumble back onto Ariadne's Thread and know we've gone in circles. We're debating whether or not to backtrack while picking up the thread when a dim light beckons us from a distant tunnel on the right.

Curious, cautious, we follow the light and find a cavern, bright and high-ceilinged—if you can call the enormous sheet of ice filtering in the sunlight from outside a ceiling. Far above our heads on the frozen roof, zigzagging patterns of windblown snow splash swirling shadows across the cavern floor.

Kato looks up, frowning. "How thick do you think that ice is?"

I scrunch my nose. "Thick enough?"

Voices carry differently in the cavern, amplified by the smooth walls and towering ceiling. When we're not speaking, it's quiet enough that I fancy I can hear my own heartbeat echoing back to me from off the sheets of ice.

It's quiet enough that there's no mistaking the distinctive twang of a bowstring when it vibrates in my ears.

We both duck on instinct, and the arrow slams into the milky-white stalagmite behind us, embedding itself deep in to the mineral deposit.

Kato reaches for me, but another twang sends us diving in opposite directions. I scramble toward another stalagmite, slipping on the ice and skidding beyond my mark. The bowstring hums again, and my right foot gets punched out from under me.

I hit the ground hard on my side and slide. Grunting, I flip onto my stomach and then scrabble back over the ice until I crash into the back side of the mineral tower.

Another arrow clatters across the ice just as I snatch in my trailing foot.

"Cat!" Kato is ten feet away, behind a stalagmite that's not even as wide as his shoulders. "You're hit!"

A colorfully fletched arrow sticks out from the heel of my boot. "It's in the sole." I yank it out and drop it next to me. "I'm fine."

"Not for long," a singsongy voice croons from a gallery of caves high up along the opposite wall of the cavern. "You're oh-so-wrong."

I take a quick look out from behind my shield, trying to discern the archer's form. "Atalanta, I presume?"

There's a pause. "She knows my name. That's not part of the game."

Twang. Crack!

She aimed high. I look up and see a huge, lethally sharp icicle speeding toward my head.

I jump out of the way, forced to forsake my shelter. Another arrow flies before I can take cover again and slams into my shoulder.

I gasp, staggering back. Then Kato has me. He shoves us both into the debris of the shattered icicle behind my stalagmite an instant before another arrow skids over the ice where I just stood.

Fuming, I grab the shaft and yank the arrow from my shoulder. Kato looks horrified.

"It hit a buckle. The armor blocked it." Mostly. Under the tough leather, warm liquid dampens my tunic, making the material cling to the side of my breast.

His eyes close briefly in relief. Then, setting me behind him, he calls, "We're here on a mission from the Gods. We don't want any trouble."

Atalanta laughs. It's a light, airy sound, like wind through trees. Preternaturally fast, she flits from cave to cave along the far wall. "So handsome. I think I'll hold you for ransom."

"What?" I say through gritted teeth.

Kato looks at me. The wariness in his cobalt eyes doesn't color his arch tone. "Now *she* can rhyme."

My jaw drops. "I can rhyme!"

"Live among bears, get covered in hairs!" Atalanta sings.

I roll my injured shoulder, testing it. It stings, but that's all. "She makes no sense. She's trying to kill us. We have to get past her."

Drawing a Kobaloi knife, I rub my thumb over the sinew while I watch the way the archer's silhouette moves. When I think I've nailed down the pattern, I throw the blade into an empty gallery, counting on her to flit through it at the same moment. She does, but she *catches* the knife, stopping it right in front of her armored chest before twirling back into the shadows.

I blink. Titos and now *this*? Those Kobaloi knives were the worst purchase of my life!

Atalanta pops into the next cave, flips my knife in her hand, and then throws it back. The blade sticks in a mini stalagmite an inch from my foot. I jerk back, thumping mad.

"It's not with a knife that you'll take my life."

I pry my knife free and then sheathe the blade again.

Twang. Crack!

Kato yanks me against him and spins to the side as another icicle falls from the roof and smashes down next to us. Shattered ice blasts our legs and scatters in a chiming wave.

"Nock an arrow, hit the marrow," Atalanta chants, letting another bolt fly.

Too late, I realize Kato isn't entirely behind the stalagmite anymore. He slaps his hand over his neck, right at the base of his skull.

Fury gathers inside me like a storm as he moves us both closer to the mineral deposit again. I reach for his wrist. "Let me see."

He lowers his red-stained fingers, and I rise to my toes, using the arm he still has around me for balance.

"It's just a scratch." But mini Titos's forked tongue is *lapping up* the blood.

I pat Kato's chest in what I hope is a reassuring way, trying to keep my eyes a normal size and my voice steady. "You're fine." Animated tattoos and vampiric snakes are *not* something he needs to worry about right now.

I pull my tunic from my pants, rip off the relatively clean hem, and then wrap the strip around Kato's neck, securing the ends with a knot. "There. Good as new."

He gives me a tight smile. "This stalagmite isn't big enough for the two of us. I'll go back to mine."

"Don't." I grab his arm. "She's too good. She'll pin you in seconds."

He hesitates and then gets behind me, pushing me right up against the frosty surface. Stuck, I can't even give Atalanta the evil eye anymore.

"I can't breathe," I eventually protest.

"Good. Then you can't move."

"And that's ever-so helpful in a fight!"

"Atalanta!" Kato calls, not moving an inch. "Zeus and Athena sent us. We're meant to bring a treasure to the Ipotane Alpha."

I roll my eyes. "Fantastic. Just tell her we're here to steal her treasure."

"It might not be hers."

"She might be guarding it," I argue.

I feel him shrug behind me. "Or she could say she was expecting us."

"Expecting to kill us," I mutter.

Kato inhales sharply, moving enough for me to lean over and see what he sees. Atalanta has stepped out onto a ledge. Framed against the gallery of caves above, she's magnificent. Wild and dark. Silky hair falls to her knees, spilling over her arms, hands, and lowered bow. Diaphanous skirts cover her long, shapely legs only to mid-thigh, and gleaming, golden upper-body armor illuminates the smooth, pale skin of her neck and face. Dark brows wing across her forehead, arching delicately. Her full mouth looks like it's been stained by kalaberries, offering an exotic splash of color against her flawless, almost translucent complexion. She's as cold and perfect as the ice crystals adorning the cavern.

Thick-lashed, elongated eyes send a shock through me. They mirror mine, glinting with the pure, light green of magic and the north.

She moves forward, her long hair swaying. "The Gods sent you to me that I might be free?"

Free? From what? "Yes!"

Kato gives me a warning squeeze, and I stick an elbow in his ribs.

Atalanta cocks her head in a perfectly savage way, reminding me of a wolf let loose in a field of unsuspecting sheep. "Please Artemis and you may depart from this."

Artemis is the Goddess? Heed the Goddess's needs.

What does that mean?

"We don't have an offering," Kato whispers in my ear.

"I know!" I grate back.

Atalanta steps so close to the edge of her perch that the tips of her boots kiss empty air. "We'll take the warrior to serve as courtier."

My insides plummet in a nauseating rush. *Is that why the Gods sent Kato in here?*

"You can't have him." I search frantically for an alternate offering. "You can have a magic cloak."

Atalanta laughs.

"Fine. Two magic cloaks."

Kato grunts. I don't think he wants to give his up.

"I'm not just handing you over!" I snap.

"Your worry can end, for we will not keep your friend."

I look sharply at the other female. "Then what do you want from him? And for how long?"

She wets her berry-colored lips. Her hands curl at her sides. "Mistress and I, we've decided to try…"

Her words trail off, an intense, heated look coming over her face. I know that look. I look at Griffin that way all the time.

Scowling, I wiggle enough to turn around and face Kato. "She looks like a wild animal in heat. I have a good idea of what they have planned for you."

"Me too."

I smack his arm. "You don't have to look so happy about it!"

Kato shrugs. "What's not to like?"

"She shot me!"

"She shot me, too."

Gah! Men! "Artemis is sworn to virginity. Her…disciple might be, too. You can't touch them."

"Heed the Goddess's needs." Kato spreads his hands like he can't help it if Artemis wants a man.

"That's not a need, it's a want! She can live without."

"She's immortal. That's a long time to live without."

"Maybe she is sick of her eternal virginity." *I would be.* "But what if you're wrong and Zeus strikes you down with a God Bolt for deflowering his daughter?"

Kato looks less keen about that. "This is part of what the

wizard said. I have to go with her. What happens next…"
He frowns. "I'll figure it out."

"It's a test." I start to panic. I don't like it. "It's a test
to see if you'll hold out, if you'll keep the Goddess pure."

"If the woman is brave," Atalanta calls down, "she'll
find her man in the second large cave."

"What second large cave?" I glance at Kato. "It took us
hours just to find this one."

"She thinks I'm your man," Kato says, surprised.

"And yet she has no problem dragging you off for an
Olympian orgy!"

"Two women is hardly an orgy," he points out.

I glare.

Kato takes my shoulders and squeezes. "This is why
it was me, Cat. Why they said only I could come into the
caves with you."

My eyebrows slam down. "What do you mean?"

"I'm the only one of us who can do this without damaging
something. I'm the only one whose heart isn't engaged."

"What? Oh…" Griffin loves me. Jocasta is clearly
something to Flynn, even if he's not sure what. And
Carver… Obviously Kato knows something about Carver
that I don't.

"There are always consequences," I say darkly.

He shrugs. "Sometimes more. Sometimes less."

My mouth flattens into a tight line. I don't like this.
"Who is Carver pining for?" No wonder he's been moody
and a little solitary lately. Whoever she is, he had to leave
her behind. "I can't be the only one who doesn't know."

Kato smiles faintly, something sad edging into his eyes.
"A ghost."

I wince. *Oh, Carver.*

Kato drops his hands from my arms. "Don't worry.

I've been in the back room of a tavern or two. I know what to do."

I don't doubt that. "You don't have to. We'll find another way."

"This was written, Cat. You know that as well as I do." Kato steps away from me. "Find me in the second cave."

My heart launches itself violently into my throat. "What if I can't?"

"You can."

I grab his wrist. "Have you seen me try to read a map? It's pathetic, and I don't say that lightly."

"You don't have a map."

"Well, that's even worse!"

Atalanta drops from her perch, landing lightly on the balls of her feet despite the impact fracturing the frost in a wide circle all around her. She strides toward us, tall, confident, and poised, possessing an animal's natural grace. Her arms are loose. Her hips sway. Her hair swoops. *Gods, it's annoying.*

I've got animal grace. I've got plenty. Definitely enough to claw her eyes out.

With a last look at me, Kato steps out from behind the stalagmite.

I jump after him, trying to pull him back. "What about the three-headed beast?"

He rubs the back of his neck, his blue eyes swimming with shadows. "I don't know, but I don't think she'll wait."

Atalanta's avid gaze is already bright with lust. She's practically foaming at the mouth. "Strip!" she commands, not bothering with a rhyme.

My jaw drops. Kato looks rather shocked himself.

"Now?" he asks, for some reason directing the question at me.

I shrug helplessly. "I guess."

Atalanta slings her bow over one shoulder and raps her fingernails against her armor. The impatient tip-tapping grates on my nerves. Everything about her grates on my nerves—the rhyming, her agility, the way she caught my knife, and how she intends to use Kato, although *he* doesn't seem to mind.

Kato strips, handing each item of clothing to me. He starts shivering almost immediately. "The temperature won't exactly enhance my performance," he mutters.

I take his pants, trying not to glimpse what they used to be covering. "I have a feeling she'll keep you warm," I say sourly.

Atalanta claps, apparently delighted with what she sees. I don't look. I *refuse* to look.

"The treasure you need, you'll receive after the deed. As you depart, it will"—she looks Kato up and down with unabashed libidinous craving, her tongue sliding along her lower lip—"warm your manly parts."

I glare at her. "That does *not* rhyme!"

She unslings her bow, nocks an arrow, and shoots me. Sort of. If she'd meant to kill me, I'd be dead. I think I lose some hair, though. In any case, Kato is faster than I am. He spins me out of the archer's path again and deposits me back behind our stalagmite. In the time before he lets me go, my face is buried in his chest. Crisp, golden hair tickles my nose and brushes my lips. His skin is still warm, and smells of man, and frost, and leather. He turns almost as fast, leaving my face against his back. I exhale, and goose bumps spread across his skin.

"I go with you now," he tells Atalanta, "and you leave her alone. You will not harm her. Ever."

Atalanta makes no response that I can hear. Maybe she

nods. I don't know. I can't see around Kato and about a mile of naked back.

He seems satisfied, but then adds, "I'm keeping my boots."

I can't help it. I look down. Before I get to his boots, though, my eyes snag on a very fine backside. I've only ever seen one naked male bottom. I tilt my head to the side. There's no real harm in seeing two.

Kato half turns, looking at me over his shoulder. My eyes jerk back up, a ridiculous blush hitting my cheeks like a thunderclap.

"Griffin will kill me for leaving you alone in here," he says.

"Griffin will kill you for being naked in the same room with me," I answer.

He grunts. "Believe me, I'd rather be dressed. It's bloody cold in here."

"Go, then," I reluctantly urge. "Atalanta will warm you up." The words almost stick in my throat. It's hard not to choke on them.

The muscles in Kato's bare arms ripple as he clenches his hands into fists. "There's still the lyre, and the monster."

I push on the middle of his back with the flat of my hand. He needs to go before he freezes to death. The warmth is already seeping from his skin. "That's my part, I guess. You just heed the Goddess's needs when you see Artemis. *Needs*," I remind him. "Not wants."

"Heed the need," he echoes, looking less enthusiastic now that he's freezing cold and actually parting from me.

Kato suddenly turns and grabs my wrist, crushing Ariadne's Thread into my skin. "Keep the string tied. No matter what, *you* find your way out."

Does he really think I'd leave him in here? "I find *you*, and then we *both* find our way out."

He looks ready to argue. He looks ready to turn this whole plan on its ear.

"Go." I give him the hard look Griffin is always giving me. "Go before I give in to my base feminine curiosity and look at your 'manly parts.'"

Kato slowly drops my wrist. "I've seen you naked. We'd be even."

"Being even isn't high on my priority list."

He grins. Then he sweeps his big hand over the top of my head, turns, and walks away.

There's a long moment when my heart forgets to beat. Atalanta takes hold of Kato's arm and drags him toward a shadowy tunnel. As she turns back to me, her long hair sweeps over his bare skin, and I wonder what she'd do if I took out a knife and sawed it all off.

Shoot me probably. For real.

"Don't follow us. Go that way." She points to the third tunnel on the left.

No rhyme this time? I bare my teeth, a horrible pressure building in my chest. I'm terrified of never seeing Kato again.

They enter the dimly lit passageway. Rows of uneven icicles hang from the rounded entrance of the tunnel, making it seem as though they're disappearing into a monster's gaping maw. Sharp teeth. Dark gullet. Ready to swallow them whole.

I shudder as they disappear from sight. To keep myself from chasing after them, I fold Kato's clothes and then tuck his things into our satchel before strapping his leather armor to the outside of the bag. His cloak is too big to fit inside, so I throw it over my shoulders and fasten it at the neck. The heat of my own cloak diminishes as the two fire-wrought garments balance their warmth together.

There's a cold spot deep in my chest, and nausea plagues my stomach as I walk toward the third tunnel on the left—into my own gaping maw. More than a foot of cloak drags on the ground behind me, sweeping my footsteps from the frost.

Find the lyre before the three-headed beast. *No problem. I'll get right on that.*

My fingers and toes are icy. I rub my hands together, muttering to myself because the sound of a voice, even my own, helps me feel less alone. Kato left me our torch, but it burned out ages ago. After a while of seeing only by the faint light of the two cloaks, I broke down and lit the second one. Since then, I've gone up, down, and around, stumbling onto my own path eight times so far. *Eight!*

The tunnel I just left has Ariadne's Thread on its slippery floor three times over. Who was the idiot who thought it would be a good idea to leave me alone in a labyrinth?

That's right! Grandpa Zeus.

He obviously doesn't know me at all. And for all of Griffin's and Beta Team's praying to Athena, she was in on this, too. So were Hades and Poseidon.

Bloody Gods. They could at least *try* not to make this so hard. You know, throw me a lyre or something.

I come to yet another fork in the tunnel and frown, worry a bitter taste on my tongue. There's a thread to the left. It's icing over, which means I was already here hours ago.

Grumbling, I go right, knowing Kato and I will walk every same, useless circle on the way back out again. Worse, we'll do it in the near pitch-dark. The torch won't last much longer, and the cloaks, even turned flame-side out, aren't actually that bright. With my luck, I'll probably stumble onto the beast just as soon as I'm blind.

A scraping noise puts a stop to my low muttering. I pause and listen, hearing a scrabbling that sounds a lot like claws on ice.

Adrenaline dumps into my system. My pulse leaps, and my muscles tense. I try to steady my breathing as I draw my sword, keeping the torch in my left hand. Before, I would have drawn a knife, but I haven't had much luck with them lately.

Click. Click. Chuff.

Great. I have the beast. I do not have the lyre.

I round a bend, moving as silently as I can. The tunnel brightens by degrees, and a thought kicks my already thundering heart into overdrive. *Is the beast guarding the second large cave?*

I'm desperate to see Kato again and to get us both out of here. By the number of times I've gotten hungry, I estimate that three days have passed since Atalanta separated us, which means we've been in the labyrinth for almost four full days. Kato left me everything we brought with us, and I've eaten sparingly, but if we can't be on our way out of here soon, meals will get truly sparse.

Being alone, and in the cold and dark, is wreaking havoc on my mind and body. Despite resting and eating at regular intervals, I'm exhausted like never before—weak and even woozy sometimes. I slept twice because my body was telling me to stop in a way I simply couldn't ignore, but both times I woke up screaming, my raw shouts echoing off the frozen walls, and not feeling rested at all.

Now, my blood drumming in my ears, I inch toward what can only be described at the moment as not total dark, my sword leading the way. I swear to the Gods, when this is over, I'm never going underground again. It's horrible, black, quiet, and incredibly lonely. I have no idea what's happened to Kato—well, *some* idea—and Griffin and the others must be freezing cold and out of their minds with worry.

The scratching gets louder. I want to turn around and find another tunnel, but there's light this way, and a three-headed beast was part of the Gods' warning. I need to face it, whether I want to or not. Unfortunately, I'm minus one lyre.

Ariadne's Thread trails from my wrist, and I wish I could somehow sense Griffin on the other end. What if something's happened to him? What if I don't make it out?

A desperate sort of anxiety clamps down on my chest, making it hard to breathe. I clutch my sword, feeling each ridge of the grip press into my palm. Fear usually makes me mad. I need to get back to that.

I plaster myself against the icy wall and creep forward just enough to get a look at what comes next. The passageway opens up, but not enough for what I'd call a cavern. It's a bigger, wider, higher tunnel, with multiple offshoots, some of which are not utterly dark.

What do those offshoots lead to? The second cavern? The first? At this point, I'm completely turned around. I could be anywhere inside the mountain. Maybe it's the exit. I could be closer to Griffin than I thought!

Quietly, I hurry toward the light until I slip on black ice and nearly land on my back. Then I step on something uneven, and my left ankle twists. Ignoring the twinge of pain, I lower the torch to see what my foot just landed on.

It's a bone. Old, crunchy, dried-up bone.

Thump! Scrabble.

I jerk my head up.

Scrabble. Thump! Thump!

I whirl, facing the darker tunnels. Something's coming down one of the passageways, but I don't know which one.

Thump! Thump! Chuff.

The middle! I dive to the right.

Wrong! The three-headed monster explodes from the right-hand tunnel.

A shot of pure fear detonates inside me. I drop and roll under a lethally clawed foot. Something razor-sharp slices my thigh, and I hiss in pain as I shove my torch up into the beast's underbelly. It bellows and skids to a stop.

I jump to my feet, my injured leg howling in protest, only to drop again when a powerful, clubbed tail whizzes over my head and smashes into the side of the tunnel. Ice shatters, and I duck as a shower of cold, sharp shards splashes over me.

The beast pivots. One of its huge heads lunges for me, and I spring back, pain pulsing in my thigh. Its jaws snap, and I back away. Six black eyes track me. They're as dark as the rest of the beast, only with a shiny, liquid gleam.

"We don't have to fight." So saying, I raise my sword.

The middle head attacks. I shoot to the side and bring my blade down hard on that skull. The impact jars me from teeth to toes.

In the flickering torchlight, I see a flash of dark horns— long, smooth, and curved low over the beast's skull. A quick sweep of the torch reveals horns protecting all three heads. They arch back over the heads and bend downward toward the jaws, protecting the vulnerable necks.

While I'm assessing the situation, the monster brings its clubbed tail around again like a battering ram. There's just enough room in the tunnel for the maneuver and nowhere for me to go. The cramped quarters work in my favor, though, because the thick, muscular part catches me in the middle while the bony club scrapes a deep furrow along the tunnel wall. I have just enough time to curl inward and throw myself backward to better absorb the impact.

I fly through the air and land sprawled on the ice on my back, the wind knocked out of me. I slide what feels like a mile down the tunnel before the top of my skull cracks against the wall. Bright lights explode behind my eyes. Pain roars through my head as momentum carries me around in a hard arc, and the rest of my body slams into the icy barrier.

For a second, there's nothing. No air. No light. No sound. Then I suck in a huge breath, and my stunned body jolts back to me. Groaning, I roll to my knees. Pain grips my head. Everything spins. I touch the sorest spot and feel the start of a huge knot, warm and wet.

I tighten my other hand around a familiar hilt. Somehow, I held on to my sword. The torch lays far down the tunnel, dimly illuminating the advancing monster from behind. I blink, trying to chase away the dizziness, but my head throbs. I can't focus on the beast, but I know it's coming for me, hulking, huge, and snarling snorts and growls that remind me of Cerberus.

Hades left me his guard dog for eight years, and I needed him a grand total of once. The Hound of the Underworld would come in really handy right now, and yet he's nowhere to be found. I'll never understand the Gods' sense of humor, or irony, or whatever it is.

Real fear, the kind I recognize like an old enemy, takes root inside of me. I'm so completely outmatched right now, there's a good chance I'm going to die.

Coming January 2017

ACKNOWLEDGMENTS

This book may never have seen the light of day without the incredible network of people surrounding me. Thank you to my wonderful agent, Jill Marsal, who read my manuscript and immediately decided she wanted to help me get this story out into the world. You gave me hope and made all those hours of work worth it the instant I got your first email. Also, thank you to my fabulous editor, Cat Clyne, this novel's most enthusiastic cheerleader. I couldn't have asked for a more dedicated, discerning, and patient editor. The entire team at Sourcebooks has lifted me up and carried me forward. It's been thrilling to know how many people are excited about this book! A special thank-you to Dawn Adams, Sourcebooks Casablanca's talented art director, and artist Gene Mollica for creating such an awesome cover, and also to Amelia Narigon for her tireless efforts to spread the word about this book. I would also like to express my particular gratitude to Dominique Raccah for taking a keen interest in this project.

To my friends and first supporters, Natasha Hall, Hannah Douglas, Marie-Laure Herrault, Marlyse Megelas, and Naomi Moulton—thank you for listening to me talk about my writing way back when it wasn't much more than a dream and we were giggling around big glasses of wine in tiny Parisian apartments. Thank you also to my friends Janet Skeslien Charles and Catherine O'Sullivan Wagner for reading all or parts of this manuscript and offering vital feedback, and to my cousin Leda in Athens for coming to my rescue on the Greek words I peppered into the manuscript. Any mistakes are entirely my own.

My family has been my cheering squad from the time I first started seriously pursuing publication, reading my writing, offering me invaluable constructive criticism, listening to my hopes and worries, and generally putting up with a (tiny) bit of neurosis. My parents, Iris and Fred Beckwith and Alan and Mary Blackmer, have given me endless guidance, love, and support. My sister, Alexis, is an incredible, real-life superhero who has somehow found the time to offer me insightful comments on hundreds of pages while also managing a full-time job, a household, and two young children. Thank you!

Sébastien, you always cheer me on, and I love the "happy first place" picture you drew for me when I won my first Romance Writers of America contest. And Séraphine, thank you for understanding that Mommy needs to work. You two light up my life.

Most especially, thank you to my hero/husband, Jean-Patrice, who works so hard both at the office and at home in order to give me the time I need to write down the stories in my head.

And finally, thank you to my amazing friend Callie Burdette. Your enthusiasm, support, perceptiveness, sharp writer's eye, and spot-on critiques have helped me through the most exciting yet daunting period of my life. I'm not sure I could have done it without you.

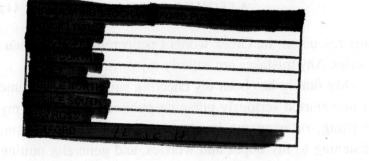

...

...you always cheered me on, and I love the Romance novels of Jane Austen... And I bet one day you'll be one of the most talented writers I know.

...

And special thanks to my husband, Sean Patrick, who worked harder... at the office and at home in order to give me the time I need to write down the stories in my head.

And finally, thank you to my amazing friend Callie (studio). Your enthusiasm, support, perceptiveness, sharp writer's eye, and spot-on critiques have helped me through the most exciting, yet daunting period of my life. I'm not sure I could have done it without you.